BOOKS BY
MAZO DE LA ROCHE

*

Whiteoak Chronicles
(*In the Order of Time*)
THE BUILDING OF JALNA
MARY WAKEFIELD
YOUNG RENNY (JALNA—1906)
WHITEOAK HERITAGE
THE WHITEOAK BROTHERS: JALNA—1923
JALNA
WHITEOAKS OF JALNA
FINCH'S FORTUNE
THE MASTER OF JALNA
WHITEOAK HARVEST
WAKEFIELD'S COURSE
RETURN TO JALNA
RENNY'S DAUGHTER
VARIABLE WINDS AT JALNA
CENTENARY AT JALNA

*

Other books by Mazo de la Roche
EXPLORERS OF THE DAWN
POSSESSION
DELIGHT
LOW LIFE AND OTHER PLAYS
PORTRAIT OF A DOG
LARK ASCENDING
BESIDE A NORMAN TOWER
THE VERY HOUSE
GROWTH OF A MAN
THE SACRED BULLOCK AND OTHER STORIES
A BOY IN THE HOUSE AND OTHER STORIES
THE SONG OF LAMBERT
RINGING THE CHANGES
A HISTORY OF THE PORT OF QUEBEC

WHITEOAKS
OF JALNA

WHITEOAKS
OF JALNA

BY
MAZO DE LA ROCHE

Whiteoak Edition

BOSTON
LITTLE, BROWN, AND COMPANY

WHITEOAK EDITION

Twenty-third Printing

THE ATLANTIC MONTHLY PRESS BOOKS
ARE PUBLISHED BY
LITTLE, BROWN, AND COMPANY
IN ASSOCIATION WITH
THE ATLANTIC MONTHLY COMPANY

FOR HUGH EAYRS

CONTENTS

WHITEOAKS
OF JALNA

The Whiteoak Family

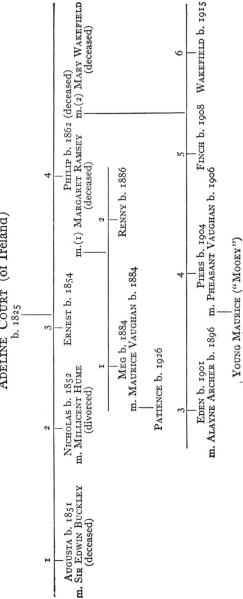

CAPTAIN PHILIP WHITEOAK (of the British Army)
b. 1815 (deceased)

m. 1848

ADELINE COURT (of Ireland)
b. 1825

1

AUGUSTA b. 1851
m. SIR EDWIN BUCKLEY
(deceased)

2

NICHOLAS b. 1852
m. MILLICENT HUME
(divorced)

3

ERNEST b. 1854

4

PHILIP b. 1862 (deceased)

m.(1) MARGARET RAMSEY
(deceased)

m.(2) MARY WAKEFIELD
(deceased)

1

MEG b. 1884
m. MAURICE VAUGHAN b. 1884

PATIENCE b. 1926

2

RENNY b. 1886

3

EDEN b. 1901
m. ALAYNE ARCHER b. 1896

4

PIERS b. 1904
m. PHEASANT VAUGHAN b. 1906

YOUNG MAURICE ("MOOEY")
b. 1926

5

FINCH b. 1908

6

WAKEFIELD b. 1915

I

FINCH

FROM the turnstile where the tickets were taken, a passage covered by striped red and white awning led to the hall of the Coliseum. The cement floor of this passage was wet from many muddy footprints, and an icy draft raced through it with a speed greater than that of the swift horses within.

There were but a few stragglers entering now, and among these was eighteen-year-old Finch Whiteoak. His raincoat and soft felt hat were dripping; even the smooth skin on his thin cheeks was shining with moisture.

He carried a strap holding a couple of textbooks and a dilapidated notebook. He was unpleasantly conscious of these as the mark of a student, and wished he had not brought them along. He tried to conceal them under his raincoat, but they made such a repulsive-looking lump on his person that he sheepishly brought them forth and carried them in full view again.

Inside the hall he found himself in a hubbub of voices and sounding footfalls, and in the midst of a large display of flowers. Monstrous chrysanthemums, strange colors flaming behind their curled petals, perfect pink roses that seemed to be musing delicately on their own perfection, indolent crimson roses, weighed down by their rich color and perfume, crowded on every side.

With the sheepish smile still lingering on his lips, Finch wandered among them. Their elegance, their fragility, combined with the vividness of their coloring, gave him a feeling of tremulous happiness. He wished that there were not so many people. He would have liked to drift about among the flowers alone, absorbing their perfume rather than inhaling it, absorbing their rich gayety rather than beholding it. A pretty young woman, quite ten years older than he, bent over the great pompom of a chrysanthemum, within which burned a sultry orange, and touched it with her cheek. "Adorable thing," she breathed, and glanced smilingly at the awkward stripling beside her. Finch grinned in return, but he moved away. Yet, when he had made sure that she was gone, he returned to the dusky bloom and gazed into it as though he would discover there some essence of the female loveliness that had caressed it.

He was roused by the sound of a man's voice shouting through a megaphone in the inner part of the building where the horse show was in progress. He looked at his wrist watch and discovered that it was a quarter to four o'clock. He would not dare to show himself at the ringside for at least another half hour. He had cut the last period at school so that he might have time to see something of the other exhibits before the events in which his brother Renny was to take part were due. Renny would expect to see him then, but he would certainly be sharp with him if he discovered that he had missed any of his lessons. Finch had failed to pass his matriculation examinations the summer before, and his present attitude toward Renny was one of humble propitiation.

He moved into the automobile section. As he was examining a lustrous dark blue touring car, a salesman came up and began to expatiate on its perfections. Finch was embarrassed, yet pleased, at being treated with deference, addressed as "sir." He stood talking with the man a few minutes, looking as sagacious as he could and keeping his books out of sight. When at last he strolled away, he threw his shoulders back and tightened his expression into one of manly composure.

He gave no more than a glance at the display of apples,

and the aquariums of goldfish. He thought he would have a look at the kennels of silver foxes. A long stairway led to this section. Up here under the roof was a different world, a world smelling of disinfectants, a world of glittering eyes, of pointed muzzles and upstanding, vigorous fur. Trapped, all of them, behind the strong wire of their cages. Curled up in tight balls, with just one watchful eye peering; scratching in the clean straw, trying to find a way out of this drear imprisonment; standing on hind legs, with contemptuous little faces pointing through the netting. Finch wished he might open the doors of all the cages. He pictured that wild scampering, that furious padding across the autumn fields, that mad digging of burrows and hiding in the hospitable earth, when he had set them free! Oh, if he could only set them free to run, to dig, to breed in the earth as they had been born to do!

Word seemed to go from cage to cage that someone had come to help them. Wherever he looked, expectant eyes seemed to be fixed on him. The little foxes yawned, stretched, shivered with expectancy. Waited . . .

A bugle sounded from below. Finch came to himself. He slouched away, hurrying toward the stairs, turning his back on the prisoners.

At the head of the stairway an elderly man was drooping mournfully before an exhibit of canaries. He accosted the boy, offering him a ticket in a lottery. The prize was to be a handsome bird in full song.

"Only twenty-five cents for the ticket," he said, "and the canary is worth twenty-five dollars. A regular beauty. Here 'e is in this cage. I've never bred a grander bird. Look at the shape and color of 'im. And you ought to 'ear 'im sing! What a present for your mother, young man, and Christmas coming in another six weeks!"

Finch thought that if he had had a mother living it would have been an extremely nice present for her. He pictured himself presenting it, in its glittering gilt cage, to a shadowy lovely young mother of about twenty-five. He fixed his hungry light eyes on the canary, trig and sleek from special feeding, and muttered something incoherent. The exhibitor produced a ticket.

"Here you are — number thirty-one. I shouldn't be a bit surprised if it was the lucky number. Sure you wouldn't like to buy two? You might as well buy two while you're about it."

Finch shook his head, and produced the twenty-five cents. As he descended the stairs he cursed himself for his weakness. He had been short enough of funds without throwing away money. He tried to picture Renny's being chivied into buying a lottery ticket for a canary.

After this expenditure he refrained from buying a programme of events for the horse show. The cheaper seats were so filled that he was obliged to take one near the back among a varied assortment of men and youths. The man next him was rather the worse for liquor. He held the bulky paper-bound programme for the events of the week so close to his nose that they almost touched.

"Damned shilly programme," he was muttering. "Each page shillier than page before."

Judging was taking place inside the ring. The tanbark was dotted with men holding their mounts. Three judges, notebooks in hand, strolled from horse to horse, now and again consulting together. The horses stood motionless, all but one which capered pettishly at the end of the reins. The exhilarating odor of tanbark and good horse-flesh hung on the air, which was still cool in spite of the closely packed spectators.

The man with the megaphone announced the winners. Ribbons were presented, and they disappeared after the defeated competitors into the regions behind. The band struck up.

"Damned usheless programme," sounded in Finch's ear. "Make nothing of it."

"Perhaps I can," said the boy, longing to look at the programme, yet not wanting to be seen in conversation with such a person.

"Buy one for yourshelf!" returned the man loudly. "Don't imagine you're going to shponge on me for one."

There was a laugh from the near-by spectators. Finch slumped in his seat, crimson, humiliated. He was thankful for the crash of music from the band that heralded the Musical Ride.

His spirits rose as he watched the glossy creatures, ridden by soldiers from the barracks, trip coyly and yet contemptuously through the intricate convolutions. He allowed himself to be carried away by the sensuous harmony of sound, of movement, of color. The lights suspended from the lofty ceiling, shrouded by bright flags and bunting, quivered in the metallic vibrations of the air.

The next event was the judging of ladies' saddle horses. There were fifteen entries, among them Silken Lady, ridden by Finch's sister-in-law, Pheasant Whiteoak. She came in at the tail of the string, a large number 15 on a white square attached to her waist. Finch felt a sudden leap of pride as he watched Lady circle the tanbark, showing her good blood and her pride of life in every step. He felt a pleasant sense of proprietorship in Pheasant, too. She was like a slender boy in her brown coat and breeches, with her bare, closely cropped head. Odd how young she looked, after all she'd been through. That affair of hers with Eden that had nearly separated Piers and her. The two seemed happier now. Piers was awfully keen that Pheasant should make a good showing in the jumps. A hard fellow, Piers — he must have given her a rough time of it for a while. A good thing that Eden was safely out of the way. He'd made trouble enough — been a bad brother to Piers, a bad husband to Alayne. All over now! Finch gave his mind to the riders.

A stout man in the uniform of a colonel put them through their paces, sending them trailing, now swift, now slow, around the ring. Pheasant's pale face grew pink. Ahead of her rode a short plump girl in immaculate English riding clothes, a glossy little bell-topped hat, a snowy stock. A youth next to Finch told him that she came from Philadelphia. She had a noble-looking mount. The judges were noticing him. Finch felt a sinking of the heart as the American horse swept rhythmically over the tanbark. When the riders dismounted and stood in various limp attitudes beside their horses, Finch's eyes were riveted on Pheasant and the girl from Philadelphia.

It was as he feared. The blue ribbon was attached to the bridle of the plump girl's horse. Silken Lady did not even get the second or third. They were awarded to horses from other towns in the province. Pheasant, her little face immobile, rode out with the troop of the defeated.

The Ladies' Hunters class came on. The sense of pleasurable anticipation was enhanced by the joyous throbbing of the drums beneath the martial air played by the horns. The first rider entered, his mount, with arching neck and polished hoofs, spurning the tanbark. With a gay air of assurance he sped lightly toward the four-foot gate. Then, as the rider dropped his head for the jump, he swerved aside and galloped easily along the track. The tension was relaxed into amusement. Laughter rippled over the boxes and broke loudly from the rear seats. Rider wheeled horse sharply and rode him again at the gate. He leaped it with ease. Without mishap he jumped the wall, then the first oxer, but as he cleared the bars he kicked the top rail and it clattered to the ground. Another try! Again the balking at the gate, again the leap, but this time two rails were scattered. A bugle sounded. Rider and horse disappeared, the man dejected, the beast ingenuously pleased with himself.

Two more entries came and went without creating a stir. The next rider was the girl from Philadelphia. The beautiful horse looked too tall for the plump little figure in the perfect riding habit. But he knew his business. He threw himself whole-heartedly into the jumping. Only one mishap in the twice around — a tick behind. They sailed off amid a steady beat of handclaps.

Then Pheasant on The Soldier, half brother to Silken Lady. Finch's heart beat heavily as they trotted into the arena. It was no joke to manage The Soldier. He was scarcely a fit mount for a slim girl of twenty. He approached the gate sidewise, showing his teeth in a disagreeable grin. Pheasant trotted him back to the starting point, and again headed him with soft encouragement toward the gate.

" Give him tashte o' whip! " advised the man beside Finch.

Again The Soldier balked at the jump. Again Pheasant wheeled him and made a fresh start, but this time a sharp cut as they approached the gate sent him flying over it like a swallow. Then over each of the tall white gates he flew, the white " socks " on his hind legs flashing, his ginger-colored tail streaming.

Finch was grinning happily. Good little Pheasant. Good boy Soldier. He violently added his applause to the storm that commended them. Still, his eyes were anxious as he awaited the second time around. This time there was no balking, but a swift triumphant flight over gate, over hedge, over double oxer. But one never knew what The Soldier would do. At the last gate he swerved aside, galloped past it, and, amid handclaps and laughter, disappeared.

The Philadelphia girl, Pheasant, and three others were recalled for a jump off. All five did well, but the American horse was the best. Sadly, Finch agreed that the judges were right when he was awarded the blue ribbon, and The Soldier the red. "But the girl can't ride like young Pheasant, anyhow," he thought.

Now came the Corinthian class, gray and chestnut, bay and black, streaming along the track close on each other's heels. Ah, there was Renny! That thin, strong figure that looked as though it were a part of the long-legged roan mare. A quiver of excitement ran through the crowd, like a breeze stirring a field of wheat. As the sound of the band died away the thunder of hoofs took up the music, sweeter by far! Finch could not bear to remain in his seat. He slid past the knees of those between him and the aisle, and descended the steps. He joined the line of men that lounged against the paling that surrounded the track.

Here the tanbark looked like brown velvet. Here one heard the straining of leather, the blowing, the snorting of the contesting glossy beasts, their heavy grunts as they alighted on the ground after the clearing of the hedge. His eyes were directed toward its greenness. He looked up at each horse as it rose, at its rider bending above it, their two muscular organisms exquisitely merged into the semblance of a centaur.

No women in this contest. Only men. Men and horses. Oh, the heart-straining thrill of it! As Renny's horse skimmed the barrier, the hedge, flew through the air, dropped to its thudding hoofs again, and thundered down the tanbark, its nostrils stretched, its mouth open, its breath rushing from its great barrel of a body, it seemed the embodiment of savage prehistoric power. Renny, with his carven nose, his brown eyes blazing in his narrow, foxlike face, his grin that had always something vindictive in it, he too seemed possessed by this savage power.

No woman in this contest? What of the mare? That gaunt roan devil that carried him, leaped at the tug of his rein, galloped like the east wind speeding across the waves with him! Ah, she was feminine enough! Every inch of her. Hadn't she whinnied from her stall cries of challenge to the velvet-eyed stallion? Hadn't she stood in the straw and given from her gaunt body a big-boned foal that had not yet been broken? Hadn't she suckled that foal, nozzling it gently, snuffing the sweetness of it? She was feminine enough, by God, thought Finch.

The boy's imagination, liberated by the tumult of plunging horses whose breath comes in warm gusts against his face as they pass, spreads itself like a fantastic screen between him and the reality of the scene before him. He sees Renny's mare, galloping toward him, continue to bear upon him instead of following the track. He sees her galloping across him, trampling him, crushing him under hoof, annihilating him. . . . He next witnesses the release of his soul from the trampled body. He sees his soul, opaque, iridescent, strangely shaped, leap to the back of the mare, behind Renny, clasping him about the waist with its shadowy yet savagely strong arms, and soaring with him above the circling riders, above the hand-clapping spectators, up among the lights which rise in rushing billows of color toward a thunderous sky above. The drums beat, and the soaring music of the horns accompanies them. . . . He stands clinging to the paling, a lanky boy with hollow cheeks, hungry eyes, one bony shoulder blade projecting a sharp ridge through his coat. His expression is so ridiculous that Renny, trotting tranquilly around the track, the blue ribbon fluttering against the roan's neck, on suddenly discovering him thinks, "Good Lord, the kid looks little more than an idiot!"

His greeting to Finch, when the boy sought him out among the groups of men and horses in the enclosure behind the arena, was only a nod. He continued his conversation with a rigid-looking officer in the uniform of an American lieutenant. Finch had seen this man taking part

in several jumping events. He had followed Renny with
the red ribbon.

Finch stood humbly by, listening to their talk of horseflesh and hunting. Mutual admiration beamed from their
eyes. At last Renny, glancing at his wrist watch, said,
"Well, I must be getting on. By the way, this is my young
brother. Finch, Mr. Rogers."

The American shook hands with the boy kindly, but
looked him over without enthusiasm.

"Grown fast, I suppose," he commented to the elder
Whiteoak, as they turned away together.

"Oh, yes," returned Renny. "No bone to speak of," and
he added, apologetically, "He's musical."

"Is he studying music?"

"He was, but I stopped it last summer after he failed in
his matric. I feel regularly up against it with him. Now
the music is cut off, he has taken to play-acting. It seems
that he'd rather do anything than work. But I dare say
he'll turn out all right. Sometimes the most unpromising
colt, you know, . . . "

They were now crossing an open paved space, unlighted
save by the blurred beam from a motor car cautiously moving among the horses that were being led to stable or station
by shouting attendants. However, a murky daylight made
it still possible to distinguish one face from another.

A hostler, running across the yard, slipped on the thin
layer of mud that covered the pavement and plunged forward, his bullet head coming in violent contact with the
stomach of a burly fellow leading a rearing blanketed horse.

He roared, "Keep your blurry 'ead out of my stummick,
will yer? Wot do you think this is, a soccer match?"

The hostler returned a volley of abuse which was drowned
by the whinnying of the horse, outraged by the delay in
seeking his supper. Inside the building the band could be
heard playing "God Save the King."

The moving shadows in the yard now became indistinguishable as darkness fell like a palpable covering over all. The rain, which had been fitful, now blew in wildly from the east, and at the same moment the roaring of the lake increased in volume, as though the elements, weary of the activities of men and beasts, had united to obliterate them.

Renny Whiteoak and the American parted, and Finch, who had been slouching behind, moved to his brother's side.

"Gosh, it's cold," mumbled the boy.

"Cold!" exclaimed his elder, in astonishment. "Why, I'm hot. The trouble with you is that you don't get enough exercise. If you'd go in for sports more, you'd get your circulation up. A foal just dropped wouldn't feel the cold to-night."

A voice called from the car which they were approaching: —

"Is that you, Renny? I thought you were never coming. I'm getting beastly cold."

It was young Pheasant.

Renny got in and turned on the lights. Finch clambered in beside the girl.

"What a pair!" said Renny, letting out the clutch. "I'll need to keep you in a nest of cotton wool."

"Just the same," she persisted, "it's very bad for Baby, my getting chilled, and I've been away from him too long already. Can't you get the car started?"

"Something's gone wrong with its blasted old innards," he growled, then added hopefully, "Perhaps the engine's just a bit cold." He did various spasmodic things to the antiquated mechanism of the car, unloosing at the same time, in a concentrated undertone, the hatred of seven years. Loving and understanding horses, he was bewildered by the eccentricities of a motor.

Pheasant interrupted, "How did I do?"

No answer came for a moment, then he growled, "Not so

badly. But you need n't have touched The Soldier. Much better not."

"Well, I came second, anyway."

"Might have come first if you had n't. Lord, if ever I get this cursed old bus home!"

Pheasant's voice was indignant. "Look at that American girl's horse! It was a perfect peach!"

"So is The Soldier," muttered her brother-in-law, stubbornly.

Finch reclined in a corner of the car, in a state of depression. The enveloping, dank blackness of the premature night, the thought of the hours of study in his cold bedroom that lay before him, seemed like hands reaching up out of the sodden ground, dragging him down. He was famishing. He had a piece of chocolate bar in his pocket, and he wondered if he could extract it and negotiate its passage to his mouth without Pheasant's becoming aware of it. He felt for it, found it, cautiously extricated it from its battered silver paper wrapping under cover of a sudden fierce outburst from Renny which distracted her attention. He crammed it into his mouth, sinking lower into the seat and closing his eyes.

He was beginning to feel comforted when Pheasant hissed in his ear, "Horrid little pig!"

He had forgotten how shrewd was her sense of smell. She was going to get even, too. She fumbled in her pocket, produced a cigarette case, and the next instant the sharp flare of a match lighted up her little pale face and showed the sarcastic pucker of her lips cherishing the cigarette. Sweet-smelling smoke lay heavy on the damp air. Finch's last cigarette had been smoked that noonday. He might, of course, have asked Renny for one, but it was scarcely safe to approach him when he was baffled by the car.

Presently the eldest Whiteoak threw himself back in his seat with a gesture of despair.

"We may walk home for all of her," he observed, laconically. He too lighted a cigarette.

Smoke and gloomy silence pervaded the car. Rain slashed against the sides, and with each flutter of the ill-fitting curtains a chill draft penetrated the interior. Rain-blurred lights of other cars slid by.

"But you were splendid, Renny," said Pheasant, to lighten the depression. "And got the blue ribbon, too! I'd come around, and I saw the whole thing."

"I couldn't help winning on the roan," he said. "God, what a mare!" Then, after a moment, he added pointedly, "Though if I'd been ass enough to take the whip to her, I should probably have come only second."

"Oh, how cold I am!" exclaimed the girl, ignoring the thrust. "And I can't help thinking of my poor little baby."

Finch was suddenly filled with intense irritation toward them both, sitting there smoking. What had they to do when they did get home but lounge about a stable or suckle a kid? While he would be forced to lash his wretched brains to the study of trigonometry. He swallowed the last of his chocolate, and said, in a hoarse voice, "You seemed to be thick enough with that fool American 'lootenant.' Who was he?"

The abandoned impudence of the words shocked him, even as he uttered them. He would not have been surprised if Renny had turned and felled him to the floor. He was sure he felt a shiver of apprehension from Pheasant's corner.

But Renny answered quietly enough, "I knew him in France. A splendid chap. Very rich, too." And he added, enviously, "Got one of the finest stables in America."

Pheasant moaned, "Oh, my poor little Mooey! Am I never to get back to him?"

Her brother-in-law's tone became testy. "Look here, my girl, you must either give up riding in horse shows or having babies. They don't fit."

"But I've just begun both in the last year," she pleaded, "and they're equally fascinating, and Piers likes me to do both."

Finch growled, "Quote someone besides Piers for a change."

"But how can I? He's the only husband I've got."

"He's not the only brother I have, and I'm tired of hearing his words chanted as though he was the Almighty."

She leaned toward him, her face a white blur against the dark. "Anyone who is as self-centred as you are naturally doesn't want to hear about anyone else. Anyone who would devour a bar of chocolate with a starving young mother at his side. Anyone—"

"Say 'anyone' again," bawled Finch, "and I'll jump out of the car!"

The altercation was cut short by a vehement jolt. The motor had started. Renny gave a grunt of satisfaction.

He slouched behind the wheel staring ahead into the November night. The roads were almost deserted when they had passed beyond the suburbs. Even the streets of the villages through which they speeded were almost empty. The vast expanse of lake and sky to the left was a great blackness, except for the beam of the lighthouse and two dusky red lights denoting the presence of a schooner ploughing against a head wind.

His mind flew ahead to the stables at Jalna. Mike, a handsome gelding, had got his leg badly cut by a kick from a vicious new horse that morning. He felt much disturbed about Mike. The vet had said it might be a serious business. He was anxious to get home and find out what sort of day he had passed. . . . He thought of the new horse that had done the damage. One of Piers's purchases. He himself had not liked the look in the brute's eyes, but Piers cared nothing about disposition if a horse's body was right. Piers would make over the disposition to suit himself. That seemed to be his idea. Well, he'd better make this new nag's temper over and be sharp about it. . . . He scowled in a way that always moved his grandmother to exclaim ecstatically, "Eh, what a perfect Court the lad is! He can give a savage look when he's a mind to!"

He thought of a foal that had been dropped that morning by one of the farm horses. She was a clumsy, ugly-looking beast with a face like a sheep and large flat feet, but, lying there in the box stall with her foal beside her, she had seemed changed. Something noble about the poor beast, as a gaunt, ugly woman may give a sudden impression of nobility bending over her newborn child. Extraordinary things, horses — Nature, an extraordinary thing altogether. The differences between one mare and another — between a farm horse and a hunter. The strange, unaccountable differences between members of the same family. His young half brothers and himself. The boys more difficult to handle than horseflesh, by a long shot. They shouldn't be, for they were the same flesh and blood, got by the same sire. . . . Yet what two boys could be more unlike than little Wakefield, so sensitive, affectionate, and clever, and young Finch, whom one couldn't browbeat into studying or shame into taking an interest in games, who was always mooning about with a sheepish air? He had seemed more odd, more mopey than ever of late. . . . And then Piers. Piers was different again. Sturdy, horse-loving, land-loving Piers. They were very congenial, he and Piers, in their love of horses, their devotion to Jalna. . . . And Eden. He uttered a sound between a growl and a sigh when he thought of Eden. Not a line from him since he had disappeared after his affair with Pheasant, nearly a year and a half ago. That showed what writing poetry could do to a chap — make him forget decency, spoil the life of a girl like Alayne. What a disgraceful mess it had been, that affair! Piers had been quieter, more inclined to moods ever since, though the coming of the baby had done a good deal to straighten things up. Poor kid, he must be howling for his supper by now.

He increased the speed regardless of the slippery road, and called over his shoulder, "Home in ten minutes now, so cheer up, Pheasant! Have either of you got a cigarette? I've smoked my last."

"I've done the same, Renny. Oh, I'm so glad we're nearly there! You've made wonderful time considering the night."

"Have you any, Finch?"

"Me!" exclaimed the boy, rubbing one of his bony knees, which had got cramped from sitting so long in one position. "I never have any! I can't afford them. It takes all my allowance, I can tell you, to pay my railway fare, and buy my lunch, and pay fees for this and that. I've nothing left for cigarettes."

"So much the better for you, at your age," returned his brother, curtly.

"Chocolate bars are much better for you," purred Pheasant, close to his ear.

Renny peered through the window. "There's the station," he said. "I suppose your wheel is there. Shall you get it? Or had you sooner stop in the car with us?"

"It's a beast of a night. I think I'll go with you. No — I'll — yes — oh, Lord, I don't know what to do!" He peered forlornly into the night.

Renny brought up the car with a jolt. He demanded over his shoulder, "What the devil is the matter with you? You seem to have a perpetual grouch. Now make up your mind if it's possible. I think myself you had better leave the wheel where it is and walk to the station in the morning."

"It'll be a beastly walk in such weather as this," mumbled Finch, moving his leg with his hands to bring life into it. "My books'll be all muddy."

"Well, get one of the men to run you down in the car."

"Piers will want the car early. I heard him say so."

Renny stretched back a long arm and threw open the door beside the youth. "Now," he said quietly, but with an ominous chest vibration in his voice, "get out. I've had enough of this shilly-shallying!"

Finch scrambled out, giving a ridiculous hop as his numb foot touched the ground. He stood with dropped jaw as the door was slammed and the motor rattled away, sending a spray of muddy water against his trouser legs.

He moved heavily under a weight of self-pity as he went toward the station house. In the room behind the station master's office he found his bicycle propped against the scales. It might not be a bad idea to weigh himself, he thought. He had been drinking a glass of milk every day of late in the hope that he might put on a little flesh. He mounted the scales and began dubiously moving the weights. The sound of men's voices came from the inner room, argumentative voices, and high-pitched. The scale balanced, he peered anxiously at the figures, then his face brightened — a clear gain of three pounds. A childlike grin lighted his features. The milk was doing him good, all right. He was gaining flesh. Not so bad that, three pounds in a fortnight. He would drink more of it. He stepped from the scales and was about to remove his bicycle when he discovered that a pedal was pressing on the platform of the scales. Suspicion clouded his brow. Might it not be possible that the pressure of the pedal had something to do with the increase in his weight? He set the wheel aside and again mounted the scales. Eagerly he examined the trembling indicator. The weight flew up. He moved the brass slide. Four pounds less. He had not gained! He had lost. He had lost. He weighed a pound less than he had a fortnight ago!

Gloomily he picked up the bicycle and steered it out of the station. He heard one of the men ask, "What's that noise out there?" And the station master's reply, "I guess it's the Whiteoak boy that goes into town to school. He leaves his wheel here." The voices were lowered and Finch could imagine the disparaging remarks they were making about him. He flung himself on to the saddle and pedaled doggedly along the path beside the rails. Darn the old bike! Darn the rain! Above all, darn milk! It was making him thinner instead of stouter. He would have no more of it.

The driveway that led to the house was a black tunnel. Hemlocks and balsams walled it in with their impenetrable resinous boughs. The heavy scent of them, the scent of the fungus growths beneath them, was so enhanced by the continuous moisture of the past two weeks that it seemed a palpable essence dripping from the dense draperies of their limbs, oozing from the wet earth beneath. It was an approach that might have led to a sleeping palace, or to the retreat of a band of worshipers of some forgotten gods. As the boy passed through the oppressive, embalmed darkness he felt that he was moving in a dream, that he might glide on thus forever, with no light, no warmth, at the end to greet him.

In there peace came to him. He wished that he might have ridden on and on among these ancient trees till he absorbed something of their impassive dignity. He pictured himself entering the room where the family would be gathered, wearing like a cloak about him the dignity of one of these trees. He pictured his entry as casting a chill over the rough good spirits of these less austere beings.

As he emerged to the graveled sweep about the house, the rain beat down on him with increasing violence, and the east wind caused the shutters to rattle and the bare stalks of the old Virginia creeper to scrape against the wall. Warm lights shone from the windows of the dining room.

He put aside his imaginings and made a dash for the back entrance.

He pushed his bicycle into a dark passage in the basement and went into a little washroom to wash his hands. As he dried them he glanced at his reflection in the speckled mirror above the basin — a lank fair lock hanging over his forehead; his long nose, his thin cheeks, made pink by the wind and rain. He did not look so bad after all, he thought. He felt comforted.

As he passed the kitchen he heard the nasal voice of Rags, the Whiteoak houseman, singing: —

> "Some day your 'eart will be broken like mine,
> So w'y should I cry over you?"

He had a glimpse of the red brick floor, the low ceiling, darkened by many years of smoke, of Rags's buxom wife bending over the hot range. His spirits rose. He raced up the stairway, hung his wet raincoat in the hall, and entered the dining room.

II

THE FAMILY

THERE was a special dish for supper that night. Finch was
aware of that, before ever he sniffed it, from the ingenuous
air of festivity brightening the faces of those about the board.
Doubtless Aunt Augusta had ordered it because she knew
that Renny would be famished after his long day and stren-
uous exertion in the horse show. Finch was supposed to
have a hot dinner at school, but he preferred to husband his
allowance by buying a light lunch, and so having a respectable sum left for cigarettes, chocolates, and other luxuries.
Consequently he had always an enormous appetite by night,
for he did not get home in time for tea. The amount of
food that disappeared into his bony person without putting
any flesh upon it was a source of wonderment and even
anxiety to his aunt.

The special dish was a cheese soufflé. Mrs. Wragge was
particularly good at a cheese soufflé. Finch's eyes were
riveted on it from the moment when he slid into his chair,
between his brother Piers and little Wakefield. There was
not very much of it left, and it had been out of the oven
long enough to have lost its first palate-pleasing fluffiness,
but he longed passionately to be allowed to scrape the last
cheesy crust from the bottom of the silver dish.

Renny, after helping him to a thick slab of cold beef, fixed
him with his penetrating gaze and, indicating the soufflé by
a nod, asked, "Want the dish to scrape?"

Finch, reddening, muttered an assent.

Renny, however, looked across the table at Lady Buckley.
"Some more of the soufflé, Aunt Augusta?"

"No, thank you, my dear. I really should not have eaten

as much as I have. Cheese at night is not very digestible, though cooked in this way it is not so harmful, and I thought that you, after your —"

The master of Jalna listened deferentially, his eyes on her face, then he turned to his uncle Nicholas. "Another helping, Uncle Nick?"

Nicholas wiped his drooping gray moustache with an immense table napkin and rumbled, "Not another bite of anything. But I should like one more cup of tea, Augusta, if you've any left."

"Uncle Ernest, more of this cheese stuff?"

Ernest waved the offer aside with a delicate white hand. "My dear boy, no! I should not have touched it at all. I wish we might not have these hot dishes for supper. I am tempted, and then I suffer."

"Piers?"

Piers had already had two helpings, but, with a teasing look out of the corner of his eye at Finch's long face, he said, "I shouldn't mind another spoonful."

"Me, too!" exclaimed Wakefield. "I'd like some more."

"I forbid it," said Augusta, pouring her third cup of tea. "You are too young a boy to eat a cheese dish at night."

"And you," put in her brother Nicholas, "are too old a woman to swill down a potful of tea at this hour."

The air of dignified offense, always worn by Lady Buckley, deepened. Her voice, too, became throaty. "I wish, Nicholas, that you would try not to be coarse. I know it is difficult, but you should consider what a bad example it is for the boys."

Her brother Ernest, desirous of preventing a squabble, remarked, "You have such excellent nerves, Augusta, that I am sure you can drink unlimited tea. I only wish that my digestion — my nerves —"

Augusta interrupted him angrily: "Whoever heard of tea hurting anyone? It's coffee that is dangerous. The

Whiteoaks, and the Courts, too, were all indefatigable
drinkers of tea."

"And rum," added Nicholas. "What do you say, Renny,
to having a bottle of something really decent to celebrate the
prowess of our nags?"

"Good head!" agreed Renny, spreading a layer of mustard over his cold beef.

Piers in the meantime had helped himself to more of
the soufflé, and then pushed the dish to Finch, who, gripping
it in one bony hand, began savagely to scrape it clean with
a massive silver spoon.

Wakefield regarded this performance with the patronizing
wonder of one who had shared the dish in its first hot
puffiness. "There's a little stuck on there, just by the
handle," he said, helpfully pointing to the morsel.

Finch desisted from his scraping long enough to hit him
a smart blow on the knuckles with the spoon.

Wake loudly cried, "Ouch!" and was ordered from the
table by Lady Buckley.

Renny shot a look of annoyance down the table. "Please
don't send the kid away, Aunt. He couldn't help squeaking
when he was hit. If anyone is sent away it will be Finch."

"Wakefield was not hurt," said Augusta, with dignity.
"He screams if Finch looks in his direction."

"Then let Finch look in another direction." And Renny
returned to the consumption of his beef with an air of
making up for lost time, as well as putting an end to the
matter.

Nicholas leaned toward him. "What do you say, Renny,
to a bottle?" he rumbled.

Ernest checked him, tapping his arm with a nervous white
hand. "Remember, Nick, that Renny is in the high jumping
to-morrow. He needs a cool head."

Renny began to laugh uproariously. "By Judas, that's
good! Aunt Augusta, do you hear that? Uncle Ernie is

afraid that a glass of spirits will make my head hot, and look at the color it is already!" He rose energetically from the table.

"Can't Rags get it?" asked Nicholas.

"Of course. And swipe a bottle for himself. . . . The key of the wine cellar, please, Aunt." He went around to Augusta and looked down on her Queen Alexandra fringe and long, rather mottled nose. She took a bunch of keys from a chatelaine she wore at her waist.

Wakefield bounced on his chair. "Let me go, please do, Renny! I love the cellar and I hardly ever get there. May I go to the cellar for a treat, Renny?"

Renny, key in hand, turned to Nicholas. "What do you suggest, Uncle Nick?"

Nicholas rumbled, "A couple of quarts of Chianti."

"Oh, come now, I'm in earnest."

"What have you got?"

"Besides the keg of ale and the native wine, there's nothing but a few bottles of Burke's Jamaica and some sloe gin — and Scotch, of course."

Nicholas smiled sardonically. "And you call that a wine cellar!"

"Well," replied his nephew, testily, "it's always been called the wine cellar. We can't stop calling it that, even if there is nothing much in it. Aunt?"

"I thought," said Ernest, "that we had half a bottle of French vermouth."

"That's up in my room," replied Nicholas, curtly. "A little rum and water, with a touch of lemon juice, will suit me, Renny."

"Aunt?"

"A glass of native port, my dear. And I really think Finch should have one, too, studying as he does."

Poor Finch did not wait for the ironic laughter which followed this appeal in his behalf to slump still lower in his chair, to crimson in deprecatory embarrassment. Yet, even as he did so, he felt a warm rush of love toward Augusta. She was not against him, anyhow.

Renny moved in the direction of the hall, and, in passing Wakefield's chair, he caught the expectant little boy by the arm and took him along, as though he had been a parcel.

They descended the stairs to the basement, where their nostrils were assailed by the mysterious smells that Wake loved. Here was the great kitchen with its manifold odors, the coal cellar, the fruit cellar, the wine cellar, the store-room, and the three tiny bedrooms for servants, of which only one was now occupied. Here the Wragges lived their strange subterranean life of bickerings, of mutual suspicion, of occasional amorousness, such as Wake had once surprised them in.

As soon as their steps were heard by Rags he appeared in the doorway of the kitchen, the stub of a cigarette glowing against his pallid little face.

"Yes, Mr. W'iteoak?" he inquired. "Were you wanting me, sir?"

"Fetch a candle, Rags. I'm after a bottle."

The light of sympathy now brightened the cockney's face. "Right you are, sir," he said, and, dropping the cigarette stub to the brick floor, he turned back to the kitchen, re-appearing in a moment with a candle in a battered brass candlestick. They had a glimpse of Mrs. Wragge, rising from the table at which she had been eating, and assuming an attitude of deference, her face as much like the rising sun as her lord's resembled the waning moon.

With Rags leading the way, the three passed in Indian file along a narrow passage that ended in a heavy padlocked door. Here Renny inserted the key, and the door, dragging stubbornly, was pushed open. Mingled with the penetrating chill were the odors of ale and spirits. The candlelight discovered what was apparently a well-stocked though untidily arranged cellar, but in truth the bottles and containers were mostly empties, which, in accordance with the negligence characteristic of the family, had never been returned.

Renny's red-brown eyes roved speculatively over the shelves. A cobweb, hanging from a rafter, had been swept off by his head, and was now draped over one ear. He whistled through his teeth with the sweet concentration of a hostler grooming a horse.

Wakefield, meanwhile, had espied an old wicker fishing basket pushed under the lowest of a tier of shelves. He dragged it forth and saw in the candlelight three dark squatty bottles, cobwebbed, leaning toward each other as though in elfin conspiracy. A liquid clucking sound came from them as they were disturbed, and, as he cautiously drew one out, a lambent bronze light played beneath its dusty surface.

"Oh, I say, Renny," he exclaimed, in awed tones, "here is something stimulative!"

Renny had made his selection, but he now set the bottles on a shelf and, snatching Wakefield's treasure from him, restored it to its fellows and pushed the basket hastily out of sight.

"If you had dropped that, you young devil's spawn," he observed, "I should have put an end to you on the spot." And he added, grinning at his henchman, "A man must have a secret in his life, eh, Rags?"

A secret in his life! The little boy was filled with ecstasy at the thought. What magic potion had his splendid brother hidden in this subterranean place? What stealthy visits did he perhaps make here, what charms, what wizardry? Oh, if Renny would only make a partner of him in his secret doings!

He was told to hold the candle while Rags locked the door. He saw Renny's eyes fixed shrewdly on the servant's grayish-white hands. He saw the eyes narrow; then Renny

transferred one of the two bottles he carried to his armpit
and, with the hand thus freed, gave a sharp tug to the pad-
lock. It slipped off into his palm. "Try again, Rags,"
he said, and his carven face with the long Court nose looked
uncannily like his grandmother's.

Rags remarked, this time successfully securing the door,
"I never did know 'ow to manage them blinkin' padlocks,
sir." He was unabashed.

"Not with me looking on, Rags. There, take the candle
from the youngster. He's got it tilted sidewise."

"Yes, sir. But just before I do, let me remove that cobweb from your 'ead, sir."

Renny bent his head and Rags unctuously lifted off the
cobweb.

They formed an odd procession, with something of the
quality of a strange religious rite. Rags, in advance, might
have been some elfish acolyte, the full light from the candle
showing sharply the bony structure of his face, the shallow
nose, the jutting chin, the impudent line of the jaw; Wakefield, in his wistful absorption, a young altar boy; Renny,
carrying a bottle in either hand, the officiating priest. The
narrow brick passage along which they passed had a chill
that might well have been associated with the crypt of some
ruined cathedral, and from the kitchen, where Mrs. Wragge
was, as usual, burning something on the range, drifted a
thin blue veil of smoke, like incense.

At the foot of the stairway Rags stood aside, holding the
candle aloft to light the others as they mounted upward.
"A pleasant evening to you, sir," he said, "and good luck
to the Jalna 'orses. We'll be drinkin' yer 'ealth down 'ere —
in *tea,* sir."

"Keep it weak, Rags. Better for your nerves," adjured
his master, callously, as he pushed the door at the top of
the stairs shut with his heavy boot.

In the dining room Nicholas sat waiting, his large shapely

hand, adorned by a heavy seal ring, stroking his drooping moustache, an expression of humorous satisfaction in his eyes. Ernest's expression was already one of regret, for he knew that he would drink and he knew only too well that his digestion would suffer for it. Still, a kind of tonic gayety was in the air. He could not help smiling rather whimsically at the faces about him, and at the foreshadowing of his own lapse!

Augusta sat admirably upright, her cameo brooch and long gold chain rising and falling on her breast, which was neither large nor small, but corseted in perfect accordance with the model of her young-womanhood. She drew back her head and regarded her nephew expectantly. He dusted the bottle of port and set it down before her.

"There, Aunt. The corkscrew, Wake. . . . Uncle Nick —Burke's Jamaica. . . . That rascal, Rags, was for leaving the cellar door unlocked, so he could sneak in and swipe something for himself. But I caught him, thank goodness."

"He's an incorrigible rascal," said Nicholas.

"He deserves to be flayed alive," agreed Ernest, pleasantly.

"I'd have done the same, myself," laughed Piers.

Pheasant had come downstairs and had drawn up a chair beside his. She was eating a bowl of bread and milk, and the sight of her brown cropped head and childish nape bent over it brought an amused yet tender smile to Piers's lips. He stroked her neck with his strong sunburnt hand, and said, "How you can like that pap beats me."

"I was brought up on it. Besides, it's frightfully good for Mooey."

"Put a little rum in it," advised Nicholas. "You need something to warm you up after that long cold drive. Incidentally it would be good for young Maurice, too. Help to make a Whiteoak and a gentleman of him."

"He's both, already," said Pheasant, sturdily, "and I'll

not encourage my offspring in a taste for spirits even at second hand."

Augusta looked upon the redness of the wine in her glass and remarked, "Our old nurse used to put a little wine in the bottom of our shoes when we went out in the wet to prevent our taking a chill. We did not know what it was to wear rubbers, and we never had colds."

"You forget, Augusta," interposed her brother Ernest. "I had severe colds."

Nicholas said, "That was because you were always kept in when it was wet."

"I can remember," went on Ernest, "looking down from the nursery window when I had one of my colds and watching you two — and, of course, Philip — romping on the lawn with the little pet lamb we had. By and by Papa would come along. He would pick up little Phil and ride him on his shoulder. I can see him. He looked so magnificent to me. I can remember how the wood pigeons were always calling then. . . . I used to shout to him and throw kisses down from my window."

He had had but one glass of rum and water; it took only that to imbue his gentle spirit with sentimental melancholy.

"Yes, I remember," said his brother. "Poor little beggar that you were, you would have a red flannel bandage about your throat, and, likely as not, your ears stuffed with cotton wool, smelling of camphor."

"Good Lord!" said Renny. "If only the wood pigeons were thick as that now! What shooting! Eh, Floss? Eh, Merlin?"

His tone, the word "shooting," which they perfectly understood, aroused the two clumber spaniels sleeping on either side of his chair. They sprang up with joyous barks.

Above the barking of the dogs Finch raised his voice: "I think I might have something. A fellow going on nineteen can stand a drink or two, I guess."

Renny gently cuffed his dogs. "Down, Merlin. Down, Floss, old pet. What's that, Finch?"

There was silence now and Finch's voice boomed loudly but with an ominous break in it. "I say I'm eighteen and I don't see why I can't have a drink."

Piers said, "Give him a sip of your wine, quickly, Aunt Augusta — he's going to cry."

Finch with difficulty controlled his temper, gazing down at the remnant of apple tart that had been saved for him from the family dinner.

"Give the boy a glass of rum," said Nicholas. "Do him good."

Renny put out a long arm and pushed the decanter, which he had filled with port, across to Finch. "Help yourself, Finch," he said, with a suddenly protective air.

Finch selected a glass and took up the decanter. He was afraid that his hand was going to shake. He set his teeth. He would not let it shake. . . . Not with the eyes of all the family on him. All the family hoping he would do some fool nervous thing. . . . Piers's white teeth showing already between his lips, all too ready for a jeering laugh. . . . He would not let it shake. Oh, God, he was saying to himself, keep my hand from shaking! He knew that he no longer believed in or feared God, yet the less he believed in and feared Him, the more often he flung out these silent invocations for His support.

His hand was steady enough until the glass was almost filled; then it began to shake. He barely escaped slopping the wine on to the table. By the time he had set the decanter down he was trembling from head to foot. He quickly tweaked his cuff over his thin wrist and threw a furtive glance at the faces of those about him.

Everyone at the table had begun to talk at once. Not noisily or confusedly, but pleasantly in accord. Smiles flickered over their faces as visible signs of the geniality

emanated from within. Aunt Augusta began to tell of the
old days at Jalna, when Papa and Mamma had entertained
in lavish fashion, had even entertained a Governor-General
and his lady. Then, of course, she drifted to social life in
England in the eighties and nineties, when, she now liked to
imagine, she had held an important social position. Nicholas,
too, talked of London, but of a different London, where he
and his wife, Millicent, had enjoyed themselves in the racing
set till his funds gave out, and she left him, and he was
obliged to return to the shelter of Jalna.

After two glasses, the mind of Ernest was centred on one
thing only — what he should wear to the horse show the
next day. He had a new fall overcoat of expensive English melton, made by the best tailor in town, such an ex-
travagance as he had not indulged in for years. It had been
bought with an eye on the horse show, yet the weather was
so cold and wet that Ernest, with his dread of afflicting his
delicate chest, was in a quandary. The tailor had told him
that he had never seen a man of his age with such a slender,
upright figure. Not much like poor old Nick, Ernest
thought, who had grown so heavy and who generally had to
lean on a stick because of his gouty knee. . . . Yet what
about the delicate chest? A severe cold at that time of year
might lead to anything. "Now, Renny," he was saying,
"what about the atmosphere in the Coliseum? Was there
a noticeable chill there to-day?"

"Chill!" ejaculated Renny, interrupted in a rhapsody
on the powers of the high jumper he was to ride the next
day. "Why, there was no chill at all! It was like a conservatory. A flapper might have gone there in a chiffon
shift, and felt none the worse for it."

He hugged Wake against his side, and gave him a sip
from his glass. The little boy, anxious to be in the very
heart of the party, had asked, "Renny, may I sit on your
knee?"

And his elder had demanded, "How old are you?"

"Eleven, Renny. Not so awfully old."

"Too old to be nursed. I mustn't coddle you. But you may sit on the arm of my chair."

Piers exclaimed, as Renny hugged the child, "Well, if that isn't coddling!"

"Nothing of the sort," retorted Renny. "It's cuddling There's all the difference in the world, isn't there, Wake? Ask any girl."

Piers no longer sat. He stood by the side of the table smiling at everyone. He looked remarkably well standing thus, with his stocky figure, his blue eyes softly shining. He talked of the land and the crops, and of a Jersey heifer he was going to trade for an exquisite bull calf.

Pheasant thought, "How darling he looks standing there! His eyes are as bright as Mooey's. Dear me, that huge bottle is almost empty! Strange that I should have come from a father who is far too fond of his glass to a husband who is inclined that way, too, when I am naturally prohibitionist in my sentiments! I'm never going to encourage my little baby in taking spirits when he gets big."

Aunt Augusta whispered to Finch, "You must go to your studies, my dear. You should learn a great deal to-night, after those two nice glasses of wine."

"Huh-huh," muttered Finch, rising from the table obediently. He took up his books from a side table where he had laid them, sighing at the thought of leaving this genial, relaxed atmosphere for the grind of mathematics. As he turned away, the lottery ticket fell from between the leaves of his Euclid to the floor.

Wakefield sprang from the arm of Renny's chair and picked it up. Finch was already in the hall. "He's dropped something," and the little boy peered at it inquisitively. "It's a ticket — look, number thirty-one! Hello, Finch, you dropped something, my boy!"

Finch turned back angrily. Patronizing little beast, with his cheeky "My boy"!

"Let's see," said Piers, taking the ticket from Wakefield and examining it. "Well, I'll be shot if it isn't a lottery ticket! What are you going in for, young Finch? You're a deep one. Out to make a fortune, eh, unknown to your family? You're still a schoolboy, you know,"—this taunt because of his failure to matriculate,—"and you're not supposed to gamble."

"What's this?" demanded Renny, suspiciously. "Fetch it here."

Piers returned the ticket to its owner. "Take it to your big brother," he advised, "and then run upstairs for his shaving strop."

Finch, glaring, thrust the ticket in his pocket and lunged toward the hall.

"Come back here!" ordered Renny. "Now," he continued, "just say what that lottery ticket is for."

"Good Lord!" bawled the goaded Finch. "Can't I buy a lottery ticket if I want to? You'd think I was an infant in arms!"

"You may buy a dozen if you wish, but I don't like the way you are acting about this one. What is it for?"

"It's for a canary, that's what it's for!" His voice was hoarse with anger. "If I can't buy a lottery ticket for a goddam canary it's a funny thing!"

The outburst of merriment that leaped from the lungs of his brothers and uncles could have been equaled in volume and vitality by few families. After the roar had subsided, Renny gave another of his metallic shouts. "A canary!" he repeated. "Next thing he'll be wanting a goldfish and a rubber plant!" But, though he laughed, in his heart he was deeply ashamed for Finch. He was fond of the boy. It was humiliating that he should be such a sissy—wanting to own a canary, of all things!

A vigorous thumping came from the bedroom across the hall.

"There now," cried Ernest, irritated concern clouding his features, "what did I tell you! You've wakened her. I knew you would. It's very bad for her to be disturbed like this at her age."

Augusta said, without flurry, "Wakefield, go to my mother's room. Open the door quietly and say, 'There is nothing wrong, Grandmamma. Please compose yourself.'"

The picture thus conjured of this scene between his small brother and his ancient grandmother caused Piers to emit a snort of laughter. His aunt and uncle Ernest looked at him with disapproval.

Ernest remarked, "It is just as well, Piers, to teach the boy to be polite."

Wakefield crossed the hall, solemn with the weight of his own importance. He opened the door of his grandmother's room and, gliding in, looked almost fearfully about that dim chamber, revealed, rather than lighted, by a night light placed on a low table near the head of the bed. Before he spoke, he closed the door behind him to shut out the robust mingling of voices from across the hall. He wanted to frighten himself a little — just a little — with the strangeness of being alone with Grandmother in this ghostly light, with the rain dripping from the eaves outside her windows, and a single red eye glowing on the hearth, as though some crouching evil spirit were watching him. He stood very still, listening to her rather wheezy breathing, just able to make out the darkness of her face upon the pillows and the restless movement of one hand upon the crimson quilt.

The flowers and fruit painted on the old leather bedstead which she had brought with her from the East glowed duskily, less bright than the plumage of the parrot perching there. A sigh from the bed quivered on the heavy air like the perfume from some forgotten potpourri of petals gathered long ago. The bygone memories of the bed were drawn upward in the sigh. In it Augusta, Nicholas, Ernest, dead Philip, father of all the turbulent young Whiteoaks, had been conceived, in it all four had been given birth. There Philip, their father, had died. What tremors, what pains, what ecstasies, what perversities and dreams the bed had known! Here Grandmother now spent the greater part of her time.

Her hand rose and hung above the quilt. A tiny red beam shone from the ruby ring she always wore. She was feeling for her stick. Before she was able to grasp it and rap again, Wakefield trotted to her side. He said, like a little parrot, "There is nothing wrong, Grandmamma. Please compose yourself."

He enjoyed the dignified words Aunt Augusta had put into his mouth. He should have liked to say them over again. Indeed he did repeat, "Please compose yourself."

She peered up at him. Her nightcap had got askew and one eye was completely hidden by it, but the other fixed him with peculiar intensity.

"Hey?" she demanded. "What's that?"

"Compose yourself," he reiterated, earnestly, and patted the quilt.

"I'll compose this family," she said, savagely, "with my stick! Where's my stick?"

He put it into her hand and then backed away a little.

She thought a moment, trying to recall what she had wanted, then a burst of half-smothered laughter from the dining room reminded her.

"What's that noise mean? What are they shouting about?"

"About a canary, Gran. Finch has a lottery ticket for one." He came close to her now, looking eagerly into her face to watch the effect of his words.

The effect was terrible. Her features were contorted by

rage. She glared up at him, speechless, for a moment, then articulated thickly, "A canary — a bird — another bird in the house! I won't have it! It'll put Boney in a rage. He won't bear it — he'll tear it to pieces!"

Boney, disturbed by the sound of his name, took his head from under his wing and thrust it forward, peering down at his mistress from his perch on the painted headboard.

"Haramzada!" he cried wildly in Hindu, "Haramzada! Iflatoon! Paji! Paji!" He rose on his toes and flapped his wings, creating a little gust of warm air that fanned Wakefield's face.

Old Mrs. Whiteoak had heaved herself up in the bed. She had protruded from under the quilt her large feet in purple bed socks, and followed them by long yellowish legs.

"My dressing gown," she gasped. "On the chair there. Hand it to me. I'll show them whether I'll have a chit-chat flibbertigibbet canary in the house."

Wakefield knew that he should have run to the dining room and called one of his elders. It was an unprecedented thing that Grandmother was doing, getting up without Aunt Augusta or one of the uncles to help her. But his desire for novelty, for excitement, was greater than his prudence. He brought the heavy purple dressing gown, and helped her to put it on. He put her stick into her eager, shapely old hand.

But to get her on to her feet! That was a different matter. Drag as he would at her arm, he could not budge her. "Ha!" she would grunt with each heroic effort, her face getting more and more the color of her dressing gown.

At last she laid down the stick. "No use," she muttered. "No use. . . . Here, take both my hands, and pull me up." She held her two hands up to him, an eager, expectant look in the one eye which her nightcap did not conceal. It was evident that she was quite hopeful that the little boy could perform the task. But, when he took her hands and strove with all his might, the result was that his feet slipped on the

rug and his small body collapsed into her arms. She broke
into sudden laughter and clutched him to her, and he, half
laughing at the predicament, half crying at his own im-
potence, began to play with the strings of her nightcap.

"Paji! Paji! Kuza Pusth!" cried Boney, beating the air
with his bright wings.

Mrs. Whiteoak pushed Wakefield from her.

"What were we doing?" she asked blankly.

"I was trying to get you up, Granny."

"What for?" Her eye gleamed suspiciously.

"Why, the canary, Gran. Finch's canary, don't you
remember?"

On the instant her old face was alight with rage.

"Remember! Of course I remember. A canary in the
house! I won't have it. I'll stir things up. I'll make a
scene. I must get out to the dining room."

"Shall I fetch Renny?"

"No. No. No, no, no. He'd put me back in bed.
Cover me up, the rascal. I know him. I must get to the
dining room and give 'em all a fright. And I must do it
quickly or one of them will be in here. Ernest will come
whining, or Nick mumbling, or Augusta rearing up her
head. No, no."

"What about creeping, Gran?"

His grandmother threw him an infuriated look. "Creep,
eh? One of my family creep! A Court creep! A Court,
let me tell you, never creeps or crawls, even before his
Maker! He walks upright, even if he has to lean on someone else to do it. Let cowards creep — let snails creep —
let snakes creep —" She looked about her rather wildly.
"What was I saying?"

"You were saying all the things you'd let creep, Granny.
You'd just got to snakes."

"But what was I going to make a scene about?"

"About the canary. Gran."

"Ah, yes. We must attend to that. Try pushing me from behind, Wakefield. Mount the bed."

Nothing loath to try his force from another angle, the little boy scrambled on to the bed, and, kneeling behind her, pushed mightily against her shoulders.

Grunting, straining, her eye prominent with the exertion, she rose. Rose so thoroughly, in fact, that she all but toppled forward on her face. But she balanced herself. Like some unseaworthy old vessel, battered by a storm, she still could ride the waves on occasion with a staunch front.

Leaning heavily on Wakefield's shoulder, she appeared in the doorway of the dining room, and cast an authoritative look over her descendants gathered there. Shock and concern displaced hilarity on their strongly marked countenances. Piers, who was nearest her, jumped to his feet and came to her side. Ernest brought a chair, and together they placed her in it.

"Mamma, Mamma," chided Ernest, adjusting her cap, so that her other too bright eye was discovered, "this is very bad for you."

Augusta said, sternly, "Wakefield, you are a very naughty boy. You deserve a whipping."

"Let the child be," rapped out her mother. "He minds his business, and he does what he is told, which is more than you do."

Lady Buckley fingered her cameo brooch and looked offendedly down her nose.

Reassured that nothing was wrong with her, Nicholas beamed across the table at his ancient parent. Her unflinching spirit, her temper, delighted him. "Game old girl," he murmured to himself. "She's marvelous, and no mistake."

"Are you hungry, Gran?" asked Renny. "Is that what brought you out?"

"No, no, no," ejaculated Ernest. "She's not hungry!

She had a large bowl of cornflakes and puffed rice before she went to bed."

His mother turned her hawklike face on him. "Cornflakes," she muttered. "Cornflakes — silly leaves . . . puffed rice — silly seeds . . . leaves and seeds — fit food for a silly canary." She dropped her chin on her breast turning a word over in her mind. "Canary." Her brain fumbled over it like a blind old tigress trying to discover the nature of a strange morsel. "Canary." Of what did it remind her? Her deep dark eyes roved over the faces of the clan till they fell on young Finch in the doorway. He was gazing at her in sheepish fascination. The instant she saw him she remembered why she had risen so vehemently from her bed. A *canary!* Finch's canary in that house! A little chirping, squeaking, hopping bird at Jalna! She wouldn't have it!

Her face became dark with anger. She found it difficult to speak.

Renny said, "Give her something to eat. She's getting in a fine old rage."

Wakefield tendered a plate of biscuits and cheese in her direction. With a savage look she poked it away with her stick.

"Finch," she articulated. "I want Finch."

The boy hesitated.

"Come close where she won't have to shout at you," said Nicholas.

Finch slouched into the room, grinning deprecatingly.

"Now," she said, peering at him from under her shaggy rust-colored brows with sudden, lucid firmness, "what's this I hear about a canary?"

Finch, staring into her eyes with a bewitched feeling, could only stammer, "Oh, look here now, Gran — look here — there's no darned canary at all —"

"There *is* a canary," she shouted, thumping her stick on

the floor. "A nasty, flibbertigibbet canary that you've smuggled into the house. Fetch it here and I'll wring its neck for it!"

"Oh, I say, Gran, it's only a lottery ticket. There's not one chance in a hundred that I'll win. I don't want the thing anyway."

"Ha!" she retorted, furiously. "You'd lie, would you? Come here!"

He approached guardedly, but she was swifter than he gave her credit for. With the sweeping gesture of one indulging in some sport, she caught him a blow on the knuckles, so sharp that it skinned three of them and doubled him up with the sting of it.

"Such a disgraceful temper!" cried her daughter.

"Steady on, Mamma," growled Nicholas.

Ernest rose from his chair, trembling. "Mamma, this is very bad for you. You might have a stroke."

"Stroke, is it?" she shouted. "I gave the brat a stroke —a stroke he'll remember. I drew the blood, I did! Put out your hand, boy, till I see it." She was purple with excitement.

Renny set down his glass of rum and water. He came and leaned over her. "Don't you want to be kissed, Gran?" he inquired on a coaxing note.

She raised her eyes and, from under the rim of her cap, peered into his face. Its lean redness, thus suddenly brought close to hers, shutting out her view of the others; his strongly carved nose, resembling her own; his lips, drawn back from his strong teeth in a smile, hard, yet still somehow tolerant and tender, caught her attention, submerged her in an enchantment she could not resist. Renny, bone of her bone, a Court of Courts, one of the old stock — nothing puling about him.

"Kiss me," she ejaculated. "Kiss me quick!"

Finch, under screen of the embrace, slipped from the

room. Going up the thickly carpeted stairs, he could hear the loud exchange of kisses.

Panting a good deal, the old lady looked around the room triumphantly after Renny had released her, — she seemed to have gathered strength from his pressing vitality, — and, giving a valiant tug to her cap which again disposed it over one eye, she demanded, " My teeth! I want my teeth. I 'm hungry. Somebody get my teeth."

" Will one of you please get the teeth for her ? " murmured Augusta, resignedly.

Wakefield blithely danced back to the bedroom, reappearing instantly with the two sets of teeth in a tumbler of water. Mrs. Whiteoak leaned toward him as he approached, and stretched out her hands. She could scarcely endure the waiting for them. The little boy joggled the tumbler before her.

" For pity's sake be careful, child," exclaimed Augusta.

" He should never have been allowed to fetch them," observed Ernest, and, despising himself for doing it, he poured a little more rum into his glass.

It had been a good evening, Renny thought. What a supper the old lady had made! And how the old boys had enjoyed their spot of rum! He had never known Uncle Nicholas more entertaining than when the women were gone and the four men were alone, the glasses refilled, and the crimson curtains drawn close. A good day. His horses had done well. He had done well. He was conscious of a pleasant ache of honorable fatigue in legs and arms. Not perhaps so much an ache as a wholesome consciousness of every muscle. How the mare had pulled, had striven!

The eldest of the young Whiteoaks, his lean body curved in an armchair, his bony weather-beaten face drooping above the dark wood of the table which reflected the lights of the prismed chandelier, would have made a satisfying model for an artist who desired to paint a picture entitled "The Huntsman at Night." He would have found, in the disposal of his limbs, in the lines of his head, a perfect example of the relaxation of a man whose joy was in vehement primitive pursuits.

Rags was clearing the table. As he lifted the bottle of spirits, of which a small part remained, the master of Jalna, nodding toward it, observed curtly, "Yours, Rags."

III
THE HOUSE AT NIGHT

WHEN the order and calm of night had descended upon the turbulence of Jalna, the old house seemed to settle under its roof with an air of snuggling, as an old man under his nightcap. It seemed to hunch itself against the darkness and draw inward. It appeared to tie the strings of its night-cap under its chin, the jutting porch, and mutter, " Now for dreams." Like nightclothes it wrapped the outside dark-ness around it, and pressed its bulk against the earth. And, as one more dream added to its weighty store, the thoughts and movements of those inside its walls flitted shadowlike in room after room.

Finch's room was under the sloping roof of the attic. Its one window was closed against the dripping leaves of the Virginia creeper which clung to that side of the house. Up here there was always a faint smell of damp plaster, and the dreamy mustiness of old books. The roof needed mend-ing, and the old books — which were mostly discarded farm journals, dog-eared manuals on horse breeding and showing, and thick catalogues of equine events — needed throwing away, but there was no haste at Jalna, no too urgent attempt to arrest natural decay. When the roof should leak sufficiently to form a puddle on the floor, when the cupboards should no longer be capable of containing more trash, then, and then only, repair and clearing out would begin.

Finch, seated under an oil lamp, shaded by a green paper shade on which were pictured the heavily smiling faces of two German girls, was writing in his diary : —

" All but missed train. Rotten day at school. *Must* swat

for math exam. Had interesting talk with Leigh in spare
hour. Horse show. Renny simply great. Best in the
show. Pheasant not bad on The Soldier. Red ribbon.
Motored home. Row about lottery ticket for canary. Gran
absolutely awful. Had two glasses of port!! Saw Joan."

He sucked the abrasions on his knuckles and let his eyes
run over the entries of the preceding days. There was
more or less variety in these. School was more or less rotten. There were noted several good times with Leigh, and
a "h—— of an evening" with George and Tom. One pe-
culiarity was common to all the entries. They all ended with
the name "Joan." It was either "Saw Joan" or "Did not
see Joan."

In looking over the entries, Finch saw nothing either pathetic or ridiculous in them. Nevertheless he took care to
conceal the diary behind some textbooks on the shelf before
he began his evening's work. He did not intend to run any
risk of its being discovered by the prying eyes of Pheasant
or young Wake.

He took out his Euclid and laid it on the table before him.
The upper right-hand corner had to be placed on an old ink
stain in the wood. The book had a habit of opening of
itself at page 107. He hoped it would not do that to-night
because, if it did, he might be unable to study. His jaw
dropped and his hand shook as he raised the cover — 107
stared up at him. . . . The pencil he held between his fingers fell with a small clatter to the floor. He was afraid
he would not be able to pick it up. He stared blankly at
the number on the corner of the page — 107. Why did he
fear it? 1 — that was the same as I . . . I, Finch Whiteoak. Oh — that was nothing . . . he, Finch, was nothing!
Ah, he was getting at it! That was why he dreaded the
number, and no wonder! Then, 7 — that, of course, was
magic. Magic 7. I, Finch, am *nothing*. He closed the
Euclid sharply and opened it in a fresh place. Page 70 this

time. Again the magic 7, and after that naught. Magic followed by nothingness, void. . . . That was life, magic, with naught to follow! He tried again. Page 123. Again the I. Then two . . . I and another. Two of us. . . . Then three. I and the other have made a third. Three of us. . . . He saw himself, himself and Joan together in a bedroom. They were bending over the crib where lay the Third which they had made, as he had seen Piers and Pheasant bending over Mooey's crib. Joan, to whom he had never spoken a word! She was a girl to whom he had been introduced at a football match by his friend, Arthur Leigh. He had only bowed, but she had said, "How do you do," in a clear piping voice, and had snuggled her round white chin into the fur collar of her coat, and had drawn in one corner of her mouth, producing by the action a tremulous yet persistent dimple in her cheek.

The thought of her had troubled him a great deal during the month that had since passed, but he had made no effort to become acquainted with her and had never spoken of her again to Leigh, though he should have liked to know her surname, which he had not caught at the moment of introduction.

She went to a girls' school not far from his own school, and few days passed without an encounter on the street. One swift glance was all he ever gave her as he took off his cap, but his meeting or not meeting with her always provided the last words for the day's entry in his diary. It was always either "Saw Joan," or "Did not see Joan."

On the nights when he was obliged to write the negative he felt invariably depressed and heavy, settling down doggedly to his work. But when he had seen her, as to-day, he was even more troubled, unable to settle down at all.

Of course, he reflected, these unhappy moods were nothing new. He had always had strange thoughts. He supposed that if he had never met Joan he would have found some other instrument with which to torture himself. If only he had passed his exams, and Renny had not in consequence stopped his music lessons! He felt that to-night, if he had been allowed to spend an hour at the piano, it would have quieted him, lifted him into happiness, freed him from the sense of longing, of fear. He did not question the justness of Renny in stopping the piano playing. He knew that he had spent a lot of time — wasted it, he humbly admitted — hanging over the keyboard, when he was not practising but feverishly attempting to compose. How happy he had been at those times! He could not in his heart of hearts believe that they had been bad for him — even bad for his school work.

Resolutely he opened his Euclid at the problems and deductions he was to study for the next day. He placed the corner of the book exactly on the blot on the table. Then he dropped his pencil again. A bad beginning to drop one's pencil. . . . He looked down at it where it had fallen on a discarded sheet of paper on which was written a French exercise. He wondered at what word the tip of the pencil pointed. But he would not be so silly as to look. He would pick up the pencil and set to work. . . . Still, it would be interesting to know the word . . . perhaps he really ought to know the word . . . perhaps there was a meaning in this — something to help him.

He dropped to his knees and bent over the pencil, narrowing his eyes to decipher the blurred letters. The point of lead rested on the word *âne*. He felt shocked. "Ass"! That's what he was — a silly ass! Thank God, no one could see him! But stay — he had been mistaken in the word. It was not *âne*, but *âme* — "soul"! Ah, that was different. His soul — that was groping in the darkness. Strange that he should be kneeling there with the tip of the pencil pointing out the word "soul." It made him think of the times he had knelt by that chair, afraid of God, praying. He

wanted suddenly to pray now, but words would not come.
He remembered one night, more than two years ago, when
Piers had made him get out of bed to say his prayers, just
to rag him, and he had been able to remember only two
words—Oh, God! *Oh, God!* What boundless, what terrible words! Words that unchained one's soul, whirled it
upward, dissolved it. . . .

If once he gave way and began to pray, to let the words
of prayer free his soul, there would be no study for him
that night. He would pick up his pencil and begin to work.

But he found that he could not pick it up. Three times his
fingers wavered above it, but they could not close on it. He
groaned, hating and fearing himself. . . . He began to
count the dim medallions of the carpet. He found that he
was kneeling on the sixth medallion from the north end of
the room, and the fifth from the west. Six and five were
eleven—it was the eleventh day of November. Six times
five—thirty. Thirty was the number of his locker at
school. Thirty was the number of marks he had taken in
the Euclid examination when he had failed . . . Christ was
thirty years old when He had been crucified. . . .

He thought that if he had a cigarette to smoke he might
be able to pick up the pencil and begin his work. He got to
his feet and stole cautiously down the attic stairs. The door
of the bedroom occupied by Piers and Pheasant stood ajar.
A lowered lamp cast a peaceful light over the white bed and
Mooey's cradle beside it. It was the same solid hooded cradle that had rocked all the infant Whiteoaks. Both the
uncles had wept, and slumbered, and crowed in it. Meg and
Renny, Eden, Piers (the most beautiful baby of all), himself (he could imagine the poor squalling wretch he had
been), little Wake, whom he could remember gazing from
under the hood with great dark eyes. . . . And two or
three babies had died in it. Finch wondered how Mooey
could sleep so quietly there.

He opened the top drawer of the chest of drawers where he knew Piers sometimes kept an extra package or two of cigarettes. Ah, there they were — Piers was good to himself! A large-size tin box of Players, more than half full. A package containing at least a dozen Turkish cigarettes. Finch helped himself, but with caution, and closed the drawer.

As he turned to go he bent over the cradle and looked in curiously at young Maurice. He was curled, sweet and warm, in baby sleep. One round fist, curved against his mouth, pressed the moist flower-petal lips to one side. There was a damp spot on the pillow where he had been slobbering a little. Finch went suddenly weak with tenderness as he looked at him. He put his head under the hood of the cradle and sniffed him, as a dog might sniff at a sleeping puppy. He kissed his cheek and felt his own blood turn to some mild sweet nectar, and his bones to nothing but a tender desire for love.

He took the baby into his arms and bent over him, his lank blond forelock falling over the little head. He kissed the head, the cheeks, the mouth extravagantly. He could not be satisfied. He poured out his soul in love. His eyes filled with tears, which dropped on to the little hands. My God, was it possible that Piers felt that way?

Voices were in the hall below. Pheasant and Aunt Augusta were coming up. . . . He thrust the child back into the cradle and drew the covers over him. Not for anything would he have been caught caressing his young nephew.

Upstairs he found he was no longer the victim of his nerves. He picked up the pencil, the Euclid, lighted one of Piers's cigarettes, and set to work.

Lady Buckley had laid aside her bracelets, her brooch, and her gold chain. She had taken off her black satin dress, her long black silk petticoat, and now, in her camisole and short white underpetticoat, was brushing her still abundant hair. Even in such jaunty apparel as this, her appearance of being on her dignity was not lessened. She regarded her reflection in the glass with her accustomed air of mingled complacence and offense. Her complexion had never been good — now it was mottled and liverish; her eyes had a peculiar glassy dullness, unlike her mother's, which still retained a clear fire. But her features were excellent. Her nose — the Court nose, though in a modified form. Not the fierce, carven feature that her mother and Renny thrust into the world. An improvement, she thought. More becoming to a lady, the widow of an English baronet. She began to think of her husband. . . .

How insignificant her parents and her brothers had thought him, with his pale side whiskers, and his mild eyes, and his neat little feet! He had had a little lisp, too. She could almost hear him, even now, calling her: "Auguthta!" But what character! He had never lost his self-control, no matter what happened. Nothing ever surprised him. Even when the word had come from England that two sudden deaths had brought the baronetcy to him, together with an old house and a respectable income, he had shown no surprise. He had merely turned from the cablegram in his hand and remarked, "You had better begin packing our bags at once, Lady Buckley. We are going home." Heavens, what a start it had given her! To be addressed as "Lady Buckley" in that cool tone, without a syllable of preparation. She had not known whether to laugh or cry. She had never ceased to be grateful that she had done neither, but had replied with undismayed dignity, "You will need new flannels for the sea voyage, Sir Edwin." . . . Lady Buckley! How the title had always stuck in her mother's throat! How disagreeable it was of her mother, always pretending that she could not remember her name! Speaking of her to friends as "my daughter, Lady Bunkley" — or perhaps "Bilgeley." If her mother had not been a Court she would have called it ill-bred. But, of course, the Courts were like that. Nicholas was very much like that. So overbearing. He always seemed to think that he and that dreadful wife of his — Millicent — had been of more importance in England than she and Edwin had been. She was sure of that because of the jocular tone he used about the little circle the Buckleys had moved in. Well, at any rate it had been a much better behaved circle than the horsy one wherein he and Millicent had splurged and lost everything!

She thought of England. How she longed to be back there! She thought of the hedgerows, the beds of geraniums about her own house (she did hope the tenants were keeping things in order), the song of the linnets on the moist sweet air, her friends. She had been away from all these things for a year, and it seemed like two. But it was her duty to remain in Canada till her mother's death. Surely Mamma — well, she was a hundred and one. It almost frightened Augusta . . . what if Mamma were to live forever! But then, no one lived forever!

She put on her flannelette nightdress, buttoned up to the chin, with silk featherstitching at the wrists. Little knobs of hair in wire wavers stuck out on her head. She drew the curtains closely across the two windows. How the rain beat! Voices came from the dining room below. Renny's voice, exclaiming, "Never! Never!" How odd that he should exclaim "Never" that way, as though in answer to her thoughts. . . . She caught sight of her reflection in the pier glass, as she stood against the long dark curtain. She drew back her head and stared. A stately figure she made, truly. An upright, noble-looking creature, she could not help thinking. She raised one hand and placed it palm downward across her brow in the attitude of one searching the horizon for a sail, in the attitude of one standing on the edge of a cliff, buffeted by the wind, with the stormy sea below.

She posed thus for a moment like a statue, then turned out the light and sought her bed.

Ernest had felt a little odd coming up the stairs, almost light-headed, but when he got to his own room he was quite himself, except that he had a feeling of agreeable exhilaration. He very much liked the rose-colored shade for his lamp that Alayne had sent him from New York on his birthday. It made his room so pretty and cheerful, even on such a night as this. Really, since this wet dark spell of weather had set in, he could hardly wait to light the lamp. Even in the daytime it made a charming spot of color in the room. Alayne had always been so sweet to him. Her going had left a real blank in his life. And Eden, too, he missed him greatly. It was such a pity that their marriage had turned out as it did. They had been such a lovely young couple, intellectual, good to look upon.

He stood meditatively, enjoying the soft pink glow that was diffused over the room. It imparted a fragile liveliness to the Dresden china figures on the mantelpiece, a tremulousness as of sunrise on the water colors on the gray walls. He was lucky to have such a room. Well, not altogether *lucky,* for his own good taste had made it what it was, though, of course, the view over the meadows and winding stream was much to be preferred to Nick's view, which was blocked by a huge cedar, and beyond it only the ravine.

The little china clock between the shepherd and shepherdess chimed twelve. What an hour for him to be getting to bed! But what a jolly evening! He hoped and prayed that the rum and water would do him no harm. Yes, and he had had a glass or two of wine before the rum. . . . He hoped and prayed that Mamma would be all right after that second supper of hers. How roguish she had been! He smiled when he thought of her. Really, one could scarcely believe that he was seventy-two with Mamma so active. . . . He hoped and prayed that he would be like that at a hundred and one. If he could manage to live that long. There was no reason why he should not live to a ripe old age. He took such good care of himself, though, of course, there was his chest — a handicap, certainly.

He remembered his new overcoat. Not a bad idea to try it on now when he was looking his best, flushed a little, his eyes bright. He got it from its hanger in the tall wardrobe and turned it round, looking it over very critically, his lips stern, his eyes knowing. "A damned fine coat!" He uttered the words aloud in the tone one might use in similar praise of mare or woman. Gad, it was a handsome coat!

He put it on, and it slipped over him with a firm yet satiny embrace. He stared at his reflection in the glass. No wonder the tailor had complimented him on his figure! Slender, upright (when he used a little will power), with an air of elegance such as one did not associate with the colonies.

Suddenly he felt the colonial's strange nostalgia for England. He remembered a top hat he had bought once in Bond Street. He remembered exactly what the shopman had looked like, and his pleasantly deferential manner. He remembered buying a flower for his buttonhole from such a sweet-faced flower seller that same morning. He recalled the agreeable elation he had felt as he had walked lightly down the street. It had never taken a great deal to elate him. He had a happier disposition than either his sister or his brother. Eden was like him in that. They both had a way of seeing the beauty of life — poetic temperament, though, of course, one couldn't say so before the family. Certainly he missed Eden's little visits to his room — to say nothing of Alayne's. Such a pity about that marriage. . . . Twenty years ago he had bought that hat in England, and he had not been back since! Perhaps when Mamma died.

and Augusta returned to her home, he would go back with her on a visit.

When Mamma died! The thought of her death always brought a tremor of apprehension with it. There was first the dread of losing her, and, added to that, the prolonged uncertainty as to who would inherit her money. Not a hint had dropped from her lips. She had thought it enough for them to know it was willed in its entirety to one member of the family. Thus her power over them was kept undiminished through the years. And their suspense. She must be worth between ninety and a hundred thousand, all in reliable bonds and stocks. Ah, if she should leave it to him, he would have independence, power in the family! He would do so many nice things for the boys! Dear boys, it would be best for them if the money were left to him. . . .

Looking steadily into the glass, his cheeks flushed, his body erect, he was sure that he did not look more than fifty, or fifty-five at the most. The coat was so warm, as well as so becoming, he would wear it to-morrow — no more shilly-shallying about it.

Before he got into bed he went to the basket where his cat, Sasha, lay sleeping with her kitten beside her. He looked down on them with a wry smile. Sasha, at her age, — she was twelve, — to have a mongrel kitten! And not only have it, but be brazen about it! He had thought she was past the age for having kittens, — especially mongrel ones, — and then, one morning, she had had this one on his bed. Just given one yell, about six in the morning, and had it. It had sounded like a yell of triumph, rather than an outcry of pain. What a jolt it had given him at that hour in the day! He'd scarcely been able to eat any breakfast. It wasn't only the sudden birth on his quilt, but the thought that Sasha . . . it wasn't as though she were a silly young female to be intrigued by a pair of handsome whiskers!

He murmured, "Kitty, kitty," and touched her with his fingers. It was as though he had touched a vital nerve that controlled her whole body. She unfolded like a fan, uncurling her body to its full length, raising the great golden plume of her tail. She opened her eyes, and then grinned impudently up at him—a great three-cornered grin that showed the roof of her mouth and her curling tongue.

"Naughty, naughty," he said, tickling her.

Her kitten butted its little bullet head against her. It should have been drowned, but his love for Sasha made him weak. It showed no sign of its mother's pure Persian birth, but there was something charming about its snow-white underpart, pink nose, and pointed gray ears. It had white paws, too, that looked large for it—working-class paws. The father was evidently a handsome fellow, but of the people.

Even after he was in bed he stretched out his hand and felt for the pair in the basket. It was amusing to lie in bed with one's hand snuggled against those warm furry bodies. It was comforting.

Piers found Pheasant already in bed, her shingled brown head quite off the pillow on the edge of the mattress, her bright eyes gazing into the cradle.

"Piers, do you know, Mooey's perfectly wonderful! What do you suppose he'd done? Got in between *quite* different layers of the blankets! I don't see how he managed it. Goodness, you've been a long time."

"We got to talking." He came over and looked down at the five-months-old baby. "Looks pretty fit, doesn't he?"

"Oo, the precious! Hand him in to me. I want him beside me while you get ready."

"Don't be silly. I shan't be five minutes. You'll only disturb him."

"I want to see his little toes, don't you?"

"Pheasant, you're nothing but a baby yourself. . . . I say, someone's been at my top drawer!"

"Not me! Not Mooey! Oh, Piers, if you'd only seen the face he made then! His mouth just like a pink button and his eyebrows raised. He looked positively supercilious."

"If I thought young Finch had been at my cigarettes . . ." He muttered as he undressed.

"Well, he had none of his own to-night. I know that. What would you do?"

"I'd show him. . . . Good Lord, I wish you had heard Uncle Ernest going on about his new coat after you left! I'll bet you a new silk undie thing to a pair of socks that he ends by wearing his winter coat after all."

"Then you'd go and say something to discourage him. Just a few words from you like 'Some day, this, Uncle Ernest,' or you might simply come into the house shivering."

"Well, you're free to tell him how balmy it is, and how perfect his shoulders look in the new coat."

"No. I'm not going to bet. It's against my principles. From now on I've got to be setting a good example to my little baby."

Piers sputtered with laughter. He was in his pyjamas now. "Shall I put out the light?"

"Piers, come here, I want to whisper."

He came and bent over her. Lying relaxed on the bed, her hair rumpled, a white shoulder showing above the slipped-down nightdress, she seemed suddenly very tender and appealing to Piers. She seemed as sweet and delicately vigorous as one of the young silver birches in the ravine.

His heart quickened its beat. "Yes? What does she want?" His eyes glowed softly into hers.

She hooked an arm around his neck. "I'm hungry, Piers. Would you — like a darling?"

He looked genuinely shocked. "Hungry! Why, it is n't any time since you were eating."

"Yes, it is. It's ages. You forget how long you 've been sitting downstairs talking. Besides, I 've fed Mooey. There's practically all the good of my own supper gone. Anyway . . . will you, Piers?"

He thought, as he descended the steps into the basement, "I 'm spoiling her. Before the kid came she'd never have dreamed of sending me downstairs for food for her at this hour. She'd have jolly well got it herself. She 's getting just like those American wives in the magazines."

Nevertheless, he sought earnestly in the pantry for something to stay her. He could hear Mrs. Wragge's succulent snore from the room beyond the kitchen. He could hear the old kitchen clock ticking the night away as eagerly as though the game were fresh to it instead of seventy years repeated. He lifted an enormous dish cover. Under it three sausages. He looked between two plates turned together. Cold salmon. He opened a door. The last of the joint, cold boiled potatoes, beet roots in their own juice, the carcass of a fowl — that looked promising. No, *high!* Whew! He shut the door. . . . What quantities of bread and buns all tumbled together in the breadbox! He chose a bun, split it, buttered it. That was that. Rather doubtfully he laid a sausage beside it. Cold rice pudding, packed with raisins. That was the thing! A saucer of that with cream. . . . Ha! What was this? Plum cake. He cut a slab and devoured it like a schoolboy. Indigestible, that stuff, for a nursing mother. . . .

Pheasant, round-eyed, sat up in bed. "Oh, how scrumptious!"

She clutched him and kissed him before she ate.

The light out, Pheasant tucked up close to him. Mooey making comfortable little snuggling noises in his sleep like a puppy. The rain beating on the windows, accen-

tuating the snugness and warmth of the indoors, the
peace. The peace. Why was it that at times like these
Eden's face should come out of the darkness to trouble him?
First as a pale disturbing reflection on the sea of his content, like the reflection of a stormy moon. Then clear and
brilliant, wearing his strange ironic smile, the blank look in
his eyes, as though he never quite clearly knew why he did
things. Piers shut his own eyes more tightly. He clenched
his teeth and pressed his forehead against Pheasant's
shoulder, trying not to think, trying not to see Eden's face
with its mocking smile.

He tried to draw comfort from her nearness and warmth.
She was his! That awful night when Finch had discovered
the two in the wood together was a dream, a nightmare.
He would not let the dreadful thought of it into his mind.
But the thought came like a slinking beast, and Piers's
mouth was suddenly drawn to one side in a grimace of pain.
Pheasant must have felt his unease, for she turned to him
and put an arm about his head, drawing it against her
breast.

Nicholas could not sleep. "Too damn much rum," he
thought. "This comes of drinking scarcely anything
stronger than tea. You get your system into such a state
that a little honest spirits knocks your sleep into a cocked
hat."

However, he didn't particularly mind lying awake. His
body was in a tranquil, steamy state, and pleasant visions
from his past drifted before his eyes. The glamour of
women he had cared for long ago hung like an essence in
the room. He had forgotten their names (or would have
had to make an effort to recall them), their faces were a blur
but the froufrou of their skirts — that adorable word
"froufrou" that had no meaning now — whispered about
him, more significant, more entrancing, than euphonious

names or pretty faces. And their little hands (in days when women's hands were really small, and "dazzling" was a word not too intense for the whiteness of their flesh) held out to him offering the flowers of dalliance. . . . His thoughts became poetic; there was a kind of rhythm to them. Realizing this, he wondered if it were possible that Eden had taken his talent from him. That would be rather a joke, he thought. What if he began to write poetry himself! He believed he could at this moment if he tried.

Nip, his Yorkshire terrier, who was curled up against his back, uncurled himself suddenly and began to scratch the quilt with concentrated vehemence. "Spider," growled Nicholas, "catch a spider, Nip!" The little dog, giving vent to a series of yelps, tore at the quilt, snuggled into it, and at last recurled himself against his master's back.

Nicholas loved the feel of that compact ball against him. He lay chuckling into the blanket he had drawn pretty well over his head. He began to get drowsy. . . . What had he been thinking of? Oh, yes, old days. Affairs. When Nip had begun that bout of scratching he had been recalling a little affair with an Irish girl at Cowes — it must have been quite thirty-five years ago, and the memory of it as fresh as her skin had been then! Ha — he had it! Adeline, that had been her name — the same name as his mother's. His mother. How she had hung on to Renny and kissed! And how they had stared into each other's eyes! A thought came to him with a nasty jolt. Suppose Renny were trying to get around her — get on the inside track after her money. . . . One never could tell . . . That red head of his. He might be as crafty as the devil for all one could tell. Nicholas remembered suddenly how as a child Renny could get things out of his grandmother. . . . What if all his caresses were calculated?

Nicholas became blazing hot, his brain a hotbed of suspicion. He flung the covers from his shoulders and put his

arms out on the quilt. Nip began to smack his lips as though
he were savoring the imaginary spider he had caught. The
rain dripped steadily. Nicholas lay staring into the darkness, going over in his mind encounters between the two —
little things trivial in themselves, but which seemed to indi-
cate that Renny's influence was unduly strong with the old
lady. Good heaven, if Renny were worming his way in
there, how dreadful! He would never forgive him!

He heard a step in the hall, Renny's step. He felt that
he must speak to him, see his face, discover perhaps some
telltale predatory gleam in his eye. He called, "Is that you,
Renny?"

Renny opened the door. "Yes, Uncle Nick. Want something?"

"Light my lamp, will you? I can't sleep."

"H'm. What's the matter with this family?" He
struck a match and came toward the lamp. "Wake's been
having a heart attack."

Nicholas growled sympathetically. "That's too bad.
Too bad. Poor little fellow. Is he better of it? Can I do
anything?"

"I shouldn't have left him if he hadn't been better. I
think he overdid it helping Gran to get up. He gets excited
about things, too. . . . Is that high enough?" The clear
flame of the lamp illumined the strongly marked features
that looked as though they had been fashioned for the facing
of high winds, carved more deeply the line of anxiety between the brows, accented the close-lying pointed ears.

Nothing underhand, self-seeking, in that face, Nicholas
thought, but I mustn't let the old lady get too doting about
him. He's the kind of man that women . . . "One thing
that was keeping me awake," he observed, peering shrewdly
into the illumined face, "was the thoughts of Mamma.
Her spirit, isn't it amazing?"

"A corker."

"It seems impossible to think that some day . . . Renny, has she ever said anything to you about how she's left her money?"

"Not a word. I've always taken it for granted that you'll get it. You're the eldest son and her favorite — a Court and all that — you ought to have it."

Nicholas's voice was sweet with reassurance. "Yes, I suppose that's the natural thing. Just set the lamp on the table here where I can reach it. Thanks, Renny. Good night, and tell Wake that he's to go straight to sleep and dream of a glorious trip to England Uncle Nick's going to take him."

"Righto. Good night."

He took from the mantel his special pipe, the sweet instrument of his bedtime smoke, and filled it. He stretched his leather-legginged legs before him, and, as he pressed the tobacco down into the bowl with his little finger, he gazed thoughtfully at Wake sleeping on the bed. Poor little beggar! What a time he'd had with him! A rotten bad spell, and that after weeks and weeks of seeming so well. He supposed it was the raw chill of the weather they'd been having that had pulled him down. That and heaving Gran about. He was such a game youngster, he'd tackle anything.

Wake's hair, rather long for an eleven-year-old, lay in a dark halo around his face. With his beautifully marked eyebrows, his fringed white lids, and his breath coming flutteringly through his parted lips, his appearance was such that it hurt Renny to look at him. Dash it all — would he ever rear the kid? Well, thank goodness, he was a little devil sometimes! He leaned forward and gently took the little thin wrist in his, felt the pulse. Quieter, more even. Wake lifted his lids.

"Oh, hello, Renny!"

"Hello. What are you awake for?"

"I don't know. I think I'm better. I say, Renny, may I go to the horse show to-morrow?"

"Not if I know it. You'll wait and go with the other kids on Saturday."

"How much can I have to spend?"

"Spend! What on?"

"Why, you know. They take around ice cream and chocolates and lemonade."

"Twenty-five cents."

"Oh. But last year there was a fortune-telling place just outside the restaurant part. I'd like to get my fortune told."

"Better not. You might hear something bad."

"What do you mean bad? Like dying?"

Renny scowled. "Good Lord, no! Like getting a sound hiding."

"Oh . . . I was thinking I might hear of a fortune being left me."

Renny's voice hardened. "What are you talking about, Wake? What fortune?" What the devil had the child in his mind?

"I dunno. . . . I say, Renny, I love watching your face. The way your nostrils go. They're funny. And the way you wiggle your eyebrow. I love watching you, more 'specially when you don't know it."

How cleverly the little rascal could change the subject! Renny laughed. "Well, I guess you're the one person who does, then."

Wakefield stole a sly look at him. "Oh no. There was someone else. Alayne. She loved watching you. I often caught her at it."

His elder sent forth a cloud of smoke. "What surprises me is the number of things you know which you've no right to know, and how slow you are on the uptake with useful information."

Wakefield closed his eyes. "He's getting himself worked

up to cry," thought Renny. He asked, "How about those legs? Nice and warm now? That nasty feeling gone, eh?" He put his hand under the clothes and began soothingly to rub them.

Alayne! What was she doing to-night? Was she happy? Forgetting him? Oh no, she would n't forget — any more than he! He wished to God he could forget! It had always been so easy for him to forget — the natural thing. And now, after more than a year, a sudden mention of her name sent the same tremor through him — gave him a sudden jolt, as though his horse had stumbled. . . . He rubbed the little legs rhythmically. Wake slept. The room was dimmed by a blue-gray haze of smoke. . . . He heard Finch moving in the room above and remembered that the boy's school fees were overdue. He unlocked a drawer and took out a slim roll of banknotes. Separating three tens and a five, he put them into an envelope, addressed and sealed it.

In the attic the only sign of habitation was the rim of light beneath Finch's door. He was about to turn the knob when a bolt was shot on the inside and he heard the boy's quick breathing.

"Hello," he rapped out. "What's this mean?"

"Oh, darn it all, Renny. I did n't know it was you!" He slid back the bolt and stood sheepish and red.

"Did you think it was the canary fellow come to get the lottery ticket?" He grinned down at Finch sarcastically.

Finch mumbled: "Thought it was Piers."

"Why? Had you been pinching something of his?"

The random shot went home. The boy's flush deepened, he stammered a weak denial, and Renny's grin exploded in a laugh. "You're certainly going to the dogs! What was it — ties? Cigarettes?"

"Cigarettes."

"H'm. . . . Well, here is your fee for the term. I should have sent it by cheque, but — the truth is, my account is a bit overdrawn. Just hand it to the bursar—and no frenzied finance on the way!" He laid a dollar on the envelope. "Get some fags for yourself, and cut out this light-fingered business. Also, keep inside your allowance."

Finch's hand shook as he took the money. He brought the lamp to light his elder down the stairs. "Is Wake feeling rocky to-night?" he asked, heavily.

"Yes."

"Gosh, I'm sorry."

He watched the lean figure descend, noticing how the lamplight sought the warm russet of leather leggings and close-cropped head. He wished to God he'd some of Renny's ginger!

Strength from music—that was what he wanted. He thought of the ivory expanse of the keyboard, and felt an ache through his soul, a quiver through his arms. . . .

Carefully he placed the notes in a shabby leather pocketbook; then from his desk he took an old mouth organ. He went into the clothes closet and shut the door. Then, putting his head under the tail of a heavy overcoat to muffle the sound, he laid his lips against the instrument and began wistfully to play.

IV

FINCH — THE ACTOR

ONE afternoon, a month later, Finch was standing among a group of amateur actors in the narrow passage between the stage and the row of dressing rooms in the Little Theatre. They were dispersing after a rehearsal of St. John Ervine's *John Ferguson*, and Mr. Brett, the English director, had just come up. Hands in pockets, he lounged over to Finch, and, with an eager smile lighting his clever, humorous, actorish face, observed, "I want to tell you, Whiteoak, how awfully pleased I am with your performance to-day. If you keep on as you're going now, you are going to make a really splendid Cloutie John."

"Thanks — Mr. Brett," stammered Finch. "I'm glad you think I'm all right." He was crimson from embarrassment and deep joy. Praise! Warm praise, before all of them!

Arthur Leigh broke in: "Yes, that's just what I've been telling Finch, Mr. Brett. He's simply splendid. I'm certain of this, that I'm doing my own part better since he's been playing Cloutie John. He brings a feeling of absolute reality into it."

Finch stared straight ahead of him, his fixed expression a burning mask for the confused elation of his spirit.

"Well, I'm very, very pleased," reiterated Mr. Brett, pushing toward the door — he was yearning for his tea. "To-morrow at the same hour, then, and everybody on time."

The door at the end of the passage was opened and a gust of crisp December air rushed in. The players drifted in a small body on to the stone steps. The walls of the university rose about them, showing here and there a lighted window. The arch of the Memorial Tower glistened in a bright armor of ice. Leigh turned to Finch as they reached the last step.

"I wish you lived in town, Finch," he said. "I'd like to see something of you. But there's always that beastly train to be caught."

"I'm afraid I've missed it to-night. I'll have to take the late one. Ten-thirty."

Leigh looked rather pleased. "That's good news. You'll come home with me to dinner, and we can have a talk. Besides, I'd like my mother and sister to meet you. I've been talking about you to them." He turned his clear, rather feminine gaze eagerly on Finch.

"Sorry. . . . Sorry," muttered the boy.

"What utter nonsense! Of course you can come. Why not?" He slipped his arm persuasively through Finch's.

"Oh, I don't know. At least — well, my clothes aren't right. And besides . . . you know I'm no good with women — ladies. Your mother and sister 'd think me an awful dud. I'd have nothing to say, and — and — look like — Cloutie John."

Leigh broke into delighted laughter.

"If only you would! If only you would both look and act like him! They'd throw themselves on your neck and embrace you. Come along, don't be an idiot!" He drew Finch on through the delicate drift of snowflakes, the air on their faces icy, yet somehow crisply caressing. Other young figures were moving quickly through the park, silhouetted against the whiteness.

Finch had, from the first moment of acquaintance, liked and admired Arthur Leigh, been flattered by the attraction he so evidently had for the other, but now he experienced a sudden outrush of warmth toward him which filled him with wonder. He felt that he loved Leigh, wanted to be his near, his closest friend. The pressure of Leigh's slender, small-boned body against his made him feel stronger than he had ever felt before. "Very well," he said, "I'll go."

They boarded a street car and stood together, swaying, hanging by the straps, smiling into each other's eyes, oblivious of the other passengers. They recalled amusing moments of the rehearsal, muttered lines of their parts, were almost suffocated by laughter. They were so happy they scarcely knew what to do.

But as Leigh put his latchkey into the lock, and Finch stood behind him before the imposing doorway of Leigh's house, young Whiteoak felt again an overwhelming shyness.

"Look here," he began, "look here, I — I — " But the door was open and he was inside the hall, where bright firelight was dancing over the surfaces of polished wood and brass, where there was such a look of immaculacy and order as Finch had never before beheld. The sound of girls' voices laughing together came from the drawing-room. The two youths darted up the stairway.

"Friends of Ada's," Leigh said, leading the way into his own room. "If once they captured us, they'd never go home. Mother hates the dinner to be late, and besides we must have a decent time for talking before you go. I refuse to hand you over to a parcel of girls."

They threw off their coats and caps. Finch endeavored to hide his stupefaction at the sight of so much luxury in a boy's room. Of course, Leigh was scarcely a boy, — he was twenty, — but he had never talked about his home, never seemed to be especially affluent, though he had plenty of pocket money. Finch had no idea what business or profession his father was in.

His host threw open a door and revealed a bathroom of virgin white and blueness. On a small table by the enamel tub stood a bowl of white narcissi just breaking into bloom.

"I like to look at lilies while I'm in the tub," said Leigh. "I bathe my soul in them while I bathe my skin in suds."

Finch stared, first at the narcissi, then at his friend.
"You're rather like that chap yourself," he mumbled.

"What chap?"

"Narcissus. I mean—you're so—well, it's not hard
to picture you gazing at your reflection in a pool—looking
awfully picturesque and all that."

Leigh looked delighted. "How I wish I had been Narcissus! The rôle would have suited me perfectly—gazing
and gazing, and adoring—myself! We'd better go ahead
and wash, old fellow. The girls are gone, and I hear the
first dinner gong." He flung a snowy-white embroidered
towel to Finch and went back to the bedroom whistling. He
knew that young Whiteoak was embarrassed, shy, and he
wanted to put him at his ease.

He wanted very much to gain Finch's confidence, even his
love. He felt extraordinarily drawn to the boy, whom he
looked upon as much younger than himself, though the
difference was only two years. Still, Finch was at school
yet, while he was in his second year at Varsity. There was
something in Finch's gaunt face and sad eyes that he found
himself constantly remembering, trying to clarify into a
definite attraction. From chance phrases, allusions that
Finch had let fall, he felt that he was misunderstood at
home, that there was no one there to appreciate the sensitive
depths of his nature, no one to love him with understanding and sympathy. He himself had been always so enfolded
in love and understanding. He must ask Finch about his
family, try to learn something that night of the setting of
his life. He could not quite make him out. He knew that
his grandfather had been an officer in India, that his family
owned a lot of land, but Finch was so rough at times, so almost uncouth. . . . He brushed his waving brown hair before the glass till it shone.

Finch had not been able to bring himself to the point of
using the embroidered towel. He had hung it carefully

among others of its kind on the glass rack, and had rubbed his face and hands dry on a corner of a bath towel. He now appeared in the doorway very shining, with a damp lock on his forehead and his long red wrists protruding pathetically from the sleeves of his blue serge coat.

In the drawing-room they found Leigh's mother and sister. Two sisters, Finch thought at first, the mother looked so young.

"My friend Finch Whiteoak," Leigh introduced him, a protective hand on his arm. "This is my mother, Finch, and this ill-looking young person my sister Ada."

In turn their soft hands lay in Finch's bony one. In turn he saw the soft pale oval of each face, the drooping locks of bronze hair, the heavy-lidded gray eyes. But the mother's hair had a tinge of gold, her eyes a tint of blue, and the amused and tolerant expression of her mouth made him afraid of her.

"Brothers will say such cruel things about their sisters," she said, with an adoring smile at her son. "I suppose you do it occasionally yourself."

Finch, breathing heavily, stammered, "Well — I suppose so — at least, I really don't know."

"Honestly now," said Leigh, "don't you find Ada distressingly ill-favored?"

She returned their gaze serenely, and Finch stammered again, "Oh, look here, Leigh . . ."

Mrs. Leigh observed, "Arthur has talked of you a great deal. He thinks your acting of the idiot boy quite wonderful."

"That's easy for me," grinned Finch. "The idiot part."

"Mother," broke in Leigh, "how can you? Cloutie John isn't an idiot. He's mad. Absolutely, gloriously mad."

Ada Leigh said, in a low deep voice, with a look into Finch's eyes which set them definitely apart from the others, "Is that easy, too, for you? The madness, I mean."

Her brother answered for Finch, fearing that he would give another stammering, grinning reply. "The easiest thing in the world, my child. All he has to do is to be himself. He's absolutely, gloriously mad also. Just wait until you see the play. When Cloutie John comes on the stage, madness, like an electric current, is going to thrill the soul of that simple-minded audience. We're all thrilled by him, even at rehearsals."

Ada continued to gaze into Finch's eyes as though Leigh had not spoken.

"I expect I am a little mad," he answered, feeling now not shy, but oddly troubled.

"I wish you would teach me how to be mad. I am far too sane to be happy."

"I couldn't teach anyone anything except how to play the fool."

Mother and son were leading the way to the dining room.

Finch saw that the table, delicately bright, was laid for four. Evidently Mrs. Leigh was a widow, though she did not look at all like Finch's idea of one. Perhaps her husband was merely out of town.

Nothing could draw him into conversation. With set face he ate his way slowly and solemnly through the intricacies of the meal. Leigh, depressed by the sense that his friend was making no impression but one of stupidity on his mother and sister, talked little. Ada seemed to make no effort to please anyone but herself, and her pleasure apparently lay in making Finch aware of the insistent gaze of her long, heavy-lidded eyes. Mrs. Leigh alone kept the talk from dying into silence. Her voice, lighter and higher than her daughter's, flowed brightly on, though Finch had the feeling that her thoughts were far away. Across her brightness a shadow fell once when she referred to the "time of my husband's death, five years ago."

When dinner was over she left them, returning only for

a moment to the drawing-room in an ermine evening cloak to say good-bye before she was whirled away in a dove-gray limousine. They had followed her to the stone porte-cochère to see her off. Leigh had tucked her in and kissed both her hands.

"Isn't she the most adorable mother to own?" he demanded, as they returned to the fireside.

"Rather," agreed Finch, his eyes on Ada. She had settled herself among the cushions of a deep couch, her narrow sloping shoulders, her slender arms, from which open filmy lace sleeves fell away, seeming almost transparent in their whiteness. Between her rather pale lips she held a Chinese-red cigarette holder.

Leigh suddenly found his tongue. He talked eagerly of the play to Finch, criticized Mr. Brett's directing of it, rehearsed one of his own important speeches, appealing to Finch for criticism.

"Come, Finch," he said, at last, determined to show off his friend before his sister, "let's do our scene together where you come to the house at night, after I've killed Witherow. Have you got your whistle here?"

"Oh, no. I can't possibly. I'd feel a frightful fool."

"If it's because of Ada, I'll send her away."

"I wish you would do it to please me," said Ada. "I should love to see it."

"She's likely to fly into a passion if she doesn't get what she wants. Aren't you, Ada?" asked her brother.

"You can't make me believe that," said Finch.

"Just the same she's a very determined young person, so you may as well give in. Wait, I know what we need to loosen things up. A whiskey and soda. That wine at dinner was native and there's simply nothing to it but gas on the stomach. Come along to the dining room. You won't want anything, will you, Ada?"

"No, thanks. I'll just wait here."

In the dining room Leigh said, "I don't think we need whiskey, Finch. Nothing so common. A nice little *crème de menthe* or Benedictine, eh? I said whiskey before Ada merely to put her off the scent; she doesn't like it. But she does like liqueurs, and I don't think they're good for a young girl, do you? I really have to look after Ada, you know, my father being dead. What will you have?"

"Oh, I don't care." Finch stared at the glittering array of glasses in the cabinet Leigh opened.

"Benedictine, then. We'll both have Benedictine. Isn't the color of it glorious? I want you to come and stay the week of the play with me, Finch. You can't possibly go home at night after the performance." At that moment he definitely made up his mind to take young Whiteoak into his intimate circle, to make him his most intimate friend. He perceived his sister's intense interest in him. She too was sensitive to the inner things of life. She recognized something peculiar, different, beautiful in Finch.

"I'm afraid I can't."

Leigh was astonished. He had expected Finch to be gratefully eager to accept any offering of friendship from him.

"But why not?"

"Oh, I don't know. But I think I'd better not. Thanks just the same."

Leigh had been accustomed all his life to doing exactly what he wanted to, to having whatever he desired. His face showed the calm brightness of youth whose will has never been crossed.

"What nonsense. Of course you'll come. You're only shy. We need see very little of my mother and Ada, if it's that you mind."

"No. The truth is," Finch burst out, "I should never have gone into this thing."

Leigh said nothing, only looked at him with bright questioning eyes.

"I believe I'll have another glass of that — er — Benedictine."

"I don't think I would if I were you. It's rather potent. . . . You were saying —"

Finch carefully set down his empty glass, fragile as a bubble. "You know I failed in my matric, Leigh."

"Certainly. Consequently you'll not need to swat at all this year. Take it easy."

"But my family —"

"Tell me about your family, Finch. You've never spoken of your parents to me."

"They're dead. My eldest brother runs things."

"Your guardian, eh? What sort of chap is he? Hard to get on with?"

"Oh, I don't think so. He's sharp-tempered if you don't toe the mark. But he's awfully kind sometimes."

"What makes you think he won't be kind this time?"

"He's got no opinion of theatricals and things of that sort. He's all for horses."

"Ah, I remember. I saw him ride gloriously at the horse show. I'd like to meet him. I might be able to persuade him that play-acting is good for you."

"You're quite wrong there, Leigh. He stopped my music lessons because of the matric business."

"Good heavens!" Leigh restrained himself from saying, "What a beast!" He asked, "And you were keen about music?"

"Awfully."

"More than about acting?"

"Much more."

"And you've never mentioned it to me!" His tone expressed hurt.

"We were always talking about sport or the theatre."

Leigh, with a gesture almost of petulance, turned to the sideboard. He refilled his own glass and that of Finch.

"You are amazingly reticent," he said coldly. "I thought we were friends."

Finch sipped his Benedictine. He did not question why it was so suddenly given, after having been withheld. He saw Leigh in a glittering aura, a beautiful and desired being who would go through life choosing his paths, his friendships, with princely ease. He exclaimed eagerly, "But we are! We are! At least, I am yours — I mean, you are mine. . . . Only, you can't understand. I did n't think you 'd be a bit interested in my family or what I cared about. Like music, you know. . . . I 'll be awfully glad to spend that week with you, Leigh, if you want me. I 'll manage it somehow."

His long, hollow-cheeked boy's face was flushed with emotion, his eyes glistened with sudden tears.

Impulsively Leigh put his arm about his shoulders. "We are friends then — for always. I can't tell you what you mean to me, Finch. I 've been attracted by you from the first moment I saw you. You 're unlike any other fellow I know. I 'm positive you 've genius, either dramatic or musical. We 'll see. Tell me all about it, anyhow."

"There 's nothing much to tell — Leigh."

"Call me Arthur."

Finch's eyes lighted. "Oh, may I? Thanks awfully. I 'll like that. . . . There 's nothing much to tell, Arthur. I can't play decently yet, but I 'd rather be doing it than anything. I think it 's chiefly because I can lose myself doing these things. Forget that I 'm Finch Whiteoak." He stared in silence at the floor for a moment, his hands thrust in his pockets, then he raised his eyes to his friend's face and asked ingenuously, "It 's wonderful when you 're able to forget yourself completely, is n't it?"

"It must be. . . . But I could n't do it, Finch. I 'm so damned self-conscious. I 'm always posing. I don't want to forget myself. My great joy in life is watching my own stunts. But," he added seriously, "my feeling about you ís not self-conscious. It's real. As real as you are, and you're as real as one of those spirited horses your red-headed brother rides so well."

Finch uttered one of his sudden guffaws. "I'm real enough, but I'm no more spirited than a — than a — why, I guess Renny'd take a fit if he heard anyone call me spirited."

"Well, I suppose I should have said sensitive, highly strung. . . . And this — Renny — stopped your music lessons, eh? Because you failed to pass your matric. Had he given you a good teacher?"

"Splendid. When Renny does anything, he does it thoroughly — even if it's swearing. I've never heard anyone who can curse like Renny."

"He seems a thoroughgoing beast, but I like him in spite of myself. Is he married?"

Finch shook his head, and he thought of Alayne.

"Doesn't care about women?"

"They fall for him."

"Are any of your brothers married?"

"Yes. Eden's married; that is — well, he's separated from his wife. She's in New York. Her name is Alayne. Piers is married, too. He and his wife live at Jalna."

"Jalna?"

"Yes, that's the name of our place. Indian military station. My grandfather was stationed there."

Leigh exclaimed, "Look here, Finch, you must ask me out. I'm eaten up with curiosity to meet this family of yours. You're like a picture without its frame. I want to be able to see you in that frame. Just give me a chance to use my charms on your Renny and there'll be no trouble about the week in town. We'll even have him in to see the show."

Ada's voice came from the drawing-room. "If you are not coming back, I wish you'd tell me. I'd find a book to read or go to bed."

"What a shame to desert her so!" exclaimed Leigh. He returned with his quick, graceful movements to the couch where she lay, and bent over her. "Sorry, little one. Finch has been telling me about his family. He's invited me to go out to meet them. Aren't you jealous?"

"Frightfully."

"Now we're going to rehearse our scene for you. . . . Come, Cloutie John, rumple your locks, and show Sis how truly mad you are."

But the rehearsal was a failure. It was impossible for Finch to abandon himself to his part in that room, with Ada Leigh's critical eyes fixed on him. Leigh, after a little. saw how impossible it was and gave up the attempt.

He asked Finch to play. Time after time Finch's eyes had been drawn to the shining ivory of the keyboard, flushed by the rose-shaded light. He longed for the feel of it under his hands. He longed to feel the sense of power, of freedom, that always came with that contact. And this was a noble-looking grand piano. He had never touched one in his life. . . . His awkwardness fell from him as he slid on to the polished seat and laid his hands on the keys. Leigh noticed then what shapely hands he had despite their boniness. He noticed the shape of his head. Finch was going to be a distinguished-looking man some day. He was going to help Finch to attain his full spiritual growth, foster with his friendship the genius that he felt sure was in him. "Play," he said, smiling, and leaned across the piano toward him.

The piano was a steed. Finch's hands were on the bridle. A moment more and he would leap into the saddle and be borne away over wild fields of melody under starry skies. The steed knew him; it thrilled beneath his touch. His foot felt for the pedal. . . . What should he play?

He raised his eyes to Leigh's face, smiling encouragement. He saw Ada's eyes on him, too, mysterious behind a faint veil of smoke. He wished she were not there. Her presence dimmed the brightness of his contact with the keyboard, as the smoke dimmed the brightness of her eyes. He felt confused. He did not seem able to remember one piece from another.

"What shall I play?" he appealed to Leigh.

"Dear old fellow, I don't know what things you've done. Can you play Chopin? You look as though you could."

"Yes. I'll try one of his waltzes."

But, though his fingers ached to gather the notes, his brain refused to guide them.

"Oh, hell!" he muttered to Leigh. "I'm up against one of my fool fits!"

Late that night he wrote in his diary, at the end of the account of his day's doings, not the usual item concerning Joan, but in black, desperate-looking characters, the words "Met Ada."

V

LEIGH'S INFLUENCE

In the days that followed, the friendship between Finch and Arthur Leigh strengthened into one of those sudden, passionate attachments of youth. They wished always to be together, but, as Finch was still at school and Leigh was a second-year student at Varsity, this was impossible. Leigh, however, had a car of his own, and he made it his habit to call for Finch every noon hour and take him out with him for luncheon. After the rehearsals it became the custom for Finch to return to the Leighs' house for dinner and to take the late train home. Finch explained this to Renny by saying that he had made a friend of a clever Varsity fellow who was willing to help him with the mathematics which were his weakness. This was partially true, for Leigh would now and again work with him for an hour. At the end of these periods Leigh, who had a bent toward mathematics, found himself nervously exhausted. It was impossible to make Finch really understand even simple problems. The most that Leigh could do was to teach him certain tricks, and to show him how to make use of his excellent memory.

Finch never forgot the lines of his part. The director of the Little Theatre told him that if the stage were not in such a bad way he would advise him to make acting his profession. He could not feel any great elation over Mr. Brett's praise because he was at the moment greatly harassed by the necessity of spending the last fortnight before the play in town. More and more rehearsals were demanded. At last he agreed that his friend should come with him to Jalna to see what his influence could do toward softening the heart of the eldest Whiteoak on the subject of play-acting. He had put off the visit several times when Leigh had suggested it, but at last, in desperation, he threw himself on Leigh's protection and resource.

It was a Saturday afternoon in the New Year. The January thaw had come and gone. The weather had become cold again, but there was no snow. It was an iron day. An iron sky and iron earth, a wind, the metallic iciness of which might well take the heart out of even a strong man. Arthur Leigh was not strong, and, as he and Finch strode northward along the road toward Jalna, it took all his courage to keep up the pace without complaint. He cast a sidelong glance at Finch. He saw his tall figure bent against the blast, the end of his long nose getting pink, a drop of moisture like a tear trickling from his eye. He had a dogged look as though he had faced such a wind along this road many a time.

Leigh gasped out, the words whistling between his teeth, "I say, Finch, do you do this walk every day — in all kinds of weather? Deep snow — and sleet — and all that?"

"Of course I do. Are you cold, Arthur?"

"I've been warmer. Don't they ever send a car for you?"

"Good Lord, no. Sometimes I get a lift. We'll soon be there now."

They strode on.

A little later Leigh exclaimed petulantly, "I was never made for such a climate. As soon as I get through college, I'll cut these winters out."

"Atlantic City, eh?"

"Oh, my dear, no! The south of France. The Lido. You and I'll go together, Finch."

Finch grinned at him lovingly. He did not see where he would ever get money for traveling, but the thought of being in Europe with Arthur was beautiful. Leigh never called him "my dear," or "darling Finch" without his heart beating a little more quickly as in glad response. He had never been able to call his friend by any term of endearment, though in secret he had used them many a time. Often the last words that came into his head before he dropped asleep were " Darling Arthur " or " My dearest Arthur." Once, in a whim, he had toyed instead with the words " Darling Ada," but it did not do at all. It made him ashamed. She was not his darling, and never would be. She was just a strange and disturbing girl who had a way of haunting his dreams. But he could say " Darling Arthur " in his mind with a caressing inflection, just as Arthur said " Darling Finch " aloud without any embarrassment.

Leigh was looking so chilled that Finch was glad when he was able to steer him at last up the driveway behind the shelter of the spruces and hemlocks. " Here we are! " he announced, rather boisterously, because he felt nervous about introducing his friend to his family. It was the first time he had ever brought a friend home with him from town.

Leigh paused to look at the old house. It stood solidly before him, its façade, crisscrossed by the bare stalks of the Virginia creeper, dark red like some ruddy old weather-beaten face, seamed by wrinkles, yet expressing great power and endurance. The upper windows were veiled by a coating of frost, but through the lower ones he could see the dancing brightness of firelight. The wind shrieked about him. Every shutter on the house seemed to be rattling. He thought, " So this is where Finch was bred."

A great round stove in the hall sent forth a blasting heat. They hung their coats and hats on an old-fashioned hatrack, ornamented on the top by a carved fox's head. An old bob-tailed sheep dog lay by the stove. He did not rise when Finch bent and patted him, but rolled over on his back and waved shaggy deprecating paws.

" Is he old? " asked Leigh.

" Just four years younger than I am."

" Likes the heat, eh? " Leigh held his hands, rigid with cold, toward the stove.

From the drawing-room came the crackle of flames and the sound of a strong old voice talking steadily.

"Now I've got you. Cornered, eh? Ha, no you don't! No getting away from me. . . . Bang, there goes your man! Checkmate!"

A clear treble replied, with a petulant note, "You're not playing chess, my grandmother; this is backgammon."

"Of course it's backgammon."

"Then why do you use the terms of chess, Gran?"

Silence for a moment, then the old voice, with the tremor of a chuckle in it: "Because I like to fuss up my opponent."

"I'm not fussed up."

"Yes, you are. Don't contradict me. I won't have it."

"Anyhow, there goes one of your men. Bang!"

"And here goes one of yours! Bang! Bang!"

"Why, Granny, you're on one of the wrong points!"

"Very well. I took the trick, didn't I?"

"Now you're talking as though it were a card game."

"Now I've got you fussed up!"

"But don't you honestly forget when you use those wrong terms?"

"Of course I don't forget. . . . Your play, now."

"But," persisted the treble, "you forgot when you moved on to the white point."

"Bosh! I've made people believe black was white before this."

Overcome by curiosity, Leigh moved to the doorway and stared into the room. He saw a large, high-ceilinged parlor, the walls of which were covered by an ornate gilded paper and hung with oil paintings. Dark red curtains cherished it against the January daylight. A fresh fire of birch logs gave it light and heat from within. Leigh wondered if the furniture with which the room was crowded could be real Chippendale. If it were, he was sure it would be worth a fortune. With greater intensity he wondered if the figure before the fire could be real, that old, old woman in the purple velvet tea gown, the large lace cap with gay rosettes of ribbon, the carven, sardonic face. The effect of the little boy sitting opposite her was one of bright fragility. And yet he bore a strange resemblance to her, as a little running brook might bear the reflection of an ancient tree.

Leigh, amazed and delighted, turned to look at Finch. Finch was grinning deprecatingly at him. " My grandmother and my young brother," he whispered, and he took out a large handkerchief and blew his nose, as though to hide his embarrassed face behind it.

He had tooted his long nose so loudly that the faces of the players turned toward the door, not so much in inquiry as in resentment at the interruption.

" Ha, Finch," said his grandmother, " I 'm beating Wakefield. Got him all fussed up."

" That 's right, Gran."

" Come and kiss me. Who 's the nice-looking boy ? "

He kissed her on the cheek. " My friend, Arthur Leigh. Arthur, my grandmother."

Old Mrs. Whiteoak held out her hand, a shapely hand, though the fingers now had a clawlike curve to them. Leigh was astonished by the number of rings she wore, the brilliance of her rubies and diamonds, astonished too by the grip of her fingers, for he saw now that she was very old indeed.

" How old do you suppose ? " she asked, as though guessing his thoughts.

" Old enough to look very wonderful and wise," he answered.

She showed all her teeth in a pleased grin. " A good speech. Very good. Not many young men are so apt today. . . . Well, I 'm past one hundred. A hundred and one. And I can beat this young man at backgammon. And I can walk to the gate out there with the help of my two sons. Not bad, eh ? But I don't venture out in this weather. Oh, no, no. I stick by the fire. My next walk will be in April—three months off. You must come and see me do it."

The parrot, which had been perched in his wooden ring at a short distance behind her chair, now took his head from under his wing and, after blinking for a moment, as though dazed by the firelight, flew heavily to her shoulder and pressed his head against her cheek. Their two old beaks were turned with preposterous solemnity on Leigh. He felt as though he were in some strange dream.

"My parrot," she said. "Boney. I fetched him from India over seventy years ago. He's had two or three different bodies, but the soul's the same. Moves from one body to another. Transmigration of souls. Ever hear of that? We learned all about that sort of thing in the East. . . . He can speak Hindu, too, can't you, Boney?"

The parrot cried, in a nasal voice, "Dilkhoosa! Dilkhoosa!"

"He's making love to me! Ah, you old rascal, Boney! Again—again—say it again! *Dilkhoosa*—Heart's delight!"

"Dilkhoosa!" cried the parrot, pecking at the hairs on her chin. "Nur Mahal!"

"Hear him! Light of the palace, he's calling me. Nur Mahal. Say it again, Boney!"

"Nur Mahal!" rapped out the parrot. "Mera lal!"

Finch, very much pleased by Leigh's evident delight in the scene, observed, "I've never seen him in such a good humor. He's usually swearing or sulking or screaming for food."

"Life's a game," said Mrs. Whiteoak, sententiously. She peered up into Leigh's face with a quizzical, mocking light in her eyes. Her hand hovered above the board as though she were about to make a move, a steady red beam settling on one of her rubies. Wakefield watched her eagerly. Boney made guttural noises and thrust forward his green breast.

But the play was not made. Slowly her chin sank, her lace cap drooped toward the board, and a gusty breath whistled between her lips.

"She's asleep," said Finch.

"Oh, bother!" exclaimed the little boy. "Just when I was going to beat her!"

Finch looked at his watch. "A quarter to four. If we're going to see Renny before tea," he said, hesitatingly, "we had better look him up. Is he at the stables, Wake?"

"Yes. May I come too?"

"It's too cold for you, and you know it. Don't act like a six-year-old."

Wakefield raised his large dark eyes to Leigh's face. "It's sad, isn't it, always to be taking care of oneself? I'm always being told to stick by the fire and not be silly wanting to do things like other boys."

"There's nothing you like better than taking care of yourself," interrupted Finch, gruffly. He heard the sound of his uncles' voices upstairs. In a moment they would be descending. From the dining room came the nasal flow of cockney excuses for some misdemeanor pouring from Rags's lips into Lady Buckley's unreceptive ear. Far off Mooey began angrily to cry. In the hall the old sheep dog rose, shook himself, and uttered a deep-toned bark. All the house was stirring as the time for tea approached. Grandmother rubbed her long nose and peered out hazily into her firelit world.

"Life's a game," she announced, as though imparting a morsel of rare wisdom.

"Let's get out of here," said Finch.

He snatched their caps from the rack and handed Leigh his.

"What about our coats?" gasped Leigh, as they faced the blast at the opening of the side door.

"We'll sprint to the stables. It's warm enough there."

Running together, they passed a young fellow in leggings

with a fine color in his cheeks. He picked up a frozen winter pear from the ground and sent it after Finch's legs.

"That is my brother Piers," said Finch, as they entered
the stables.

They found Renny in a loose box, arranging the forelock
of a coy-looking mare with great exactness. Finch made the
introduction without enthusiasm. He hoped little from this
meeting.

"How do you do?" said the eldest Whiteoak, with a sharp
glance at the visitor.

He was indeed formidable, thought young Leigh. He did
not blame Finch for being afraid of him. His face, under
its peaked tweed cap, looked as though wind and weather,
strong passions, and a high temper had hammered into it a
kind of fierce immobility. . . . God, thought Leigh, he will
be like the old lady when he is her age, if he doesn't break
his neck while riding before he reaches it!

The youths discussed the mare together, her master —
rather ostentatiously, Leigh fancied — turning his back on
them, and continuing his caressing arrangement of her mane
and forelock. No admiring comment or carefully provocative question from Leigh drew more than a monosyllable
from him. Still they persisted. He could not spend the
entire afternoon over the mare's toilette. . . .

No, apparently he was satisfied. He looked her over;
then, taking her head quickly between his hands, he pressed
a kiss on her nose. "My pretty one," Leigh heard him say.
The mare's eyes were two beaming orbs of contentment, her
forehead the very throne of love. She uttered a deep sigh.

Renny came out of the loose box.

"What is her name?" asked Leigh.

"Cora."

A stableman was carrying buckets of water along the passage to the various stalls. He placed one before the occupant
of the stall nearest them, and a long gray head was thrust

forward, yearning lips were plunged into the cold drink.
Renny pushed past the boys and went around into the stall.

"How is the leg, Wright?"

"Fine, sir. Couldn't be mendin' better."

They bent over a bandaged hind leg.

"It was wonderful, sir, you getting him the way you did.
He's going to make his mark, I'm sure of it. And, for my
part, I don't believe he's spoiled for flat racing, say what
they will."

Renny and the stableman stared with concentration at the
bandage. The water in the bucket was lowered three parts
of the way down. Coaxing whinnies, the indolent jangle of
buckles, the petulant stamp of a hoof, were the only sounds.

"How did he get hurt?" asked Leigh, in an attempt to
draw nearer to the master of Jalna through the horses which
were so plainly his absorbing interest.

"Kicked himself." He was pressing a practised thumb
along the dappled gray flank.

"Really! How did he happen to do that?"

"Shied." He straightened himself and turned to Wright.
"How is Darkie's indigestion?"

"Better, sir, but he'll have those attacks just as long as
he bolts his oats the way he does. He's more like a ravening wolf than a horse with his feed."

A shadow fell across Renny's face. "Has he had his
oats?"

"Yes, sir. I divided them into two lots, like you said
to. After he'd had the first lot, I made him wait ten minutes. I've just give him the last half now."

Renny strode with irritable swiftness to a stall farther
down the passage, where a tall black horse was feeding with
ferocious eagerness. He ceased champing his oats for a
second to look back at his master entering the stall, then,
with his mouth full, the oats dribbling from his lips, he
plunged his face once more into his feed box.

Renny caught his head and jerked it up. "Cut out that guzzling!" he ordered. "Are you trying to kill yourself?"

The horse tried to shake him off, straining desperately toward his oats, his great eyes rolling in anger at the interruption. After a few moments he was allowed to fill his mouth once more, and again restrained. The rest of the meal was a struggle. He bit at Renny. Renny cuffed him. He snorted his outraged greed. Renny became suddenly hilarious and broke into noisy laughter.

"I should think that such irritation would be worse for the beast's digestion than bolting," observed Leigh.

"Should you?" grinned Finch, highly pleased with his brother.

The horse now was showing his big teeth, as though he too felt a kind of grim amusement.

Finch whispered to Leigh, "Now would be a good time to speak to him about the play. At least," he added, rather pessimistically, "as good as any."

Leigh looked toward the red-haired Renny with some apprehension. "I suppose so," he said. Then he had an idea —impulsive, extravagant, but one to break the ice between himself and Finch's brother.

He said, "I wonder, Mr. Whiteoak, if you could tell me where I might buy a good saddle horse. I have been wanting one for some time,"—he was in truth afraid of horses,—"but I haven't found—haven't been quite able" —his sentence broke down weakly.

There was no need for him to finish it. The arrogant face before him softened into an expression of almost tender solicitude. Renny said, "It's a good thing young Finch brought you out. It's a serious matter, buying a horse if you are inexperienced. Especially a saddle horse. I was talking the other day to a young fellow who had paid a fancy price for one and it had turned out not only nasty-tempered but a wind-sucker. A handsome beast, too. But he'd got badly stung. I have "— he hesitated, examining a bleeding knuckle which Darkie had jammed against the manger.

"Yes, yes," said Arthur, eagerly, though he felt a certain resentment at the ease with which the barrier between had been swept away when the possibility of a deal in horseflesh had appeared.

Renny took the knuckle from his lips. "I have a lovely three-year-old here — by Sirocco, out of Twilight Star — the image of his sire. You've seen Sirocco, of course?"

Arthur shook his head.

Renny regarded him pityingly. "You haven't? Well, I'll take you around to see him. Every stallion, you must know, — that is, every really great stallion, — reproduces himself absolutely only once. And Sirocco has only done it once. But perhaps" — he had been about to lead the way down the passage, but he wheeled, as though by an arresting thought — "perhaps you don't care much about breeding points, and just want a —"

"Not at all," interrupted Arthur. "It must be a real beauty, everything you say —"

"Horse like that can't be bought cheaply, you know."

"Oh, that doesn't matter." Then he reddened a little, thinking he might appear pretentious, too affluent, and added, "The fact is, I've been saving up for a saddle horse for a very long time."

The eldest Whiteoak had already heard, though without great interest at the time, that Leigh had inherited a large fortune, and that he would shortly be of age. He said, cheerfully, "Well, in that case" — and led the way to the stallion's loose box.

Finch followed, wondering what all this would lead to, worrying over the thought of Arthur in Renny's grip for the sake of him. From the loose box to the stall where the three-year-old was they proceeded, and Leigh learned more about saddle horses in half an hour than in all his preceding life. He thanked God that the day was wild, for otherwise he knew he would have been forced into a trial ride on the scornful-looking beast that cast suspicious glances at him down its nose.

The sound of small feet running came to them, and Wakefield dashed along the passage, a coat thrown over his head beneath which his face looked out, bright-eyed and scarlet-cheeked.

"I simply *flew* over," he panted, "to tell you to come to tea. It's five o'clock and there was a perfectly 'normous cake and it's nearly gone and there's a fresh pot of tea made for *you*, Renny. And for Mr. Leigh, o' course."

The snow had come at last. He was feathered all over with it.

"You should not have come out in this gale," said Renny. "Was there no one else to send?"

"I wanted to come! Which nag is that? Is he a good jumper? I must run around and see my pony. Shouldn't you like to see my birthday pony, Mr. Leigh?"

Renny caught him by the arm. "No. Don't go around there. Wallflower is in the next stall and she's feeling very nervous to-day. Go to the house, Finch, and tell Aunt that Mr. Leigh will follow you in a little while. Tell her to keep the tea hot for him. Send Rags over with a pot for me, and some bread and butter. I'll take it here." He picked up Wakefield as though he had been a parcel, and deposited him on Finch's back. "Give this youngster a ride. He's got nothing but slippers on. You deserve a good cuffing, Wake. And see that you keep that coat over your head." He raised his voice and shouted, "Open the door for this thoroughbred, Wright!"

Wakefield clutched Finch about the neck, delighted with this sudden return to the days of pickaback. Finch, however, looked rather glum when the stableman laughed as he passed them. He thought he detected a jeering note in his laughter. Wake was much heavier than he would have believed possible. But when the door had slammed behind them and the wind had caught him in the back he felt that they would be swept along without an effort on his part.

The snow came with a flourish across the ravine. The white flakes rushed endlessly one on another. Already the ground was white. The lights of the house looked far away. Finch lurched, bent forward, as though the next moment he would go on his nose.

"I don't suppose," said Wakefield, "you could caper a bit."

"What the hell—" bawled Finch. "Caper! What do you think I am—a draft horse? Caper! Caper!"

But his sense of fun was roused. He began to caper indeed, skipping, whirling awkwardly on the gale, feeling suddenly wildly happy. Wake no longer seemed a drag on him. They were one—a hairy, gamboling centaur, frisking in the January dusk, stung by the snowflakes into animal hilarity.

From side to side they swayed and rocked. Far away they heard the breakers crashing on the beach.

"Centaur," gasped Finch. "Prancing centaur."

Wakefield, believing that he was uttering the cry peculiar to centaurs, gave a shrill treble neigh that quavered and died among the snowflakes. He too was happy. The coat had fallen from his head, which he held high, fancying it to be adorned with a great fanlike beard and a fierce crest of hair. Again he neighed and again, and in answer to his neigh came the bellow of the waves.

So, noisy, riotous, snowy, they staggered into the side door. Finch, depositing Wakefield on the floor, leaned against the wall, his hand to his side.

"Winded?" asked Wakefield, looking kindly up at him.

"You bet."

"Do you know, I think a beef, iron, and wine mixture would be good for you. You've grown too fast and you can't stand much, and you look right now as if you were going to fall in a heap."

The virtue was indeed gone out of Finch, the madness, the gayety, but he did not want medical advice from this patronizing youngster. With a grunt he turned away and slouched to the dining room.

In the stable Renny had remarked, a shadow on his face, " A delicate boy, that."

"Yes, so I gathered," returned Leigh. "Perhaps he'll outgrow it. They often do, don't they? I wasn't a very strong kid myself."

Renny looked him over. "Hmph," he observed, without any note of encouragement; then added, more cheerfully, "I'd like to take you to my office and show you the horse's pedigree." He led the way to a small room partitioned off from a corner of the stable. He switched on a dangling electric bulb, and, after placing a kitchen chair for Leigh, seated himself before a yellow oak desk and began to look over a file of papers.

As he sat engrossed, beneath the hard white light, Leigh studied him with an access of interest. He tried to put himself in Finch's place, to imagine how it would feel to be obliged to ask this stern-looking fellow for permission to do this and that, to face him after failure in an exam. He was so sensitive himself, he had been so surrounded by understanding and sympathy, that he could not imagine it. . . . He wished very much that he were not going to buy the horse. It would be necessary to board it out; it would be necessary to ride it, and he did not care for riding. Renny Whiteoak's performance at the horse show had left him quite unmoved. He was infinitely more impressed by the sight of him sitting in his chair under the electric bulb, searching with complete concentration through his records. He had been driven to buying the horse in order to create a meeting place where he and Finch's brother could talk about Finch. But how was he to begin?

His reflections were broken by a piercing cry somewhere outside, followed by a cascade of blood-freezing screeches. He turned white with terror.

Renny Whiteoak remarked laconically, " Pig. Killing it."

Leigh felt relieved, but still shocked. " Oh," he said, and, looking out at the darkness, he observed, " It seems an odd time for killing a pig."

" Yes, does n't it?" He raised his eyes from the papers and, seeing Leigh's face, said, " It will be over in a minute."

It was. Silence fell. Leigh shivered, for the room seemed to him very cold with a damp chill that he supposed penetrated from the stable.

" Ah, here we are! Now, just draw your chair up to the desk."

Leigh obediently drew toward the desk, and the two bent over the pedigrees. He followed rather vaguely the intricacies of blood relationships, and was surprised at the knowledge one man might have of the qualities of various equine families.

They were still absorbed when a tap came at the door and Wragge entered with Renny's tea. Leigh began to feel desperate. His chances for pleading Finch's cause to the head of the clan seemed to be lessening. With a sudden nervous decision he closed the bargain. The payment was arranged.

Renny observed, while washing his hands in a basin on a small washing stand in a corner, " It's too bad to have kept you from your tea so long. I wish I had had Rags fetch enough over here for two. He might just as well. However, he'll take you over to the house. It's getting dark."

Leigh shivered. He was nervous, he was cold, and the thought of eating in a stable disgusted him.

"Thank you," he said. "It doesn't matter at all." He shivered again, as he noticed how Renny rubbed yellow soap on his hands regardless of the raw knuckle.

Rags set the tray on the desk. He arranged the things on it with the air of a liveried butler putting the last touches on a table laid for a banquet. He lifted the cover from a silver dish and disclosed three thick slices of buttered toast.

"Bit of a juggler I am, sir," he said, "getting the tr'y acrost in a blizzard like this and never sloppin' so much as a drop."

"Good for you," observed his master, sitting down before the tray and pouring himself a cup of tea. "But this is no blizzard. It's nothing but a fresh wind. It's good for you." He took a large bite of toast with relish.

Now, thought Leigh, is the time to tackle him. He said, "There's something I'd like to talk to you about, Mr. Whiteoak — by ourselves. I can find my way to the house without any trouble, really. I — I simply want to ask you something — explain something — that is " — he felt like a stammering schoolboy.

Renny looked surprised, but he said, "Yes? If there's anything I can do — Very well, Rags, you needn't wait for Mr. Leigh."

"It's about Finch," began Leigh, slowly, feeling his way, like a man in the darkness of a strange wood. "I'm very fond of him."

"Yes," returned Renny, the alert interest in his eyes changing to polite attention, "Finch has often spoken of you." Again his expression changed, this time to a stare at the inquisitive little cockney, who blinked back at him for a moment and then slid out of the room with a kind of impudent servility.

As the door closed behind him, words came more easily to Leigh. "I think, sir, that Finch " — he had the good sense to use moderation in his statement — "is really a very clever boy. I think he will be a great credit to you — to Jalna." His subtle mind had discovered that, more than his horses, the eldest Whiteoak loved his house. A sudden breaking up of his features into tenderness and pleasure at some praise of Leigh's for the lofty rooms, the old English furniture, had disclosed this. He went on: "I am sure he will, if he is allowed a little margin — a chance, you know, to develop in his own way. There are some fellows who can't stand the grind of study unless they have some kind of outlet —"

"Oh, he's been telling you about the music lessons, eh? Well, I thought it best to stop them for a while. He was always strumming, and he failed —"

"It was not necessarily the music that caused him to fail. Any number of fellows fail the first time who don't know one note from another. If he'd had more music in his life, he might not have failed. It's quite possible."

Renny, pouring himself more tea, burst into laughter.

Leigh hurried on: "But music has nothing to do with this. This is about acting."

"Acting!"

"Yes. Finch has great talent for acting. I'm not sure that it is not greater than his talent for music."

Renny threw himself back in his chair. Good God, was there no limit to the extraordinary talents of this hobbledehoy? "Where's he been acting? Why haven't I been told about it?"

"I'm afraid I've been to blame about that. I felt that the expression of — of some art is so necessary to Finch that I persuaded him — made him promise not to let anyone put a stop to it."

The fiery brown eyes were on him. "His promises to me are worth nothing, then!"

"But they are! I give you my word that he has not been neglecting his work. He'll have no trouble passing next year. He didn't make a bad showing, you know. I believe it was more nerves than anything that made him fail."

A knock sounded on the door.

"Come in," said Renny, and Wright entered. He said, "The vet's here, sir."

"Good," exclaimed Renny, rising. With a movement of suppressed irritation he turned to Leigh: "What do you want me to do?"

He was faintly suspicious of Leigh. He felt that Leigh had cornered him. He supposed that Finch had got Leigh working on his behalf. He had a way of enlisting the sympathies of susceptible people — intellectual people. There had been Alayne. How she had pleaded for music lessons for him! The thought of her softened him. He added, "I don't expect Finch to plug away and never have any fun. I don't object to anything so long as it's not going to interfere with his studies."

A clumber spaniel that had come in with Wright raised himself on his hind legs beside the desk and began to lick the buttery crumbs of toast from the plate.

A feeling of weakness stole over Leigh. His efforts seemed suddenly futile. The life of this place was too strong for him, the personalities of the Whiteoaks too vigorous. He could never penetrate the solid wall they presented to the world. Even Renny's words scarcely encouraged him.

He watched the spaniel licking the plate in a trancelike silence for a moment, then he said, with an effort, "If you would only let Finch feel that. If he could know that you don't despise him for needing something — some form of expression other than the routine of the school curriculum — of school games — "

Wright's round blue eyes were riveted on his face. The eyes of all the horses in the glossy prints and lithographs that covered the wall were riveted on him, their nostrils distended in contempt.

Renny took the spaniel by the collar and put him gently to the floor. Outside in the stable a man's voice was raised, shouting orders. There was a clatter of hoofs.

Leigh said, hurriedly, "Mr. Whiteoak, will you promise me something? Let Finch spend the next fortnight with me. I'll help him all I can with his work, and I honestly think I can help a good deal. Then I want you to come, if you will, to our place for dinner one night of the play and see for yourself how splendid Finch is. My mother and sister would like to meet you. You know you're a hero to Finch, and consequently to us, too. He's told us about what you did in the War — the D.S.O., you know."

Renny showed embarrassment, as well as impatience. "Very well," he said, curtly. "Let him go ahead with the play. But no slacking, mind."

"And you'll come one night?"

"Yes."

"Thanks very much. I'm tremendously grateful." But, in truth, he felt only relief and a weary haste to be off.

"That's all right. And I hope you will like the horse."

"I know I shall."

They shook hands and parted.

Out in the close-pressing snowflakes, the wind urging him with gusto toward the glowing windows of the house, Leigh felt Finch farther removed from him than ever he had been since their friendship had begun. He saw him now as an integral part of the pattern of Jalna. He could not now separate him, familiar and dear as he was, from the closely woven, harsh fabric of his family. He almost wished he had never seen him among his vigorous kin. And yet, if he had not, he should never really have understood him, known whence had sprung the spark which was Finch. And, too, in spite of his feeling of chill, of fatigue, of having his energy sapped by this place, he experienced an odd sense of exhilaration as he ran up the steps to the door, grasped its great icy knob in his hand, opened it, pushed it shut against the wind and snow, was met by the rush of warmth, bright color, loud voices. The uncles were now there, Aunt Augusta, Piers, and Pheasant. Meg and Maurice had come to tea from Vaughanlands, Meg with a fat six-months-old baby girl in her arms. Fresh tea was brought to him, toast, and plum jam and cakes. They all stared at him, but talked to each other, ignoring him. Never, never, he thought, could an outsider become one of them.

VI

CLOUTIE JOHN

THE opening night of the play Finch was wrought up to such a pitch of excitement that he wondered if he would ever feel natural again. At one moment he wished nothing better than that the earth might open and swallow him, put him speedily from sight before the time came for him to set foot on the stage. At the next he was walking on air in joyous anticipation, his eyes bright, his lank lock of fair hair almost into them. His lips would tremble as though he were going to cry or laugh, but his conversation consisted mainly of monosyllables.

Leigh was nervous, too. He had the part of the hero, mixture of courage and cowardice, to play, and his soul yearned over Finch, who had not only to make his first appearance at the Little Theatre, but to make it before Renny. Leigh had intended that the elder brother should see the performance late in the week, but Mrs. Leigh, un-advised by him, had sent the invitation to dinner, naming Monday. There was nothing to do but make the best of it, induce a complacent state of mind in the difficult guest by good wine and charming feminine companionship. For the latter, Leigh put all trust in his mother and sister. In his haste and perturbation, he took time to speculate as to which of them would interest Renny the more, upon which his quick glance might linger. For himself, the two so claimed his life, his love, that he wondered whether he should ever care for any other woman. He hoped not. His mother, his sister, Finch — these were enough.

Finch, coming into the drawing-room, where he now felt happily at ease, found Ada Leigh already there. She said, with her peculiar, slanting look at him, across a lighted candelabrum, "I suppose you're awfully nervous."

He was in one of his moments of elation. "Oh, I don't think so. I don't believe I'm as nervous as Arthur is."

"I think you are. You're trembling."

"That's nothing. It doesn't take anything to make me shake. Why, I can't pass a teacup without slopping the tea over."

"Ah, but this is different. You're frightened." She was smiling teasingly. He felt that she wanted him to be frightened. He drew nearer to her and saw the reflection of a pointed flame in her eyes.

"I am not afraid," he insisted. "I'm happy."

"Yes, you are afraid." There was a little gasping sound in her voice.

"Afraid of what, then?"

"Afraid of me."

"Afraid of *you?*" He tried to look astonished, but he began to feel afraid, and yet oddly elated.

"Yes . . . and I of you."

He laughed now and he ceased trembling. Quick pulses began to beat all over his body. He took her hand and began to caress her fingers. He examined her pink nails as though they were little shells he had found on some strange shore. . . .

Then she was in his arms. He who had never kissed a girl! He felt suffocated. . . . It seemed to him an unreal dream that he was kissing her. She was snuggling under his chin. . . . Over her head he looked out into the darkness beyond the window, and saw the cluster of candle flames reflected like a cluster of bright blooms. He saw the reflection of his own head, the pale green of her dress like a shimmering pool in the darkness, over which his head was bent. How unreal it all seemed! He embraced her, excited by the beautiful reflection, by a new sense of power, of daring, but he felt that he was acting a part. They kissed in a tremulous dream.

Mrs. Leigh and Arthur were coming down the stairs together. There was plenty of time for the two in the drawing-room to draw apart, he to pick up a book and she to rearrange some flowers in a black bowl. No longer the darkness beyond the window reflected the entwined figures of the impassioned pursuers of experience.

Arthur went to Finch and threw an arm across his shoulders. "Darling Finch," he said, in his low, musical voice, "I'm so glad you're not nervous any more. You've a beam of absolute assurance in your eyes. I'm the one who is nervous."

How comforting Arthur's caressing arm was! Finch rejoiced in the yoke of friendship thus laid across his shoulders. He saw Ada's eyes fixed on them, dark with jealousy.

If only Renny were not coming to dinner, he should be happy, he thought. He could not conceive of Renny's fitting into the delicately adjusted contacts of that group. Yet, when Renny came, looking distant and elegant to Finch in his dinner jacket, he fitted in marvelously well. More strangely still, he did not adjust his conversation to the light current which usually flowed easily about the table, Mrs. Leigh always guiding its course, but he brought with him something of the more vigorous, harsh atmosphere of Jalna. His red head, his shoulders that had the droop of much riding in the saddle, his sudden, sharp laughter, dominated the room.

Finch had never seen Mrs. Leigh so gay, so like a girl. She seemed younger than Ada, who was rather silent, seeming in soft veiled glances to study the newcomer. But, when her eyes met Finch's, a look of swift understanding passed between them. Finch was so exhilarated by his experience of love-making, so proud of Renny, that his face was full of brightness. He looked charming. An observer would have found it interesting to compare him with the slouching, deprecating, often sullen youth who appeared at home.

Renny ate and talked with zest. Arthur, delighted with the success of his plans, found his dislike of the elder brother turning to appreciation of his generous and fiery temper. He felt his own manhood strengthened by contact with this sharper fibre. He felt that it would be good for him to have a man of this sort coming to the house, good for Ada, too, who was beginning to expect admiration from all males.

Arthur and Finch were leaving for the theatre before the others. Mrs. Leigh and Ada were upstairs preparing to put on their evening wraps. While Arthur was ordering a car, the two brothers were left alone in the drawing-room for a moment.

Why, thought Finch, am I cursed by this sense of the unreality of things? There is Renny, sitting in the Leighs' drawing-room, smoking. Here am I, yet I can't believe we are here, that we are real. Is it because nothing seems real outside of Jalna? Are we all like that, or just I? Why do these feelings come over me and spoil my pleasure? He put his thumb to his lips and nervously bit the nail.

Renny turned his head toward him. "Don't bite your nails. It's a beastly habit."

Abashed, Finch stuffed his hand into his pocket.

"Renny," he asked, after a moment, almost plaintively, "does this room seem real to you?"

Renny's brown gaze swept the cream and rose and silver of the room. "No," he said, "I don't think it does."

Thank God, oh, thank God! Things were unreal to Renny, too!

"Well, look here," he went on, anxiously, "do you see it in a tremendous kind of haze, in a dream, still, yet moving, like a reflection in a bubble?"

Renny stared.   "It is something like that."

"And I! Do I seem unreal to you?"

"Decidedly."

He could never have let himself go like this with Renny at home.   But it was really wonderful.

"And do you seem unreal to yourself, Renny? Do you wonder why you do certain things? Wonder if you are anything more than a dream?"

"I dare say.   I think you're excited to-night.   You'd better hang on to yourself or you'll forget your lines."

"Do you suppose I'll have stage fright?"

"I think you've got it already."

"What do you mean, got it already?"

"You're afraid of life, and that's the same thing."

In a burst of nervous excitement, Finch whispered, hoarsely, "What do you think? I kissed Ada Leigh in this room to-night!"

"The deuce you did! No wonder you feel unreal.   Did she like it?"

"I think so.   We were reflected in the strangest way in the window.   Ourselves, only more beautiful."

"H'm."   Renny regarded him with genial amusement. "Are you sure she didn't ask for it?"

"Of course I am."   He reddened, but he still leaned over Renny's chair in a confidential attitude.

"Well, it's an experience for you.   She's a pretty girl." Finch breathed hard.   "Don't sprawl over me that way, snuffling in my face.   Have you a cold?"

"Oh, no."   He straightened himself again, abashed.

Leigh's voice called from outside.

"Coming, Arthur!"

Finch hastened out to his friend. . . .

Renny sat puffing at his cigarette, the glow of amusement still brightening his eyes.   Young Finch making love! And it seemed like yesterday when he had turned Finch across his knee and warmed his seat. And now he was getting to be a man, poor devil!

He looked about him. An unreal room. Not a bit like the drawing-room at Jalna. Nothing homelike about it, with all these little pictures speckled over the walls, all the delicate furnishings, the fragile ornaments. But it suited the two pretty women. Odd, mysterious women, attractive, yet uncomfortable.

He rose as Ada Leigh, her face flowerlike above a white fur wrap, entered the room.

"Mother will be down in a moment," she said, stroking the fur of her deep collar.

Renny observed her hand. "Yes? Will you take this chair?"

"No, thanks, it's not worth while sitting down. We must be going." She dropped her cheek against the fur with a feline caressing movement and drew a deep, quivering breath.

He stood near her, motionless, attentive. He thought, "What the devil's the matter with the girl?"

She raised her heavy-lidded eyes to his and said, "I wish I were not going to-night."

"I'm sorry. Are you going to tell me why?"

"There's no time to talk. . . . But I'm very unhappy."

He smiled at her in a puzzled way. He had no faith in her unhappiness. He was suspicious of her.

"You'll think me very stupid. Talking like this to you — a stranger. But you're Finch's brother. And you see — oh, I can't explain!" Her eyes were raised beseechingly to his. "I'm so frightfully inexperienced — and — and — I thought I felt something I didn't. I thought" — her expressive face quivered — "oh, I can't go on!"

He said gravely, "I shouldn't worry if I were you. That sort of thing happens to all of us. We imagine that we feel things, and then we let ourselves in for things. . . . But you'll soon forget about it."

"Oh, I wish, I wish," she exclaimed, "that I had someone like you to help me — about life. I know nothing — and Arthur, although he is such a darling to me, is ignorant. He doesn't really know any more than I do."

Renny thought, "The trouble with you both is that you know far too much." He said, "I'm afraid you have come to the wrong man for advice. I don't understand women. I couldn't possibly."

She said, slowly, "I don't quite mean advice."

"What, then, precisely?"

She pushed the white fur back from her throat. "Something more subtle, I guess. Your friendship — if it wouldn't bore you too much."

He thought, "Ha, my girl, you're one of the deep kind!" And said, "Good. We shall be friends."

In the theatre, seated between mother and daughter, he experienced a feeling of exasperation, of being trapped. The two pretty women seemed like jailers, and this place a prison. He hated the "arty" atmosphere, the cold, chaste walls, the curtain. The lack of an orchestra depressed him. For him a theatre should blaze in gilt and scarlet, the curtain should present some florid Italian scene, and his spirit should be borne on the crash of music as on an element. He hated the chatter of women's voices before the curtain rose. In the buzz of it he talked to the two on either side of him and forgot which was mother and which was daughter. He began to be unaccountably nervous for Finch. He had not wanted him to go in for anything of this sort, but now that he was . . . His throat tightened. He had trouble in taking a deep breath.

The play began. It increased his low spirits. The religion of the old man, his quoting of the Scriptures, made Renny want to howl. And Finch, when at last he appeared!

His wild hair, his dirty face, his rags, his bare feet! Something deeply conservative in Renny disliked very much the sight of bare feet on the stage. The legs of a chorus girl, that was quite different, but a man's — his brother's — bare feet were distinctly ugly. And the way Finch blew on his whistle, the mad way he danced about, and sat on the floor and jumped up again, and begged for scraps of food, and slept in the chimney corner, and was always appearing suddenly and disappearing! And his Irish brogue!

The applause thundered. Finch was the bright star of the evening. His face was white and wild with exultation as he was applauded again and again. Mrs. Leigh and Ada clapped their hands with delicate enthusiasm. Renny sat between them wearing a displeased grin very like his grandmother's when her pride had been hurt.

After the play there was a little gathering in the director's room. Friends crowded about the actors. Finch, not quite rid of his make-up, showed a dingy smear on his cheek. He trembled when he came to speak to Mrs. Leigh and Renny.

"Oh, my dear," cried Mrs. Leigh, her hand squeezing his arm, "you could not have been better! We are all thrilled by you."

Renny said nothing, regarding him with the same grin of disapproval. To Finch it seemed to say, "Wait until I get you alone, young man." His feeling of triumph was gone. He felt that he had been making a fool of himself for the amusement of the audience. Not again during the week did he recover his buoyancy and complete abandon in the part.

Returning home in the train next day, Renny thought about Finch, and not only Finch, but all those younger members of the family who were his half brothers. What was wrong with them? Certainly there was some weakness, bred in the bone, that made them different from the other Whiteoaks. The face of their mother flashed into his mind. She had been governess to him and Meg before his father had married her. They had given her rather a rough time both as governess and as stepmother. He had been the thorn in her side when she had been their governess; Meg, when she had become their stepmother. Her face flashed into his mind, coming between him and the wintry fields outside. He realized for the first time that she had been a beautiful young woman. A warm face, warm blue eyes that darkened with emotion, an exquisitely modeled chin and throat. He remembered seeing her temper flare when Meggie had sat, stolid and plump, blankly refusing to take any interest in her music lesson. He remembered her sobbing with exasperation over his misbehavior. But when she had become their stepmother she had held herself somewhat aloof from them, encircled by the love of her husband, absorbed by her too frequent motherhood.

Renny recalled vividly now the fact that when he had come upon her she had nearly always been reading. Poetry, too. What a mother for men! He had come upon her reading poetry to his father, while he stared at her, listening, his eyes enfolding her. She had loved him, and had not long survived him. Poor young Wake had been a posthumous child.

Poetry in them — music in them — that was the trouble, Eden was full of poetry, and he had inherited his mother's beauty, too. . . . Where was he now? They had heard nothing of him in the year and a half he had been away. How ghastly to think that Alayne was tied to him. . . . At the thought of Alayne an ache struck him in the breast, an ache of longing for something that he could not possess. His soul groped, searching for a way to turn aside from the longing. He wondered at himself. He, for whom it had been so easy to forget. . . .

He shifted his body on the seat, as an animal, puzzled by pain, changes its position, bending his lean red face to stare out of the window on the far side of the car. He saw a frozen stream there and the rounded black forms of a clump of cedars.

Of what had he been thinking? Ah, yes, the boys! Eden. A damned fool, Eden. But Piers was no fool. Sound as a nut. A Whiteoak, through and through. Then Finch, the young whelp, deceiving him! Posturing, play-acting before a parcel of highbrows. And mad about music, too. Well, he'd got to work in earnest now if he were going to amount to anything. . . . There was Wake, fanciful little rascal. No knowing what he'd be up to in a few years. . . .

Like an eagle whose nestlings were turning out to be sky-larks, Renny regarded his brood, his love, his pride in them, clouded by doubt.

At the station Wright was waiting for him with a dappled gray gelding harnessed to a red sleigh. The drifts were too high for motoring. Wright also brought his great coon coat, in which he enveloped himself on the platform.

As they flew along the glistening road, past drifts where the fine snow was ruffled in a silver mist, Renny felt that he could not drink in enough of the freshness of the day. He took great breaths, he let the wind whistle in his teeth. The sharp hoofs of the gelding sent hard pieces of clean snow on to the fur robe on their knees.

When they arrived at the stables Piers was there. He asked as Renny alighted, "Well, how did the matinée idol get on?"

"He took the part of an idiot. Too damned well."

"He would," said Piers.

VII

THE ORCHESTRA

BESIDES Arthur Leigh, Finch had one other friend. This was George Fennel, the rector's second son. But his friendship with George lacked the sense of adventure, the exhilaration of his friendship with Arthur. Arthur and he had sought out each other. They had bridged barriers to clasp hands. But George and he had been thrown together since infancy. Each thought he knew all there was to know about the other. Each was fond of the other and a little despised him. Their bonds were hatred of mathematics and love of music. But where Finch toiled and sweated over his mathematics, and ached with desire for music, George made no effort to learn what was hard for him, concentrating with dogged purpose on the subjects he liked, early determining that, square peg as he was, he would be fitted into no round hole. He played whatever musical instrument was handy without partiality. He liked the mouth organ as well as the piano, the banjo as well as the mandolin. He made them all sing for him of the sweetness of life.

He was a short, thickset youth, yet somehow graceful. His clothes were always untidy and his hair rumpled. Arthur Leigh thought him boorish, commonplace, a country clod. He did what he could to draw Finch away from him, and Finch, during that winter, till the time of the play, had never seen so little of George. But after the play he had yearned toward George. For some reason which he could not have explained, he was no longer quite so happy at the Leighs'. Not that his passage with Ada had made any palpable difference. He did not follow his advance by another step or by a repetition. She seemed to have forgotten it. Mrs. Leigh was even kinder than before. She asked many questions about the family at Jalna, and when she learned that one of the uncles was a student of Shakespeare, and that one of the young men was a poet, she took to talking quite seriously to Finch about literature. She was disappointed that Renny was unable — Arthur thought unwilling — to accept two subsequent invitations to dinner.

Whether it were this new interest, this refined probing into the relationships, temperaments, and tastes of his family, or some change in Arthur's attitude toward himself, which made him less happy in the Leighs' house, he did not know, but he felt the change, which was not so much a change as a development, a new aspect in Arthur's affection for him. Arthur had become oversensitive, exacting, critical of him. Finch was now often finding out that he had, by some gruff or careless remark, hurt Arthur; that he had, by some coarseness or stupidity, offended him; that, when he loudly aired his opinions, Arthur winced. Yet they had hours of such happiness together that Finch went home through the snow joyous in all his being. The trouble was, he decided, that Arthur loved him so well that he wanted him to be perfect, as he was perfect, not knowing how impossible that was.

How different with George! George expected nothing of him and was not disappointed. They could spend an evening together in his tiny bedroom in the rectory, working at an uninspired level of intelligence, chaffing, telling each other idiotic jokes, littering the floor with nutshells, and finally descending to the parlor for an hour of music before Finch must hasten home. Finch at the piano, George playing the banjo, his older brother Tom the mandolin, while the rector would sit smoking, the long pipe nestling on his beard, reading the *Churchman*, with rare imperturbability. Tom was a lazy fellow who did everything badly (except gardening, for which he had a genius) but Finch never tired of hearing George play the banjo, of watching him as he sat squarely on his chair, his thick hands playing with great dexterity and spirit, his eyes softly beaming from under his untidy hair.

George, like Finch, was always hard up. Sometimes they had not between them two coins to rub together. When Finch was with Arthur he was continually accepting favors, continually being given pleasures which he could only repay by gratitude. At times he felt that the fount of his gratitude must dry up from the unceasing flow.

"But you must not thank me!" Leigh would exclaim. "You know that I love to do things for you."

But perhaps, when Finch on the next occasion was silently pleased, Leigh would ask, with a slight frown denting his smooth forehead, "Are you pleased, Finch, old chap? Do you like the idea?"

How different with George! There was nothing about which he need be grateful to George. They were both about as poor in this world's possessions as they well could be. Each owned a few shabby clothes, his schoolbooks, his watch, and a cherished object or two, such as George's banjo and an old silver snuffbox which Lady Buckley had given Finch. When he was going to the rectory, Finch would fill his pockets with apples; Mr. Fennel would carry a plate of crullers to the boys; they would both rifle Mrs. Fennel's pantry. It was a pleasant and inexpensive give and take.

But now that George was seventeen and Finch eighteen they experienced great longing for more money to spend. Finch had tried several ways of earning it. He humbly had asked Piers if there were any work he could do for him on Saturdays, and Piers had put him to sorting apples in the twilight chill of the apple house. Between handling the icy fruit, standing on the cement floor, and the draft from the open door, he had contracted an attack of bronchitis that had kept him in his bed for a fortnight. Piers had come to the bedside.

"How long did you work?" he had asked.

"Nearly all the day," Finch had croaked.

"How many hours, exactly?"

"From nine till four, I think, and, of course, I laid off for dinner."

"A day is from seven to five. Well, here is two dollars. Better buy yourself a bottle of cough stuff. And the next time you want to earn some money, get a job in a conservatory." He had thrown a new banknote on to the quilt. Finch had later spent the money on roses for Ada Leigh.

Bronchitis was bad, but missing school for weeks was worse. He had lain, feverish, his chest torn by coughing, lonely in his attic room, listening to the sounds that came from below for companionship, unable to eat the too substantial meals Rags had carried to him, worrying all the while lest he fail again in his examinations.

But, when he was better, the urge to earn some money had come again. This time he asked Renny for work, and Renny had given him a saddle horse to exercise. All the Whiteoaks could ride, but the horses seemed to know that there was no masterfulness in Finch, and they tried all their favorite tricks when he rode them.

This one, just recovering from an accident, supposedly quiet as a sheep, had, in sportive caper, shied at her own gate, and given Finch a tumble on the driveway. Everyone, from Grandmother to Wakefield, had joked about Finch's mishap, and because the mare, elated by her riderless condition, had galloped to the woods, and an hour had been spent in capturing her, her flank grazed by a broken branch, Renny had paid Finch, not with money, but with a curse. The pain of a wrenched ankle was borne in silence, but a scowl darkened his forehead as he limped to and from the station. To be a figure of fun, that was his supreme humiliation.

One evening George said to him, "I know a fellow who would rig up a radio for us for next to nothing."

"H'm," grunted Finch, tearing a bite from a russet apple. "If we only had that next to nothing!"

"They're any amount of fun," sighed George. "You can get wonderful concerts from New York, Chicago—all over, in fact."

"Good music, eh? Piano playing?"

"Rather. You've heard Sinclair's radio, haven't you?"

"Yes, but he always tunes in for jazz."

"Why don't you interest your family in them? One would be great fun for your grandmother and your aunt and uncles."

"I'd never get near it. Besides, they wouldn't spend the money on it. All the old ones are as close as bark to a tree."

"What about Renny or Piers?"

"They detest them. Besides, money is awfully tight at home this winter. Gosh, you know I can't get any money for anything but my fees and my railway ticket. What are you talking about?"

George leaned forward, his square, roguish face twinkling. "I know how we can earn some money, Finch."

Finch flung the core of the russet into the waste-paper basket. "How, then?" His tone was skeptical.

"By getting up an orchestra."

"An orchestra! You've gone dotty, haven't you?"

"Not by a long shot. Listen here. The other day my father was making a sick call in Stead, and I drove him there. These people have a greenhouse, and while I waited outside I strolled about looking through the windows at the plants. A fellow came out and we got to talking. He was a grandson and he'd just come out from town because of the sickness. I soon found out that he plays the mandolin. He's got a friend who plays it, too, and another who plays the flute. They've been thinking for some time they'd like to get up an orchestra if they could find some fellows to play the banjo and piano. He was awfully excited when I told him we might go in for it."

Finch was staggered. "But your father—what will he say?"

"He won't know. You see, I didn't tell this fellow I was Dad's son. He thinks I'm just employed by him. I thought it was better, because one's people are so darned silly about who you go with. Of course, these other fellows are all right, but you know how unreasonable one's family can be." And he added softly, "One of the chaps is a tailor's assistant —he's the flautist—and the other works in the abattoir."

"Gee!" exclaimed Finch. "Do you mean to say he *kills* things?"

"I didn't ask him," returned George testily. "The point is that he can play the mandolin."

"So you've met them!"

"Yes. At the noon hour. They're awfully decent chaps, and they're quite old, too. The one I first met is twenty-three, and the other looks about twenty-six or so. They're awfully anxious to meet you."

Finch began to shake with excitement. He took out a box in which were two Woodbines, and offered it to George. "Have a fag?"

They lighted up.

Finch was too excited to look at George. He fixed his eyes on the stovepipe hole in the floor, through which sufficient heat was supposed to penetrate to warm George's room. He began to wonder whether their voices could be heard in the kitchen below.

"What about the pipe hole? Is the servant down there?"

"She couldn't possibly hear. Besides, she's got her steady with her."

"Who is he?"

"Jack Sims. From Vaughans'."

Murmuring voices came from below. The boys moved

softly near the pipe hole and peered down. In the light from a feeble electric bulb they saw two arms lying along the dresser. The hands were clasped. One hand, projecting from a blue cotton sleeve, was plump, a rawish pink from much washing of clothes; the other, the hairy wrist of which protruded from coarse cloth, was the gnarled hand of a middle-aged farm laborer. The voices had ceased and the only sound was the ticking of the kitchen clock.

The two intertwined hands fascinated Finch. They became for him symbolic of the mystery, the reaching out, the groping for support of life. He felt the tenderness, the fire, that each hand drew from the other and gathered like herbs of comfort for the lonely heart. . . .

George was whispering, "It's a fact, they never get any further than that."

"You mean any *nearer*, don't you?"

"I mean any *forwarder*."

They broke into suffocating giggles. They threw themselves on the lumpy couch, uttering explosive squeaks. But, though Finch giggled hysterically, his mind's eye was still peering down the pipe hole, his soul burning to know what were the thoughts of the two below.

"Why didn't you tell me about them before? We might often have taken a squint down at them."

"There was nothing to it." George's face turned glum. "Now, look here, Finch, which are you most interested in, the orchestra or those two silly spoons in the kitchen?"

Finch returned, still grinning, "There's no earthly use in talking about an orchestra to me. I wouldn't be let go to town for practising or playing at places. There'd be a hell of a row if I proposed such a thing."

"No need for you to mention it. I've got it all arranged. You don't object to making five dollars every now and again, do you?"

Finch sat up and stared. "Would I get that much?"

"Certainly. Lilly, that's the leader's name, says we can easily get twenty-five dollars a night for playing at dances in restaurants. That's five each. Not bad, eh, for strumming a few hours? Now don't interrupt. It'll be the simplest thing in the world for us to work the thing. By bolting a bit of lunch, we can get in an hour's practice at noon. Sometimes we can do it after five o'clock by staying in town for the seven-thirty train. That's easy. Now, for the dances. You remember my aunt, Mrs. St. John, has been widowed lately."

Finch nodded.

"She's a favorite with your family, isn't she?"

Again he nodded with deep solemnity.

"Very well. My aunt was saying only yesterday that she would like me to spend a night with her once a week for company. She would be pleased if I were to bring you along, and, seeing that she's a favorite of your darned old family, I don't suppose they'd object to you spending a night in her house, when she's widowed and all that, and I guess Renny thinks you're more likely to study when you're with me than with that Leigh chap." George, in his quiet way, thoroughly disliked Leigh.

"But your aunt, won't she be suspicious?"

George smiled gently. "It all fits in beautifully. Auntie is ordered to bed by her doctor at eight every night. She'll see us get our books out — the library's downstairs — and then toddle off to her bedroom and go bye-bye. The dances begin at nine. We'll see life in those restaurants, too, mind you. And five bucks apiece. . . ."

They whispered, planning together, till it was time for Finch to go home. There he sat, wrapped in a quilt, studying, to make up for lost time. But between him and the page returned again and again the vision of the two clasped hands lying on the kitchen dresser, then Ada's face with mouth tremulously smiling, quivering from the kisses he had given her. With an effort he would put these pictures away and drag his mind back to its task.

Difficult, unlikely as it had seemed, the orchestra came into being. It flourished. Lunches were bolted and the noonday period was spent in practice in the parlor above the tailor shop, into which penetrated the pungent smell of hot iron pressing damp cloth. The tailor's assistant was cousin to the tailor, and he and his girl-wife and puny infant lived also above the shop. He was the oldest member of the orchestra, being twenty-six. His name was Meech. Finch soon became well acquainted with all the family, and, as they were kind to him and admired his playing, his affection rushed out to them. Often, when the practice was over, he would stay awhile, making himself late for school, to play Chopin or Schubert before the friendly circle. Then the thin girl-wife of the young tailor would crouch at the end of the piano watching his hands as he played. She was so close to him that she was in his way, but he would not ask her to move. Sitting so, with her eyes on him, music springing up beneath his hands, he felt firm and strong, free as air.

"Come along," George would urge, his banjo under his arm, "we shall be late."

"Don't wait for me," Finch would say over his shoulder, and would be happier when the banjo, the first and second mandolins, were gone and he was left alone with the flute and his family.

Finch now saw a new kind of life, the life of shopgirls and their beaus seeking pleasure at night in cheap restaurants. On the mornings when the orchestra had an engagement to play that evening, he awoke with a start, excited in all his being. The way had always been paved the night before with his family. Poor Mrs. St. John wanted George to spend the night at her house and would like to have Finch also. There was never any difficulty. Finch found it was the easiest thing in the world to lead a double life. Aunt

Augusta would send a box of little cakes or a pot of marmalade to Mrs. St. John. His aunt, though she looked at him coldly, her head drawn back with her air of offense, had a tender spot in her heart for the boy. To his amazement, he had won the prize canary in the raffle, and had smuggled the cage to her room, swathed in paper, a present for her on her seventy-fifth birthday. It had come as an inspiration to him that the day on which he had received it was her birthday. She had told him that his winning the lottery was a good omen for his future. The two were drawn together. He often visited her room to see the canary, and they gloated over the prize together. She soon grew to love it extravagantly. Now she must always keep the door of her room shut tightly for fear old Mrs. Whiteoak should hear it sing. Grandmother would never have tolerated any other bird in the house with Boney. Then there was the fear of Sasha, Ernest's yellow Persian cat, who had taken to making her toilette on Augusta's doormat. Ernest also grew fond of the canary. He too would go to his sister's room to hear it sing, and they would gaze enraptured at the little throbbing body while it dipped its yellow head from side to side, warbling first to one long-faced listener, then to the other.

These days Finch lived in a kind of haze. He felt life changing all around him. New forces were drawing him this way and that. At times he felt an aching in his breast that was almost a pain, a yearning for what he knew not. Not for religion. Not for love, — he had not attempted to make love to Ada again, — but for something of which religion and love were only a part. His eyes were troubled, he grew thinner. Yet he was always hungry. On the days when there was no practice of the orchestra, he would go, after the school luncheon, to a large shop much frequented by the boys when they were in funds. There he would wander up and down past the glittering glass cases of tempting foods

displayed; platters of ham and tongue; fiery red lobsters, and
little pink shrimps; he would droop over the case of cheeses,
fascinated. The cream cheese, Swiss cheese, Camembert,
Roquefort, Oka, the dear little cheeses made by the Trappist
monks in Quebec. He thought he should like to be a monk
working in the cool rooms of the monastery, and he would
buy this particular cheese, though he did not much like it,
because of the thought it brought. And, at the other side
of the shop would be George, giving his money for cakes
and chocolates, and bottled fruit from California.

They would off with their spoil, and at recess they and
their friends would devour it in haste, or a feast would be
arranged after school, when they could eat at leisure. They
contrived, however, to put by a respectable sum for the radio,
and toward a camping trip in the summer. Finch would
have liked to buy presents for the family from the wealth
that poured in so fast, but where would they think he had
got the money? But he could not resist a necktie for Renny's
birthday, which fell in March. He spent a long time in the
haberdasher's choosing it—two shades of blue in a gorgeous
stripe. Renny's eyebrows flew up in surprise when it was
presented. He was touched. But when he appeared at Sunday tea wearing it, the vivid blue blazing against the highly
colored flesh of his face, his red hair, a storm of protest
arose from the family. Renny's beauty — which, they declared, required dark colors to set it off — was ruined by the
tie. Now it would have become Piers, with his blue eyes
and fair skin. And the next time Finch saw the tie Piers
was wearing it.

He had better luck with the box of water colors he bought
for Wakefield. To avoid suspicion, for it was a very good
box of colors, he said that it was a present from Leigh.
Wake, who was condemned to his bed that week, was delighted. He painted pictures day in and day out. Renny,
finding his bed littered with them, thought, with a moment's

heaviness, "By God, this poor youngster's going to be a genius, too!"

Engagements for the orchestra came thick and fast. The young musicians played with such untiring gayety; they were so obliging. Finch conscientiously slaved at his books, and, between practising and studying and loss of sleep, grew so thin that even Piers was moved to concern.

"Try to eat more," he advised. "You're growing, and you need plenty of good grub."

"Eat!" cried Finch, his nerves on edge. "I'm always eating. If I'm thin, it's my own business. Please let me alone."

"But," persisted Piers, feeling Finch's arm, "you're getting thinner. You're soft, too. Now, just feel my muscle."

"I don't want to feel your muscle. If you'd used your muscle less on me, it mightn't be so hard and I mightn't be so thin."

Just after Easter, George announced an engagement in a restaurant in which they had played several times. The members of some athletic club were having a dance. The two boys had spent the Easter holidays with Mrs. St. John and the orchestra had worked very hard learning new dance music. They had played at four dances, so Finch had twenty dollars to add to the hoard hidden on the top shelf of his clothes cupboard in an old fishing basket. Since the opening of school he had studied late into every night, apprehensive of again failing in his examinations.

On the night of the dance he was very tired. There had been trouble over spending the night in town, and only a passionate appeal to Aunt Augusta to intervene for him had made it possible. The rector, too, was beginning to think that his sister should be able to get on without George, and even Mrs. St. John herself had become a little less yearning toward her two young visitors. Finch felt that he could stand the strain no longer, that for a while the orchestra should take no new engagements or that someone else must be found to play the piano. Yet he loved it. It was life — making music, watching the dancing, the love-making, being in the streets late at night, the freshly earned money in his pocket.

Mrs. St. John had been slow to leave them that night. Her health was better, and there was no need for such early retiring. It pleased her to sit in the library with the two fresh-skinned youths, watching them at their study, the light touching their thick hair — George's brown, tousled; Finch's fair, limp, with the lock on the forehead oddly appealing to her. She liked to watch their hands — George's small, white, strong, and precise in their movements; Finch's long, bony, yet beautifully shaped, nervous, uncertain.

They had to assume a trancelike absorption before she would leave them, and when she did leave, and the strain was over, they fell into a fit of smothered laughter that, for Finch, threatened to become hysterical.

"Shut up," ordered George, recovering himself, "or she'll hear you and come back."

Finch buried his face in the crook of his arm and gave forth strange squeaks. George glowered at him.

"I never saw a chap like you. You never know when to stop anything." He looked at his watch. "Good heavens, we'll never dare risk taking a street car. I'll have to phone for a taxi." He opened the door of the library and listened. "I hear her running water upstairs. I guess she's safe, now."

He took the receiver from its hook and gave a number. He stared across the table at Finch, who stared back with wet eyes, his lips stretched in a hysterical grin. He looked so silly that George snorted into the telephone. He sputtered idiotically as he ordered the taxi. Finch was squeaking again. "Of course," said George, slamming up the receiver, "if you *can't* control yourself . . ." He tried his best to look like his father.

George went into the hall and crept up the stairway to the door of his aunt's room.

Returning, he said, "It's all right. She's getting ready for bed. . . . I've told the driver to wait around the corner. Now step on the gas, Finch, for goodness' sake!"

Rushing through the cold spring night, they were filled with the glow of adventure, thinking of the dangerous life they led. George's banjo lay across his knees. Finch held a portfolio of music. As George paid the driver, Finch stared up at a great ruby-red electric sign, advertising chocolates, hot against the heavy gray sky. "Shouldn't be surprised if we had snow," he said. "It's cold enough for it."

But inside it was hot. The room was full of young men and girls—the men, hockey players, lithe and strong, the girls, bare-shouldered, silken-legged, with laughing red-lipped faces. Some of them knew Finch by sight as a member of the orchestra, and waved to him as he sat sounding a note while the musicians tuned up. There was something about him that they liked. "I say, Doris, there's the boy with the blond hair! I think he's a lamb. Shouldn't mind dancing with him."

The flute, the two mandolins, the banjo, the piano, gave voice. They sang of the joy of the dance, of strong limbs, of supple backs, of touching electric finger tips. All the brightly colored crowd galloped like huntsmen, led by the five hounds, in pursuit of that adroit fox, Joy.

When the time came for supper, the members of the orchestra rose and stretched their legs. They had been playing for three hours. A waiter brought them refreshments. Finch, trying not to seem ravenous, was irritated when a tall black-haired girl came up to him. "My, you boys can play," she said. "I'd sooner dance to your music than any of the big orchestras."

"Oh, go on!"

"Honestly, I would."

He took another sandwich. His gaze did not rise above her shimmering shins.

"You're a funny boy. Gosh, your eyelashes are almost a mile long!"

He blushed, and raised his eyes as high as the marble whiteness of her chest.

"I wish we could have a dance together, Mister — what's your name?"

"Finch."

"Oh, and the Christian name?"

"Bill."

"Bill Finch, eh? I wish you'd come and see me some night, will you, Bill?"

"Rather."

"No. 5, Mayberry Street. Remember that? To-morrow night? Ask for Miss Lucas."

"No, I couldn't to-morrow."

"The next, then?"

"Yes," he agreed. "The next." He wished she would leave him with the sandwiches.

A stout fellow came up and took her arm. "Here, Betty," he said, "none of that." He led her off, but her bold greenish eyes laughed over her white shoulder at Finch.

He boasted to Meech, the flautist, of the advances she had made, while they hurriedly consumed cake and coffee. "That's a good sort to steer clear of," Meech counseled; "a lot of bold-looking hussies here, and no mistake."

The dance went on, the dancers displaying even more freedom of movement and brightness of eyes than before supper. They had been drinking a little, but they were not noisy. At two o'clock Burns, the mandolin player, who worked in an abattoir, passed a flask among the players. They were very tired. A little later they emptied it.

"One dance more!" the dancers begged at three o'clock. "One dance more!" They clapped their hands vigorously. Finch felt ready to drop from the stool. A tendon in his right hand ached horribly. The dancers seemed to him like vampires, sucking his blood, never tiring of the taste of it.

The tall girl disentangled herself from the blur of the crowd and rushed to the piano. She threw her arms about Finch's neck and hugged him. "Another, another," she whispered, "and don't forget your promise!" He loathed the hot, steamy smell of her. He gasped for breath, his hands lying, played out, on the keyboard. He tried to draw his head away.

"Don't be so formal, dearie," she said, releasing him, and again the thickset man came and dragged her away.

A waiter appeared with a glass jug and glasses. "Have some ginger ale?" he asked, smiling.

Finch took a glass. Something stronger than ginger ale, he discovered. A pleasant glow passed into him with the first half of the glass. After the second half he felt stronger, firmer. He looked over his shoulder at the others. George Fennel's eyes were shining under his tumbled hair. Meech, the flautist, showed a pink flush on his high, pale forehead. Lilly and Burns were laughing together. Burns said, in a heavy bass voice, "Lilly, here, can't see the strings. He's pipped, aren't you, Lilly?"

But now they discovered that they could go on. A little gush of energy swept them into "My Heart Stood Still." The dancers moved in silence, holding each other tightly. The sliding of their feet sounding like the dry rush of autumn leaves. The cruel white lights showed them as people growing old. A blight seemed to have fallen on them. And yet they could not stop dancing.

Now it was the orchestra that dragged them on. They seemed no more than manikins operated by wires. Jerkily they went through dance after dance, and with hot, moist hands clapped for more. The orchestra broke into song, with the exception of Meech, the flautist. "And then my heart stood still," they sang, for their repertory was limited, and they had to repeat their pieces time and again.

At last the dancing feet stood still. It was past four o'clock when the members of the orchestra descended the narrow stairs and went out into the darkness of the morning.

Snow had fallen deeply. The city street looked as pure as a street in Heaven. Marble whiteness everywhere, arched by a dark blue sky out of which hung a great golden moon.

The sweet coldness of the still air was like a joyful caress. They lifted their faces to it, opened their mouths and drank it in. They sought to absorb it into every region of their beings. The soft pure snow beneath their feet was beautiful. They ran in it, ruffling it up. Lilly took off his hat that his head might cool, but Burns snatched it and jammed it on his head again. "No, no, you'll take cold, my little Lilly. My pretty little Lilly," he admonished, rather thickly.

Lilly, his hat into his eyes, trudged along silently, much annoyed.

"I know," went on Burns, "of a place where we could get a good hot supper. I'm starving."

"So am I!" cried George. "Head on, O Burns! You of the significant name! Let's make a night of it."

"I ought to get home," objected Meech, "to my wife and little one."

Burns exclaimed, "Wife and little one be —"

"Look out what you say!" interrupted the flautist, standing up to him.

"Keep your shirt on," retorted Burns. "I didn't mean no harm. I only meant I know a place where we can get a good hot supper, and seeing as how we got extra pay tonight I'm willing to stand treat for the crowd. How about it now, eh?"

There was almost instant agreement, and as they tramped

along Burns remarked, "My stomach begins to think my throat is cut."

His companions grunted. They thought it was far from taste in him, a butcher, to talk of cut throats.

It was a little ill-lighted dingy restaurant to which Burns led them, but the bacon and eggs were good, and after a whispered consultation the waiter brought them a jug of beer. The five were ravenous. They scarcely noticed the other people in the room until their plates were swept clean and cigarettes were lighted. George then leaned toward his friends, whispering: "For heaven's sake keep your instruments out of sight. They'll be after us to play if they spot them."

There were about two dozen people seated at the tables. It was clear that they were regarding the youths with speculation in their eyes. It was too late to hide the mandolins and banjo.

One of the men came over to them. He said, with an ingratiating grin, "Say, couldn't you fellows give us a tune or two? Some of the girlies are feeling lively and they'd give a good deal to shake a leg."

"What do you take us for?" growled Lilly. "We've been playing all night. Besides, there's no piano."

"Yes, there is. Over behind the screen there. Just give us one little tune. The girlies'll be awfully disappointed if you don't." He wheezed unpleasantly behind Finch's ear.

The "girlies" themselves came, and added their importunities. Something from a bottle was poured into the empty beer glasses. Finch heard a strange buzzing in his head. The air in the room moved as though it were no longer air, but whispering waves. The electric lights were blurred into a milky haze. He was being led to the piano. He felt intolerably sad.

About him the others were tuning up. He heard George swearing at a broken string. He put his hands on the keyboard and blinked at it. It was a white marble terrace with little black figures of nuns in procession across it. He sat staring at them, stupefied, they were so perfect, so black, so sad. Burns said, hoarsely, "My Heart Stood Still."

"Awright," agreed Finch.

It was not he who was playing. It was only his hands, mechanisms which depended on him not at all. Over and over they played what they were told to play, firm, strong, banging out the accented notes. He could see George's face, set like a white mask, and his small white hands plucking vigorously at the strings. The flute soared and wailed in a kind of dying scream; the mandolins chirped away as though they knew no tiring. Burns's red butcher's fists had always made Finch rather sick as they hovered over the strings. The mandolin seemed like some puny little animal he was about to slaughter.

They were in the street again. They were all yelling together. They had no reason to raise their voices. Only some primitive instinct told them it was the time for yelling. They straggled along the snowy street, sometimes in file, sometimes strung across the roadway. The strange snow light — the moon had become too pale to be accounted anything more than a wan presence in the paling sky — lent an unearthly quality to their figures. Their cries seemed the cries of spirits rather than of men.

They did not know where they were going. Up one street and down another, and, coming upon the first street again, they traversed it for the second time without recognizing it. Each variation and eccentric curve was marked on the purity of the snow. Sometimes they were separated into two parties, two going in one direction and three in another. Then the far-away shouting of one group would startle into a panic the other, and they would run, calling each other by name, until they met again on some corner, and the little band would be reunited.

Once the flautist was lost by the other four. It was some little time before they noticed that one of their number was absent, though they realized that all was not well with them. From their hoarse, deep-toned shouts one high-pitched tenor cry was missing. But at last their loss was borne in upon them. They stood stock-still, staring blankly at each other. Who was gone?

Then, all at once, they knew it was Meech.

"Meech! Meech!" they shouted, and they began to run in a body, calling his name and reeling as they ran.

There was no answer, so they called him by his Christian name.

"Sinden! Sinden! Hi, Sinden Meech!"

At last they found him. He had wandered into a wide, well-lit street of the prosperous. His arms were clasped about the standard of an electric light. His head was thrown back and he gazed rapturously upward.

"This is a clock tower," he declared. "I'm trying to find out what time it is. One — two — three — four — five" — and he counted loudly up to twenty-nine. "Twenty-nine o'clock," he announced. "That's as rotten an hour as I ever heard struck."

"Go to hell," said Burns. "That ain't no clock."

"Yes, it is, too! And I'm going to stop here until it strikes again. Next time it'll strike — one — two — three — "

The rest of the quintet joined in the counting with explosive shouts.

They were interrupted by a scream from Lilly, doubled up in the middle of the road. They ceased to count, and encircled him, all but Sinden Meech, who still clasped the standard.

"What's the matter, Lilly?"

"I've got a pain. Say, you fellers, what d'ye do for a pain?"

"Where is it, Lilly?"

"In m-my belly."

"That's no kind of word to say on the street!"

"Well, what shall I call it then?"

"Diaphragm," said George Fennel.

"All right, then. I've a pain in my diagram."

They shouted with sardonic laughter, hopping about in circles like crows against the snow.

When a lull came, Meech announced, leaving the standard and reeling toward them, "My father brought up ten chil- dren on the piccolo."

They gathered about him, interested.

He continued plaintively, "Is it possible that I can't bring up one on the flute?"

They howled.

Three figures were seen approaching, a man and two women. The women were frightened, and the man himself nervous about passing this band of ruffians on the street. He clasped the arms of the women closely, set his face, and marched into their midst.

But there was nothing to fear. The five youths gazed wonderingly into the faces of what appeared to them a portentous apparition. They crowded close, but they said nothing until the three had passed. Then George called, "Bye-bye, ladies!"

And Finch cooed, "Ta-ta, gennelman."

Then a storm of bye-byes and ta-tas followed the retreat- ing figures.

A window was thrown up in the large house opposite, and a man in his night clothes appeared in the opening.

"If you hoodlums don't get off this street in double- quick time, I'll call the police. Now, get a move on!"

The members of the orchestra looked at each other. Then they burst into jeers, whistles, and catcalls. Finch packed a snowball and sent it flying through the window into the angry whiskered face. A volley of snowballs followed. The householder retreated. He was going to telephone for the police.

Almost at the moment of his disappearance a thick, helmeted figure appeared at the corner of the street. With terrified looks they snatched up their mandolins, banjo, and flute, silent participators in all this rowdyism, and fled along the street and down a lane. From there they emerged into another street, raced along it, and heard the policeman's whistle on the clear morning air.

Bright red-gold wavelets of cloud appeared in the eastern sky, forerunners of the strong tide of day. Blue shadows became visible on the snow.

Finch and George Fennel found themselves separated from the rest. They ran on for several blocks, and at last made sure that they were not pursued. They halted and looked at each other curiously as people who meet under strange circumstances for the first time.

"Where do you live?" asked Finch.

"With aunt in ole house in College Street."

After a moment's reflection, Finch observed, "I live in ole house, too. Name of Jalna."

"*In*-deed. Are you going there now?"

"I dunno. Where'd you say you live?"

"I said ole house in College Street."

"Wanna go there?"

"Absolutely. All the time."

"Tha's nice. College Street, you say?"

"Say, have you got anything against that street?"

"No, no. I'm going to take you there."

"All righ', Finch. Goo' friend to me."

Finch put his arm around George's neck and they made a somewhat uneven progression along the street. Coming upon a milkman, they asked him their way, but when he had directed them they questioned his directions so skeptically that he became irritated and whipped up his horse and left them. However, they followed him to his next place of delivery, calling, "Hi, there!"

"Well, what do you want?" he snarled, standing in the bluish snow, with a carrier of milk bottles in his hand.

"Do you stop here or there?" demanded George.

"Funny, ain't you?" sneered the milkman, crashing the carrier into the wagon, and leaping in after it.

"I suppose we can buy a bottle of milk," said Finch.

"Let's see your money," said the milkman, suspiciously, and his horse began to plod heavily along the accustomed route.

Finch, trotting alongside, held up a silver coin. The milkman drew in his horse and sulkily handed out a bottle. "If you'd drunk more o' this," he said, "and less o' the other, you wouldn't be where you are."

But they discovered, when they had opened the bottle, that the milk was frozen. They tried disconsolately to dig it out with a penknife, and, failing this, they broke the bottle off the milk and left the erect frozen shape standing on the nearest doorstep.

Finch again put his arm about his friend's neck, and again they set out to find the house of Mrs. St. John.

Finch cuddled George's head against his shoulder. "What are you?" he asked.

"Goo' boy," responded George.

"Tha's a wrong answer," said Finch, very gravely. "Now tell me again, what are you?"

"Goo' boy," persisted George, doggedly.

"Tha's a wrong answer."

And thus they proceeded with question and answer until, as by a miracle, they stood before the door of the house they sought.

"You live here?" asked Finch, politely.

"Yes. . . . You live here, too?"

"No. I live in ole house named Jalna."

"Oh. . . . Well, goo'-bye."

"Goo'-bye. See you later."

They parted, and Finch on the next street took a taxi and drove to the station. During the ride he kept his face pressed to the window, observing with drunken interest the streets through which they passed.

There was only a short wait until the early morning train left. The conductor on this train did not know Finch, but he had a fatherly eye on him, and awoke him from his heavy sleep before they reached the station at Weddels', and saw him safely to the platform.

Out here in the open, the sunshine poured down in an unobstructed flood. The sun was climbing the clear blue sky, his springtime ardor unabashed by the snowfall of the night before. The snow, in truth, was now nothing more than a thin white garment on the earth. The earth was casting it aside and pushing up her bare brown bosom to the sun. She was straining her body toward him to absorb his heat.

In the ditches, bright runnels of water were gurgling. The bare limbs of the trees shone as though they had been varnished. A rut in the road made a bathtub for a little bird. He agitated his brown wings joyously and sent up a cascade of sparkling drops.

Finch splashed through the melting slush, his face heavy and flushed, his hair plastered over his forehead. Two farmers in a wagon, passing him, remarked that that young Whiteoak was growing up no better than the rest.

He met Rags as he was about to enter the house. The servant observed, with his air of impudent solicitude, "If I was you, Mister Finch, I shouldn't gaow into the 'ouse lookin' like that. I'd gaow round to the washroom and wash my fice. There's no hobject in advertising to the family, sir, wot kind of a night you've spent."

VIII

THE FOUR BROTHERS

HE went in at the side door, and descended, with rather jerky movements, the short flight of steps leading to the basement. He was too dazed by the buzzing in his head to notice the sound of voices in the washroom, and, even when he had opened the door, he did not at once perceive that it was occupied. However, as he stood blinking in the warm, steamy atmosphere, he gradually made out the figures of his brothers. Piers was kneeling beside a large tin bathtub in which a spaniel drooped, wet and shivering, its face looking pathetically wan and meek with all the fluffy hair lathered down. Standing braced against the hand basin stood Renny, pipe in mouth, directing the operations, and perched on a stepladder was little Wakefield, eating a chocolate bar.

Finch hesitated, but it was too late to retreat — all three had seen him. He entered slowly and closed the door behind him. For a space no one paid any attention to him. Renny laid his pipe on the window sill, snatched up a bucket of clear water, and poured it over the dog, Piers slithering his hands up and down its body to rinse away the lather.

"Good boy, now!" cried Wakefield. "Up, Merlin, up!"

The spaniel, released, straddled on the brick floor a moment, then shook himself mightily, sending a shower of drops in all directions.

"Hi! Hi!" shouted Wakefield. "You're drowning us!"

Renny tossed a bath towel to Piers, who, his shirt sleeves rolled up on his white, muscular arms, began vigorously to rub the dog dry.

Renny turned suddenly and looked at Finch.

"Well, I'll be shot!" he exclaimed.

Wakefield peered through the steamy air at him, and then, with a perfect imitation of the eldest Whiteoak's tone, cried in his clear treble, "Well, I'll be shot, too!"

Piers looked over his shoulder at the object of their astonishment. He made no remark, but, releasing the dog, he rose and moved a step nearer for a closer inspection. Finch stood facing them, his jaw dropped in an expression of stupid resentment, his face dirty, his collar and tie askew.

"Well," he snarled, out of the side of his mouth, "do you like the looks of me?"

"So well," returned Piers, "that I've a mind to stick your head in this tub of suds."

"You just try it! Just lay a finger on me, any of you! I want to be let alone, that's what I want. I don't want any damned interference from anybody!" He fixed his heavy gaze on Piers. "We had a fight in this room once. Say the word and we'll have another!"

"A fight!" Piers gave a sarcastic laugh. "A fight, you young ass — you don't call that a fight, I hope? You threw some water in my face and I knocked you down." He turned to Renny. "Don't you remember? You came in, and he was lying on the floor with a bloody nose, blubbering."

Finch interrupted vehemently, "I was not blubbering!"

"Yes, you were! You always blubber when you're punished. Sniveling is your long suit."

Finch, with face distorted by rage, lunged toward him, and the spaniel, exhilarated by the bath, desiring to have part in the excitement, sprang upon Finch, barking, and almost overthrew him.

This bundle of wetness pawing him was the last straw to Finch's nerves. The exuberant barks in his face confused him. He scarcely knew what he was doing when he kicked the spaniel. Even its yelp of pain hardly penetrated his consciousness. What did pierce it, with terrible distinctness, was Renny's expression of white anger. Renny looked very strange, he thought, white as a ghost, with that aghast expression.

Renny was staring as though he could not believe that Finch had kicked Merlin. Then his mouth set. He laid down his pipe, and in a stride was on him. He shook him as a terrier a rat, and then threw him on to a bench, saying, "If I thought you knew what you were doing, I'd flay you." He bent and put his hand on the dog's side, and looked reassuringly into his eyes.

Finch's eyes were on Renny's hand, that hard, strong hand that moved with such machinelike swiftness and surety. He sprawled on the bench, his back against the wall, filled with misery, anger, and self-loathing.

Wakefield remarked from his perch, "Usually I'm not on hand when there's a row." No one heard him.

"Now," said Renny, taking up his pipe again, "I want you to tell me where you were last night."

"In town," mumbled Finch, brokenly.

"Where? You certainly weren't at Mrs. St. John's."

"I had dinner there."

"Yes?"

He wished Renny's eyes were not so fiercely, so mercilessly, questioning. It made it hard for him to think clearly, to put himself in a decent light if possible. Yet, what use in trying when he had kicked Merlin! If only Piers weren't there, it would be easier to make a clean breast of it!

Piers was again rubbing Merlin, but he never took his bright blue eyes from Finch's face, and he never took the small sneering grin from his lips.

"Well," Finch's voice was still more broken, "there's this orchestra I belong to. I've never told you about that But there is no harm in it really."

"A harmless bird, this!" interjected Piers.

"An orchestra! What sort of orchestra?"

"Oh, just a little one a few of us got up, so we could make a little money. A banjo, two mandolins, a flute, and I — played the piano."

"God, what an orchestra!" exclaimed Piers, standing up and drying his arms.

"Who are these fellows?"

"Oh — some fellows I know. Not at school. I — just got in with them." He must not implicate George. "We practised after school."

"Where did you play?"

"In restaurants. Cheap ones. For dances."

"That's what you were up to when you were spending the night with George's aunt, eh? Was George into this?"

"No, no. I just happened to meet these fellows —"

"They must be a pretty lot. Who are they?"

"You wouldn't know if I told you. One of them is named Lilly, and another Burns, and another Meech."

"But who are they? Who are their people?"

"How much did you get for playing?" put in Piers.

This question came as a relief. He raised his haggard eyes to Piers. "Five dollars a night."

"And how often have you played?"

"I don't — I can't remember — but we've been going out for over two months."

"What I want to know," insisted Renny, "is who these boys are. Are they students?"

"No. They work. Lilly's grandfather has a greenhouse. Sinden Meech is in some sort of tailoring establishment. Burns is in some kind of — abattoir."

"H'm. . . . And so you're in the habit of knocking about town all night drinking, eh?"

Oh, if they wouldn't stare at him so! He could not get his thoughts clear with those relentless eyes on him!

"No, no," he mumbled, wringing his fingers together. "This is the very first time. . . . We'd been playing for a dance. We got awfully tired. And they gave us something to buck us up. But not too much, mind you. It was at the other place where we went afterward that they — some-one — gave us another drink. I guess it was pretty rotten stuff, and when we came out in the street we — couldn't find our way at first — and we separated and got together again and then I took the train for home."

Renny rapped his pipe on the window sill and put it in his pocket. "You're in no condition," he said, looking Finch over with distaste, "to listen to a lecture now. Go to your bed and sleep this off. Then I'll have something to say to you."

"If you were mine," said Piers, "I'd hold your head under that tap for fifteen minutes and see if that would waken you up."

"But I'm *not* yours!" Finch cried, hoarsely. "I'm not anybody's! You talk as though I were a dog."

"I wouldn't insult any dog by comparing him to you!"

Finch's misery became too much for him. He burst into tears. He took out a soiled handkerchief and violently blew his nose.

Wakefield began to scramble down from his stepladder. "Let me out of here," he said. "I'm getting upset."

He hastened toward the door, but as he reached Piers's side he espied a half sheet of crumpled paper lying on the floor. He bent and examined it.

"What's this, I wonder," he said.

"Give it here," said Piers.

Wakefield handed it to him, and Piers, smoothing it out, cast his eyes over it. His expression changed.

"This evidently belongs to Finch," he said, slowly. "He must have pulled it out of his pocket with his handker-chief." He looked steadily at Finch. "Now that you're making a clean breast of it, Finch, will you give me leave to read this aloud?"

"Do what you darned please," sobbed Finch.

"It's a note from someone to you." He read, with distinctness: —

"DEAREST FINCH, —

"After you were gone last night, I was very much disturbed. You were preoccupied — not like your old self with me. Cannot you tell me what is wrong? It would be a terrible thing to me if the clarity of our relationship were clouded. Write to me, darling Finch.

"ARTHUR"

Piers folded the paper, and returned it to the child. "Give this back to Finch," he said. "He'll not want to be separated from it." He turned then to Renny. "Did you take it in, Renny? His friend Arthur calls him 'dearest' and 'darling.' Could you have believed it possible that one of us should ever have got into such a disgusting mix-up?"

Renny said, his eyes fixed on the spaniel, "This Arthur Leigh calls him 'dearest' and 'darling.'"

"Yes! And rants about the 'clarity of their relationship'!" He gave a flourish of his hand toward Finch. "Is it any wonder he looks a wreck — alternately boozing with butchers and tailors and spooning with a rotter like Leigh?"

"I thought you were a little fool," said the eldest Whiteoak, "but now I'm disgusted with you. You've been deceiving me, and wasting time when you should have been studying. As for this neurotic affair with Leigh — I tell you, I'm sick at heart for you."

Finch could not defend himself. He felt annihilated. He held Arthur's note in one shaking hand and in the other he gripped his handkerchief, but he did not hold it to his face. He left the misery of his face exposed to the eyes of his brothers. Sobs shook his lips. Tears ran down his cheeks unheeded.

Wakefield could not bear it. Slipping past Piers and Renny, he threw his arms about Finch's neck.

"Oh, don't cry," he implored. "Poor old Finch, don't cry!"

Renny said, "This is very bad for you," and took him under the arms and put him into the passage outside.

The little boy stood there motionless, his heart pounding heavily. He was oppressed by the strife among his elders. He had a feeling that something frightening was going to happen.

Mrs. Wragge came out of the kitchen carrying a corn broom and a dustpan. She began angrily to sweep something off the red brick floor into the pan.

"If that 'usband of mine," she affirmed, "don't quit throwin' refuge on my clean floors, it'll be the worse for 'im."

"There's another bit, over in the corner," said Wakefield, pointing.

Mrs. Wragge collected it, straightened her back, and looked curiously at the door of the washroom.

"What might they be doing in there so long?" she asked. Wakefield replied with dignity, "They *might* be doing almost anything, Maggie. What they *are* doing is washing a dog."

"I thought the master's voice sounded as though he were a bit put out over something."

"Not more than usual, Maggie."

"Well, it's none of my business."

"You bet it isn't."

"But, just the same, when Wragge told me that Mr. Finch had come 'ome with his collar hangin' loose and 'is fice dirty at this time in the morning, I says, 'Look out for squalls.'"

The door of the washroom opened. Renny and Piers, followed by Finch and the spaniel, came out. Renny picked up Wake and threw him across his shoulder. Upstairs he set him down in the hall and rumpled his hair. "Feel better?" he asked. Wake nodded, but he kept his eyes turned away from Finch. He could not bear to look at him. . . .

Finch lay on his bed all day. He was in a strange state, between sleeping and waking. He could not think clearly, and his head hurt him terribly. He felt as though the inside of it had become solid, while, over the surface, sharp pains trickled down into his neck. He had an abominable taste in the mouth. He had a light-headed, feverish feeling. It was impossible for him to arrange the events of the last twelve hours in proper sequence. He had never been so confused, so hopeless, in his life. All the muddle-headedness, the fear, the groping of his years, seemed to have harried him, jostled him, spiritually disheveled, to this. He was an outcast in his own home, unspeakably alone. He asked himself the old question, What am I? He examined his hand as it lay clenched on the quilt beside him. What was it? Why had it been formed? Given those strange and delicate muscles — the power to draw music from the aching heart of the piano. That music was more real than the hand that made it. The hand was nothing, the body was nothing. The soul surely less than the grass. He lay as motionless as though the soul had indeed left the body.

After a time, the thought of music again came to him. He remembered something by a Russian composer, which his teacher had played to him. It had been too difficult for Finch to play, but he had the power of remembering it, of inwardly hearing it, in its entirety, as though it were again being played.

He lay, letting it sing through him, through every nerve in his body, like a cleansing, rushing wind. At last he felt peaceful and slept.

IX

ALAYNE

THREE weeks later, Alayne Whiteoak sat alone in the living room of the apartment which she shared with Rosamund Trent. She had just finished reading a new book, and she was about to write a review of it for one of the magazines. She wrote a good many reviews and short articles now, in addition to her work as reader for the publishing house of Parsons and Cory.

This was an English novel of Oxford undergraduates who waved white hands, who talked endlessly and cleverly, always on the verge of the risqué. She wished they had not sent her this particular book — but then it was only one of many like it. She felt that she could not do it justice because she had come to it prejudiced. It was not her sort of book. She sighed and looked at the books piled about her. She thought of the procession of books that, in the last year and a half, since her return to New York, had passed through her hands. A strangely dressed procession, carrying brazen "blurbs," trampling her spirit, tiring her.

She had none of the angry irritation of a professional reader whose own creative power is being stifled by continuous critical reading. She had little creative power in writing. She did not even desire it, but she wanted certain things from life which life apparently was to withhold from her. She wanted open space about her, and she wanted freedom to love. She desired spiritual growth.

When she had first come back to New York, her reaction from the troubled ingrown life at Jalna was a desire to submerge her personality in the routine of work, to drown in the roar of the city remembrance of that strange house-

hold — love of Renny Whiteoak. And for a while it seemed
that she had succeeded. Rosamund Trent had been almost
pathetically glad to welcome her back to the apartment on
Seventy-first Street. "You know, Alayne dear, I never
hoped much from that marriage of yours. Not that your
young poet was not an adorable creature, but still, scarcely
the type that husbands are made of. It has been an experience for you, — I should n't have minded a year of it, myself, — but now the thing is to put it behind you and look
steadily forward." Her voice had had an exultant little
crow in it as once more she took Alayne under her wing.

Mr. Cory felt badly that the marriage had been so un-
successful. He still had a fatherly interest in Alayne, and
it had been through him that the two had met. Eden's
two slim books of poetry were still in print, but the sale of
them had dropped to almost nothing. Still, now and again
in some literary article reference was made to the wild
beauty of the lyrics, or to the fresh vigor of the long narrative poem, *The Golden Sturgeon.* No new manuscript
had been submitted to the publisher by Eden, but once, in a
magazine, he had come upon a short poem by him which
was either childishly naïve or horribly and deliberately
cynical. Mr. Cory, after reading it several times, could
not really decide. In either case he had a poor opinion of
it. He had been uncertain whether or not to show it to
Alayne. He had cut it out and saved it for her, but when
next she came into the office, and he looked into her eyes,
he decided against it. No, she had had enough suffering.
Better not remind her of the cause of it. So, instead, he
begged her to come oftener to his house, insisted that she
come to dinner that very night, and when he was alone he
tore the poem into small pieces.

To-night Alayne felt stifled by the air of the city. She
went to the window, opened it wide, and sat on the sill,
looking down into the street. There were few pedestrians,

but a stream of motor cars flowed by, like an uneasy, tortured river that could find no rest. The smell of oil, of city dust, dulled the freshness of the spring night. The myriad separate sounds, resolved into one final roar, sucked down human personality as quicksand human flesh and blood. Looking down into the city, a spectator might fancy he saw wild arms thrown upward in gestures of despair, as by drowning people.

Alayne thought of Jalna. Of the April wind as it came singing through the ravine, stirring the limbs of the birches, the oaks, the poplars, to response. She remembered the smell that rose from the earth in which their roots were twined and lovingly intertwined, a smell of quickening and decay, of the beginning and the end. She saw, in imagination, the great balsams that guarded the driveway and stood in dark clumps at the lawn's edge, shutting in the house, making a brooding barrier between Jalna and the world. She saw Renny riding along the drive on his bony gray mare, drooping in the saddle, and somehow, in that indolent accustomed droop, giving an impression of extraordinary vigor and vitality. . . . He was no longer on his horse. He stood beside her. His piercing red-brown eyes searched her face. He moved nearer, and she saw his nostrils quiver, his mouth set. . . . God, she was in his arms! His lips were draining the strength from her, and yet strength like fire had leaped from his body to hers. . . .

Alayne made a small, moaning sound. She pressed her hand to her throat. Was she to have no peace? Was the remembrance of Renny's kisses to torture her always? Ah, but if she could, would she part with the delight of that torture?

She remembered his last passionate kiss of good-bye, and how she had clung to him and breathed, "Again," and his putting her away from him with a sharp gesture of renunciation. "No," he had said, through his teeth. "Not again." And he had moved away and taken his place among his brothers. Her last sight of him had been as he stood among them, taller than they, his hair shining redly in the firelight.

To-night she felt invisible cords, charged with desire, drawing her toward Jalna. She experienced a mystic ecstasy in the secret pull of them. She gave herself up to it, all her senses absorbed. She became unconscious of the strangely compounded street roar. She did not even hear, until it was twice repeated, the buzz of the bell of her own door.

When at last she heard it, she was startled. She had a feeling approaching apprehension as she went to the door and opened it. In the bright light of the hallway stood young Finch Whiteoak. Like a ghost created by her thoughts he stood, tall, hollow-cheeked, a tremulous smile on his lips.

"Finch!" she exclaimed.

"Hullo, Alayne!" He got out the words with an effort. His face broke up into a smile that was perilously near the contortion of crying.

"Finch, my dear, is it possible? You in New York! I can scarcely believe it is you. But you must tell me all about it."

She drew him in, and took his hat and coat. It seemed so strange to see him away from Jalna that she felt she might be laying eyes on him for the first time.

"I ran away," he muttered. "I just couldn't stand it. . . . I've been here three weeks."

Alayne led him to a sofa and sat down beside him. "Oh, Finch! Poor dear. Tell me all about it." She laid her hand on his. Isolated thus, they were intimate as they had never been at Jalna.

He looked at her hand lying on his. He had always been moved by the whiteness of her hands.

"Well, things seemed absolutely set against me — or me

against them. Darned if I know which. Anyhow, I failed
in my matric. I suppose you heard that. Aunt Augusta
and you write sometimes to each other, don't you? Well,
Renny stopped my music lessons. I wasn't even allowed
to touch the piano. And I guess that was all right, too, for
I'd sort of gone dotty about music. I couldn't forget it
for a minute. But I'm like that, you know. Once I get a
thing on the brain, I'm done for." He sighed deeply.

Her hand which was lying on his clenched itself. She
withdrew it and repeated, "He stopped your music."
Between her and Finch rose a vision of Renny's carved
profile, its inflexibility denying the warmth of the full face.
"Yes? And then what?"

"Well, it seemed as though I'd got to have something
besides plain work. A kind of ballast. I felt that I
couldn't stick it unless there was something. So I went to
play-acting. The Little Theatre, you know. I'd made a friend
of a splendid chap named Arthur Leigh. He's perhaps a
bit girlish — well, no, not girlish, but overrefined for the
taste of my brothers. Anyhow he liked me, and encouraged
me a lot about my acting. He even got after Renny and
persuaded him to come and see the play I was in. Well, it
all turned out badly. I was taking the part of a half-witted
Irish boy, and Renny thought it came too darned easy to
me. I did it too well. He was frightfully fed up with me
and my talents, he said."

He sat silent a moment, pulling at his flexible underlip;
then he said, "You can't imagine, Alayne, how beastly life
seems to me, sometimes."

"Can't I?"

"Oh, I know you've had a lot of trouble — Eden, and
all that — but still, in yourself, you're a reasonable being
and . . . oh, dash it all, I can never express myself!"

"I know what you mean, Finch. And perhaps it is so.
I don't believe I am capable of suffering as you are."

"Well, I always bring it on myself. That's one thing," he said, darkly.

"Is it possible that Renny could not appreciate the fact that you were doing a piece of good acting?" How she loved to drag in that name, to caress it with her tongue, even while her heart was angry against him!

"The trouble was," answered Finch, "that he hated seeing me in that part. I was in my bare feet, and dirty. I hadn't much on but an idiotic expression. Renny's awfully conventional."

"But think of some of the men — horse dealers, and such — that he goes about with, seems to make friends of. That's not conventional."

"If you said that to Renny, he'd say, 'Yes, but I don't get up on a stage with them and charge people admission to watch my antics.' Most of all, it was the half-wittedness of the part. He thinks I'm a bit that way already." He pulled his lips again, and then went on more quickly, so that the tale of his misdeeds might be done with. "So there was no more play-acting. The next thing was an orchestra. George Fennel — you remember the boys at the rectory, Alayne — and myself and three other chaps got it up — a banjo, two mandolins, a flute, and the piano. All the practising was done on the sly. We played for club dances. You know the sort of club it would be. Cheap restaurants. But we made quite a lot of money — five dollars apiece, each night."

Alayne looked at him with a mingling of admiration and amusement. "What amazing boys! Had you planned to do anything special with all this money?"

"We bought quite a good radio. We had that at the rectory, of course."

"Where did Mr. Fennel think that came from?"

"Oh, he never asks many questions. He's awfully unpractical. He probably thought we'd rigged it up out of some odds and ends of wire. Then some of the money went toward hearing some good music — Paderewski, Kreisler. But I saved most of it. That's how I got here, to New York. And then too we'd blow in quite a bit on grub. I'm always hungry, you know."

There was a peculiar expression on his face, as he said this, that startled Alayne. A sudden break in his voice. She thought, "Is it possible the boy is hungry now?" She said, "You're like I am. I'm always getting hungry at odd times. Here it is, only half-past eight, and I'm starving. But of course I didn't eat much dinner. Supposing, Finch, that you tell me quickly how things came to a head, and then we can have the details over some supper."

He agreed, in his odd, hesitating way, and then, in a muffled voice, told of the last performance of the orchestra, of his return to Jalna, of the scene in the washroom. "It was only that I'd been lit, and was feeling dazed — oh, absolutely awful — but there was something else. I'd pulled my handkerchief out of my pocket, and with it a note from Arthur Leigh. There was nothing to that, but he'd called me 'darling Finch,' and Renny and Piers went right up in the air over it." His face twitched as he remembered the scene.

"Finch, do you tell me that they read your letter?"

"I told Piers he might."

"But why?"

"I forget."

It was useless; she could never understand them. "But why should they have been angry? It was harmless enough, surely."

He flushed a dark red. "They didn't think so. They thought it was beastly. Neurotic, and all that. Oh, you can't understand. It was just the last straw." He clasped his hands between his knees, and Alayne saw that he was shaking. She got up quickly. She was afraid he was going to cry, and she could not bear that. Something in her would give way if he cried. She must hang on to herself. She said, almost coldly, " So it was then you decided to run away?"

"Yes. I stayed in my room all day. Lay on the bed trying to think. Then, when night came, I sneaked out with a suitcase of clothes and got a late bus into town on the highway. In the morning I took the train for New York."

" And you've been here three weeks?"

"Yes. I've never written home either."

"What have you been doing, Finch?"

"Trying to get a job." He raised a miserable young face to hers. "I thought it'd be easy to get one here, but I simply can't round up anything. There seemed to be dozens ahead of me whenever I answered an advertisement. Gosh, it's been awful!"

She looked down at him with compassion. "But why in the world didn't you come to me before? It hurts me to think that you've been walking the streets here looking for work, and have never come to see me."

"I didn't want to come until I had got something, but to-night—I just gave in. . . . I—I was so frightfully homesick." He reached out, took her hand, and pressed it to his forehead. "Oh, Alayne, you've always been so good to me!"

She bent and kissed him, then she said, assuming a businesslike tone, "Now we must have something to eat. There are cigarettes. You smoke while I forage in the pantry."

In the glittering little pantry, with its air of trig unhomeliness, she discovered some potato salad bought at a delicatessen shop, a tin of vermicelli with tomato sauce, a lettuce, and some dill pickles. She and Rosamund took only their breakfast and lunch in the apartment.

Strange fare, she thought, as she arranged the things on the tea wagon, for a Whiteoak! She had made coffee, and now she remembered some jars of preserves given to her by the aunts who lived up the Hudson. She chose one of black currants in a rich syrup. Last, she added some slices of rye bread and some little chocolate-covered cakes.

Finch's back was toward her as she entered the living room. His head was enveloped in tobacco smoke. He was examining her books. She noticed how loosely his coat hung on him. The boy looked half-starved, she thought.

"Great Scott," he exclaimed, turning round, "what a lot of new books, Alayne! How do you ever get the time to read them all?"

"By not getting time for anything else," she returned. "That one you have in your hand is very interesting. Take it along with you, Finch. I believe you might like it."

"Poetry," he commented, turning over the leaves. . . . He looked up from the book. Their eyes met, and he took a quick step toward her. "Alayne — have you ever — seen *him* — heard of him?" His face grew scarlet.

"Eden?" She said the name with composure. "I've never seen him or heard from him, but Miss Trent, who shares the apartment with me, insists that she saw him one night last fall outside a theatre. Just a glimpse. She thought he looked ill. Your aunt told me in a letter that you had heard nothing."

"Not a thing. I've been afraid ever since I came here that I'd run up against him. He and I had an awful scene" — oh, Lord, why had he recalled that time to her? — "I guess he hates me, all right."

She had begun to set the supper things on a small table. He came to her and touched her arm timidly. "Forgive me, Alayne. I shouldn't have spoken of him."

She looked up with continued composure. "It doesn't upset me to speak of Eden. He is nothing to me now. I don't believe I should feel greatly disturbed if I met him face to face. Now do sit down, Finch, and try to imagine

that this food is not so sketchy. If only I had known you
were coming . . ."

How hungry the boy was! She talked incessantly to
cover the fact, to give him a chance to eat without interruption. He swept the plates clean, and drank cup after
cup of coffee. Over coffee and cigarettes he gave her news
of each separate member of the family. Finally he told her
in detail of the last performance of the orchestra, of the
wild night in the streets afterward. He began to laugh.
Finch's laughter was infectious. Alayne laughed too, and
as he imitated the maudlin outpourings of the different
players they could no longer restrain themselves, and laughed
till they were exhausted. Alayne had not given way to such
primitive emotions since leaving Jalna, had had no impulse
to do so.

Rosamund Trent, returning, discovered them thus abandoned to hilarity. She was astonished to find this lank
youth sprawling in the Chinese-red leather armchair, a fair
lock dangling over his forehead, making himself tremendously at home. She was still more astonished to find
Alayne deeply flushed, weak with laughter.

Finch got to his feet, embarrassed by the arrival of
the sophisticated-looking middle-aged woman whose small
bright green hat looked as if it were moulded to her head.

"Rosamund," said Alayne, "my brother-in-law, Finch
Whiteoak."

Miss Trent looked at him keenly, smiled humorously, and
shook his hand heartily.

"I'm glad you came," she declared. "I don't often find
Alayne in such spirits."

She took to Finch at once. When she heard that he was
looking for a position, she was instantly ready to take him
under her wing, to place him where he would have an excellent chance of advancement. She was in the advertising
business.

"The very thing for him!" she exclaimed to Alayne, energetically snapping her cigarette lighter. "I'll see about it first thing in the morning."

But Alayne could not picture Finch in an advertising office. She had already made up her mind to see Mr. Cory about him. It required courage to oppose Rosamund when she had set her mind on taking someone under her wing, but Finch helped her by boldly saying that he felt a greater urge in himself toward publishing than toward advertising.

Before he left, Finch helped to carry out the supper things, and in the kitchen Alayne gave him some money — it was to be only a loan — and learned from him that he had been forced to pawn his topcoat and his watch.

In a few days Finch was installed in a minor clerk's position in the publishing house, and Rosamund Trent had had to satisfy her instinct for managing by finding him a more comfortable lodging.

It was only a week later that Alayne had a letter from Lady Buckley, written in a long, graceful hand, with frequent underlinings.

JALNA,
18th April 1927.

MY DEAR ALAYNE, —

I was so *pleased* to receive your last, and to hear that you are in good health and as good spirits as possible, under the *circumstances.*

We are in fair health, excepting my brother Ernest, who has been suffering from a cold. My brother Nicholas is troubled by gout, as usual with him in the spring. I re-iterate the word *diet* to him, but it has little effect. My mother is excessively well, considering her great age. Has come through the winter with no more serious ailments than occasional attacks of *wind* on the stomach. Renny is in good health, as always, but is limping about on a stick as the result of a severe kick on the knee from a vicious *horse*. Luckily the veterinary was in the stable at the time and administered *first aid.*

It is really at Renny's instigation that I am writing to you about our trouble. He is greatly upset in his mind, as indeed we all are, excepting perhaps Mamma, who seems singularly callous about it all. I am sure that by now you are quite *wrought up* by curiosity, so I shall relieve it by coming to the point at once. Finch has *disappeared*.

Knowing what a closely knit, affectionate family we are, you can imagine our *state* of *mind*.

He has been gone four weeks and we are now thoroughly alarmed. Wakefield quite threw us into a state at the dinner table yesterday by suggesting that perhaps Finch has been *murdered*. What a dreadful word that is! I doubt if I have ever written any so *low* word in my correspondence hitherto.

Renny has had a private detective on the search for Finch, and has traced him to New York. He now declares that, unless he is found inside of the week, he will *publicly* advertise for him. This would be very humiliating for us, as we have given out that he is away on a visit for his health. As a matter of fact, it was none too good. I think the poor boy worried a great deal over being denied access to a pianoforte, and I firmly believe this was at the root of the *disaster*.

You are so sympathetic, dear Alayne. You understand, as no outsider could, our extreme devotion as a family, in spite of little *surface* flurries. I trust you will be able to send us some word of Finch. Remembering how fond he was of you, we think it quite probable that he has sought you out. Pray heaven we shall not have to go through the agony of *publicly* advertising for him. Renny has already gone to the length of writing a *complete* description of him, and it sounded *so* unattractive when read aloud.

Hoping to hear good news from you,

In urgent haste,

Ever affectionately,

AUGUSTA BUCKLEY.

P.S. Wakefield sends his love. His heart has been very troublesome. The Canadian winter inevitably pulls him down, as it does me. A. B.

Alayne wrote by return post: —

DEAR LADY BUCKLEY, —

It is as you have guessed. Finch has been to see me. He is quite well, and has a position in which he has a good chance of advancement. If I were you (and by you, I mean the entire family) I should not interfere with him, or try to get in touch with him. For the present, at any rate. Finch has been through an unhappy time, and I think he should be left quite to himself for the present.

I will see him regularly, and send you a report of him frequently, but you may tell Renny that I absolutely refuse to send his address.

I am glad you got through the winter as well as you did, and I am sorry to hear of the various disabilities, especially that Wake's heart has been troubling him. Please tell him that I often, often think of him, and wish I could see him.

I really do not think you need to worry about Finch.

Yours lovingly,

ALAYNE.

X

ERNEST'S ADVENTURE

RAGS carried in the mail and laid it before Renny, who was sitting on one side of the fireplace, his injured leg propped on an ottoman, the top of which was worked in a design in green and silver beads, portraying an angel carrying a sheaf of lilies. On the opposite side of the fireplace sat Nicholas, his gouty leg supported by an ottoman of exactly similar pattern, a glass of whiskey and soda at his elbow. He was chuckling deeply over a month-old copy of *Punch*. At a small table sat Ernest, stringing afresh a necklet of enormous amber beads for his mother. His long face drooped above the task in hand with an expression of serene absorption. Old Mrs. Whiteoak, leaning forward in her chair, watched every movement of his fingers, gratifying from the glow of the amber in the firelight her love of color, as a heavy old bee might extract sweetness from a flower. Her breath came and went more noisily over her thrust-out underlip than was usual, partly because of her attitude, and partly because of the effort of concentration. This gusty breathing and the occasional chuckle from Nicholas were the only sounds as Renny read his letters, and they served but to emphasize the seclusion of the room, the sense of an excluding wall against the rest of the world which a group of Whiteoaks always achieved.

None of his elders inquired for letters of Renny. Not one of the three received more than one or two in the whole year, and then it was, as likely as not, an advertisement.

Wakefield came into the room. "Aunt Augusta wants to know," he said in his clear treble, "if there are any letters for her."

"Two from England." Renny gave them to him.

"How nice for her!" said Wakefield, looking over his shoulder. "Why, there's another, Renny, with an American stamp. It's addressed to Lady Buckley, isn't it?"

"Take her what I gave you," said his brother curtly, and Wakefield trotted off to tell Augusta that Renny was holding back some of her mail.

When time enough had passed for her to read the two letters from England, she appeared in the doorway.

"Are you sure you have not overlooked one of my letters, Renny?" she asked. "I was expecting another."

He patted the seat of the sofa beside him. "Come and read it here," he said.

Lady Buckley looked annoyed, but she came and placed herself beside him, very upright, with eyebrows almost touching her Queen Alexandra fringe.

"I'll open it for you," he said, and with a large paper knife, the handle of which was formed of the foot of a fawn, he carefully slit the envelope, taking time with the business, as though he liked to touch this particular letter. She divined whom the letter was from.

She perched her eyeglasses on her nose and took the letter with an impassive face, but she had barely read a line when she exclaimed on a deep note, "Thank heaven, he is safe!"

Renny hitched his body nearer to her and peered at the letter. "Well, I'll be shot!" he muttered.

"Read," she commanded, in a whisper, and they perused the letter together.

When they reached the line, "You may tell Renny that I absolutely refuse to send his address," she pointed to it with a dramatic forefinger, and Renny's teeth showed in a smile that was an odd mingling of chagrin and gratification.

Wakefield, behind the sofa, intruded his head between

theirs and asked, "Is it about Finch? Has anything happened to Finch?"

Hearing the name, Ernest looked up quickly from his beads. "Is anything wrong?" he asked. "Any bad news of the boy?"

"He is found," announced Augusta. "He is in New York. He is well."

"The young devil," said Nicholas, laying down his *Punch*. "He ought to be brought home and given a sound hiding!"

For once the gentle Ernest agreed. "He ought indeed. I've worried myself ill over that boy."

"Who is the letter from?" asked Nicholas.

"Alayne. Keep still and I will read it to you." Impressively she read the letter aloud.

"I'm the only one she sent a message to," cried Wakefield, "excepting Renny, and his isn't a nice one. She says she won't tell him where Finch is, doesn't she?"

"Hush," said Augusta. "We don't wish to hear any of your chatter at a moment like this."

"Alayne," asserted Nicholas, "put ideas in that boy's head from the very first. It was she, you'll remember, Renny, who persuaded you to give him music lessons."

"You play the piano yourself," retorted his sister, tartly.

Nicholas puffed at his pipe imperturbably. "I do. But I don't lose my head over music. I could never become hag-ridden by art. Finch was not sane about it, and it did him no end of harm."

Renny said, "To think of his having the guts to go to New York alone! He must have saved all the money he made from that fool orchestra."

"The question is," said his aunt, "what is to be done? It is shocking to think of Finch exposed to the temptations of that terrible city."

"He must be brought back at once!" exclaimed Ernest, dropping a bead in his agitation.

So long as he had been faithful to his task, handling the honey-colored spheres with delicacy and precision, old Mrs. Whiteoak had chosen to pay no heed to the conversation, but now she raised her massive head in its beribboned cap and threw a piercing glance into the faces about her.

"What's the to-do?" she demanded.

They looked at each other. Had they better tell her?

The look did not escape her. She rapped with her stick on the floor. "Ha! What's this? What's the to-do? I will not be kept out of things."

"Easy on, Mamma," said Nicholas, soothingly. "It's nothing but young Finch. We've found out where he is."

A feeling of breathlessness came over the room, as always happened when a piece of news had just been broken to her. How would she take it? Would there be a scene? Every eye was fixed on that hard-bitten, smouldering old face.

"Finch, eh? You've found out where Finch is!"

"He's in New York," went on Nicholas. "We have had a letter from Alayne. She's seen him."

"Ha! What's he doing there?"

"He seems to have some sort of job. I fancy Alayne got it for him."

"Oh, did she? I had always thought she was well connected." She dropped her chin to her breast. Was she thinking deeply, or was she fallen into one of her dozes? Boney hopped from his perch and began to peck at the ribbons on her cap. He pulled at the ribbons till the cap was a trifle askew.

Suddenly she raised her head and said, emphatically, "I want him. I want to see Finch. Take the bird away. He's disarranging my cap."

Ernest gingerly replaced Boney on his perch, but not until he had received a wicked peck on the wrist.

"Haramzada!" screamed Boney, flapping his wings. "Iflatoon! Chore! Chore!"

Renny observed, "I think it would be a damned good idea to leave him there for a while. He'll soon get sick of it. Teach him a lesson."

Grandmother arched her neck and turned her beaklike nose toward him. "You do, eh? You would, eh? And you his guardian! Always ready to cross my will! Unnatural grandson! Unnatural brother!" Purplish red suffused her face.

"Nonsense," said Renny. "I'm nothing of the sort."

"You are! You are! You like nothing so well as to cross people. You'd like to be a tyrant like my father. Old Renny Court. Red Renny, they used to call him in Ireland. He cowed all his seven children but me. Me he couldn't cow." She shook her head triumphantly, then was transported by rage. "To think that I should bring another like him into the world!"

"Thanks for nothing!" retorted the master of Jalna. "You didn't bring me into the world."

"Didn't bring you into the world!" she cried. "You dare contradict me? If I didn't bring you into the world, I should like to know who did!"

"You forget," he returned, "that you are my father's mother, not mine."

"Well, I should like to know who you'd have been without your father! An English gentleman, and your mother only a poor flibbertigibbet governess."

His face was nearly as red as hers. "Now you're confusing me with his second family. My mother was Dr. Ramsay's daughter. Surely you don't forget how you hated her."

"Haramzada!" added Boney, rocking on his perch. "Iflatoon! Iflatoon!"

Nicholas broke in, rumblingly, "Stop baiting her, Renny! I won't have it. Look at the color of her face, and remember that she's over a hundred."

His mother turned on him. "Look at the color of your own face! You 're only envious that you haven't our hot blood. What we want is to have our quarrel out in peace."

"It 's very bad for you, Mamma," said Ernest.

"Go on with your bead-stringing, ninny!" ordered his mother.

Augusta cried, "Can we never discuss anything without dissension?"

"Would you serve beef without mustard?" replied the old lady.

"I wonder," observed Wakefield, "if Finch will get into the crime wave they 're having in that country. Rags was telling me about it."

"The child has touched the keynote of the matter," said Augusta. "Finch will be sure to come under some bad influence if he is left in New York. How could Alayne watch over him? What can she know of the temptations that befall a young man?"

"Man!" rumbled Nicholas. "Callow boy!"

"He must be fetched," said Grandmother, "and that at once. Ernest shall go for him."

If Ernest had been told that he was to join an Arctic exploring party, he could not have looked more surprised. "But, Mamma," he said, "why me?"

"Because," she responded, vigorously, "Nick cannot travel on account of his knee. Renny cannot travel on account of his leg. Piers is too busy, and, besides, he has never been there. Eden—what 's become of Eden?"

"He 's away, Mamma."

"Hmph. I don't like this going away. I want the young folk about me. You had better fetch him, too. You 're the one to go."

"I quite agree with Mamma," said Augusta.

Mother and daughter looked at each other, amazed to find themselves in accord.

Old Mrs. Whiteoak moved and settled her teeth into a more efficient position in her mouth with a crunching noise.

"Mamma, must you do that?" asked Ernest.

She disregarded the question, but, with a grim grin at her daughter, remarked, "Well spoken, Lady Bunkley."

After the first consternation had worn off, Ernest was thrilled through all his being by the adventure of going to New York. He had always intended to visit it again. Europe seemed out of the question. But he had procrastinated, because of lack of money and indolence, till the intention had become more and more shadowy, and would have melted into the shadow of other unfulfilled intentions had not the family forced him to action.

Two days later he was eating his dinner in the train. He felt extraordinarily pleased with himself as he bent his head above the menu under the deferential black gaze of the waiter, and felt beneath him the deep, purposeful throbbing of the wheels. He even enjoyed the unaccustomed ice water.

As he sipped his coffee at the end of the meal, he did not worry in the least about his digestion. He felt firm and strong. He gazed out of the window at the wooded ravines, at the dark blue hills and ridges slipping by. His eyes delighted in the vineyards, in the peach orchards, where thousands of little peach trees, white with bloom, marched above the rich red loam, dyed redder by the setting sun. The ground beneath the cherry trees was white with their lost petals. All the farmlands beamed and shone with promise.

The dark hand of the waiter taking up the tip pleased him, the faces of the other passengers interested. Round-faced, shrewd-looking New York business men, some of them. He thought rather ruefully, "Been looking after their interests in Canada, I suppose. . . . Well, if we haven't the initiative or capital to develop our own country,

and if the Mother Country does n't do it, why, there's nothing for it but to let the Americans undertake it."

In the smoking compartment he had a cigar. He would
have liked to engage the man nearest him in conversation,
but as soon as the man showed a disposition to talk Ernest
looked down his nose with an expression of absorption. He
could not talk to a stranger, much as he would have liked
to discuss some of the great questions of the day with
someone besides his family and his few intimates. Of
the last there were really only two: Mr. Fennel, whose
interests were centred in protecting his vegetable garden
from insects and his parish from ritualism, which two
elderly married ladies and a single young man were determined to introduce; and a Mr. Sinclair, the last survivor of
another English family, whose father had also retired from
the army and built a house five miles from Jalna. But as
he lived alone, and so had no one to talk to, he came to his
discussions with Ernest so full of explosive vitality that he
left him exhausted, and as he believed nothing that was not
in the London *Times,* and it was three weeks old when he got
it, companionship with him had its limitations.

Ernest had traveled little in America, and had forgotten
the dreadful publicity of the sleeping cars. He had difficulty,
too, in putting out his light. When at last he was tucked
in, the man in the berth above him snored so persistently
that he could not sleep for a long while. Still, sleep came
at last, fitful, restless because of lack of air, but still better
than lying awake. By sunrise he was propped on one elbow
peering out of the window. He was among the first to
enter the dining car, having already bought a New York
paper and exchanged a dignified good-morning with two of
his fellow passengers. He was glad that they could not
know how long it was since he had traveled by night.

How good the bacon and eggs and coffee were! How
interested that handsome blonde woman at the table opposite!

Every time he raised his eyes she was looking at him. He hoped there was nothing wrong with his collar or tie. He passed his hand over his head to make sure that his hair was smooth. A faint color rose in his cheeks.

His heart was thudding uncomfortably as they neared the Grand Central Station. His knees trembled as he stood while the porter brushed his clothes. Then came terrible suspense as the man disappeared with his bag, a good English bag that he had bought himself at Drew's in Regent Street. Then relief at the capture of the bag on the platform. And scarcely had relief raised its head, like a too early spring flower, before it was frozen into dismay by the sight of a "redcap" darting into the throng, the bag clutched in his hand.

By the time the bag was recaptured, Ernest's head was wet with sweat. He sank on to the seat of a taxi, and, taking off his hat, mopped his brow, gazing meanwhile anxiously through the window into the unbelievably crowded street. He had directed the driver to take him to the Brevoort, because it was there that he had stayed during his last trip to New York twenty years ago.

XI

ERNEST'S TACT

ALAYNE'S amazement on seeing Finch at her door was a mild emotion compared with that which she experienced when it opened upon Ernest. She would scarcely have been more taken aback had one of the tall old trees of Jalna drawn up its roots and journeyed to visit her. She suffered him to shake her hand, to imprint a kiss on her cheek. She put him into the Chinese-red chair, and even then she could not believe in his reality. Her eyes sought the door half expecting to behold the rest of the procession — Grandmother and Boney, Nicholas and Nip, Renny and his spaniels, Piers and Pheasant, little Wake.

"But, my dear child," said Ernest, "how good it is to see you!"

"Yes, indeed," said Alayne, sitting down near him and trying to make her voice natural, "it is delightful to see you, too."

"You're looking pale, dear Alayne."

"Ah, well, you know what winter in the city is. I've been tired to death sometimes."

She realized, now that the shock of surprise was passing, why he had come. He had come to take Finch home, and, if possible, she would prevent it.

She turned a look of defense on him. "I suppose you've come to see Finch," she said.

Ernest was embarrassed. He wished she had not come so directly to the point. He would have liked to have a little pleasant conversation, and then have led up delicately to the object of his visit.

"Well, my dear Alayne, I suppose I shall see Finch, now

that I'm here, but it really gives me a much deeper pleasure to see you."

"You're not really going to insist on the poor boy going back with you, surely!"

"No, no, no. But I want to talk to him, to find out how he is living—in short, to satisfy the family about him. It's really dreadful, you know, for a mere boy of his inexperience to be turned loose in New York."

"He's working! And he's treated with more consideration than he was at home. I hope you don't mind my saying that. You know yourself that Finch was not always treated fairly."

Ernest remained invincibly placid. "My dear girl, I don't believe you understand us. Our family circle is very closely knit."

"I do understand! It's so closely knit that you won't let one of your number escape. You want to reach out and drag him back again. I know I'm being awfully rude, but I cannot help it. It is the way I've always felt about your family."

"We didn't reach out after Eden."

"You knew it was no use. You couldn't control Eden. And you had no inkling as to where he was."

Ernest regarded her with curiosity. "Do you mind if I ask you something?"

"What is it?"

"Have you seen Eden since you came back?"

"No, I have not. I suppose I shall never see him again. I don't want to."

"I'm very sure you don't. You suffered too much because of him." Ernest was relieved that he had successfully switched the conversation into a more sympathetic channel. He laid his long white hand on hers and gently pressed it. She experienced a sudden warmth and sense of security in being treated with affection by a much older person. It was

nice, and he was nice — she had forgotten how nice, how
kind. She had forgotten, too, how distinguished his appearance, and how agreeable to the ear his voice. Really,
he was a dear, and she must not be too hard on him.
He was less to blame than the others for the tyranny of
Jalna.

He exclaimed in admiration at the compactness, the
charm of the apartment. She led him about, showing him
all the trig electrical devices. They delighted him. He had
never seen anything like them. He must press the electric
buttons and observe all the resulting phenomena. Ernest
said that he wondered how she had ever endured the dis-
comforts of Jalna.

Returning, arm in arm, to the living room, the subject
of Finch was reopened, with more restraint on the part of
Alayne and even greater amiability on the part of Ernest.
She gave him particulars about Finch's work, his chances of
advancement.

Ernest listened with sympathy.

"But where," he asked, "does his chance of continuing
the study of music come in?"

"I'm afraid it doesn't come in at all," she replied sadly,
"but then, neither does it apparently at Jalna."

"Oh, I think Renny may relent on that score."

"Tell me, Uncle Ernest," she demanded, looking him in
the eyes, "was it Renny who urged you to come to see Finch
or was it to please your mother? I know how she hates the
thought of any of the boys leaving home."

He was pleased at being "Uncled" by Alayne.

"My dear child," he said, "I did not need any urging.
I wanted to see the boy, and I thought what an opportunity
for seeing you. You know, I had grown very fond of you."

"And I of you! You see, I had no — no —"

"No nice old uncles," he continued for her. "Of course
not. Nice old aunts are one thing, but nice old uncles are

quite another. Their position is unique. . . . Now, as to
Renny. If you had heard him talking to me just before I
left, you would have realized how keen he is to have Finch
back."

"When I lived at Jalna," she said, thoughtfully, "I used
to think that very often in those family conclaves of yours
Renny was urged"—she longed to say "harried"—"into
taking a stand that—"

"No, no, no! Renny is a man of quick decisions. He
knows what he wants and goes for it."

"Yes, I know," she agreed, in a low tone.

"When we hold those conclaves, as you call them, Renny
usually has his own opinion from the beginning, but it is
only after the matter has been thrashed out by the family
that he gives voice to his decision, and because his decision often coincides with the conclusion the family has
reached—"

"Do the family ever reach a unanimous decision?"

"If you could have heard how fully agreed we were that
Finch must come home—"

"Oh, that I can understand! I wish I had not told you
where he is working."

"My dear, I shall not try to force Finch in the very least.
You shall be present, if you will, when we meet, then you'll
see that I only want an affectionate talk with him."

"But what are you going to do, then? Bribe him to go
home with the promise of music lessons? Has Renny descended to bribing the boys?"

Ernest answered impressively, "Renny had no intention
of stopping Finch from playing the piano except till his examinations should be over. Once he has written on them,
Renny intends, and has intended all along, that Finch shall
begin taking lessons again. He may spend the whole summer making music if he likes."

"Hmph," muttered Alayne, grudgingly. She wished she

could have felt more enthusiastic over the family's plans for Finch.

Nevertheless, Ernest was a dear. She loved to see him sitting in her most comfortable chair making attractive but rather vague gestures with his graceful hands. She was proud of him when Rosamund Trent came in and discovered them. She had the feeling that when she had talked of Eden's uncles Rosamund had pictured two rather frowsty old men, quaint relics of a bygone day. Now she saw that Rosamund found Ernest charming. She was impressed by the pleasant modulations in his voice. These he had acquired at Oxford, along with the notion that, while it might be well for some to slave, it was not well for Ernest Whiteoak.

Ernest invited the two to luncheon with him. As he walked along Fifth Avenue with them beside him, there was spring in his step and in his blood. Alayne had a look of breeding; he admired that in a woman above all things. Rosamund looked essentially a woman of the world; and he hankered for the world. Again and again he wished old Nicholas could see him. As a gesture of complete abandon, he ordered lobster. His guests ordered it, too, but without any air of recklessness. With the three bright red mounds before them, he could not help but talk of meals in Victorian London. He told of sitting at a table near Oscar Wilde, and of having seen Lily Langtry in her prime. He recalled how Nicholas had rowed for Oxford.

After luncheon they returned to the apartment and Rosamund brought out a bottle of liqueur. She had prepared a strange cocktail before they had set out.

"But I thought," exclaimed Ernest, sipping from the diminutive green glass, "that you had Prohibition here!"

"We have," returned Miss Trent, in her deepest contralto, "but we also have the speak-easy."

"Speak-easy?" repeated Ernest. "But what in the world is that?"

"Happily there is no need for you to become acquainted with them. They're stupid places. I may tell you that they are thicker than the flowers in May here."

"Ah, we could never get on with Prohibition," said Ernest.

"Of course you couldn't!" she commented. "Do you like that liqueur?"

Alayne wished that Rosamund were not so keenly interested in the subject of drinking. It had an almost morbid fascination for her. It repelled Alayne to hear the solid, middle-aged woman using the current tags about Prohibition, talking as though she were a seasoned drinker. Yet it was really only a harmless affectation, the desire to be intensely modern. Rosamund was a good honest soul, a loyal, sympathetic friend.

"We couldn't do with Prohibition at home," said Ernest, didactically. "Our population is too small." Miss Trent's cocktail, the excitement of the crowded streets and restaurant, the liqueur on the return, had gone to his head. His brain was active, but his thoughts somewhat kaleidoscopic. "Think of our Boundary Line, three hundred miles of it from coast to coast — or is it three thousand? — without a single fort! Oh, no, Prohibition would mix things up dreadfully."

His audience looked properly impressed, but Alayne suggested that he sit down. He refused, and continued to stand gracefully, holding his glass. "See what Prohibition has done for you! Why, I am told that our Nova Scotian fishermen have given up fishing. It is more profitable to smuggle. You get all you want through them."

"Life is a strange muddle," observed Rosamund.

"It is. And the women's vote has made it still more so," he murmured. "Luckily our women are British in their training, and vote as their men do. But look at the situation in the Province of Quebec! There the women have no vote. 'We are Latins!' their Premier exclaims. 'We adore our women, but we will not give them the vote. It is against all our instincts.' And I must say I admire them for it."

"Yet they haven't Prohibition, have they?" asked Miss Trent, bewildered.

"No, and never had! Their greatest grievances are Orangeism in Ontario, emigration to the States, and, of course, smuggling, which is sometimes a source of Revenue. But the real trouble with the whole Dominion is the Boundary Line — and these Arctic expeditions — and Transatlantic flights." He sat down abruptly.

Very soon his slight confusion passed, and he was himself again. It must be arranged when he was to see Finch. Alayne suggested that they meet in the apartment, go out to dinner together, and then to the theatre. Ernest desired that Finch should not be told of his arrival. It would be a pleasant surprise for the boy to find his uncle awaiting him. "Because, you know, dear Alayne, I'm not going to scold or threaten him. Nothing at all of that sort."

"I should say not," said Alayne, truculently.

But she would not agree to Finch's meeting Ernest without preparation. She telephoned him, asking him to come to see her that evening, and announced the arrival from Jalna. She delivered Ernest's reassuring message.

Nevertheless Finch was shaking when he came into the room. If it had seemed strange to Alayne to see one of the older generation of Whiteoaks in New York, for Finch it was an almost staggering experience. He felt as though he were viewing his distinguished-looking elderly relative for the first time. He could not remember Uncle Ernest's ever having been away from Jalna, and he had never been away himself till now in all his life. Even when they shook hands, and Ernest spoke kindly to him, he had a sense of unreality and, in spite of Alayne's reassurance, a sense of foreboding.

He did not know just what he feared. His uncle could

not force him to go home. At his back he had the strength of Alayne's staunch loyalty. That day he had actually had a word of praise in the office.

"Upon my honor," exclaimed Ernest, putting his hand on the boy's shoulder, "you're taller than ever, old fellow! And thin! He's really thinner, Alayne, though I shouldn't have thought it possible. And how are you getting on?"

Finch braced himself with as much manliness as he could muster, and replied, "Oh, fine, thanks. That is — all right, I think."

"I'm glad of that. They'll be so glad to hear at home."

Finch was embarrassed. "Were they worrying?" he mumbled.

"Indeed they were. We were all of us greatly worried. But no need to talk; I can tell them now that you are well and safe." No word of his going back. Finch breathed easier, and yet there was a queer ache at his heart. The truth was, in the past few days he had been suffering acutely from homesickness. Under the delicate May sky, the dusty never-resting traffic of the city had made him feel as he had never before felt in springtime — heavy, tired, stifled, trapped. His feet dragged, longing for the springing grass. His nostrils seemed unable to draw in sufficient air to satisfy his lungs. It was only by a great effort that he could keep his mind on his work. Each night he dreamed of Jalna, and waked half expecting to find himself in his room under the eaves. More and more he remembered all that had been beautiful and kindly and pleasant in his home.

Alayne had intended that they should go to a play, but Ernest suggested grand opera because Finch was so fond of music. She had acquiesced, and Rosamund Trent had been able to arrange about the tickets. While they were at dinner, Alayne had suddenly seen Ernest's sweet thoughtfulness in a new light. She remembered having heard him say that above all things he disliked grand opera. "He is a sly old

man," she thought. "He intends to work on Finch's feelings through his love of music."

The opera was *Aïda*. Finch had never heard it before.
Tears of happiness filled his eyes, his heart was heavy with
the sweetness of music. Yet it was not the music of the
orchestra or the singers that moved him. It was the music of
the old square piano at home. It was Beethoven's Opus X,
which in imagination he was playing. The keys, alive,
eager, rose to meet his fingers. With one part of his brain
he heard the music of *Aïda*. With another he followed himself through the intricacies of the movement.

Every now and again Ernest slid a speculative look
toward him. He wondered whether the boy were happy
or unhappy, whether he should have difficulty in persuading
him to come home. The thought of leaving Finch in New
York was intolerable to him. The thought of Jalna without
Finch seemed insupportable. Not that he had ever found
him but a commonplace, rather irritating boy. But he was
a Whiteoak, one of themselves. Eden's defection had been
the first break. If Finch left home, it would seem that dis-
integration of the family had set in. Besides, there was
Mamma. It was bad for her to be worried.

He felt suddenly rather tired. It had been an exciting
day for him, full of unusual activities. He felt weighted
by his responsibility. At the same time he experienced a
sense of elation at being at the opera in company with these
two well-turned-out women. Ah, if old Nicholas could only
see him! Alayne, he thought, was lovelier than ever. Sorrow and fatigue had brought out the inward brightness of
her, as the brightness of a jewel is accentuated by calculated
and delicate cutting. And there was a kind of recklessness
about her that seemed new to him. He remembered her as
always wearing an air of reserve, of awareness. Now it
seemed that she was one ready to throw off bonds which
chafed her, one craving a broader sweep of air. She fas-

cinated him. He longed to know what she was thinking.
Ah, how tired he was! Would the opera never end? He
stifled a yawn.

But as the crowd surged out, and he felt the cool night air
on his face, he revived. It was like a return to his prime to
find himself steering an evening-cloaked female through a
crowd. Really, he must make a trip to New York every
now and again after this. It was not well to let one's self
become frowsty. And with his figure, his carriage, it was a
downright waste. He pressed Miss Trent's firm arm a little
as he guided her. An exquisite perfume rose from the soft
fur of her collar. . . .

They had a little supper in the apartment. Delicate food,
Pall Mall cigarettes, bought specially for him; gay conversation, for Ernest found it easy to shine before this audience,
so uncritical, so, if he could have known, tolerantly amused
by him; and, added to their tolerance and amusement, a
sentimental desire to look through his mind back into the
strange glamour of another day. He sighed as he said
good-night. He was not a bit tired now, and he hated to
think how soon this charming interlude would be over.

It was not till he and Finch were back in his hotel bedroom that there returned to him with force the consciousness of his mission. He had arranged that the boy should
spend the night with him, and had got a room for him next
to his own. He shrank from the thought of a clash of wills
at that late hour. He wished he could simply pack Finch
into his portmanteau the next day, with his clothes, and
carry him back to Jalna. It was such a nuisance having to
be politic with him, tactful and understanding. It was really
a pest the way boys grew up.

There was a distinct air of embarrassment between them
when they found themselves alone in the hotel bedroom
together. It was abominably stuffy, and Ernest went to the
window and threw it up.

He looked out for a moment on the confusion of roofs and blinding lights, at the orange- and ruby-colored signs that flashed on and off, at the sinister-looking black spaces beyond which lay one knew not what, at the white-lettered signs which were painted, tier upon tier, on the side of a building in the next street, at the strange, blurred sky which might as well be a stretch of canvas for all its apparent reality. Up here the sound of the traffic was deadened to a dull rumble that seemed resentful of the spring night.

Ernest found that he had smudged his finger ends in opening the window. He went into the bathroom to wash his hands. Finch had dropped into a chair by the table, looking very young and wan under the hard electric light. He had picked up the shiny black Bible belonging to the hotel and was looking at it with a queer smile. An uncomfortable boy, Ernest thought. He lathered his hands, and examined his face in the mirror above the basin. He was looking well.

On returning to the bedroom he said, "I hate very much to go back to Jalna without you, Finch. Everyone at home will be disappointed."

"I can't see them disappointed because I don't go back."

"But they will be. You don't understand. You're one of us, aren't you?"

"The odd one."

"Nonsense. We're all more or less oddities, I fancy. And we're proud of you, though you may not think so."

Finch grunted sarcastically. "You should have heard Renny and Piers telling me how proud they were of me!"

"Come, come, don't take things so hard. Piers has a rough tongue —"

"He's as hard as nails! With me, anyhow."

"He doesn't always mean it, and, if he does, he's not the important one. It's Renny who matters."

"Renny thinks I'm an ass."

Ernest sat down beside him. He put all the persuasiveness, all the eloquence of which he was capable, into his voice. "Renny loves you. He wants you to come home like a good boy, without any further trouble. He is willing, after you've tried your examinations, to let you take music lessons again — to play as much as you want to. All you have to do is to try your exams."

"What if I fail?"

"You won't fail. You'll pass. You did not fail badly last time. You're sure to pass."

"And if I do — what then?"

"You have all your life before you. You'll make something fine of it."

"I don't see myself," said Finch wearily.

"Finch, you had a very clever and very lovely mother. She would have wanted you to develop your talent — to be a credit to us."

"Good Lord!" exclaimed the boy. "This sort of talk is new to me! My talents — my mother —"

"But, my dear child," cried Ernest in exasperation, for his head was beginning to ache, "families will make remarks. You don't expect —"

"Gran often makes sneering remarks about her — my mother. I hear her, though I've pretended not."

"Your grandmother is a hundred and one. Your mother has been dead eleven years. What have their relations to do with the question in hand? . . . Really, you are wearing me out! The point is this." Ernest made a supreme effort. "What is there for you in New York? Crowds, crowds, crowds. Struggle, struggle. You, a Whiteoak, struggling in a foreign mob! Uncongenial work. Homesickness. You know you're horribly homesick, Finch. I've been watching you. You're homesick."

"Don't!" cried the boy in anguish, putting his head on the table. "I can't bear it! Oh, Uncle Ernest, do you really think I'd better go back?"

XII

EDEN DISCOVERED

Two evenings later Eden Whiteoak was sauntering along lower Fifth Avenue, one hand thrust in a pocket of a rather shabby tweed jacket, the other carrying a light stick. The change in him since he had disappeared from Jalna was remarkable. He had become thin almost to emaciation. His movements were still graceful, but the bright vigor of his carriage was gone. He seemed to progress only by an effort of the will, either because of bodily weakness or because of extreme despondency. If he had removed his hat, one would have seen that his hair, which had lain like a shining metal casque upon his head, was now rough and unkempt. Above the hollows in his cheeks two feverish spots burned where had been only a fresh glow. The beauty of his large blue eyes seemed accentuated. They still retained their peculiar unseeing expression, which sometimes disturbed one in company with him, and his lips still curved in their odd half-smile.

He was feeling himself near the end of his tether, and he was filled with a cynical dislike toward the moving mass of people who shared the pavement with him. This dislike, through some whim or perhaps some old resentment, was directed chiefly toward those of the opposite sex. And his aversion was at the moment centred upon their legs, which, like the sleek antennæ of insects, moved mechanically past him. It seemed to him that if ever he should look back upon this night of humid, unseasonable heat, he would recall it as being borne along its course by innumerable silk-clad legs.

Four girls approached abreast, wearing French heels and flesh-colored stockings, their eight legs flashing in quick rhythm. "Beasts," he thought. "Beasts. Why cumber ye the earth? Why, in God's name? I wish I could help you off it. Four. Why should there be four of you, all alike?" He glanced up at their faces, heavy-eyed, smooth-cheeked, crimson-mouthed faces. He scowled at them. Beasts. A little later he singled out one walking with a thin, undersized youth. Her skirt was very short. Her calves large, caught inward abruptly at knee and ankle. Her feet ridiculously short. Oh, the grotesque shape of her! Why should she exist? Why, oh, why? How could the spotted-faced youth endure her?

The darkness of his brow deepened. He kept his eyes on the pavement, trying not to see the women. But presently he was jostled by one. He almost staggered, her progress had been so relentless, so direct. He turned his head and his angry eyes swept her. He saw her heavy middle-aged legs, her huge, pallid, aggressive face, her heavy breasts, smothered beneath a brassiere, her close hat pulled over one eye, the other eye glowering through horn-rimmed spectacles. Why, oh, why should she exist? Why cumbereth ye the earth, fat beast? They exchanged looks. She thought, "Oh, if we could only *really enforce* the law to protect lovely young men like that! I'm sure he's been drinking. He stumbled right against me."

There was no air. The air seemed to have been sucked out of the street, leaving it a vacuum through which a dream-like procession marched, a procession so dreamlike that it required no air. The faces, the legs, passed in a blur before Eden's eyes, until at last the form of an old woman stood out clearly. She was in rusty black, wearing an old-fashioned bonnet, the strings of which were tied in a greasy bow beneath her withered, jutting chin. Her slate-colored eyes, which had once been as blue as Eden's, were fixed in the unseeing stare of one who had looked too long on life and could bear to look no more. Her sunken upper lip

gnawed always the pendulous lower one. The turned-out toes
of her large shoes could barely be seen beneath the heavy
width of her draggled skirt. Instantly she appeared as something precious to Eden. His heart leaped. He surveyed her
appraisingly, feeling a new joy in the poetry of life. Here
was a woman who had meaning. One could understand
why she existed, not cumbering the earth, gracing it —
beautiful. Ah, the gracious, exquisite reality of her waddling legless form! There she was — a woman. He was
jostled, almost pushed from the curb as he stared. He drew
a banknote, his last, from his pocket, and hurried after her.
He pressed it into her hand. The hand, a claw, closed over it.
She shambled on without a glance at him.

He felt elated, and suddenly rather hungry. A row of
people sitting on high stools before a counter in a drug store
attracted him. He went in. There was only one empty
stool, between two young girls. He would not take it, but
stood waiting until there was a space at the end, beside an
elderly man. He ordered tomato soup and wafers. As he
drooped over the mug containing the thick liquid, which
tasted as though it were of the tinned variety, a fit of coughing came on him. He had difficulty in suppressing it, and,
by the time he had, his appetite was gone. He drank the
rest of the soup, but left the wafers. Out in the street he
found that there was now a faint movement of air. He
entered the little garden in Madison Square, sat down on
one of the benches, and lighted a cigarette. A feeling of
extreme lassitude crept over him, from the legs upward,
at last reaching his head and making him drowsy. The
figures passing through the park became shadowy. He saw
as in a dream the twilight arch of the sky, the far-off hazy
moon, the rows of lights, like strings of bright beads in the
surrounding buildings.

He was weary with a deep sickness of dejection. He remembered his young strength, his gifts — and they had

come to this! And he was twenty-six! Surely he was held in derision of the gods. He remembered Jalna, his brothers, Alayne. He had harmed them all in one way or another, he supposed. But he did not think of them clearly. Himself only he saw with great clarity. His own white face, like the face of a drowning man, risen for a moment on the crest of a wave.

What was there for him to do? He could not now earn his living. He could not go home. He had parted from the woman with whom he had been living because he could no longer contribute to their joint expenses. She would have been glad to have paid all — but, Christ, he had not come to that! How they had quarreled, and she had rained tears whom he had thought too hard ever to shed one! How he had grown to hate her heavy arms! To be free of them — that was the one bright spot.

The smell of damp earth rose from the roots of the new grass about him. The sound of traffic was lulled to a deep hum. He felt isolated, as though he were on an island in the midst of a lonely sea. He was alone. Utterly alone. A wave of loneliness swept over him, so engulfing that beside it the homesickness of Finch was little more than a ripple. He sank back on the bench, his chin on his chest.

Two people had come and seated themselves beside him. They were talking steadily, but in low tones — a mellow old voice and a boyish one. He scarcely heard them. Another fit of coughing came upon him, and he clung to the back of the bench for support. When it was past he took off his hat and wiped his forehead with his handkerchief. The elder of the two men leaned forward and looked toward him with compassion. Eden, embarrassed, took out a cigarette, struck a match. His face was illuminated.

"My God!" cried Ernest, springing up. "Eden, is it you?"

Eden looked up at him, too astounded for speech.

"Speak, Eden! Tell me what is the matter."

Eden's mouth quivered. "Everything, I guess."

"But that cough! It's simply terrible. How long have you had it?"

"Several months. Don't bother. It will be all right when the warm weather comes."

"But the weather is hot now!"

"It's unseasonable. Probably be cold again to-morrow. . . . Please don't trouble about me. Tell me why you are here. Is that young Finch?"

Finch got to his feet, trembling. He was bewildered, frightened by this sudden meeting with Eden. He remembered his last encounter with him. That summer night when he had discovered Eden and Pheasant in the birch wood together. His mind fastened on an incident strikingly similar in both meetings, and yet how dissimilar! On each occasion Eden had, at a moment of climax, struck a match, illuminated a face. But in the first instance it had been the white, terrified face of Finch; now it was his own, hollow-cheeked, feverish. Then he had exclaimed bitterly, "What a worm you are, brother Finch!" Now he said, in a low tone of reckless self-possession, "Hullo, Finch! You here, too? God, what a meeting!"

"Hullo!" returned Finch, but he could not hold out his hand. His heart sank when he looked at Eden. He had helped to bring him to this.

"Eden, Eden!" cried their uncle. "I am distressed to find you looking so ill. I could not have believed —"

"Oh, I'm not in such bad shape as I look." He stared at these newly arrived members of his family in satiric mirth. "Lord, what a quaint pair you are! When did you come here, and why?"

Ernest and Finch glanced at each other uncomfortably.

"I — he —" mumbled the boy.

"He — I —" stammered Ernest.

Eden broke into laughter. "I see it all! You ran away, Finch, and Uncle Ernest came to fetch you. Or was it the other way about? Never mind, it's enough that you're here! I wouldn't have believed you'd have the guts."

"You must come back to my hotel," said Ernest.

"I wish I could invite you to my lodgings, but they're too tough for you, by a long shot."

Ernest was greatly upset. He turned to Finch. "Get a taxi. Eden isn't fit to walk."

On the way to the hotel, Eden asked, "Have you seen Alayne?"

"Yes, I've had dinner with her—and luncheon. M-yes. She's looking lovely, Eden."

"She would! Some women thrive on marital troubles. They find them more stimulating than babies."

In the hotel bedroom Ernest said, "What you need is a good hot toddy, but how am I to get you one? Do you know if there is one of those—er—'speak-easy' places about?" His heart failed him as he spoke. The thought of searching for such a place was abhorrent to him.

"No, thanks," said Eden. "I couldn't possibly take anything." He drank a glass of water and fidgeted about the room, talking in a way that seemed to Ernest rather strange and wild. Finch sat by the window smoking, and took no part in the conversation. Eden did not speak to him.

After a time Eden announced his intention of going, but just as he took up his hat he was attacked by another fit of coughing. His last strength seemed to go into this. After it was over, he flung himself on the bed and shivered from head to foot. He was plainly so ill that Ernest was distraught. He sent Finch running downstairs to inquire about a doctor. Next morning he sent a telegram to Renny:—

HAVE FOUND EDEN VERY ILL PLEASE COME AT ONCE CANNOT COPE WITH THIS.

E. WHITEOAK.

XIII
THE CIRCLE

On the morning that followed, another member of the Whiteoak family might have been seen ascending in the hotel lift, attended by a porter carrying a rather shabby suitcase. When they alighted, he limped vigorously after the man and knocked with impatience on the designated door. It was opened by Finch.

When the porter had been tipped and the door closed behind him, Renny swept his eyes over the boy and gave a grunt, half of satisfaction at beholding him, half of derision.

Finch, red in the face, drew a step nearer. The elder took him by the arm, then kissed him. Finch seemed to him little more grown up than Wakefield. Joy and pure love surged through Finch. Animal joy and love that made him want to leap on Renny and caress him roughly like a joyous dog. He stood still, grinning sheepishly.

"Where's Eden?" demanded Renny.

"In there." He nodded toward the next room. "Uncle Ernest's with him."

Ernest himself then entered. He looked white and drawn.

"Heavens above!" he exclaimed. "I'm thankful you've come," and he gripped Renny's hand.

"This is a pretty mess," said Renny. "Have you a doctor? How ill is he? What's the matter with him?"

"It is indeed," returned Ernest. "I don't know when I've been so upset. I called a doctor as soon as he was taken badly. I think he's a good one. He's got a German name, but I dare say he's all the cleverer for that." He braced himself and looked Renny in the eyes. "Renny, it's the boy's lungs. They're in a bad way. He's in great danger, the doctor says."

Renny's brow contracted. He set the point of his stick in the centre of the geometrical pattern of the rug and stared at it. He said in a low voice, "His mother died of consumption."

"Yes. But none of the children have shown any tendency that way. I suppose he's been exposing himself."

Renny began to limp nervously up and down the room. Ernest asked, solicitously, "How is your knee? It is a shame to have brought you here, when you're not fit, but I — you understand — "

"It's nothing. I wish I had our own doctor to see him. This man may be an alarmist."

"I don't know. I hope so. He says that he must have the very best care."

"We must take him home. . . . What does Alayne think of this?"

"She's terribly upset, naturally. She's shocked. There's no hatred in her toward Eden. She thinks that he simply can't help being what he is. Unfaithful. I agree, too. What do you think?"

"I think he's a damned nuisance. All these brothers of mine are." He turned his incisive gaze suddenly on Finch. "I hope you're going to behave yourself, now," he said.

Finch pulled at his underlip.

Ernest put in, "It's God's mercy that the boy ran away. We should never have heard of Eden till too late."

Both men stared at Finch. He writhed inwardly, not knowing whether he was being commended or jeered at.

Ernest continued, "Alayne had got him quite a decent position in a publishing house, as costing clerk. I saw this Mr. Cory and got him to let him off at once. I had to have his help with Eden. I couldn't be alone here, not knowing what might happen. I little thought, when I left home, the time I'd have."

"Well, it's a good thing he's been of some use," replied Renny. "Now, you'd better take me in to Eden."

Eden was propped up in bed, not seeming so ill as Renny had expected until he had taken the hot dry hand and felt the thinness of it, noticed the sharp outline of the limbs under the coverings.

Renny seated himself on the side of the bed and surveyed his brother. "You have got yourself into a pretty state, haven't you?"

Eden had been told that Renny was coming, but it seemed too unreal to see his family thus gathering about him. It frightened him. Was he so dreadfully ill? He withdrew his hand quickly from Renny's and raised himself in the bed. He said, excitedly, "I don't like this at all! What in hell's the matter? Does that doctor say I'm going to die?"

"I haven't been told anything of the sort," returned Renny, with composure. "Uncle Ernest wired me that he had come across you, and that you were on the rocks. Well, you are, aren't you? What are you getting up in the air about?"

Sweat stood on Eden's forehead. "He wired you! Show me the telegram!"

"I can't. It's at home. For heaven's sake, keep your hair on! You don't feel like dying, I suppose." He grinned as he asked the question, but he was filled by a great anxiety. All that was sturdy in him rushed out toward Eden to protect him.

"Tell me what he said! Had he seen the doctor yet?" He dropped back on the pillow. "Never mind. You wouldn't tell me the truth."

"I'm going to take you home."

Eden's agitation had subsided. He stared at his brother hungrily. "God, it looks good to see you sitting there! But I wish you'd take a chair! You make the bed sag. You're no featherweight, Renny. . . . Look at my arm." He thrust it out from the sleeve, thin, dead-white, blue-veined. Renny scowled at it.

He got up, dragged a chair to one side of the bed and reseated himself.

"I can't think how you got yourself into such a state. You don't look as though you'd had enough to eat. Why haven't you sent to me for money?"

"Should you have sent it?"

"You know I should."

"And now you want to take me home?"

"That's why I'm here."

"Good old patriarch! The two lost lambs. Young Finch and I. . . . But what about Piers? He'd not stand for that. God, I should like to see his face if it were suggested!"

"I did see it. I told him I might fetch you if you were fit to travel."

Eden laughed, suddenly and maliciously. "Poor Piers! What did he say? That he'd poison all his pigs and then take a dose himself?"

"No," Renny returned, sternly. "He remarked that you were a waster and always would be. He said that if you were coming home to — to —"

"To die. . . . Go on."

"That he'd take Pheasant away till it was over."

Again Eden was moved to mirth, but this time there was a hysterical note in it.

"It's a good thing you're amused," Renny observed calmly. "I should say that the joke is on you." He thought, "I wish I knew what is in the bottom of his mind. I wish I knew what he's been up to the past year."

But Eden's laughter brought on a fit of coughing. Renny watched him, his hard, thin frame tense with misery. "Can I do anything?" he entreated.

Eden raised his head, which he had buried in the pillow.

His hair was plastered in damp locks on his forehead, his face flushed crimson.

"Look here, Renny."

"Yes."

"My mother died of lung trouble, didn't she?"

"The doctor called it that, but I think she simply pined away after Wake's birth. Father's death was hard on her."

"That's the way I'll go!"

"You've not been having a posthumous baby."

"Might that bring it on, do you think?"

"If a woman were inclined that way."

"Well, I'm free from that cause."

"But perhaps you've been begetting one!"

"If I have, it will be posthumous, poor little devil."

"If you are determined to look on the black side of this trouble, you'll die and no mistake," declared Renny, emphatically. "Buck up! Be a man! I'm going to take you home. You'll get good care — the best care —"

"Who will take care of me?"

"A nurse, I suppose."

Eden answered, hoarsely vehement: "Like hell she will! I tell you, I hate women! I won't have a nurse about me. I loathe them — starchy, flat-footed, hard-eyed — I'll not go home if you make me have a nurse! I'll die first!"

Ernest, his face puckered by anxiety, came into the sick room. Finch, drawn by morbid curiosity, slunk after him.

Ernest said, reproachfully, "This will never do. The doctor says he must be kept quiet. I don't think you realize how ill he is, Renny." He poured something into a glass and brought it to Eden.

Renny regarded the proceeding with intense irritation and concern. He remarked, "I realize that he's making this affair as difficult as possible."

Ernest, looking down his nose, smoothed Eden's pillow.

"Perhaps you expect Uncle Ernie to nurse you," observed Renny, sarcastically.

Finch guffawed.

Renny wheeled on him. "What —" he began. "What —"

"Let the lad be," said Ernest. "Finch, my boy, fill the hot-water bottle and fetch it."

Eden did not want the hot-water bottle, but he pretended that he did, since the need of it made him appear rather more ill-used. Finch, with Renny's eye on him, slunk out with the bottle.

"I'll die before I'll have a nurse," Eden persisted, in a weak voice, after a silence broken only by the running of a tap.

The hot-water bottle was put in with him. Ernest patted his back, and said, "If it were not for Meggie's baby, she would be the very one! She would be perfect. She is almost perfect in every way."

"Yes," agreed Renny. "She is."

"Couldn't she get someone to look after the kid?" asked Eden.

"She has a sort of companion, but she'd never trust it to her entirely. She's a perfect mother." After a little he continued, hesitatingly, "Do you know, I have an idea. It may not be feasible, but" — he looked from one to the other — "but the whole affair is so unusual . . ."

"What is your idea?" asked Renny.

"Oh, I'm afraid it would be impossible. We'd better not discuss it. We had better think of someone possible. . . . Eden, if the thought of a trained nurse is so intolerable to you, how would it do if we engaged some elderly woman who has had experience —"

"I saw one on the street!" interrupted Eden. "Wonderful old body! Tatters, and a face like one of the Fates."

Renny asked of Ernest, "Do you think he's a little light in his head?"

Finch gave a muffled snort of laughter.

"Not at all," said Ernest. "You don't understand him, that is all. . . . Now the person I have in mind is Mrs. Patch. She is reliable. She has had experience in nursing —"

Finch, unable to stop himself, interjected, "She ought to do. She's buried three of her own with T.B."

"Finch," said his uncle, sternly, "that remark was in very bad taste. I'm surprised at you!"

"Don't mind me," said Eden, faintly smiling. "Only please tell me about this idea of yours. Whom had you in mind?"

Ernest answered, looking, not at him, but at Renny, "I was wondering whether Alayne might be persuaded to nurse him."

This sudden mention of her name seemed to conjure Alayne's bodily presence before the occupants of the room. A subtle embarrassment dimmed their vision of each other. Ernest, after uttering the words, was moved to wish that he could recall them. They had seemed to him to besmirch her present aloofness, to drag her again into the shame and darkness of her last days at Jalna. He looked rather pathetically into the faces of his nephews, seeing each in his relation to those days.

Renny, experiencing a feeling of shock by the proposal, stared at Eden lying on the bed, disheveled, ill, beautiful. He saw him as again the possessor of Alayne. He felt in himself the pain for something he could never possess. No, she must not do such a thing. It would be cruel to ask her, and yet . . . if she could bring herself to do it . . . he thought of her as standing reluctant in the room, midway between himself and Eden. . . .

"She's not quite a saint," he said.

Finch, crouching in a big chair, twisted his fingers together. Figures in a dream, that was what they were — gesticulating, hiding their troubled eyes, disappearing and reappearing, beckoning one who had eluded them to return, seeking to draw her again into the circle. Again, in spite of himself, he spoke. "Do women," he asked, "ever take a man back after a thing like that?"

His brothers regarded him in silence, too astounded to speak. It was Ernest's mellow voice that answered.

"Many a woman has taken a man back to her bed after such an escapade. . . . I was only suggesting that if Alayne could be persuaded to return to Jalna with us — to help look after Eden — how splendid it would be. . . . I was thinking of her hands. They're so cool, so capable."

"You must think she's without character," said Renny.

"Not at all! I think she has great strength of character, or I should not suggest such a thing. . . . She's sick and tired of her life as it is. If she should return to Jalna she might never leave it again. Mamma is really too much for Augusta."

Renny turned to Eden. "What do you think? Should you like Alayne to nurse you?"

Eden rolled over, hiding his face in the pillow.

Finch exclaimed, "He doesn't want her! He doesn't want her!" He could not bear the idea of Alayne's being drawn again into Jalna, as into a whirlpool in which she would be sucked under.

"Let him be," said his uncle. "Let him have time to think."

The three sat with their eyes on the hunched-up figure on the bed. In and out, through the mazes of their thoughts, the shape of Alayne moved, in a kind of mystic dance. The roar of traffic from below rose as a wall around them.

At last Eden rolled over and faced them. "I give you my word," he said, "that unless Alayne comes to help me get well, I shall die." His eyes were challenging, his mouth feverish.

Finch said over and over again to himself, "It's a shame —a shame to ask her."

"You are the one to ask her," said Ernest to Renny. "You must see her at once."

"How soon can he travel?"

"In a few days."

"I think you are the one to ask her. You've been talking to her."

"No—no. It must be you, Renny."

"I will bring her here, and he shall ask her himself."

"I am afraid it will upset him."

"I'll prepare her, but he must do the asking."

"Very well," said Eden. "Bring her here to see me. She can't refuse that."

Renny's feelings, as he stood waiting for Alayne to answer her door, were a strange mixture. He had a disheartened, hangdog feeling at being forced, through his solicitude for Eden, to come on such an errand. He had scarcely slept for two nights. In a city he was miserable, as a wild animal trapped. Yet stirring all through him was a ruthless exhilaration at the thought of once more becoming a moving force in Alayne's life, in tearing her from her security and exposing her to the tyranny of passions and desires which she had thought to set aside.

As she stood before him, his thought was that she was in no way striking, as he had pictured her in his fancy. She was less tall, her hair was a paler gold, her eyes more gray than blue, her lips closed in a colder line. Yet, his reaction to this meeting was greater than he had expected. He felt a magnetic fervor coursing in his blood as his hand held hers. He wondered if this were palpable to her. If it were, he marveled at her self-control.

Alayne's sensations were the very reverse of his. Standing before her in the flesh, his characteristics were even more intense than in her memory. He was taller, more incisive, his eyes more burning, his nose larger, more

arrogantly curved at the nostrils. Inversely, his effect on
her was less profound than she had feared. She was like
a swimmer who, dreading the force of current, finds himself
unexpectedly able to breast it. She felt that since she had
last seen him she had gained in self-confidence and maturity.

With the conflict of these undiscovered emotions surging
between them, they entered the living room.

He said, "One after another we are appearing. Only
wait and you shall have Gran at your door with Boney on
her shoulder."

She gave a little laugh, and then said, gravely, "But it
is too bad that it is trouble that brings you."

"Yes." He looked at her shrewdly. "You know how
serious Eden's condition is?"

"I have talked about it with your uncle." Her face was
quite calm.

He said, his eyes devouring her, "God, it seems strange
to see you!"

"And you!"

"Has the time seemed long or short to you?"

"Very long."

"Short to me. Gone like the wind."

"Ah, well, you have your horses, your dogs, your family.
I am rather a lonely person."

"But you're busy." He glanced at the books on the
writing table.

She gave a little shrug, and then said, "I am afraid I
think too much and take too little exercise."

"You should have more exercise. I do my best thinking
on horseback. Do you remember our rides together? You
thought I was a stern riding master, didn't you?"

"Our rides together," she murmured, and in a flash saw
herself and Renny galloping along the lake shore, heard the
mad thud of hoofs, the strain of leather, saw again the
shining, flying manes. Her breath came quickly, as though

she had indeed been riding. "How is Letty?" she asked. Letty was the mare she had ridden.

"Beautiful as ever. Ready — waiting for you to ride her again."

"I am afraid I shall never do that," she said, in a low voice.

"Aren't you ever coming to visit us?"

"Renny," she said with sudden passion, "we said goodbye on that last night. You should not have come here to see me."

"Have I disturbed you?" he asked. "You look cool enough in all conscience."

"That is what I wish to be. I — I want to forget the past."

He spoke soothingly, as to a nervous horse. "Of course. Of course. That's right, too. I should never have come if I weren't so worried about Eden."

She opened her eyes wide. "I cannot do anything for Eden," she said, abruptly.

"Not come to see him?"

"Go to see Eden! I could not possibly. Why should I?"

"When you have seen him you won't ask that question. He's a sick man. I don't believe he'll get over this. His mother went in consumption, you know."

Consumption! They would still call it that at Jalna. What a terrible word!

"I am the last person Eden would want to see."

"You're mistaken. He's terribly keen to see you."

"But why?"

"There's no accounting for the desires of anyone as ill as Eden. Possibly he has something to say to you that he thinks is important."

"That is what has brought you here?"

"Yes."

A flash of bitter disappointment pierced her. He had

not sought her out because he must set eyes on her, but for Eden's sake. She said, "I cannot see him."

"Oh, but I think you will. You couldn't refuse."

He sat doggedly smoking, endeavoring to override her opposition, she felt, by his taciturn tyranny.

She murmured, "It will be a difficult scene for me."

He replied, "There will not necessarily be a scene. Why should women always expect scenes?"

"Perhaps I learned to expect them in your family," she retorted.

He showed his teeth in the Court grin, which, subsiding, left his face again dogged.

"You will come, Alayne," he said. "You can scarcely refuse to see him for five minutes."

"Do you know," she said, "I believe I guess what he wants. He is frightened about himself and he wants me to look after him — nurse him back to health!"

"That may be," Renny replied, imperturbably. "At all events he absolutely refuses to have a trained nurse. I don't know how Aunt Augusta and Mrs. Wragge will make out with him. Uncle Ernest suggested old Mrs. Patch, and Finch said at once that she ought to know something of nursing consumption, as she had buried three of her own with it!"

He looked shrewdly into her eyes to read the effect of his words there, and saw dismay, even horror.

"Mrs. Wragge — Mrs. Patch," she repeated. "They would be the end of him!" Her mind flew to the scene of Jalna. She saw Eden, beautiful Eden, lying on a bed, neglected by Mrs. Wragge or Mrs. Patch. Another thought struck her. "He should not be in the house with the boys — Wakefield, Finch. It would be dangerous."

"I had thought of that," said Renny, "and I have an idea. You remember Fiddler's Hut?"

Was she likely to forget it? "Yes, I remember."

"Very well.   Early this spring I had it cleaned up, painted, made quite decent for a Scotch couple who were to work for Piers. Something went wrong. They did not turn up. Now, I'm wondering whether it might not be made quite a decent place for Eden. We have quantities of furniture at Jalna that could be spared. If some pieces were taken to the cottage and some rugs, it wouldn't look so bad. It might be made quite nice. And if only you would see Eden and use your influence —"

"My influence!"

"Yes. You have a great deal of influence over him still. You might persuade him to have a trained nurse. God, if you only knew how troubled I am about him!"

Suddenly he seemed, not domineering, but naïve to her; pathetic in his confidence in her. She did not look into his eyes, which for her were dark and dangerous, but at the troubled pucker on his forehead, above which the rust-colored hair grew in a point.

She pictured the mismanagement of a sick room at Jalna. She thought of Fiddler's Hut, embowered in trees and rank growths. And Eden terribly ill. All her New England love of order, of seemliness, cried out against the disorder, the muddle-headedness of the Whiteoaks. She was trembling with agitation, even while she heard herself agreeing in a level voice to accompany him to the hotel.

In less than an hour she found herself, with a sense of unreality, by Eden's bed, pale, with set lips.

He lay, his fair hair wildly tossed, his white throat and breast uncovered. She thought of dying poets, of Keats, of Shelley sinking in the waves. Young as they had been, both older than he. And his poetry was beautiful, too. She still loved his poetry. She knew it by heart. What might he not write if he could only be made well again! Was it her duty to Art? To the love she still felt for his poetry, his beauty? Ah, he had been her lover once, lying with that same head on her breast! Dear heaven, how sweet their love had been, and — how fleeting!

Their love had been a red rose, clasped, inhaled, thrown down to die. But the faint perfume of it lingering made her soul stir in pain.

Eden caught her hand and held it. He said, huskily, "I knew you'd come! You couldn't refuse me that — now. . . . Alayne, don't leave me. Stay with me — save me! You've no idea how I need you. I refused to have a nurse because I knew it was only you who could help me. It's your strength — your support . . . I can't get well without it."

He broke into a passion of tears, and, with his eyes still wet, fell into a paroxysm of coughing.

She looked down on him, her face contorted like a child's, in the effort to keep from crying. She heard herself promise in a broken voice to accompany him back to Jalna.

XIV

THE ARM OF JALNA

The train seemed to be flying with passionate purpose through the night. The engine shot forth smoke and sparks, its bright eye glared, its whistle rent the air. Its long hinderpart, trailing after it, the intricate, metallic parts of which revolved with terrific energy, seemed no less than the body of some fabulous serpent which, having swallowed certain humans, hastened to disgorge them in a favored spot. In the steel cavern of its vast interior their tender bodies iay secure and unharmed. It seemed to Finch, imaging it thus, that its journey was made for the sole purpose of returning five souls to the walls of Jalna, from which they had wandered.

Eden had borne the journey well. Renny had taken a compartment for his comfort, and had shared it with him that he might be on hand to wait on him. Ernest, Finch, and Alayne had had berths at the other end of the coach. The four — for Eden had not been visible to the other occupants of the coach — were the subjects of much conjecture. The men — tall, thin, absorbed in themselves and their female companion — made their numerous passages from end to end of the coach in complete obliviousness of the other travelers. Thus the Whiteoaks revealed their power of carrying their own atmosphere with them. With calculated reserve they raised a wall about themselves, excluding the rest of the world. In the smoking compartment not one of them exchanged more than a glance, which itself lacked any appearance of friendliness, with any other passenger.

They were met on their arrival by two motor cars. One

was of English make, a very old car but still good, owned
by Maurice Vaughan, Renny's brother-in-law, and driven
by him. Eden was installed in it, and with him went Ernest
and Renny. Watching their departure, Alayne wondered
why Renny had not chosen to ride with her. She was relieved that the propinquity of a long drive had not to be
endured, but she felt a quick disappointment, even resentment, that he had shunned her. His mixture of coldness
and fire, of calculation and restrained impulse, had always disturbed her. To be near him was to experience
alternate moods of exhilaration and depression. She was
glad that she was not to be in the house with him. Fiddler's
Hut was near enough.

As she settled herself in the familiar shabby car of the
Whiteoaks beside Finch, beheld the remembered form of
Wright, the stableman, driving, and dressed to the height
of his power for the occasion, she wondered what had been
the force which had impelled her to this strange return.
Had it indeed been the shadow of her dead love for Eden —
springing desire to cherish his life for the sake of his poetry?
Or was it that, knowing Renny willed it so, she had no self-
denying power to resist? Or was it simply and terribly
that the old house — Jalna itself — had caught her in the coil
of its spell, had stretched forth its arm to draw her back
into its bosom?

Finch and she said little. An understanding that made
words no obligation had been born between them. He too
had his moving thoughts. He was passing through the town
where his school was. What a great city it had seemed to
him until he had seen New York! Now it looked as though
it had had a blow on the head that had flattened it. Its
streets looked incredibly narrow. The crowd, which had
seemed to him once to surge, now merely loitered. They
had different faces, too, less set, more good-humored. And
how jolly the policemen looked in their helmets!

When they had left the town and were flying along the country road, past fields of springing corn and gardens bright with tulips and heavy with the scent of lilacs, Finch's face was so happy that Alayne said, with a half-rueful smile, " Glad to be home after all, are n't you?"

He assented with a nod. He longed to tell her that part of his gladness was due to her presence, the miracle of her riding beside him in the spring, but could not. He tried to make her understand by a look, and turned toward her with his wide, not unattractive smile.

She smiled in return and touched his hand, and he thought she understood, but she was only thinking, "What will become of him now? Is this a good or a bad step for him?"

They came to the low white cottages of Evandale, the blacksmith's, Mrs. Brawn's tiny shop, the English church on its high, wooded knoll, the vine-covered rectory. The wind blew, high and fresh, scattering the last of the orchard blossoms. They entered the driveway of Jalna just as the occupants of the other car were alighting. Renny had Eden by the arm.

They were crowded together in the porch. The lawn seemed less spacious than Alayne had remembered it. The great evergreen trees, with their heavy, draped boughs, seemed to have drawn nearer, to be whispering together in groups, observing the return.

Rags flung wide the front door, disclosing, as in a tableau, the grandmother, supported by Nicholas and Augusta. Her face was set in a grin of joyous anticipation. She wore her purple velvet tea gown, her largest cap, with the purple ribbons. Her shapely old hand, resting on the ebony stick, bore many rich-tinted rings. Behind her, down the hall, the sunlight, coming through the stained-glass window, cast strangely shaped bright-colored patches. Still grasping her stick, she took a step forward and extended her arms.

The arrival had been well timed for her. After a sound

night's sleep, she had just arisen refreshed, her initial vitality
not yet lowered by the agitations of the day.

"Ha!" she exclaimed. "Ha! Children. . . . All my
children. . . . Kiss me quick!"

They pressed about her, almost hiding her — Ernest,
Renny, Finch, Eden. Loud smacks were exchanged.

"Dear me, Nicholas," said Ernest, with some anxiety, as
his mother embraced Eden, "do you think she should do
that? The contagion, I mean."

"She'll scarcely catch anything at her age," rejoined
Nicholas, composedly. "God, how changed the boy is!"

"Yes. . . . What a time I've had, Nick! If only you
knew what I've been through! The responsibility and all!
How has Mamma been?"

"Marvelous. Renny's letter has given her a new lease of
life. I wonder what prompted him to write to her instead
of to Augusta."

Ernest stared, incredulously. "You don't mean that he
wrote to Mamma about Alayne's coming and getting the
cottage ready for them?"

"He did. Right over Augusta's head. The old girl is
nettled, I can tell you. And serve her right. She's too
hoity-toity about here by far."

"H'm! He should not have done that. It wasn't fair to
Augusta. And Mamma is so helpless. What could she do?"

Nicholas gave one of his subterranean chuckles. "Do?
Do? She has driven us nearly crazy. If she had had her
way most of the furniture would have been carried from the
house to furnish Fiddler's Hut. Things haven't been dull
here! Look at her now."

Old Mrs. Whiteoak was again seated in her own chair.
To protect her from draft a black and gold Indian screen
had been placed at her back. On top of the screen Boney,
in brilliant spring plumage, was perched, his beady eyes
fixed on her cap, the gay ribbons of which intrigued him.

On ottomans on either side of her she had commanded Eden and Alayne to sit. She took a hand of each. It was almost a sacramental act.

Her mind had never grasped the fact that Eden and Alayne were estranged, separated. She saw them now only as an inseparable pair who had disappeared for a long time and were now returned miraculously to her. Her activities of the past days had brightened her eyes and reset her strongly marked features in the mould of authority.

"Ha!" she ejaculated. "And so you're here! At last, eh? My young couple. Bonny as ever. Lord, what a time I've had getting ready for you! What a to-do! Eh, Augusta? A to-do, eh? Alayne, my dear, you remember my daughter, Lady Bunkley? She's failing. I notice it. This climate don't agree with her. It takes an old war horse like me to stand it. I've lived through India and I've lived through Canada. Roasting and freezing. All one to me."

Augusta looked down her nose. She was greatly chagrined by the old lady's remarks. She said, "It is no great wonder if I am unwell. It has been a trying time." She directed her offended gaze toward Renny.

He did not see it. His eyes were fixed on his grandmother. He was absorbing her aspect, delighting in her. Some perversity of his nature had impelled him to write to her, asking her to oversee the furnishing of the Hut for Eden and Alayne—she was the one above all who would see to it that the Hut was made comfortable. This he wrote, knowing that she was capable only of making things difficult for his aunt. His feeling toward Augusta was not altogether dutiful, though, on occasion, he would be demonstratively affectionate. She too often interfered with the boys. She too often sounded the note of England's superiority, of the crudity of the Colonies. He admired her, but he resented her. He admired his grandmother and re-

sented not her most flagrant absurdities. Now her air of
hilarity, of the exaltation of a superior being, moved him
to tenderness toward her. He forgot for the moment his
anxiety over Eden. He forgot his smouldering passion for
Alayne. He was satisfied to see her sitting at his grandmother's right hand, for a while, at least, a member of his
tribe. He felt the tug of those unseen cords between himself
and every being in the room.

Eden's exhaustion after the journey was, for the moment, forgotten in the excitement of the home-coming. He
felt the cynical bliss of the prodigal. He was at his own
hearth again, he was loved, but he knew he was unchanged.
He smiled mockingly at Alayne across the purple velvet
expanse of grandmother's lap, across the glitter of her rings
as they pressed into the flesh of the two captured hands. He
felt an exquisite relief in the knowledge that Alayne would
be with him at Jalna, to care for him as she had done once
before when he was ill. He could not have borne anyone
else about him. If he were to die, it would not be quite so
horrible with her beside him. . . . But he could not help
that mocking smile.

"I am trapped," Alayne thought. "Why am I here?
What does it all mean? Is there some plan, some reason
in it all? Or are we just mad puppets set jigging by the
sinister hand of a magician? Is the hand this old woman's?
Not hard to think of her as Fate. . . ."

"Shaitan! Shaitan ka batka!" screamed Boney, suddenly perceiving her as a stranger.

"Tell the bird to hold his tongue!" cried Grandmother.
"I want to talk."

"Hold your tongue, Bonaparte!" growled Nicholas.

Alayne thought, "Is Eden going to die? And if he does
— what? Why am I here? If I can nurse him back to
health, can I ever care for him again? Ah, no, no — I could
not! What are Renny's thoughts? Why was I such a fool

as to think that his presence no longer swept over me like
a wave of the sea. Oh, why did I come?" Her brow contracted in pain. Old Mrs. Whiteoak's rings were hurting
her hand.

"Shaitan! Shaitan ka batka!" raged Boney.

"Nick!"

"Yes, Mamma."

"Ernest!"

"Yes, Mamma."

"Tell the bird to hush. I'm asking Alayne a question."
They composed the parrot with a bit of biscuit.

"Are you glad to be home again, child?"

"Y-yes. Oh, yes."

"And where have you been all this time?"

"In New York."

"It's a poor place from what I hear. Did you weary of
it? Had Eden a good position?"

All the eyes in the room were on her. She hedged. "I
went away once for a change. To visit cousins in Milwaukee."

The strong rust-colored eyebrows shot upward. "Milwaukee! China, eh? That's a long way."

Nicholas came to the rescue. "Milwaukee's not in China,
Mamma. It's somewhere in the States."

"Nonsense! It's in China. Walkee-walkee — talkee-
talkee! Don't you think I know pidgin English?" She
grinned triumphantly, squeezing Alayne's hand.

"Walkee-walkee — talkee-talkee!" chanted Wakefield.

"Nicholas!"

"Yes, Mamma."

"Hush the boy. I must not be interrupted."

Nicholas put out a long arm and drew Wake to his side.
"Listen," he said, with a finger up; "an improving conversation."

Grandmother said, with her dark bright eyes on the two

beside her, "What's the matter? Why haven't you got a child?"

"This is too much," said Augusta.

Her mother retorted, "It's not enough. . . . Pheasant's had one. Meggie's had one. May manage another. . . . I don't like this business of not having children. My mother had eleven. I should have done as well. I started off smartly. But, look you, when we came here the doctor was so hard to get at, Philip was afraid for me. Ah, there was a man, my Philip! The back on him! You don't see such straight backs nowadays. No children. . . . H'm. In my day, a wife would give her husband a round dozen—"

"Shaitan!" cried Boney, his biscuit gone and his eye on the stranger.

"—and, if there was one of them he wasn't quite sure about, he took it like a man—ha!"

"Shaitan ka batka!"

"He knew even the most reliable mare . . . skittish now and then."

"Ka batka!"

"Hey, Renny?"

"Yes, old dear. Great days those!"

Eden withdrew his hand from his grandmother's. There was a look of exhaustion on his face. He got to his feet; his lips were parted, his forehead drawn in a frown. "Awfully tired," he muttered. "I think I'll lie down for a bit." He looked vaguely about.

"Poor lad," said the old lady. "Put him on the sofa in the library."

Eden walked slowly from the room. Ernest followed him, solicitous, a little important. He covered him with a rug on the sofa.

Grandmother's eyes followed the pair with satisfaction. She then turned to Alayne. "Don't worry, my dear, we'll soon have him well again. Then let's hope you'll—"

" Mamma," interrupted Nicholas, "tell Alayne about the Hut. What a time you've had, and all that."

This was enough to distract her attention from the necessity of multiplying. She now bent her faculties to a description of the downy nest she had prepared.

Nicholas said in an undertone to Renny, "It was appalling. The Hut could not possibly have held the furniture she insisted on sending to it. There was only one thing to do, and that was to carry the things out at one door and bring them back through another. Augusta, poor old girl, was at her wit's end."

The master of Jalna showed his teeth in appreciation. Then, his face clouding, he asked, "What do you think of Eden? Pretty sick boy, eh?"

"How bad is he? I couldn't gather much from your letter."

"I don't quite know. I must have Dr. Drummond see him. The New York doctor says his condition is serious. Not hopeless."

"American doctors!" observed Nicholas with a shrug. "Fresh air. Milk. We'll soon fill him out. . . . Gad, what a trump that girl is! Gone off in looks, though."

"Nonsense," denied Ernest, who had come up from behind. "She's lovelier than ever."

Renny offered no opinion. His eyes were on her face. He read there spiritual acceptance of her changed condition. A calm embrace of even Boney. A trump? No. A proud spirit subdued by passion. He moved circuitously to her side among the pieces of heavy, inlaid mahogany. He sat down on the ottoman that had been occupied by Eden.

"I want to tell you," he said, "how happy it makes me to have you here."

Old Mrs. Whiteoak had fallen into a doze. Fate seemed to be napping. Alayne and Renny might have been the

only two in the room, each so felt the isolating power of the
other's proximity.

"I had to come. He wanted me—needed me so terribly."

"Of course. He needs you. . . . And when—he gets
better?"

"Then I shall go back."

But the words sounded unreal to her. Though she had
left her possessions in the apartment, had made preparations for only a summer's stay, the words sounded unreal.
The apartment with its artistic rugs, its pretty lamps, its bits
of brass and copper, seemed of less importance than the
ebony stick of this sleeping old woman. Rosamund Trent
seemed of no importance. This room spoke to her. Its
cumbersome furniture had a message for her. Its thick
walls, enclosing that subjugating atmosphere, had a sig-·
nificance which no other walls could have. She might not
grasp the unqualified meaning of it. She had not courage
for the attempt. The room might be only a trap, and she—
a rabbit, perhaps—a limp, vulnerable rabbit—caught!

His tone, when he spoke again, was almost crisp. "Well,
you've come, and that's the great thing. I can't tell you
what a load it takes off my mind. I believe it will mean
recovery for Eden."

She must work, she must strain for Eden's recovery. And
that was right. One must obey the laws of one's order. But
what a fantastic interlude in her life this summer was to be!

Augusta had gone out. Now she reappeared in the doorway and motioned them to come. They rose and went to
her, moving cautiously so as not to awaken the grandmother.

"He has fallen asleep," said Augusta. "Done out, poor
boy. And you must be so tired, too, my dear. Shouldn't
you like to come up to my room and tidy yourself before
dinner? I'll have a jug of hot water taken up to you."

Alayne thanked her. She would be glad to change her
dress and wash.

"Then," continued Augusta, "I shall take you to the cottage — I think we had better drop that horrid name of Fiddler's Hut, now that you are going to live there — and show you our preparations. I suppose I should say my mother's preparations." And she directed a reproachful look at Renny.

He returned her look truculently. "I like the old name," he said. "I don't see any sense in changing it."

"I shall certainly never call it that again."

"Call it what you please! It's Fiddler's Hut." He gave an angry gesture.

"Why one should cling to low names!"

"You'll be sneering at Jalna next!"

Alayne thought, "Have I ever been away? Here they are, wrangling in exactly the same fashion. I don't see how I am to bear it. What has come over me now I am in this house? A mere movement of his arm disturbs me! In New York it was possible — here, I cannot! I cannot! Thank God, I shall be under another roof!"

A red patch of light, projected through the colored glass of the window, rested on Renny's head. His hair seemed to be on fire. He said, contemptuously, "The *cottage*, eh? Better call it Rose Cottage, or Honeysuckle Cottage. Make it sweet while you're about it!" It was a passion with him that nothing about the place should be changed.

The front door was thrown open, and Wakefield ran in. With him came a rush of spring wind and three dogs. The two spaniels began to bark and jump about their master. The old sheep dog sniffed Alayne and wagged the clump of fur that was his tail. He remembered her.

Wakefield held out a small bunch of windflowers. "I've brought these for you," he said. "You're to keep them in your room."

Alayne clasped him to her. How adorable his little body felt! So light, so fragile, and yet how full of life! "Thank

you! Thank you!" she breathed, and he laughed as he felt
the warmth of her mouth against his ear. He wrapped himself about her.

"Child," admonished his aunt, "don't be so rough with
Alayne! She is coming to my room now. She is tired.
You're dragging her down."

Renny removed the little limpet, and Lady Buckley took
Alayne by the arm.

As they mounted the stairs, she said, "You have done
nobly and rightly. I cannot express how I admire you for
it. I wish I could say that I am sure you will be rewarded
for your self-sacrifice, but I have not found it so in life."
And she sighed. "I have discovered a nice young Scotch
girl who will come from the village every day to work for
you at — you know where. I refuse to call the cottage by
that odious name, even though Renny be disagreeable
to me."

They sought Augusta's room, and she poured water from
the heavy ewer into the basin, that Alayne might wash her
face and hands.

Finch, too, had gone to his room. The creak of the attic
stairs, as he ascended, was to him the voice of the house.
It welcomed him, and chided him. The attic complained
that it had been so long deserted by him. No one there, all
those weeks, to listen to the voice of the house at night. All
that he might have heard it say on those nights was now lost
to him forever. The walls of his room did not seem to be
standing still. They seemed to move, to quiver in consciousness of him. The faded flowers of the wallpaper stirred as
in a gust. He stood there, snuffing the familiar smells: the
plaster, damp in one spot where the roof leaked — there was
his water basin just where he had left it, placed to catch the
drops; the faded carpet, not swept too thoroughly by Mrs.
Wragge — it had a peculiar, fuzzy smell; the mustiness of

the old books in the cupboard; and, permeating all, the essence of the house itself, which held a secret never to be told, though he thought he came near to guessing it.

He threw open the window and let in the air. The trees, sombre and friendly, exhaled their teasing, resinous scents. Little rosy cones, like tiny candles for a fête day, stood upright on a mossy spruce. All the trees showed a green film of moss on that side of the trunk nearest the house, as if a visible sign of their communion with it. The leaves of the deciduous trees, in their newly opened freshness, were of a gloss unimpeachable and pure. Beyond the trees, the meadows, moist and verdant; the paddock, where a group of leggy foals stood in awe of their own newness; the apple orchard, where the pinkish-white blossoms were falling with every breeze to the dark red earth, like flowers before the feet of June, young Summer's bride. The stream, its surface broken in a thousand sunny splinters, hastened down into the ravine, where only the trunks of the silver birches stood bright against the shade. A mourning dove uttered its pensive, wooing call.

Finch threw out his arms and drew the beauty of it into his soul. He sent his spirit out of the window to meet the morning. His spirit returned to him, laden with the morning, heavy with the sweetness of it, as a bee with honey.

He thought of his last day in this room, its humiliation. He had dreaded the home-coming as ignominious. But Piers had not been present to jeer at him. He had crept back, scarcely noticed, under the screen of Eden's illness. Only Uncle Nicholas had growled, under his moustache, "Well, young man, I hope you're ashamed of yourself. What you need is a good hiding."

And Renny, overhearing, had remarked, curtly, "If it hadn't been for the kid we'd never have found Eden."

Cantankerous, magnificent Renny!

Behind him he heard a light step. He turned and saw

Wakefield in the doorway. The dignity of his bearing, the gravity of his small countenance, showed him to be in a mood which Finch detested. A darned patronizing mood that expressed itself in the most high-flown words at his command, words garnered from his conversations with Aunt Augusta and Mr. Fennel.

"I see," he said, enunciating clearly, "that you have repented you of your folly."

Finch hung on to himself. It was hard to keep his hands off the insufferable little fellow, but he must. A bad way that would be for reinstating himself. He wondered why Wakefield had no respect for him. Other small boys had for their seniors. In the house of one of his school friends he had seen an inquisitive young brother dismissed with a mere nod of the head.

No harm in trying that on Wake, anyhow. He suspended the brush he had begun to use on his hair, and gave his head a peremptory jerk toward the door. The expression of his face, reflected in the looking-glass, was one of cold authority.

Wakefield did not move. He said, "I knew full well that you would repent you of your folly."

Finch threw down the hairbrush and bore down upon him. But you could not really hurt anything as fragile as this youngster. Why, his bones were only gristle! Finch flung him over his shoulder and ran down the stairs with him hanging limp and unresisting. But the instant Wake was set on his feet in the hall, his cock-a-hoop air returned, and he deftly placed himself at the head of the procession now entering the dining room.

"Aha!" cried Grandmother, showing every tooth, "that's what I like to hear! Young lads racketing about!"

They were around the table, with the portraits of Captain Philip Whiteoak in his uniform and old Adeline in her heyday smiling down on them. Behind their chairs glided the form of Rags, his expression that queer mixture of servility and impudence, his shiny black coat, dragged on in haste at the last minute, very much up at the nape.

There they were, consuming large slices of underdone roast beef; potatoes roasted in the pan; turnips smothered in brown gravy; asparagus weltering in drawn butter; a boiled pudding with hard sauce; and repeated cups of hot tea. Alayne was touched because they had remembered that she did not eat pudding. There were jam tarts for her. "Baked in the little shell pattypans you like!" Grandmother pointed out. And there was sherry to drink, too. A New York clubman would have paid a pretty price for such sherry as this. How old Adeline liked it! She threw back her head, her cap ribbons trembling, to drain the last drop. Renny whispered, "I'll send some of this sherry to Fiddler's Hut for Eden. Some good porter would buck him up, too. Do him more good than milk." Alayne's thoughts flew on swift wings of compassion to Eden, stretched on the sofa in the next room. She had had a glimpse of him as she passed, covered with a magenta crocheted afghan. Confusing for him, she thought, all this robust conversation. Nicholas, Ernest, their mother, were all talking at once. About food. What Ernest had had to eat in New York; what Nicholas had eaten in London, twenty-five years ago. What Grandmother had eaten in India, seventy-five years ago. Augusta, in contralto tones, extolled the flavor of English strawberries, lettuce, and cauliflower. There was an altercation among Augusta, Renny, and Wakefield as to whether or not the child should eat the fat of his beef. Only Finch was silent, eating as though he would never get enough.

Sunshine, coming through the yellow blinds, bathed them all as in the thunderous glow of a Turner sunset. The salient features of each were mordantly emphasized. Grandmother's cap, her eyebrows, her nose; Augusta's fringe, the carriage of her head; Nicholas's shoulders, the sardonic droop of his moustache; Ernest's long white hands; Wake's glowing dark eyes; Renny's red head, his Court nose. And in the essence of them there was no conformation to a standard. Life had not hammered them, planed them, fitted them to any pattern. After the weary wit of the talk to which she had listened, rather than taken part in, at dinners of the past year, all this gusto, this spendthrift tossing away of energy! But perhaps they were right. Perhaps they had some secret which others had lost or were losing. They did not save themselves. They were built on a wasteful plan. Like shouldering trees, they thrust down their roots, thrust out their limbs, strove with each other, battled with the elemental. They saw nothing strange or unlikely in themselves. They were the Whiteoaks of Jalna. There was nothing more to be said.

XV

VAUGHANLANDS

THAT same afternoon Renny and Wakefield descended the slope that led from the lawn into the ravine, crossed the bridge over the stream, and reascended the opposite slope, along the winding diversities of the continued path which led them, at last, to an open oak wood, the property of Maurice Vaughan. The house itself stood in a hollow, and so thick was the foliage of the surrounding trees, following a month of rains, that only the smoke from one of its chimneys, rising in a delicate blue cloud, was visible to them, though they could hear the sound of a woman's voice singing inside.

A field of corn lay between them and the lawn. In it a village boy stood beating indifferently on a pan to ward off the crows. The crows circled above him or fed at a short distance, with derisive side glances in his direction. Walking among them were two white gulls, flown all the way from the lake for this inland recreation.

The boy was startled by having his pan and stick snatched from him. "Think you'll frighten crows by those feeble taps?" demanded Renny. "Listen to this!" He created a terrible din, not far from the boy's ear. The crows rose straight in the air, screaming. The gulls, flying low abreast, sailed in the direction of the lake.

The brothers walked on, the little one clutching his elder's sleeve. By the time they had reached the gap in the cedar hedge which bordered the lawn, the beating on the tin had grown faint, and did not noticeably oppose the full clear tones of the woman's voice, singing inside the house.

"Renny!" Wakefield tugged at the sleeve. "Why did

Piers bring Pheasant and Mooey over here, just when Eden and Alayne have come?"

"Because Piers can't abide Eden."

"Why?"

"You couldn't understand."

"Did Piers and Pheasant come over here so that Eden could come home and be nursed?"

"Yes."

"But I thought Meggie couldn't abide Pheasant."

"Well, she's made friends with her for Piers's sake — and Eden's."

Wakefield's eyes, though dark with thought, were troubled. "I find it hard," he said, "to keep things straight in my mind."

"You don't need to. The less you think about them the better."

"But I've got my own ideas, just the same." His tone was truculent.

"You've too many ideas. You're too inquisitive."

Wakefield raised his eyes, with the perfect touch of appeal in them. "I suppose it's my delicate health," he said. How well he gauged his elder! He was drawn against his side as they went into the house.

No one in the dim parlor. The sitting room, the dining room, empty. Still, the sweet, full woman's voice flooded the house. They went up the stairs. Wakefield ran along the hallway, knocked on a door, and, almost immediately, opened it.

The room discovered was splashed with sunshine coming through the swaying branches of trees. It was bright with highly glazed, gayly colored chintz. A vase holding daffodils stood on the centre table. On the table also was a silver tray bearing a teapot, a plate of scones, and a small piece of honey in the comb. Meg was enjoying one of her little lunches.

"Ha!" said Renny. "Nibbling as usual, eh?" He bent and kissed her.

Wakefield pressed against her back, holding his hands over her eyes. "Guess who it is!"

She drew down his hands till they lay on her breast, and turned her face back to his. They kissed. "Oh," he exclaimed, "I taste honey on you!" He looked greedily at the square of honeycomb.

"I had no appetite for dinner," she exclaimed, "so I began to feel a little faint, and had this brought to me. I don't really want it. You may finish it, Wake, darling."

He took the honeycomb in his fingers and began to devour it, Meg regarding him with indulgence, Renny with affectionate concern.

Renny asked, "Do you think that is wholesome?"

"Oh, yes. It's a natural food. It couldn't possibly hurt him."

"To think," she exclaimed, "that you have been in New York since I saw you last!" She regarded him as if she expected to find something exotic in him. "What you must have seen! But before any of that, tell me about Eden. This is a great shock. Is he very ill? If he is in danger, I don't know how to bear it. Poor lamb. And he was always so well. Everything started with that wretched marriage of his. The day he first brought that girl to Jalna, I saw trouble ahead." She screwed up her courage. "Renny, is Eden going to—" She glanced at the child. He must not hear anything terrible.

"Well, he has a spot on one lung. He's very thin. . . . I think he isn't quite so ill as that doctor made out. But he'll need a lot of nursing." He thought, "What will she say when I tell her that Alayne is here?" He continued, "Everything depends on fresh air and good nursing."

Meg exclaimed, "I should be the one to nurse him! But there's Baby. I can't expose her."

He reckoned with her indolence. "What about this 'mother's help'—whatever you call her—couldn't she look after the youngster?"

Meg moved on her chair to confront him. Her short, plump arm lay across the table, her milk-white, sensuously curved hand drooping over the edge. Her voice was reproachful. "Trust my baby to Minny Ware! She's a featherbrain. One never knows what she will do next! Sometimes I wish I had never seen her."

They were silent a moment. The voice of the singer came cooingly from a distant room. He could not tell Meg yet that Alayne was at Jalna.

She said, "It seems terrible to me to banish Eden to the Hut."

"It isn't safe to have him in the house with the boys."

"And Finch is back! What a frightful responsibility life is for some people! While others . . . That is what takes my appetite—worry."

"Finch will be all right, now. . . . He's a queer young devil. You can't get at him."

She observed, with complacence, "Finch would never have run away if I had been at home. Aunt Augusta simply cannot understand boys."

Renny was listening to the voice. He asked, "Is that girl always singing?"

His sister nodded, as though in confirmation of inexpressible things. She bent toward him, whispering, "You know, it's going to be terribly trying for me having Pheasant here. Nothing but my love for Piers would induce me. She made up to Minny Ware at once. Already they are talking together in corners. . . . I ignore them."

A heavy step was heard in the hall. A knuckle touched the panel of the door.

Meg's smooth brow showed a pucker, but she murmured, "Come in."

The tap came again. "He didn't hear you," said Renny. "Hello, Maurice!"

The door opened and Vaughan appeared. His graying hair was rumpled, his Norfolk jacket hung unevenly from his broad shoulders.

"Been having a nap?" asked Renny.

He nodded, grinning apologetically. "Anything private under discussion? I only came for my pipe. Left it some-where about." He thought, "Why does Meggie look at me that way? A damned funny look."

"I was just asking Meggie whether Miss Ware ever stops singing," said Renny. "A joyous sort of being to have about. I wish we could borrow her for Jalna." He thought, "Marriage is the devil. She's got old Maurice just where she wants him."

Meg thought, "Why is it that I can never have my own brother to myself? Is there no such thing as privacy when one is married?"

Vaughan had found his pipe and tobacco pouch. He filled the pipe deftly, considering that his right hand had been crippled in the War.

Meg's full blue eyes were fixed on the crippled hand, and the leather bandage worn about the wrist. It was the sight of that which had melted her heart toward him. Yet now its movement had the power to irritate her. It was ab-normal, even sinister, rather than pathetic. She said, re-proachfully, "Renny says that he does not think Eden is very seriously ill. You had me so terribly frightened." She turned to her brother. "Maurice said Eden looked half-dead."

"He looked that way to me," Vaughan said, doggedly.

"He did look pretty seedy after the journey," agreed Renny. "But he had a sleep and something to eat, and he's more like himself now. We've got him moved into Fiddler's Hut." In a moment more he must tell her that Alayne was returned. He felt a constriction in his throat.

She asked eagerly, "How did you get him there? Could he walk so far over rough ground?"

"Wright and I took him. Half carried him. . . . They've rigged it up very comfortably. You'd be surprised. Gran had a glorious time ordering everyone about, and Aunt Augusta has the hump." No, he could not tell her yet. . . .

Vaughan knew what was on Renny's mind. He observed, staring at the bowl of his pipe, "He'll take a lot of nursing. Lord, did you notice his wrists and knees?"

"There you go again!" cried his wife. "You seem determined to frighten me." She placed a hand on her heart. "If you knew what a weight I feel here!"

"I'm sorry," said Vaughan. "I seem destined to put my foot in it. . . . I only meant — "

"Please stop," she interrupted, dramatically. "Let me see for myself how he is." . . . Her agitation found vent in correcting Wakefield. He was wiping his fingers on the edge of the traycloth.

He was sticky, argumentative. Before he was quelled, another knock sounded on the door, this time a quick tattoo, signaling a delicate urgency.

"It's Baby," said the singer's voice. "She's been crying for you."

Wakefield flung wide the door. A blonde young woman stood there, holding in her arms a plump infant.

Meg's face was smoothed into an expression of maternal adoration. Her lips parted in a smile of ineffable sweetness. She held out her arms, her breast becoming a harbor, and received the child. She pressed a long kiss on its flower-petal cheek.

At forty-two she had been made a mother by Vaughan, and he had realized his dream of becoming the father of her child. But their inner selves had not been welded together

by the birth. She who had never yearned toward motherhood now became extravagantly maternal, putting him outside the pale of that tender intimacy. Sometimes he found
himself with the bewildered feeling of a dog whose own
door is closed against it. He loved this child as he had
never loved Pheasant, who had been so lonely, so eager for
love. Meg had named it Patience. "But why?" he had
exclaimed, not liking the name at all. "Patience is my
favorite virtue," she had replied, "and we can call her Patty
for short."

It was an odd thing that while "Mooey," as he was nick-
named, the child of the boy and girl, Piers and Pheasant,
was a serious infant, staring out at the world from under a
pucker in his brow, Patty, the child of middle-aged parents,
was lively, with inconsequent exuberance. She bounced
now on her mother's lap, kicked out her heels, and showed
her four white teeth in a hilarious grin.

Her uncle poked her with his finger. She reached for
his red hair. "Ha," he said, "you young vixen! Look at
her, Maurice."

"Yes. She can give a good pull, too."

Meg turned smiling to Minny Ware. "Don't go," she
said, graciously. "Sit down, please. I may want you to
take Baby again."

Minny Ware had had no intention of going. The infant
had not so longed for the society of its mother as she had
longed for the society of men. It was ill going for her when
there was a man about and she not bathed in his presence.
At this moment of her life it was her hot ambition to
capture the master of Jalna. But he had a wary eye on her.
She almost feared that he scented her desire.

She sat with crossed knees, watching the family group
about the baby. A bright blue smock, very open at the
throat, showed her rather thick milk-white neck and full
chest. The smock was short, and beneath it were discovered

excessively pink knickers, and stockings such as only a London girl would have the courage to wear.

She had, as a matter of fact, been born, not in London, but in a remote part of England, where her father had been rector of a scattered parish. She had rarely known what it was to have two coins to rub together. When her father had died, two years after the close of the War, she and another girl had gone up to London, keen after adventure, strong and fresh as a wind from their native moor. For several years they had earned a precarious living there. They managed to preserve their virtue, and even kept their wild-rose complexions. But life was hard, and after a while they thought of London only as a place from which they longed to escape. Mercifully, the friend had a small legacy left to her, and they decided to go to Canada. A short course was taken at an agricultural college. Armed with this experience, they set out to run a poultry farm in Southern Ontario. But they had not sufficient capital to support them while they became accustomed to conditions so different. The seasons were unfavorable; the young chicks died in large numbers from a contagious disease; the turkey poults were even more disappointing, for they succumbed to blackhead. The cost of putting up the poultry houses had been greater than they had expected. Grain was very expensive; food was dear. At the end of two seasons they were stranded, with just enough left to pay their debts. They did this, for they were inherently honest, and turned their thoughts again cityward.

If they had been stenographers, they might easily have got situations. As it was, they tried unsuccessfully to get taken on by the proprietors of small high-class shops, as doctors' or dentists' assistants. At long last they got employment as waitresses in a tea shop. A year of this, and Minny Ware's feet became afflicted. To stand on them all day, to carry heavy trays, was an agony too great. One night she read an advertisement for a "mother's help" and companion — a Mrs. Vaughan the advertiser. The place was in the country, the child an infant. She longed for the country, and she "loved babies." She applied for the position by letter in excellent old-country handwriting. She explained that she was the daughter of a clergyman, and had come to Canada to raise poultry. Having failed in that, she felt that nothing would be so congenial to her as a position in charge of a young child. She did not mention her experience as waitress. The fact that she had failed in an undertaking commended her to Maurice. He had always a fellow feeling for failures. Meg liked the idea of her being the daughter of a parson. Minny Ware had now been with them for five months.

As soon as there was an opportunity, she said in a low tone to Renny, "New York must be great fun."

"I suppose it is," he returned. "I wasn't there for fun. I dare say you would like it. Do you want to go there?"

"Who doesn't? But do you think they would let me across the line?"

"Not with that London accent, I'm afraid."

She gave a rich, effortless laugh, which, having passed her lips, left her face round and solemn, like a child's. She said, "You must teach me how to speak, so they will take me in."

"Are you so restless, then?" His eyes swept over her, resting on the freckles that accentuated the whiteness of her rather thick nose. "You have looks that are unusual. You've got a voice. What are you going to do with them?"

"Exploit them in the States. There's nothing to keep me here." Her eyes, of an indeterminate color, narrow above high cheek bones, looked provocatively into his.

The frustrated torrent of his passion for Alayne turned, for a moment, toward this girl. As he realized this, he felt an intense, inexplicable irritation. He looked beyond Minny Ware to his sister.

"Alayne," he said, "has come back to look after Eden." Let Meggie fly into a rage, if she would, before an outsider.

"Alayne come back . . ." she repeated the words, softly, curling her lip a little.

"Eden begged her to come."

"She has not much pride, has she?"

"She's full of pride. She's too proud to care what you or anyone else thinks."

"Even you?" Her lip curled again.

Minny Ware looked eagerly from one face to another. Could she make herself a place here?

Renny did not answer, but his eyes warned Meg to be careful.

She sat, winking very fast, as though to keep back tears or temper, her full cheek rested against her closed hand. She was, in truth, blinking before a new idea. . . . If Alayne and Eden were reconciled, so much the better. Let Alayne provide for the poor darling. There was no use in Alayne's pretending she was poor. Americans always had plenty of money. Eden might be delicate for a long time. And if he — if Alayne fancied that he were not going to recover — that she could capture Renny through Eden's death — she would find how mistaken she was!

In any case Renny must be protected from Alayne. There was only one way by which he could be protected. A wife. And here, at hand, was Minny Ware. Meg's perceptions, slow but penetrating, left no doubt in her mind that Alayne loved Renny — that Renny was intensely aware of Alayne. Very different this controlled awareness from the calculated passion and abrupt endings of his affairs with other women, which Meg had sensed rather than observed. Affairs which her stolid pride had made her overlook.

She absorbed the picture of Renny and Minny Ware

side by side. Should she, she asked herself, be willing to
see them so attached for the rest of their days? Her
heart's answer was in the affirmative. Though she was
ready to find fault with Minny,— for being careless, for
making up too readily to Pheasant, — it was certain that
Minny was the one woman she would be willing to accept
as a sister. She knew already what it was to hate two
women married to her brothers. From the first, Minny's
lavish light-heartedness, her physical exuberance, her good
temper under correction, her willingness to be at another's
beck and call, had caused Meg to look on her with favor,
even an approaching affection.

Could Renny have a wife better suited to him? People
would say that he had married beneath him. That prospect
did not trouble Meg. It was her opinion that, no matter where
a Whiteoak should seek his mate, the fact that he married
her placed her above questioning. And, whatever Minny
had been forced to do, the fact remained that she was the
daughter of a clergyman, and had been nicely reared. Even
though her skirts were too short and her stockings strange —
well, life in post-war London was doubtless strange. She
had rebuked Minny for the flamboyancy of her clothes,
but the girl had been adamant. She had said, in effect,
that, if Mrs. Vaughan did not like her clothes, she would
go. She could not dress soberly to fit her situation. It
would break her spirit.

To understand Meg Vaughan, it must be remembered
that she had led a life of extraordinary isolation. She had
been educated by governesses. She had made no friends.
Her brothers, her elderly uncles, her grandmother, had
sufficiently filled her life. During the long years of her
estrangement from Maurice, she had acquired a taste for
solitude. Those long hours in her chamber — what did she
do with them? Brush her long hair that showed a feather
of gray above the forehead? Eat comforting little lunches?

Dream, with her head supported on her short plump fore-
arm? In winter three weeks would pass in which she would
not set foot out of doors, except to go to church.

Now here she was, with a husband and a baby, and a
companion whom she desired to marry to her favorite
brother. She was as comfortable as a plump rabbit in its
burrow. She longed to secure Renny in a peace as nearly
approaching hers as was possible to his turbulent nature.
One's mate must not matter too much, if one were a Whiteoak. Maurice did not; Minny would not. One's children
mattered terribly. Her breast rose in a heavy sweet breath
when she thought of Baby.

Meg did not know what it was to be socially ambitious.
How could she, since they were the most important people
thereabout? She did not take into account rich manufac-
turers or merchants who had built imposing residences only
a few miles away on the lake shore. She had not changed
the position of a piece of furniture since she had come to
Vaughanlands.

During the rest of Renny's stay she was sweetly, solidly
acquiescent toward him. He left thinking how perfect she
was. In Maurice's stable, looking over a new mare from
the West, he told Maurice that Meggie was perfect, and
Maurice agreed.

When the two women were alone, Minny Ware exclaimed, "Let me brew a fresh pot of tea. They spoiled
your little lunch."

"Do," said Meggie. "We'll have it together."

They looked into each other's eyes and smiled. Then
Minny's eyes filled with tears. She snatched up the infant
and kissed it extravagantly.

XVI

WOODLAND MEETINGS

EDEN was pathetic. He was like a capricious child, weak and tyrannical. He could not in those first weeks bear Alayne out of his sight. There was so much to be done for him that only she could do to his satisfaction. The young Scotch girl came every day to help; their meals were carried to them in covered dishes by Rags, from the house. But Alayne must move his hammock from place to place, following the sun; she must make his eggnogs, his sherry jelly, read to him, sit with him at night by the hour when he could not sleep, encourage and restrain him. Like a child, he was sweetly humble on occasion. He would catch her skirt, hold it, and say, brokenly, "I don't deserve it. You should have left me to die"; or, "If I get better, Alayne, I wonder if you could love me."

She was endlessly patient with him, but her love was dead, as his was, in truth, for her. A tranquillity, born of the knowledge that all was over between them, gave them assurance. The mind of each was free to explore its own depths, to see its own reflection in the lucent pool of summer. Eden, with his invincible desire for beauty, read poems in the opening scroll of violets, tiny orchids, hooked fern fronds that covered the woodland. He read them in the interlacing pattern of leaves, branches, the shadows of flying birds.

In all these Alayne read passion. She thought only of Renny.

She had seen little of him, and then only in the presence of Eden or others of the family. She had several times taken tea with old Mrs. Whiteoak and Augusta. On all occasions the talk was of Eden's health. He was improving. Almost from the first Alayne had been convinced that his illness was not to be fatal. He was responding to rest and good food. She could imagine his life in New York. But how weak he was! Once, adventuring across the orchard path to the edge of the paddock to watch a group of romping, long-legged foals, he had met Piers. Piers, sturdy and sunburned in the sunlight. There had passed no word, but a look from Piers, and a forward movement that had shocked the sap from Eden's legs.

He had tottered back through the orchard, and flung himself on his bed. After a while he had muttered, "I met brother Piers. God, what a look! There was murder in it. To think I'd let him see I was afraid of him!" He did not venture that way again.

Alayne brooded on this meeting for a little, and she felt angry at Piers. But her thoughts, like strong, cruel birds, flew back to Renny. Yet her care was for Eden. She wished there were more sunshine for him. June was windless, and sometimes they felt suffocated under the lush greenness that enclosed them. Fiddler's Hut was half hidden by a twisted creeper that shadowed the small-paned windows. It seemed impossible to keep Eden in the sunlight for more than half an hour without the necessity of moving him. Even the path that wound from the door across the little clearing was bordered by such a growth of fern and bracken that an adventurer along it was certain of wet knees. Here summer not only was born and flourished, but seethed with life. Each morning was fresh and lucent, as though the first morning on earth. The jeweled leaves of the wild grape and bracken scarcely dried before another dew.

Weeks ago she had asked Renny if something might not be done to let in air and sunshine. Nothing had yet been done. Enough that he brought Eden back to Jalna. It would require effort to rouse him to further action. The family now took it for granted that Eden would recover.

She had left him in a comfortable chair, a glass of milk at his elbow, a book in his hand. A splash of sunlight, of a richness suggesting autumn rather than June, gave the effect of his being a figure in a tableau, as she looked back. This effect was heightened by the pensive immobility of his attitude, and by the, one might almost think, conscious pose of his hands and beautifully modeled head. She had come near to touching his hair in a passing caress, as she had left. She was glad now that she had not. She went down the moist path, past the spring, overgrown with wild honeysuckle, and followed it swiftly, as it rose into the wood.

She must have exercise. Her muscles were aching for movement. In walking she discovered that these weeks had brought fresh physical strength to her. She distended her breast and drew deep breaths. This was her first walk since she had come to Jalna.

A bridle path, smooth with pine needles, lay through the wood. On each side of it, raising waxen bells to the light, clustered frail lilies of the valley. A clump of poplar saplings, looking pale and lost against the thick trunks of the pines, were covered by silvery unfolding leaves, as though a flock of wan butterflies had settled there. High in the pines she heard the plaintive notes of a mourning dove. Here and there rose the towering pallid bole of a silver birch, shining as though from an inner light.

The notes of the mourning dove were drowned by the rapid thudding of a horse's hoofs. Alayne drew out of sight behind a massive, moss-grown trunk. She peered out to see who the rider might be. It was Pheasant, riding bare-headed astride a slender Western pony. They passed in a flash — padding hoofs, flying mane, great shining eyes, and, above, little white face and tumbled dark hair. Alayne called her name, but the girl did not hear, and in a moment was gone beyond a curve.

It was Alayne's first glimpse of Pheasant since her return. She felt a quick out-going of warmth toward her. Poor wild, sweet Pheasant, married so young to Piers! If she had not known her, she would have taken that flying figure on horseback for a boy.

The bridle path emerged from the pine wood. Irrele·vantly appeared a field planted with potatoes. The potato plants, lusty and strong, in flower, compact in the midst of the woodland, were not unlovely. Neither was the bent old man, Piers's laborer, unlovely in his blue shirt, in his attitude of patient hoeing.

She followed the path, now in the full blaze of sunshine. The woods about were no longer pine, but oaks and birch and maple. In every hollow were gay gatherings of wood lilies, white and purplish pink, and through all the trees sounded the ring of bird song. An oriole flashed. She caught the blue of a jay's swift wing and thought she saw, but was not sure, a scarlet tanager. Then again came the hoof beats. Pheasant was returning. Alayne trembled, looking down on the path, where in the dust lay the little hoofprints.

Pheasant was beside her. She had leaped from her horse. His breathing sounded, quick and passionate. His velvet nose was introduced between the faces of the two girls.

"Pheasant!"

"Alayne!"

Their eyes embraced, their hands touched; they wavered, laughing, then kissed. The horse, puzzled, flung back his head, shaking his bridle.

"Let's sit down in the wood," cried Pheasant. "How splendid our meeting like this! Away from all the family, you know. Those people. Well, we're different, after all, you and I. We can't talk just the same, be ourselves, when they're all about us." And she added, quaintly, "I think you're noble, Alayne! But how can I tell you what I think? I'll never forget how beautiful you were to me. And now you've come back to nurse Eden!"

They sat down among the trees. The grass was long and so tender that it seemed to have grown in a day. The horse began to crop, petulantly jerking up, with a sidewise movement of the head, great succulent mouthfuls. Pheasant sat with her back against a young oak.

On her white forehead, above the pale oval of her face, a lock of dark hair lay like a half-opened fan. Alayne thought that she had never seen such beautiful brown eyes. Her mouth was small and she opened it little when she spoke, but when she laughed, which was seldom, she opened it wide, showing her white teeth.

"Isn't life a funny tangle?" she said. "It would take a lot of untangling to straighten us, wouldn't it, Alayne?"

"Does it bear talking about? Hadn't we better just talk of you and me?"

"I suppose so. But perhaps God is trying to untangle it all, or perhaps it is just that we are becoming more mellow with age. Do you think, perhaps, that we are becoming more mellow with age, Alayne?"

Alayne had forgotten how quaint, how pathetically sagacious she was.

"Perhaps we are becoming more mellow," she agreed, soberly. "Let us hope so. . . . I cannot see us as free agents — just marionettes in a strange dance." Her mouth tightened in a bitter line.

The sunshine flickered over Pheasant. She was visualizing that macabre dance. "I can picture it," she said. "Renny leads. Then the uncles, the aunt. All of us dancing after — holding hands — bowing — looking over our shoulders. Wake last, with little horns, and a pipe, playing the tune." Her eyes glowed into Alayne's. "I've such an imagination, Alayne. I can make pictures by the hour. It's a great help to have an imagination. Piers has very little, and he says he wishes I hadn't so much. He thinks I'd be a better wife and mother if I hadn't so much. What do you think?"

"I think," said Alayne, "that you're an adorable child. They tell me that you're a mother, but I can't believe it."

"Wait till you see Mooey! He's simply wonderful. Not so fat as Meg's baby, but such a look in his eyes! It quite frightens me. . . . Still, I don't believe there's any truth in the saying that the good die young. I shouldn't look on old Mrs. Whiteoak — Gran — as specially good, should you? Not that I should insinuate that she's ever been immoral, — Heaven forbid that I should cast a stone at anyone, — but I think she's been cynical, rather than pious, all her long life, don't you?"

"I do. And I should not worry about Mooey dying young if I were you. . . . Tell me, Pheasant, who is this Miss Ware? Meg brought her along once when she came with some shortcake for Eden. She seems a strange sort of girl. English, isn't she?"

"Yes. She's a sort of companion to Meg, and she's nice to me. She's mad about men. I actually have to keep my eye on her when Piers is about." . . . She plucked nervously at the grass, and added, "Meg wants to marry her to Renny."

What were the birds in the treetops doing? What strange happening had taken place among the inhabitants of the burrows underground? Through all the woodland was an inexplicable stir. Alayne felt it run along the ground, up the tree trunks, along the branches into the leaves, which strangely began to flutter. Had a shadow fallen across the sky? What had the child been saying?

Meg, with her stupid stubbornness of purpose, had set out to marry Renny to this woman whom she had chosen —

for what purpose? She saw Renny, with his air of mettle. She saw Minny Ware, her narrow, strangely colored eyes laughing above her high cheek bones, her wide red mouth smiling, her thick white neck. She heard that full, rich voice, that effortless, ringing laugh.

She forced herself to speak steadily. "And Renny, does he take kindly to the idea?"

Pheasant frowned. "How can one tell about Renny? He thinks, 'This is a fine filly.' Well, he's a judge of good horseflesh! Last night all of us went over to Jalna. Minny played and sang. Renny seemed to hang about the piano a good deal. Everybody fell in love with her singing. The uncles couldn't keep their eyes off her, and, if you'll believe me, Gran actually pinched her on the thigh! She was a success. But Renny'll never marry her. He won't marry anyone. He's too aloof."

At these last words, Alayne felt a sharp pang, and withal a sickly sense of comfort, as of the sun shining dimly through mist.

As though aware of the presence of concentrated emotion, the horse ceased cropping, raised his head, and looked startled. Pheasant went to him and took the bridle in her hand. "He's getting a bit restless," she said. "And I must go. I promised not to be long away."

They walked along the path together, Pheasant leading the horse. In the potato field the old man was leaning on his hoe, gazing pensively down on the strong plants as though in deep thought.

"What are you dreaming about, Binns?" called out Pheasant.

"Bugs is here," he answered, and fell again into thought.

The horse's hoofs sounded indolently on the firm, moist path. Overhead a network of bird song was being woven, in intricate, ever-changing pattern.

"How idle the old man is!" said Alayne.

"There is a psychological reason for that." Pheasant assumed her sagacious look. "It's because the fields are scattered, far apart, among the woods. It makes a man lazy to see the woods all about him. Noah Binns isn't earning his salt to-day." Looking back over her shoulder, she called, "Wake up, Noah!"

"Bugs is here," answered the old man, not raising his head.

When they entered the pine wood they met Minny Ware, pushing a perambulator in which sat Meg's infant, Patience. Minny wore a very short dress of vivid green, and a wide, drooping hat, fit for a garden party.

"Oh, hallo," she exclaimed, with her London accent. "The fashionable world goes a-walking, eh?" She turned, tilting the perambulator on its back wheels and surveying Alayne from under the brim of her hat.

"How do you like the weather?" she asked. "Glorious, eh? I've never seen so much sunshine in all my life."

"At Fiddler's Hut the foliage is too dense. We don't get nearly enough sunshine." Alayne's voice was cold and distant. She could scarcely conceal her antagonism for this full-blooded girl. She felt that beside her she looked colorless, listless.

"How is your husband?" asked Minny Ware. "Better, I hope. It must be rotten to have anything wrong with one's lungs. I believe mine are made of India rubber." The full, effortless laugh gushed forth. She looked ready to burst into song. "Thank you," returned Alayne rigidly. "He is getting better."

Minny Ware went on blithely, "Mr. Whiteoak was suggesting to me that I go over one day and sing to him. He thought it might cheer him up. Do you think he'd like it?"

"I dare say he would." But there was no note of encouragement in her voice.

"I should go mad without music myself," said Minny. "I suppose you get wonderful music in New York."

"Very good." Alayne's lips scarcely moved. She looked straight ahead of her.

"I'll be going there myself one day. I'll have to get you to put me on to the ropes."

Alayne did not answer.

Patience was making bubbly noises and holding up her hands toward the horse.

Pheasant laughed. "She's a perfect Whiteoak! Look at her, she's asking to get into the saddle."

With a swift movement of her white bare arm, Minny lifted the child and swung it to the horse's back, and supported it there. "How's that, Ducky?" she gurgled. "Nice old gee-gee?" She clapped the horse on the flank.

"For God's sake, be careful, Minny!" cried Pheasant. "He's nervous." She patted him soothingly.

"Is he?" laughed Minny. "He seems a docile little beast. Doesn't she look a lamb on horseback?"

Patience indeed looked charming, the downy brown hair on her little head blown, her eyes bright with excitement. She clutched the rein in her tiny hands and cooed in ecstasy.

"She's a perfect Whiteoak," averred Pheasant again, with solemnity.

Alayne did not think she cared for babies, especially Meg's baby. Perhaps it was that she did not understand them, had had nothing to do with them in her life. For something to say she admired the grace of the horse.

"He's from the West," said Pheasant. "He's been badly used. We found welts all over him, when we had him clipped. He's been branded twice. I think that must hurt, though they say not." She glanced at her wrist watch. "I think you'd better put Patience in her pram. I must be getting home."

Minny Ware took the baby in her arms. She pressed

her full red mouth to its soft cheek. "Music and babies," she murmured, through the kiss. "They're the soul and body of life, aren't they? I couldn't get on without them. In England I always had a baby about, looking after it for one of my father's sick parishioners."

Alayne saw Minny as a symbolic figure — a song on her moist red lips, a baby against her swelling breast. Songs and babies — an endless procession from her vigorous body. With a fresh pang, she saw her as Renny's wife, singing to him, bearing his children. Minny was revealed to be a fit mate for one of the Whiteoaks. One whose formidable physical strength and spiritual acquiescence could be welded into their circle. She saw herself as a disparate being; an alloy that never could be merged; a bird brooding on a strange nest, crying to a mate to whom her voice would ever be alien.

She slipped her finger into the child's tender palm. The little hand closed about her finger and drew it toward the inquisitive mouth.

Pheasant sprang to the saddle with casual accustomedness. Her loose white shirt showed a tear, revealing a thin young shoulder. She chirruped. In an instant the horse, which had been walking indolently, with drooping head, became an object of force, of speed. Its thudding hoofs sent up a spray of pine needles. The dark curve of its flank swam beneath the rider. Horse and rider disappeared behind a bend in the path.

The two young women walked on together. When they reached the point where Alayne must turn into the narrow footpath leading to Fiddler's Hut, Minny Ware said, "Shall I come one day, then, and sing?"

"Yes, do," answered Alayne. After all, Eden might like her singing. He hadn't much to amuse him, shut in among the trees. He must get tired of reading and being read to.

She found him sitting on the ground beneath a cedar tree

that rose, a pointed spire, behind him. She asked, anxiously, "Do you think you should sit on the ground? I'm afraid it's quite damp."

He pushed back his hair petulantly. "I was so beastly hot. There seemed to be more air down here."

"Sometimes I wonder," she said, looking at him with a pucker on her forehead, "if you should have come here at all. It might have been better if you had gone to the mountains or one of your Northern lakes. Even now, if you would like to go, I would go with you."

"No." He turned his head away sulkily. "I'm here, and here I'll stay. If I get better, well and good. If I don't — it doesn't much matter." He stretched out his hand, plucked a wood lily, and tore off its petals one by one.

"That's nonsense," said Alayne, sharply. "It matters a great deal. Have I come all this way for something that does not matter?"

"It does not matter to you."

"Yes, it does."

"You don't love me."

She did not answer.

"Do you love me?" he insisted, childishly.

"No."

"Then in what way do I matter to you? For God's sake, don't say my writing matters to you!"

"But it does! And you do — for yourself. Can't you understand how my feeling for you may have changed into something quite different from love — yet something that makes me want to care for you, make you well again?"

She went to him, and stood looking down on him with compassion. She must take his mind from the subject of his illness.

"I met that Minny Ware just now. She offers to come over some day and sing to you. Will you like that?"

"No." he said. "I shan't like it. I don't want her coming here. She's stupid. She's silly. I can imagine the noise she would make — stupid and silly."

On an impulse she could not restrain, Alayne said, "Meg is scheming to marry her to Renny."

His face was almost comic in its surprise. "Marry her to Renny! But why? Why should she want to marry that girl to Renny?"

His eyes, with their veiled gaze, looked into Alayne's, but she saw that his swift mind was hot on the trail of Meg's devious motives. "That girl," he repeated. "That girl. Renny. I can't see it. But wait!" The light of malicious understanding crept into his eyes. "She's afraid — that's what it is — afraid! She'd marry him to an imbecile rather than have that happen."

"Have what happen? How mysterious you are!" But her heart was beginning to beat uncomfortably.

He narrowed his eyes to two slits and peered up at her. Sunlight and leaf shadows, playing across his face, gave it a sardonic grimace. "My poor girl, don't you see? Deceased husband's brother! Meggie thinks there is a fair chance of my dying, and she's afraid you'll marry Renny. She's going to fix him up with a nice plump songstress instead. I see it all. I'll engage she'll do it. Poor Reynard. That sly red-headed fox will be helpless. She'll bait the trap with such a sleek plump pullet. And she'll lead him to it and let him sniff — God, he hasn't a chance!"

She stood looking down at him, under the flickering leaf shadows. His face looked greenish-white. Her heart sank under a weight of apprehension. She felt that they were helpless, moved inexorably by soulless forces. They were being woven into the pattern of Jalna. They could no more extricate themselves than the strands caught in the loom. Vibrating on the heat, she felt the deep-toned hum of the loom through all her being.

He was regarding her with heartless interest. "You

mind?" he queried, mischievously. "You mind as much as that?"

"As much as what?" she asked angrily, hate for him rising in her.

"Your face! Oh, your face!" He changed the expression of his own visage into one of dolor. "It's like this!"

Tears of anger, of shame, stung her eyelids.

"And now you're going to cry! Is it for me? Or Renny? Or yourself? Tell me that, Alayne!"

She could not bear it. She turned and went swiftly toward the cottage. He remained a little, savoring the moment. He said to himself, "I am alive—I am alive! The worms are not gnawing me—yet!" He turned his hand about, examining the wrist that had been so round, so firm. "No mould—yet!" He felt his pulse. "Still kicking!"

He got up—it seemed to him that he felt stronger—and followed Alayne into the cottage.

The little Scotch maid was laying the table. Rags would be here any minute with their dinner. Through a crack of the door of Alayne's room he could see her standing before the little looking-glass, her hands raised to her hair. Her arms and shoulders were bare, and the graceful sweep of their lines brought to him a moment of remembered emotion. Not so long ago those arms had held him. Not so long ago delicate and extravagant caresses had passed between them. And how soon over! The remembrance of them as meaningless as a shadow from which the substance has fled.

But the shadow disturbed him. He wandered about the room, humming a tune.

Alayne came from her room. He looked at her with curiosity. His erotic proclivities, his sensitiveness, had given him the power of putting himself in the place of one of the opposite sex, of gauging with uncanny precision emotions alien to himself. So now, beneath her studied calm, he was conscious of the turbulence of the thoughts created by his words.

She knew something of this sexual clairvoyance, but had not fathomed its dark depths. If she had realized the full knowledge he had of her at that moment, it would have been impossible for her to remain under the same roof with him.

She had changed to a thinner dress of a pale green that seemed to have caught its color from the atmosphere, for, though it was noonday, the room lay in a green twilight because of the rich foliage that was reared between its windows and the sun.

"How nice and cool you look," he said, his eyes resting on her.

She did not answer, but went to the window and looked out between the leaves of the trumpet vine. She thought of Renny, and his promise to cut away some of these creeping things. Why did he not come? Was it callous absorption in his own doings that made him neglect his brother, or did he wish to avoid her? She told herself that she was angry at him. Vehemently she asked herself why it was that her love for him should so often be driven to put on the hair shirt of irritation.

It was July when at last he came. A dim day after a week of intense heat. When they looked out in the morning, their little woodland world had been shrouded in an unearthly fog. Thin films of vapor covered the abnormally large leaves, gathering at the tips and forming clear drops. The seething summer life of the wood was silent, apparently in a deep languor after the restless activity of the past week. There was no bird song; only from the little spring, hidden under its bower of honeysuckle, came a faint murmuring, like the very breath of the sleeping grass. As the morning drew on, the fog lifted slightly and the sun was distinguishable, but almost as wan, as somnolent, as the old moon.

Each day the path that led from the door became narrower, more closed in by the urgent growth of flowers and weeds. Few used it. The visits from those at the house had become rarer, either because of the heat and lassitude of the month of July or because they were absorbed by some new inter-weaving of the threads of the pattern that was being woven at Jalna. Eden and Alayne were left very much to themselves, spending drowsy days, cut off by his illness and her shrinking from meetings with the family.

She felt apathetic now. They might go on like this forever, passing their days in that green shade, their nights in fantastic dreams. She was startled, almost afraid, when, on this morning, she saw Renny's figure detach itself from the mist which lay thick under the orchard trees, and which had made his body appear to be but another trunk, and emerge into the path. She saw that he wore a loose white shirt and riding breeches, but he carried in one hand some implement and in the other a long trailing piece of vetch, covered with little purple flowers.

He moved with such energy along the path, seemed so unoppressed by the humid air and the fog, that she fancied it moved aside for him, was lightened and dispersed at his approach.

Eden had actually been trying to write. He raised his eyes from the pad that lay on his knee and, like Alayne, looked almost startled toward the door, as Renny stood there.

An expression of embarrassment made the elder brother's features appear less carved than usual. He knew that he had been remiss, even heartless, but he had, since their return, a feeling of shy avoidance toward them. Although Alayne had come only to nurse Eden, to will him back to health, and then again part from him, she seemed now to belong to him. She must not be sought out, brooded on, hungered for, with a pain as for something one could never possess. Renny had retired, with an almost animal fatalism, to wait for events to turn out as they would. He was watchful. His instincts were invincible. He was conscious of the presence of those two in the very air he breathed, in the earth beneath his feet. Yet the summer might have passed without his going to them, had not Augusta that morning drawn his attention to the unusual growth of the vine that covered the porch, to the great size of the geranium leaves in the beds, to the difficulty of keeping down weeds in the garden, and to the need for cutting the lawn. All these evidences of rank growth drove him to inspect the still ranker growth at Fiddler's Hut. Those two might almost be enclosed now by such a hedge as enclosed the Sleeping Palace.

As he passed through the orchard he had noticed a clump of purple vetch, wound and curled about itself into a great mound, beautiful, showing through the mist. He had detached a long strand of this and brought it to Alayne. It hung dangling from his hand, almost touching the doorsill. His spaniels appeared on either side of him.

Eden was pathetically glad to see him. His face broke into a boyish smile, and he exclaimed, " You, at last, Renny! I thought you'd forgotten me! How long do you think it is since you were here?"

"Weeks, I know. I'm ashamed. But I've been —"

"For God's sake, don't say you've been busy! What must it be like to be busy! I've forgotten!"

"Did you ever know?" Renny came in and stood beside him. The dogs entered also, with great dignity, their plumed legs and bellies dripping from the wet grass. "Shall I turn them out?" he asked Alayne. "I'm afraid they're making tracks on the floor."

"No, no!" objected Eden. "I like them. How fine they look! And you, too. Doesn't he, Alayne?" The dogs went to him and sniffed his thin hands.

"He looks as he always does," she anwered, coldly. Now that he stood before her, whom her whole being had ached to see, she felt antagonism for his vigor, his detachment. How little he cared for Eden, for her, for anyone but himself!

His brown eyes were on her face. He moved toward her, half shyly, and offered the vetch.

"I picked this," he said, "in the orchard. Funny stuff. A weed — but pretty. I thought you might like it."

"We have so few growing things about us," said Eden.

Alayne took the vetch. Their hands touched. Deliberately she had manœuvred so that they must touch. She must feel the torment of that contact. . . . The vine clung to her hands as she put it into a vase. When she drew them away it still clung, was dragged from the vase, its tendrils seeming to feel for her fingers.

She sat down by the window. Renny took a chair beside Eden. He looked him over critically. "You're getting stronger," he observed. "Drummond" — the family doctor — "says you're improving steadily. He thinks you'll be almost recovered by fall."

"Silly old blighter!" exclaimed Eden. "He hasn't seen me for weeks!"

"There is nothing to do but continue the treatment. You're getting the best of care."

"Everyone avoids me," continued Eden. "One would think I had the plague! The only one who comes is Wakefield, and I must send him away. If it weren't for Rags, I should not know what is going on in the house."

"What has he been telling you?" asked Renny, quickly.

"Nothing in particular, excepting that Piers and his wife are home again. I suppose Meggie couldn't put up with them any longer."

Both Renny and Alayne wondered how he could bring

himself to repeat that bit of news. There was surely no shame in him. She looked out of the window, and Renny down at his boots. After a silence he said, "Meggie comes to see you."

"Not often. There's some excuse for her. It's a long walk, and she's getting fat. Once she brought that Ware girl. I suppose you know her?" He regarded Renny with a mocking and slightly contemptuous smile.

"Yes. I gave her a lesson or two in riding."

"Ah. . . . How does she sit a horse?"

"Like a sack of meal."

Eden broke into laughter. "I wish Meggie could hear you!"

"Why?"

"Can't you guess?"

Alayne could not bear it. He must be stopped. "Eden," she interrupted, in a harsh, dry voice, "it is time for your eggnog. I must make it." She rose and, in passing him, gave him a look of impassioned appeal. Her lips moved, forming the word, "Don't."

When the brothers were left alone, Renny demanded, "What do you mean?"

"Oh, nothing! Only that she seems to be a pet of Meggie's. But honestly, it's a deadly thing to be cooped up with one person all the time. That one face. That one voice. Those eyes. Even though you care a great deal for the person — feel all kinds of gratitude, as I do. Picture yourself here, between these four walls, day and night, with only Alayne!" With bright malice his eyes sought Renny's. They seemed to say, "You may be well, — sound as one of your own horses, — but look how I can torment you! What would you give to have what I have — and which is nothing to me!"

Renny said, imperturbably, "Well, you're improving, at any rate. That's the main thing."

If he were touched on the quick, he hid the pain well—red-headed devil!

Alayne brought the eggnog. Eden stirred it, gazing contemplatively into the yellow liquid. The two watched him, weak, unscrupulous, holding them, as it were, in the net of his mockery. There was a vibration in the air about them as if all three were antagonists, each of the other.

Renny began to talk, in a desultory fashion. News of his stables, news of the family. The uncles and Aunt Augusta stuck to the house pretty much because of the heat. Gran was well. Word had just come that Finch had passed his examinations. He was a happy boy. They'd make something of him yet!

At last he rose. "Now what about this greenery? I've shears and a saw here, and if you'll show me what you want cut down—"

"You go with him, Alayne," said Eden. "It's so beastly foggy out. I'll stop here and see if I can do anything with this."

Renny glanced at the pad on Eden's knee. What was written looked like poetry. Good Lord, was he at it again! Renny had hoped that his illness might have cured him of this other disability. But no, while Eden lived he would make verse, and trouble.

Outside, the fog still enveloped the woodland, delicate and somnolent. The pale moonlike sun scarcely illumined it. The drip of moisture from leaves mingled with the muted murmur of the spring.

"It's rather a strange morning," said Alayne, "to have chosen for cutting things. It will be hard to know what the effect will be." She thought, "We are alone, shut in by the fog. We might be the only two on earth."

"Yes," he agreed, in an equally matter-of-fact tone. "It's a queer morning. The branches seem to spring out from nowhere. However, that won't prevent their being lopped off." He thought, "Her face is like a white flower. I wonder what she would say if I were to kiss her. The little hollow of her throat would be the place."

She looked about her vaguely. What was it she wanted him to do? The path, yes. "This path," she said, "should be widened. We get so wet."

He followed it with his eyes. Safer than looking at her. "I'd need a scythe for that. I'll send one of the men around this afternoon and he'll cut down all that growth. Now I'll thin out these long branches."

Before long, boughs, heavy with their summer growth, lay all about. And all about green mounds of low growing things: dogwood, with its waxen berries; elderberry, its fruit just going red; sumach, the still green plumes of which were miniature trees in themselves; aconite, still in flower; and long graceful trailers of the wild grape. And wherever he strode, in his heavy boots, tender growths lay crushed. His dogs ran here and there, chasing into cover the squirrels and rabbits she had tried to tame. Symbolic of him, she thought, in one of those waves of antagonism which would ride close upon the waves of her love.

"No more," she exclaimed, at last. "I'm afraid to think how it will all look when the sun comes out."

"Much better," he assured her. He stopped and lighted a cigarette. His expression became one of gravity. "I must tell you the real reason why the uncles and aunt have not been to see you. You're sure Rags has said nothing to Eden?"

"Nothing." She was startled. She feared some strange development of the situation.

He went on. "We've been worried" — he knitted his brow and inhaled the smoke deeply — "about my grandmother."

His grandmother! Always that imposing, sinister, deplorable old figurehead of the Jalna battleship!

"Yes? Is she not so well?"

He returned, irritably, "She's quite well. Perfectly well. But—she's given us all a bad fright, and now she's behaving in—well, a very worrying fashion. I thought Eden had better not be told."

Alayne stared, mystified beyond words.

"Pretended she was dying. Staged a regular deathbed scene. Good-byes and all. It was awful. You couldn't believe how well she did it."

Alayne could believe anything of old Adeline.

"Tell me about it."

"Don't repeat any of this to Eden."

"Certainly I will not."

"It gave us a terrible fright. I had come in rather late. About one o'clock, I think. I had just put on the light in my bedroom. Wakefield was awake. He said he couldn't sleep because moonlight was coming into the room and the cupboard door stood ajar. It worried him. He wanted me to look into the cupboard, to make sure there was nothing there. I did, to please him. Just as I stuck my head into it a loud rapping came from below. Gran beating on the floor with her stick. The kid squeaked, he was so nervous. I left him and ran down to her room. Aunt Augusta called out, 'Are you going to Mamma, Renny? I don't see how she can be hungry, at this hour!' Well, in her room there was the night light, of course. I could see her sitting up in bed, clutching her throat. She said, 'Renny, I'm dying. Fetch the others.' You can imagine my feelings."

"Yes. It was terrifying."

"Rather. I asked her where she felt the worst, and she only gave a sort of gurgle. Then she got out, 'My children —I want to tell them good-bye. Every one. Bring them.' I got some brandy from the dining room and managed to give her a swallow of that. I propped her up on the pillows. The parrot kept biting at me, as if he didn't want anyone near her. Then I went to the telephone, and Drummond promised to be over immediately. Then I ran upstairs. Got them all up. Finch from the attic. Little Wake. God, they were a white-looking lot!"

"And she was only pretending?"

"She had us all going. We crowded about the bed. She put her arms around each one in turn. I thought, 'That's a pretty strong hug.' And she'd something to say to each. A kind of message. Tears were running down Uncle Ernest's face. Wake was sobbing. She had us all going." The red of his face deepened, as he recalled the scene.

"And then?"

"Then the doctor came. Pulled down her eyelid. Felt her pulse. He said, 'You're not dying!' And she said, 'I feel better now. I'd like something to eat.' The next morning she told us that she'd been lying awake and she'd got an idea she'd like to know just how badly we'd feel if we thought she was dying."

Alayne said, through tight lips, "I hope she was satisfied."

"She must have been. We were a sorry sight. . . . And if you'd seen us trailing back to bed! Hair on end. Night-clothes. We were figures of fun, I can tell you!"

"It was abominably cruel of her."

"Perhaps. But a good one on us. And, I guess, a great satisfaction to her."

"You were sufficiently harrowed!"

"If only you could have seen us!"

She smiled in rather bitter amusement. "I think I begin to understand you."

"Me?"

"You—as a family."

"We're easy to understand—when you know us."

"But we are friends—aren't we?"

"Are we? I don't believe I can manage that."

"Don't you think of me, then, in a friendly way?"

"Me? Friendly? Good God, Alayne! And you call Gran tormenting!"

"Well — about her. You spoke of some odd behavior." She was a fool to get on dangerous ground with him. Better talk about old Adeline.

He went on, frowning, "The trouble is this. Ever since that night she's always wanting to see her lawyer. Has him out every few days. It must be a plague for him. And it makes things tense at Jalna. I don't worry about her will. But I know the uncles are worrying. And one can't help wondering. I suppose you know that she's going to leave everything she has in a lump sum to one of us. I suppose everyone is really wondering just how sorrowful he looked that night. Rather wishes he had the chance to do it over again. You remember I told you that Uncle Ernest cried. I believe Uncle Nick thinks that Uncle Ernest feels rather cocky about that. Wishes he could have dug up a tear or two." He gave one of his sudden staccato laughs.

"If it comes to that," she said, ironically, "Wakefield cried too."

"And Mooey! Did I tell you he was down, too? The old dear missed him. She looked around and said, 'Somebody's not here! It's the baby. My great-grandson. Fetch the baby down!' Pheasant flew upstairs and brought Mooey. If you'll believe me, the little devil simply howled. And now Piers and Pheasant are hopeful about him!" This time his laughter reached Eden's ears.

He appeared in the doorway of the cottage. The fog was really dispersing. He stood, after all this lopping of branches, in a bath of vague sunlight.

"What's the joke? You might tell it to me."

Alayne called back, "It isn't really a joke. Just something Renny finds amusing. How did you get on?"

"I've done it!"

"Done what?" asked Renny.

Alayne answered, "Finished what he was writing. Didn't you notice that he was writing?"

"Oh, yes. A poem. I suppose that's a good sign." He forced his features into a grin of approbation.

"Splendid." As they drew near to the young poet she said, "I'm so glad, Eden. Is it good?"

"I'll read it. No, I'll wait till Renny's gone. I say, what a shambles you've made of the place!"

Renny looked disappointed. "When it's been raked over it will look better. Shall I trim this Virginia creeper now?"

"No. I like a little privacy."

"But you've said a hundred times—" cried Alayne.

"My good girl, never remind a person of temperament what he's said a hundred times."

"But it's dreadful to have that vine clinging round you!"

"No, it isn't. It makes me feel like a sturdy oak."

Renny examined the vine critically. "I think he's right. It would be a pity to touch it. It's always looked just like that."

"But," Alayne protested, "everything in the cottage is damp!"

The brothers agreed that the vine had nothing to do with the dampness.

A figure was approaching along the path. It was Minny Ware, in a vivid blue dress. She carried a bowl of jelly mounded with whipped cream.

"I've had such a time to find my way," she said. "It's the first time I've been in this direction by myself. I hadn't realized how large the estate is. Mrs. Vaughan sent this."

"Not so large as it once was," observed Renny, gloomily.

Alayne took the jelly and wondered what she would do with Miss Ware. Eden seemed rather pleased with her.

"Come in," he said, "and let's look at you. We'll pretend you're a bit of blue sky."

They went into the cottage. Minny Ware seated herself in a wicker chair by the open door. Eden's remark had made her radiant. Renny sat on a bench, holding the collars of his dogs. Alayne disappeared into the kitchen, carrying the bowl of jelly. She did not want to be in the room with the girl.

Minny Ware, elated at being left alone with the two men, exclaimed, " *Is n't* this atmosphere the most depressing!"

" You don't look depressed," said Eden, his eyes absorbing the freshness of her cheeks and lips, the gayety of her gown.

" It 's weather to make a man virtuous," said Renny.

This remark evoked a gush of laughter from Minny, effortless as an oriole's song.

Eden continued to be pleased with her. He said, " I wonder if you are too depressed to sing to me. You promised to, you know."

Minny Ware thought she could n't, was sure she would disgrace herself by trying to sing on such a morning as this, but after some persuading she threw back her head, clasped her hands before her, in the attitude of a good child, and sang three little English songs. Alayne remained in the kitchen. Covertly she watched the three through a crack of the door. She saw Renny's intent gaze on the throbbing white throat, the full bosom. She saw Eden's appraising eyes also fixed on the girl, who appeared to have forgotten their presence. The first song was of a country lover and his lass, with a touch of Devon dialect in the refrain. The second song told of little birds in springtime innocently building their nest. The third — yes, the third was a lullaby. This she softly crooned, her ripe lips parted in a smile. She remembered the presence of the brothers and, as she finished, her eyes sought theirs. She seemed timidly to ask for approbation.

The last long-drawn sweet note had been too much for

one of the spaniels. He raised his muzzle and gave vent to a deep howl.

"Did he hate it so?" asked Minny Ware, looking askance at the dog.

"Down, Merlin," said Renny. "He's like his master. He's not musical."

Her face fell. "I thought the other night you enjoyed it."

"I enjoyed this, too. But you sang more passionate things the other night. I suppose something else in me was appealed to then."

"Oh, I love passionate music!" She spoke with abandon. "I only sang these simple little things to please your brother, as he's not well."

"Thank you," said Eden with gravity. "That was nice of you."

"Oh, now you're laughing at me!" she cried, and filled the room with her laughter.

Alayne came in and sat down on a stiff-backed grandfather's chair. She felt icy before this exuberance. Only with the two spaniels, held by their collars, did she feel any sense of companionship in the room.

When Eden and she were alone, she said, "If your sister thinks she will bring *that* to pass, she is mistaken. He hates her. I could see it in his eyes."

"How clever you are!" he cried. "You can read him like a book, can't you?" His glance was full of merriment.

XVII
NIGHT MEETINGS

WHILE Eden and Alayne were struggling for his renewed health at Fiddler's Hut, the family group were living in a morbid complicity of emotions, the two strongest of these being fear and jealousy. Since old Adeline had, as Renny put it, staged her own deathbed scene, they apprehended, one and all, that this sudden interest of hers in her final act was but the foreshadow of the spectre itself. The thought of it hung over them like a pall. The idea that she should pass from their midst was unbelievable. . . . Captain Philip Whiteoak had died; young Philip and his two wives had died; several infant Whiteoaks had passed away in that house; but that the involved pattern Adeline had woven in and out of those rooms, round about their lives, could be shattered was incredible. Shivers of foreboding ran through this pattern, such as might run through the intricate web of a spider when the old spinner himself, curled in the very centre, is shaken by some dire convulsion.

If she was aware of any change in the atmosphere, she made no sign. She seemed in even better health than usual, and ate with increasing gusto, in preparation, it seemed to them, for the chill fast approaching. Neither did they talk to each other of what was in their minds, but of other things they talked even more than usual. Augusta, Nicholas, and Ernest sought out each other more frequently in their rooms. They discussed their pets, Nip, Sasha, and her kitten, their amazing sagacity. They grouped themselves, with chirrups and tweets, about the cage of Augusta's canary. Forced cheerfulness sapped their energy. They were like people watching each other for symptoms of some disease which it was necessary, for their peace of mind, to ignore. Each one discovered, with grim satisfaction, the symptoms he sought in the others, and believed he had successfully hidden his own.

Augusta had little hope of gain for herself. She was passionately desirous that Ernest should be the heir. Nicholas thought that they plotted against him, and he feared Renny more than the two of them together. And Augusta and Ernest feared Renny and thought he plotted against them. And Renny believed that all his three elders were plotting against him. Even Mooey, Piers's infant son, became an object of suspicion. Had not his great-grandmother demanded that Mooey be brought to her? Was she not always pushing bits of biscuit and peppermints into his hand? And she was always exclaiming, "Bring my great-grandson to me! I want to kiss him — quick."

Piers did not hope greatly for himself, though he felt a thrill of exultation when his grandmother would cry, "Boy, you're the image of my Philip! Back and thighs just like his. And those bright blue eyes of his, too!" But both Piers and Pheasant thought it truly remarkable that on her deathbed — even if it were a pretense — Grandmother should have called for Mooey. Frightfully old people were often drawn to frightfully young ones. They had things in common — thinking mostly of food and sleep — being near the beginning and the end, and all that sort of thing.

Mooey laughed every time he saw his great-grandmother. To certain of the family his laughter sounded sinister.

Wakefield, with the shrewdness of a child living among grown-up folk, was conscious of the air of dread and suspicion that had crept into every corner of the house, even to the basement, where the Wragges discussed the situation from every angle. They quarreled bitterly over it, for Wragge was of the opinion that the peppery and taciturn master of Jalna should inherit, while Mrs. Wragge, whose bias in favor of primogeniture was strong, thought that Nicholas should be his mother's heir. Nicholas too was in the habit of giving her little presents of money, when she "did" his room.

Wakefield soon discovered that his elders were troubled when he hung about his grandmother's neck and whispered in her ear. This gave him an agreeable sense of power. He began to lavish delicate attentions on her. He carried little nosegays to her, and handfuls of wild strawberries, which brought out a rash on her grand Court nose. He would steal up behind her and press his hands over her eyes, demanding, in a deep voice, "Who is it, my grandmother?" —invariably being vociferously kissed for it.

One day he announced that he was making a special prayer for her each night.

"Ha!" she cried. "Praying for me, eh? What is it that you say?"

"It depends," he replied, his palms together between his bare knees, "on what sort of day you've had. If your appetite's been not so good, I pray that it may be better. If it's been good, I pray for lemon tart next day. If you've been worked up into a rage, I pray that you may have more consideration shown you to-morrow."

"The darling!" exclaimed his grandmother. "Oh, the precious darling! Praying for his old Gran!" And she made a habit from that day of asking him each morning what his prayer for her had been the night before.

She took to giving him quite valuable things. One stormy afternoon when he was bored, she opened the door of the Indian cabinet, containing the ivory, ebony, jade, and lapis lazuli curios which he always longed to play with, but must not touch, and filled his two hands with things which she said he was to keep. Her sons and daughter were genuinely alarmed

"Mamma!" chided Augusta. "You must be crazy!"

"Mind your business, Lady Bunkley!" retorted old Adeline. "I'll give away my bed if I choose, or my head. I tell you, this child is the apple of my eye."

Nicholas and Ernest emerged from cover and conferred with each other in the open.

"It's really very worrying, Nick," said Ernest.

"The child is literally *worming* his way into Mamma's *inmost* affections. Dear knows how it will end!"

"Renny must be spoken to," said Nicholas. He spoke to Renny.

"It's very bad for my mother, to know that she is being constantly prayed for. I must ask you to put a stop to it."

"The hell I will!" rejoined Renny. "It can't hurt her to know that Wake is praying for her. It tickles her to death."

"That's exactly the danger," put in Ernest, lugubriously. "At her age it might tickle her to death. She's too old to be prayed for."

"Ha, ha, ha!" shouted Renny.

Nicholas and Ernest came to the conclusion that Meg and Renny were putting the child up to it. Wakefield's face continued to be a mask of piety, but there was a secret little smile on his lips.

Finch, scarcely noticed by the family once their rejoicing over his return had subsided, was only an observer of this drama. Tension was relaxed for him, not increased. The strain of his examinations was over. He had passed. Not gloriously, — he had come near the tail end of the candidates, — but passed, nevertheless. It was as though an aching tooth were drawn. He could look at his dog-eared textbooks without a sinking at the heart.

It was beautiful to him to spend these hot summer days in the country. He imagined with horror what they must be in New York. Yet there were moments when he remembered with a strange regret the lights in the harbor at night, the interesting foreign faces one met in the streets, the kindness that had been shown him at Cory and Parsons. He would wonder vaguely if he had missed something by coming home with Uncle Ernest, something he could never have again — a chance to get on in the world, to be respected instead of sneered at or just tolerated. But this was home, and here was music. Twice a week he went to the city and had music lessons. Two hours daily he was allowed to practise on the old square piano in the drawing-room. It was not enough, and he would have made up the deficiency by some extra practice on the piano at Vaughanlands but for an unsurmountable shyness of Minny Ware. Her presence in that house took all the virtue out of his playing. Her laughter frightened him. He felt that she regarded him as a curiosity. And there was something in her oddly colored eyes, slanting above her high cheek bones, that disturbed him to the depths of his being. Her eyes seemed to invite him while her mouth laughed at him. . . . No, he could not practise in the house where Minny was.

On the occasions when she came to Jalna he felt certain that she was making up to Renny, and he felt certain that Meg approved. Unbearable if those two were to marry. He couldn't stand that laughing, slant-eyed girl in the house. If only Renny and Alayne might be married! He was deeply conscious of their love for each other. He would have liked to talk with Alayne these days, of life and art, and the meaning of both. In Alayne he felt a stability, a clarity, which he craved for himself, but he could not go to see her because of Eden.

One day, when he was sent to the rectory on a message, Mr. Fennel questioned him about his music. When Finch told him that he was dissatisfied with the amount of practising he got, the rector offered to let him practise on the church organ, and gave him a key so that he might let

himself into the church at any time. This was the beginning
of a new happiness. Miss Pink, the organist, finding him
rather baffled by the organ, offered to help him for a while
each week after choir practice. Soon he wrung from the
old organ music so passionate that Miss Pink quite tingled
when she heard it, and wondered if it were quite right to
draw such sounds from the pipes of a church organ.

Finch went more and more frequently to the church to
play. At first he went only in the daytime, then was cap-
tivated by the mystery of playing in the twilight, and at
last, wandering along the road one night in the moonlight,
he was seized by the desire to play in the church by night.
He climbed the long flight of steps to the churchyard, passed
through the glimmering gravestones and in at the portal.
Outside it was sultry. Warm dust had lain thick on the road,
but in here there was a coolness as of death and the austere
presence of God. Finch had never been alone in the church
at night before, and he felt the Presence there in the moonlight as he never felt it when people sat in the pews and Mr.
Fennel moved about in the chancel.

Finch's belief in God seemed to be something that would
not die. In spite of the boyish blasphemies of his school-
mates, or the half-amused tolerance of young men like
Arthur Leigh, or the cynical references to Christ as a
curiosity which he had heard among the staff in the publishing house, his belief in Him remained secure, terrible,
and strangely sweet, somewhere deep within him. Music
had freed him from the terror of God that had troubled
his boyhood, but there in the church he felt in his every
fibre the power of the Almighty Presence.

On that first night he played little. He sat with his long
hands on the keys, searching his heart, trying to find out,
if he could, what was in it of good and evil. Now its
depths seemed less turgid than usual. He looked into it
and saw a white light glimmering. God living in him.

Not to be beaten down. The white light, pointed like a flame, quivered, drew upward. Sank, writhed as though in agony. He brooded over his heart, trying to discover its secret.

Had this white flame anything to do with the pale shape that sometimes, in moments of exaltation, emerged from his breast and floated for a space, face down, close beside him, before it was dissolved into the darkness? That pale shape he knew was himself, his innermost essence, drawn from his body by some magnetic force. Did the shape — himself — emerge from the body in search of something without which it would never rest? If the white flame he saw in his heart was God in him, was this white shape perhaps himself in God?

In this dark tangle of thought one thing was clear to him: he was being searched for, as he was searching. Not by God, whose eye already held him; not by Christ, who had one awful night shown him His pierced hands; but by that Third Person. It was He who strove to speak in the white flame. It was He who, at last, after Finch had sat long before the organ in the moonlight, touched the boy's fingers on the keys; and the night was full of music. The moonlight sang through the dim aisles. Through the stained glass a lyric light swept singing across the chancel. The organ, though Finch's fingers did not move, filled its every gilded pipe with divine melody.

The white flame in his heart struggled, writhed in agony no more. It filled his heart to overflowing. . . .

Afterward he wandered for a long while up and down the empty aisles. He touched the walls with his hands. His hands were full of magic. He raised his eyes to the memorial windows, in memory of his grandfather, his father, and the mother of Meg and Renny. There was none in memory of his own mother. Sometime, he thought, he would place one there. The central figure would be that of a youth, with a distraught face and a breast open to expose his heart, in which a pale light would shine. No one but himself would understand the significance of the window, and he would come, a mature man, and sit beneath it, remembering this night.

He went out into the churchyard and stood in the moonlight. Below, on the road, he saw two men whose figures he knew. One was Chalk, the blacksmith, reeling slightly, the other was old Noah Binns, a laborer at Jalna. He descended the steps and followed them at a little distance. Chalk talked without ceasing in an argumentative tone, until he turned in waveringly at his own door next the smithy. Finch caught up to Binns and walked abreast of him, where the blacksmith had been. Binns plodded on, not seeming to notice the change of companion. Finch wondered greatly what were the thoughts of an old man like Binns. Had he ever experienced anything such as he had just experienced in the church? He could play the fiddle a little. Had he ever felt music as Finch had felt it to-night? Finch kept staring into his face, and at last the old man turned and looked into his. He showed no astonishment, only a flicker of pleasure that one had come to whom he could impart information. He clumped along several paces in silence, choosing carefully the words in which the portentous news should be phrased. Then he said, "Bugs is here."

"Eh, what?" said Finch, startled.

"Tatie bugs," said Binns. "They've come."

"Ho!" said Finch. "What's the cure?"

"Paris green. Ain't no other."

They clumped on through the soft, moonlit dust.

At last they came to Binns's cottage on the outskirts of Evandale. Binns opened his gate. He stood looking up at the full moon, then he turned to Finch: "There's a curse on it all," he said.

Finch shivered. "Do you think so?" he asked.

"Yes," returned old Binns. "Every year bugs comes. And more bugs. It's a curse on us for our sins." He went into his cottage.

Finch could not bear to go indoors. He kept to the road that led past Jalna, through the village of Weddel's, down to the lake. This was four miles from the church. A rush of cool air rose from the lake. It was stirring softly, as though in its sleep. It glittered in the moonlight like a great monster, clothed in bright armor. As it slept, white foam curled from its lips along the shore. Finch undressed and ran out into the water. He plunged, he swam, he floated on its dark, bright surface, his body white as foam. It seemed that he could not sufficiently surrender himself to it. He wanted to be one with it, to make it one with him. He felt that if he could completely surrender himself to the lake he would be able to understand life. He rested on its glimmering darkness, as on the rise and fall of a deep bosom. He closed his eyes tightly, and saw the unnamable color of life. It swam in intermingling circles, wave upon wave, before his closed eyes. He felt inexpressibly powerful and pure. He felt completely empty of thought. The flame within him had consumed all thought, and left only instinct, the instinct to become one with the lake. . . .

His eyelids lift. He stares into the glowing face of the moon, fascinated. The lake speaks to him. It speaks with his own voice, for it is he. He hears the words rise from its dark bosom, floating on the golden air. "My beloved spake, and said unto me, Rise up, my love, my fair one, and come away. For, lo, the winter is past, the rain is over and gone; The flowers appear on the earth; the time of the singing of birds is come, and the voice of the turtle is heard in our land. . . . Arise, my love, my fair one, and come away. O my dove, that art in the clefts of the rock, in the secret places of the stairs, let me see thy countenance, let me hear thy voice; for sweet is thy voice, and thy countenance is comely."

Suddenly he turns over, swims strongly, plunging, wrestling with the lake. It is no longer a part of him, but an antagonist. At last he is tired out, and, wading to the shore, he lies down on the smooth sand and watches the moon sink behind the tree tops.

This was the first of many nights. More and more often he slipped out of the house and went to the church to play. The church, which on week days seemed to belong to no one, on Sundays to the Whiteoak family, at night belonged to him. He would play for hours, afterward wandering about the fields or along the roads, and, on warm nights, going to the lake. At night he was fearless and free. In the daytime, depressed by lack of sleep and nervous excitement, he had an air of slinking, of avoiding the others. Renny, noticing the shadows under his eyes, told Piers to give him some work on the farm land to set him up. For a terrible week he was subject to Piers, to his robust ragging, while his back ached, his palms blistered, and he felt ready to drop from fatigue. No music those nights. A dead-beat stumbling to bed. Finch could see that the farm laborers, the stablemen, were vastly amused by his weakness, his stupidity. They would let him struggle with a task too heavy for him, without an offer of assistance, while they tumbled over each other to wait on Piers. He could not understand it. Things came to a head at the end of the week in a quarrel. Finch was kicked. He retaliated with a blow from his bony fist on Piers's jaw. The next day Finch had to stay in bed, and Renny ordered that he should be allowed to go his way in peace. No use to trouble about him. He was a problem that could not be solved.

The next night he resumed his playing in the church.

Returning home past midnight, he let himself in at the side door of the house and was just passing his grandmother's room when her voice called, "Who is there? Come here, please."

Finch hesitated. He had a mind to steal up the stairs without answering. He did not want her to know that he had been out till that hour. She might get to watching him. Questions might be asked. Still, she might really need someone. Worst of all, she might be about to stage another deathbed scene. That would be appalling.

As he hesitated, she called again, sharply, "Who's there? Come quickly, please!"

Finch opened the door of her room and put his head inside. By the night light he could see her propped up on her two pillows, her nightcap shadowing her eyes, her old mouth sunken. But her expression was inquiring rather than anxious; her hands were clasped with resignation on the coverlet.

He felt suddenly tender toward her. He asked, "Want a drink, Grannie, dear? Anything I can do?"

"Ha, it's you, is it, Finch? Well, well, you don't often visit me at this hour. You don't often visit me at all. I like boys about me. Come and sit you down. I want to be talked to."

He came to the bedside and looked down at her. She took his hand and pulled him close, and closer till she could kiss him.

"Ha!" she said. "Nice smooth young cheek! Now sit here on the bed and be a nice boy. You are a nice boy, aren't you?"

Finch gave his sheepish grin. "I'm afraid not, Gran."

"Not nice! Who says so?"

"I don't think anyone has ever called me a nice boy, Gran."

"I do. I do. I call you a very nice boy. If anybody says you're not a nice boy he'll hear from me. I won't have it. I say you're a very nice boy. You're a pretty boy, too in this light, with your lock hanging over your forehead and your eyes bright. You've got an underfed, aye, a starved look. But you've got the Court nose, and that's something to go on. Life will never down you altogether when you've got that nose. You're not afraid of life, are you?" She peered up at him, with so understanding a look in her deep old eyes that Finch was startled into saying, "Yes, I am. I'm awfully afraid of it."

She reared her head from the pillow. "Afraid of life! What nonsense. A Court afraid of life! I won't have it. You mustn't be afraid of life. Take it by the horns. Take it by the tail. Grasp it where the hair is short. Make it afraid of you. That's the way I did. Do you think I'd have been here talking to you this night — if I'd been afraid of life? Look at this nose of mine. These eyes. Do they look afraid of life? And my mouth — when my teeth are in — it's not afraid either!"

He sat on the side of the bed, stroking her hand. "You're a wonderful woman, Gran. You're twice the man I'll ever be."

"Don't say that. Give yourself time. Mother's milk hardly dry on your lips yet. . . . How's that music? I hear you thumping away at it. Coming on?"

"Pretty well, Gran." He stopped stroking her hand and held it tightly in both of his. "There's nothing I like quite so much."

Her arched eyebrows went up. "Really! Well, well. I expect you get that from your poor mother. She was always tra-la-la-ing about the house."

He closed his eyes, picturing his mother singing about that house. He said, in a low voice, "I wish she had lived, Gran."

Her fingers tightened on his. "No, no. Don't say that. She wasn't fit to cope with life. She was one of those people who are always better dead — if you know what I mean."

"Yes, I know," he answered, and added to himself, "Like me!"

What was the boy thinking? She peered up at him. "Don't get ideas in your head," she said, sternly.

"I'm no good, Gran."

Her voice became harsh, but her eyes were kind. "None of that now! What have I been telling you? Piers has been knocking you around. I heard about it."

He reddened. "I landed him a good one in the face."

"You did, eh? Good for you! H'm. . . . Boys fighting. Young animals. My brothers used to fight, I can tell you. In County Meath. Take their jackets off and at it! My father used to pull their hair for it. Ha!"

Her eyes closed, her hand relaxed. She fell into a doze.

Finch looked at her lying there. So near to death. A year or two at the most, surely. And how full of courage she was! Courage and a good digestion — she'd always had both. And in what good stead they had stood her! Even in her sleep she was impressive — not pathetic, lying there, toothless, with her nightcap over one eye. He tried to absorb some of her courage into himself. He fancied it might be done. Here alone with her at night in her own stronghold.

A gust came down the chimney and the night light flickered. Boney, perched on the head of the bed, stirred, and made a clucking noise in his sleep. Finch thought it would be best for him to go, while she slept. He was withdrawing his hand, but her fingers closed on it. She opened her eyes.

"Ah," she muttered, "I was thinking. I didn't doze. Don't tell me I dozed. I like a spell of thinking. It sets me straight."

"Yes, Gran, I know. But it's not good for you to lose so much sleep. You'll be tired to-morrow."

"Not a bit of it. If I'm tired, I'll stop here and rest. It's the family that makes me tired, fussing over me. Fuss, fuss, fuss, ever since that night." She looked at him quizzically. "You remember the night I nearly died?"

He nodded. He hoped she wasn't going to try anything like that again.

She saw anxiety in his eyes and said, "Don't worry. I shan't do that again. It might be boy and wolf. They mightn't come running when I'd really need them. But they fuss, Finch, because I have Patton out. I like to see my lawyer. I keep thinking up little bequests for old friends — Miss Pink — the Lacey girls — even old Hickson and other folk in the village." A shrewd gleam came into her eyes. "I suppose you're not worrying about who I'm going to leave my money to, eh?"

"God, no!"

"Don't curse! Too much God and hell and bloody about this house. I won't have it."

"All right, Gran."

"I'm going to give you a present," she said.

"Oh no, Gran, please don't!" he exclaimed, alarmed.

"Why not, I'd like to know?"

"They'd all say I'd been sucking up to you."

"Let me hear them! Send anyone that says that to me."

"Well, please let it be something small, that I can hide."

"Hide my present! I won't have it! Stick it up! Put it in full view! Invite the family to come and look at it! If anyone says you're sucking up send him to me. I'll take the crimp out of him!"

"Very well, Gran," agreed Finch, resignedly.

Her old eyes roved about the room. "I'll tell you what I'm going to give you. I'm going to give you that porcelain figure of Kuan Yin — Chinese goddess. Very good. Good for you to have. She's not afraid of life.

Lets it pass over her. You're no fighter. You're musical. Better let it pass over you. But don't let it frighten you. . . . Fetch her over here, and mind you don't drop her!"

He had seen the porcelain figure all his life, standing on the mantelpiece, amid a strange medley of bowls, vases, and boxes — Eastern and English, ancient and Victorian. It was so crowded on the mantelpiece that he felt reasonably hopeful that the little goddess would not be missed by the family. He lifted her gently from the spot where she had stood for more than seventy years, and carried her to his grandmother. The old hands stretched out toward the delicate figure, closed round it eagerly.

"If you could see the place," she said, "where I got this! Another life. Another life. Most of the English out there were down on the East, down on the Eastern religions — but I wasn't. They understand a lot that we don't. Western religions are flibbertigibbet beside Eastern religions. Don't tell that I said that! Here, take her" — she put the goddess into his hands — "something for you to remember me by."

"As though I could ever forget you, Gran!"

She smiled mockingly, and for a flash he saw, toothless and all as she was, Eden's smile on her face. "Well, time will tell. . . . Look in her face! What do you see?"

He knitted his brow, his face close to the porcelain oval of the statuette's. "Something very deep and calm. . . . I — I can't quite make it out."

"Well, well, take it along. You'll understand some day. Good night, child, I'm tired. . . . Wait — do you often prowl about like this?"

"Sometimes."

"What do you do?"

"You won't tell on me, Gran?"

"Come, come, I'm over a hundred. Even a woman can learn to keep her mouth shut in that time!"

He said, almost in a whisper, "I go to the church, and play the organ."

She showed no surprise. "And you're not afraid alone there at night, with all the dead folk outside?"

"No."

"Ah, you're a queer boy! Music, always music with you. Well, a church is an interesting place once you get the parson and the people out of it. Real music can get in then, and a real God! Nothing flibbertigibbet about religion then."

She was very tired; her voice had become a mumble; but she made a last effort and said, "I like your coming in like this. My best sleep is over by midnight — just catnaps after that. Night's very long. I want you, every time you've been at the church, to come for a chat afterward. Does me good. Come right in — I'll be awake." And as she said the word "awake" she fell asleep.

And so these strange night meetings began. Night after night, week after week, Finch crept out of the house, had his hours of happiness, of faunlike freedom, and crept in again. He never failed to go to her room, and always she was awake, waiting for him. Her eyes, under their rust-red brows, fixed on him eagerly, as he glided in and drew the door to behind him. He looked forward to the meetings as much as she. Bizarre assignations they were, between the centenarian and a boy of nineteen. Like secret lovers, they avoided each other in the presence of the family, fearing that some intimate look, some secret smile, might betray their intimacy. Finch came to know her, to understand the depths of her, sometimes mordant, sometimes touchingly tender, as he was sure no other member of the household understood her. She no longer seemed old to him, but ageless, like the Chinese porcelain goddess she had given him. Sometimes, in the beam of the night light, propped in her richly painted bed, she looked beautiful to him, a rugged reclining statue carved by some sculptor who expressed in it his dreams of an indomitable soul.

One night in August, she startled him by asking abruptly, "Well, boy, whom shall I leave my money to?"

"Oh, don't ask me that, Gran! That's for you to say."

"I know. But, just supposing you were in my place, whom would you leave it to? Remember, it's going in one lump sum to somebody. I won't have my bit of money cut up like a cake! Right or wrong, my mind's fixed on that. Now then, Finch, who's to get it, eh?"

"I say — I can't possibly —"

"Nonsense! Do as I tell you. Name the one you think is most deserving. Don't pretend you haven't thought about it. I won't have it."

"Well," he answered with sudden determination and even a look of severity on his lips, "I should say, since you ask me, that there's only one person who really deserves to have it!"

"Yes? Which one?"

"Renny!"

"Renny, eh? That's because he's your favorite."

"Not at all. I was putting myself in your place, as you told me to."

"Then because he's head of the house?"

"No, not that. If you can't see, I can't tell you."

"Of course you can. Why?"

"Very well. You'll be annoyed with me, though."

"No, I shan't. Out with it!"

"Well, Renny's always hard up. He's brought up the lot of us. He's had Uncle Nick and Uncle Ernie living here for years. Ever since I can remember. You've always made your home with him. He likes having you. It wouldn't be like home to him if you weren't here. And he likes having the uncles and Aunt Augusta. But, just the same, he's at his wit's end sometimes to know where to dig up money enough to pay wages, and butcher bills, and the vet, and all that."

She was regarding him steadfastly. "You can be plain-spoken," she said, "when you like. You've got a good forthright way with you, too. I can't see eye to eye with you on every point, but I'm glad to know what you think. And I'm not angry with you." She began to talk of something else.

She did not bring up the subject again, but talked to him of her past, recalling the days when she and her Philip were young together, and even went back to the days of her girlhood in County Meath. Finch learned to pour out to her his thoughts, as he had never done to anyone before, and probably never would again with such unrestraint. When at last he would steal up to his room, something of her would be still with him in the figure of Kuan Yin, standing on his desk.

XVIII
DEATH OF A CENTENARIAN

OLD Adeline was being dressed for tea by Augusta. That is, she was having her hair tidied, her best cap with the purple ribbon rosettes put on, and her box of rings displayed before her. She had felt a little tired when she waked from her afternoon nap, so she had had Augusta put a peppermint drop into her mouth, and she mumbled this as she looked over her rings. She chose them with especial care, selecting those of brilliant contrasting stones, for the rector was to be present, and she knew that he disapproved of such a show of jewels on such ancient hands, or indeed on any hands.

Augusta stood patiently holding the box, looking down her long nose at her mother's still longer one curved in pleasurable speculation. Adeline chose a ring — a fine ruby, set round with smaller ones. She was a long time finding the finger on which she wore it, and putting it on. The box trembled slightly in Augusta's hand. Her mother bent forward, fumbled, discovered her emerald ring, and put it on. Again she bent forward, dribbling a little from the peppermint on to the velvet lining of the box.

"Mamma," said Augusta, "must you do that?"

"Do what?"

"Dribble on the velvet."

"I'm not dribbling. Let me be." But she fumbled for her handkerchief and wiped her lips.

She put on six rings, a cameo bracelet, and a brooch containing her Philip's hair. She turned then to the mirror, adjusted her cap, and scrutinized her face with one eyebrow cocked.

"You look nice and bright this afternoon, Mamma," said Augusta.

The old lady shot an upward glance at her. "I wish I could say the same for you," she returned.

Augusta drew back her head with an offended air and surveyed her own reflection. Really, Mamma was very short with one! It took a lot of patience. . . .

Adeline stretched out her ringed hand and took the velvet-framed photograph of her Philip from the dresser. She looked at it for some moments, kissed it, and set it in its place.

"What a handsome man Papa was!" said Augusta, and surreptitiously wiped the picture with her handkerchief.

"He was. Put the picture down."

"Indeed, all our men are good-looking!"

"Aye, we're a shapely lot. I'm ready. Fetch Nick and Ernest."

Her sons were soon at her side, Nicholas walking less heavily than usual because his gout was not troubling him. They almost lifted her from her chair. She took an arm of each and said over her shoulder to Augusta, "Bring the bird along! Poor Boney, he's dull to-day."

The little procession moved along the hall so slowly that it seemed to Augusta, carrying the bird on his perch, that they were only marking time. But they were really moving, and at last had shuffled their way to where the light fell full upon them through the colored glass window.

"Rest here a bit," said their mother. "I'm tired." She was tall, but looked a short woman between her sons, she was so bent.

She glanced up at the window. "I like to see the light coming through there," she observed. "It's very pretty."

They were in the drawing-room, and she was established in her own chair, with Boney on his perch beside her. Mr. Fennel rose, but he gave her time to recover her breath before coming forward to take her hand and inquire after her health.

"I'm quite well," she said. "Don't know what it is to have any pain, except a little wind on the stomach. But Boney's dull. He hasn't spoken a word for weeks. D' ye think he's getting old?"

Mr. Fennel replied, guardedly, "Well, he may be getting a little old."

Nicholas said, "He's moulting. He drops his feathers all over the place."

She asked Mr. Fennel about a number of his parishioners, but she had difficulty in remembering their names. Augusta, who had begun to pour tea, said in an undertone to Ernest, "I seem to notice a difference in Mamma. Her memory . . . and what a long time she was coming down the hall! Do you notice anything?"

Ernest looked toward his mother anxiously. "She did seem to lean heavily. Perhaps a little more than usual. But she ate a very good dinner. A very good dinner indeed."

Finch had come up behind them. He overheard the words, and thought he knew the reason why his grandmother showed a certain languor in the daytime. It would be strange if she did not, he thought, remembering her vigor, her clear-headedness of the night before. He had a guilty feeling that he was perhaps sapping her vitality by his midnight visits. . . . He came to his aunt's side.

Augusta handed him a cup of tea. "Take this to my mother," she said, "and then come back for the crumpets and honey."

Crumpets and honey! Finch's mouth watered. He wondered if he should ever get over this feeling of being ravenous. And yet he was so thin! He felt discouraged about himself. He wished his aunt would not send him about with tea. He invariably slopped it.

Old Adeline watched him with pursed mouth as he drew

an occasional table to her side and set her tea on it. Her greed equalled his own. Her hands, trembling a little, poured what tea had slopped into the saucer back into the cup, raised the cup to her lips, and drank gustily. The rings flashed on her shapely hands. Mr. Fennel marked them with disapproval.

His voice came muffled through his curly brown beard. " Well, Finch, and how goes the practising? "

" Very well, thank you, sir," mumbled Finch.

" The other night I was in my garden quite late. About eleven o'clock. I was surprised to hear the organ. You are quite welcome to use it in the daytime, you know." Gentle reproof was in his tone.

"I rather like the practising at night, sir, if you don't mind."

His eyes moved from Mr. Fennel's beard to his grandmother's face. They exchanged a look of deep complicity like two conspirators. Her gaze was clear. The tea had revived her.

She said, setting down the empty cup, "I like the boy to practise at night. Night's the time for music — for love. . . . Afternoon's the time for tea — sociability. . . . Morning's the time for — er — tea. Another cup, Finch. Is there nothing to eat? "

Pheasant appeared with tea for Mr. Fennel, and Piers with the crumpets and honey. He was in white flannels.

" Ah," observed the rector, " it is nice to see you looking cool, Piers! You looked pretty hot the last time I saw you."

"Yes, that was a hot spell. Things are easing off now. Late August, you know. The crops are in. Small fruit over. Apples not begun."

" But there is always the stock, eh? "

"Yes, always the stock. I don't get much time for loafing. But this is Pheasant's birthday, and I 'm celebrating it by a day off and a clean suit."

"Her birthday, is it?" said Mr. Fennel. "I wish I had known! I would have brought some offering, if only a nosegay."

Grandmother blinked rapidly; she smacked the honey on her lips. "Pheasant's birthday, eh? Why wasn't I told? Why was it kept from me? I like birthdays. I'd have given her a present." She turned toward Meg, Maurice, and Renny, who had just come into the room. "Did you know, my dears, that we're having a birthday party? It's Pheasant's birthday, and we're all dressed up for it. Look at the rector! Look at Piers! Look at me! Aren't we trig?" She was all alive. She grinned at them, with the malicious and flashing grin for which the Courts had been famous.

Meg approached her and dropped a kiss on her forehead. "I had heard nothing of any birthday," she said, coldly.

"Maurice," exclaimed Grandmother, "haven't you brought a birthday present for your daughter? Are you going to neglect old Baby just because new Baby's on the scene?"

Maurice slouched forward somewhat sheepishly. "I must do something about it," he said.

Pheasant's little face was scarlet with embarrassment. She surveyed the family with the startled, timid gaze of a young wild thing.

"She's blessed," said Piers glumly, "for she expects nothing."

Grandmother absorbed this saying. "H'm," she said. She swallowed a piece of crumpet, and then added, "It's the unexpected that happens. She's going to get a present. And from me!"

A chill of apprehension fell on the company.

Mr. Fennel, feeling it, observed, "There's nothing so pleasant, I think, as an unexpected present." But even to himself his words sounded lame. He could utter no ghostly comfort that would calm these troubled waters.

Old Adeline finished her crumpet with dispatch, drank another cup of tea. Then she demanded, "How old are you?"

Despite Renny's encouraging look, the word came in a whisper. "Twenty — "

"Twenty, eh? Sweet and twenty! I was twenty once — ha! 'Come and kiss me, sweet and twenty! Youth's a stuff will not' — what was it? My old memory's gone. Come here, my dear!"

Pheasant went to her, trembling.

Adeline spread out her hands, palms down, and examined her rings. Meg, with unaccustomed agility, sprang to her side. "Granny, Granny," she breathed, "don't do anything rash! A bit of lace. A little money to buy herself something pretty. But not— not — " She caught her grandmother's hands in hers and drew the jeweled fingers against her own plump breast.

"Mamma," said Ernest, "this excitement is very bad for you."

"Bring the backgammon board," said Nicholas. "She likes a game of backgammon after tea."

"I've not finished my tea," rapped out his mother. "I want cake. Not that white wishy-washy cake. Fruit cake."

Never was fruit cake so swiftly, so passionately, produced. She selected a piece, laid it on her plate, and, as though there had been no interruption, again spread out her hands, palms downward.

She shot a glance at Meg, kneeling by her side.

"Get up, Meggie," she said, brusquely but not unkindly. "You've nothing to be humble about." But Meg still knelt, her hands to her breast, her eyes jealously guarding the rings.

With a decisive movement, Adeline removed from the

third finger of her right hand the ring of glowing rubies.
She took the girl's thin brown hand in hers and put it on
her middle finger. She looked up into her face, smiling.
"Give you color, my dear. Give you heart. Nothing like
a ruby. . . . I'll try some of that pale cake now."

Pheasant stood transfixed, reverently holding the bril-
liantly decorated hand in the hand that wore only her wedding ring. Her eyes were starry.

"Oh," she half-whispered, "how lovely! What beauties!
Oh, you darling Gran!"

Piers was at her side, sturdy, defiant, all aglow.

"Splendid!" exclaimed Renny. "Let me see how it
looks on your little paw!"

But Wakefield intervened, took her hand, and fluttered
his long lashes, examining the stones. He said, judicially,
"You've got a fine ring there, my girl. I hope you take
care of it."

Meg still knelt, her eyes damp, her hands clenched. "It's
unjust," she gasped. "It's unfair to me and my child!"

Renny put his hands under her arms and heaved her to
her feet. He whispered vehemently into her ear, "Don't
make a show of yourself, Meggie! Remember, Mr. Fennel's
here." Inwardly he thanked God for the presence of Mr.
Fennel. It had certainly saved them from a terrible scene.
She relapsed against his shoulder.

The rector himself was wishing that the tea party had
been more placid. He observed, pulling at his beard, "I
always think that an unexpected present is the most delightful." He could not resist adding, "And jewels are so
beautiful on young hands."

Adeline appeared not to have heard. She finished her
cake, eating the moist crumbs from her saucer with a spoon.
But after a little she extended her bereft right hand toward
him, with a flourish, and said, "You don't think they suit
my old hands, eh?"

He knew how to mollify her.

"I have never seen hands," he said, "better shaped for the wearing of rings."

She clasped them on her stomach and surveyed the scene before her. There was trouble in the air, and she had brewed it. She had, directly or indirectly, made almost every being in the room. The pattern of the room was centrifugal, and she was the arch designer, the absolute centre. She felt complacent, firm, and strong. She fixed her eyes on Renny, and gave him a waggish nod. She knew he did not mind young Pheasant's having the ruby. He grinned back at her. He had Wakefield on his knee.

Adeline kept on wagging her head at Renny, but now with reproof. "Too old to be nursed," she said.

"I know," replied Renny, "but he will clamber over me." He pushed Wakefield from his knee.

"Poor darling! He looks like a young robin pushed from the nest! Tell me, did you pray for me last night?"

"Yes, my grandmother."

She looked triumphantly about her. "He never misses a night! And what did you pray?"

Wakefield drew up his eyebrows. "I prayed — let's see — I prayed" — his eyes lit on Pheasant's hand — "that you would give a present to-day, and — get one!"

She struck the arm of her chair with her palm. "Ha! Listen to that! A present! Now who would give me a present? No, no, I must do all the giving. Till the last. Then you can make me a present of a fine funeral. Ha!"

Nicholas growled to Ernest, "I shall have to cuff that young rascal before he'll stop this mischief of praying."

"It's very depressing for Mamma," said Ernest, gloomily. "It must be stopped."

"A game of backgammon will divert her."

Ernest looked dubious. "The last time I played with her she wasn't very clear about it."

"Never mind. She must be diverted. She's in the mood to give presents all round. I don't know what has come over her."

He found the backgammon board, and the velvet bag containing the dice and dice boxes. He said to Wakefield, hovering near, "Ask your Grandmamma and the parson if they will play backgammon. Place the small table between them. I shall cuff you if you persist in this praying business."

"Yes, Uncle Nick."

The little boy flew away, held whispered conversations, flew back.

"Uncle Nick!"

"Yes."

"I've placed the table, and the parson, and Gran. They said they were nothing loath."

Finch said, "He made that last up. They didn't put it in those fool words."

"You are odious, Finch," retorted Wake. He adored his Aunt Augusta's vocabulary and had no self-consciousness in employing it.

The opponents faced each other. Bearded, untidy Mr. Fennel; gorgeous, ancient Adeline.

"I'm black," she said.

Very well, he was white. The men were placed on the tables. The dice were thrown.

"Deuce!" from the parson.

"Trey!" from Grandmother.

They made their moves. The dice rattled. The emeralds on her left hand winked.

"Doublets!"

"Quatre!" She pronounced it "cater."

The dice were shaken; the players pondered; the men were moved.

"Deuce!"

" Trey ! "

" Cinq ! "

" Ace ! "

The game proceeded. Her head was as clear as ever it had been. Her eyes were bright. She fascinated Finch. He stood behind Mr. Fennel's chair watching her. Sometimes their eyes met, and always there was that flash between them, that complicity of conspirators. "Afraid of life!" her eyes said. "A Court afraid? Watch me!"

He watched her. He could not look away. Across the chasm of more than eighty years their souls met, touched fingers, touched lips.

One by one she got her men home. One by one she took them from the board. She had won the first game!

" A hit ! " she cried, striking her hands together. " A hit ! "

Two groups had formed in the room, away from the players and Finch, who stood behind the rector, and Wakefield perched on the arm of his grandmother's chair. One of these groups consisted of Meg, Nicholas, Ernest, and Augusta, who in undertones discussed what portent the gift of the ring might have. The other group was composed of Piers, Pheasant, Maurice, and Renny, who talked rather loudly, in an effort to appear unconscious that there was trouble in the air. As Grandmother cried, " A hit ! " the faces of the members of both groups turned toward her, and they clapped their hands, applauding her.

" Well played, my grandmother ! " cried Wakefield, patting her on the back.

Finch's eyes sought hers, found them, held them. She felt suddenly tired. She was very tired, but very happy.

" You have me badly beaten," said Mr. Fennel, stroking his beard.

" Ah, yes. I'm in good form to-day," she mumbled. " Very good form — to-night."

Boney shuffled on his perch, shook himself, gaped. Two

bright feathers were loosened, and sank slowly to the floor.

Mr. Fennel stared at him.

"He does n't talk now, eh?"

"No," she answered, craning her neck so as to see the bird. "He does n't talk at all. Poor Boney! Poor old Boney! Does n't talk at all. Does n't say curse words. Does n't say love words. Silent as the grave, hey, Boney?"

"Shall we have another game?" asked Mr. Fennel.

The two groups had resumed their preoccupations. Renny's laugh broke out sharply.

"Another game? Yes, I'd like another game. I'm white!"

Mr. Fennel and Wakefield exchanged glances.

"But, Gran," cried Wakefield, "you were black before!"

"Black! Not a bit of it, I'm white."

Mr. Fennel changed the men, giving her the white ones.

The men were placed. The dice shaken. The game proceeded.

"Deuce!"

"Cinq!"

"The Doublet!"

But her head was no longer clear. She fumbled for her men, and could not have got through the game had not Wakefield, leaning on her shoulder, helped her with the play.

She was beaten, but she did not know it.

"A double game!" she said, triumphantly. "A double game! Gammon!"

The rector smiled indulgently.

Finch felt himself sinking beneath a cloud.

"But, my grandmother," cried Wakefield, "you're beaten! Don't you know when you're beaten?"

"Me beaten? Not a bit of it. I won't have it! I've won." She was staring straight ahead of her into Finch's eyes. "Gammon!"

Mr. Fennel began gathering up the men.

"Another game?" he asked. "You may make it back-gammon, this time."

She did not answer.

Wakefield nudged her shoulder. "Another game, Gran?"

"I'm afraid she's a little tired," said Mr. Fennel.

But she was still smiling, looking straight into Finch's eyes. Her eyes were saying to him, "A Court afraid? A Court afraid of death? Gammon!"

Again Boney shook himself, and another feather fluttered to the floor.

Nicholas had risen to his feet, and was looking across the room. Suddenly he shouted, "Mother!"

They were all on their feet, except Wakefield, who still hung on her shoulder, realizing nothing.

Her head sank.

Finch watched them as they gathered about her, raising her head, holding smelling salts to her long nose, forcing brandy between her blanched lips, wringing their hands, being frightened, half-demented. He had seen her spirit, staunch and stubborn, leave the body. He knew it was futile to try to recall it.

Boney watched the scene with one detached yellow eye, apparently unmoved, but when they carried her to the sofa and laid her on it, he left his perch with a distracted tumble of wings and fluttered on to her prostrate body, screaming, "Nick! Nick! Nick!" It was the first time in years he had ever been known to utter a word of English.

He was with difficulty captured and taken to her bedroom, where he took his position on the head of the bed and re-lapsed into stoical silence.

Piers telephoned for the doctor. Meg was sobbing in Augusta's arms. Ernest sat beside the table, his head buried in his arms across the backgammon board. Pheasant had flown upstairs to her bedroom to bedew the ruby ring with tears. Nicholas drew a chair to his mother's side and sat with his shoulders bent, staring blankly into her face. The rector dropped his chin into his beard and murmured a short prayer over the body, stretched out so straight that the feet, in black slippers, projected over the end of the sofa. Again she looked a tall woman.

Mr. Fennel was about to close the eyes. The heavy lids resisted. Renny caught his arm.

"Don't close her eyes! I won't believe she's dead! She can't have died like that!"

He put his hand inside her tea gown and felt her heart. It was still. He brought a mirror and held it before her nostrils. Its bright surface was undimmed. But he would not have her eyes closed.

Soon Dr. Drummond came and pronounced her dead, and himself closed her eyelids. He was an old man, and had brought all the younger Whiteoaks, from Meg down, into the world.

Ernest rose then and came to her, trembling. He stroked her face, and kissed it, sobbing, "Mamma . . . Mamma." . . . But Nicholas sat motionless as a statue.

Renny could not stay in that house. He would go to Fiddler's Hut and tell Eden and Alayne what had happened. He flung out through the side door into the grassy yard where the old brick oven stood. A waddling procession of ducks cocked their roguish eyes at him; Mrs. Wragge and the kitchenmaid peered after him with curiosity from a basement window. Galloping colts in the paddock came whimpering to the fence as he hurried past. Red and white cows in the pasture, heavy-uddered, turned their tolerant gaze after him. He entered the orchard. The days were already shortening. The red sun showed between the black trunks of the trees. He noticed that all colors were intensified into a sombre brightness. Little rosy mushrooms were rosetted here and there in the lush grass. The orchard fence was smothered in goldenrod.

Between the orchard and the "old orchard" lay a field of potatoes. Old Binns was digging them and laying them in shallow ridges on the black loam. In that long day he had done perhaps a half-day's work. He leaned on his spade and shouted, "Hi! Mr. Whiteoak! Hi!"

Renny stopped.

"Yes?"

"What do you s'pose be here now?"

"What?"

"Blight. Blight be here."

Renny threw up his hand.

"Put down that spade!" he shouted. "No more work here to-day!" He strode on.

No spade should stir the surface of the land she had loved. That land must lie quiet, mourning for her to-day, and to-morrow, and the next day.

Old Binns watched Renny disappear into the glowing density of the old orchard. He was aghast. Never in his life before had he had such an order. He must be going to lose his job! He thrust his spade deep into the soil and turned up three potatoes. Feverishly he thrust and grubbed for the potatoes. Never before had he worked with such vehemence. He kept muttering angrily to himself, "Blight he here, anyhow. Dang him!"

The old orchard, unpruned since a decade, displayed a fantastic exuberance of foliage. The branches of the apple trees, which later would be weighted with ripe fruit, never to be garnered, swept to the ground. Among them grew clumps of green hazel and sumach, with its rose-red plumes. Creepers of various kinds had caught at the lowest boughs and clambered up them, as though striving to drag the trees themselves to the earth. A discarded mowing machine was hidden beneath a rank growth of wild grapevine, its presence never to be guessed. As Renny moved along the path, wild rabbits bounded from his way, and heavy moths sometimes blundered against his face. As he neared the cottage he heard the spring talking secretly among the grasses.

Doors and windows of the cottage stood open, but there was no sound of voices. He went to the front door and looked in. Alayne was writing at a table, and Eden lay on the sofa, a cigarette between his lips and a book drooping from his hand. His face and body had filled out, his cheeks were brown, but Alayne looked pale and more slender. They had not heard Renny come up, and to him the room and its occupants, in the intense sunset glow, appeared unreal as in a tableau. It seemed unreal, fantastic, that they should be sitting unmoved, aware of nothing.

He made some incoherent sound, and, as though a spell had been broken, they both looked up. The pallor of Alayne's cheeks, which had seemed intensified by the reddish light, appeared now to be touched into flame. Eden smiled, and his smile froze. He started up.

"Renny! What's the matter?"

Alayne too rose.

He tried to speak to them, but no words would come. He stood silent, leaning against the doorpost, his face contorted into a forbidding grimace.

The two stood petrified, until Eden got out, "For Christ's sake, Renny, speak to us! Tell us what's wrong?"

He looked at them, filled with a strange antagonism for them, and then said, harshly, "She's dead. . . . Gran. . . . I thought I should let you know."

Avoiding their eyes, his face still contorted, he turned hastily down the path and disappeared into the pine woods.

XIX

JALNA IN MOURNING

THERE she lies, the old woman, in her coffin; wreaths, sprays, crosses of sweet flowers, all about her. She has been bathed, embalmed, dressed in her best black velvet dress. Her hands are crossed on her breast, but they have left her only her wedding ring, worn to a mere thread of gold. If one could see inside the ring, one might decipher the words "Adeline, Philip, 1848." She wears her best lace cap that has long been put by in a lavender-scented box awaiting this occasion. On a silver plate on the coffin is engraved the date of her birth, her death, her name, including her Christian names — Adeline Honora Bridget. All has been done for her that it is possible to do. All is arranged, perfected for her burial. She has been on this earth a long time, but now she is to be put into it for an infinitely longer period.

There is an ineffable air of dignity, of pomp, about her. She looks like an ancient empress, with that faintly contemptuous smile on her lips, that carven nose. She might have lived as the centre of court intrigues, instead of having passed three quarters of her life in this backwater, with only her family to lord it over. Ireland and India, two countries the names of which begin with "I," have left their mark on her. Her life has been lived, dominated by "I."

At her head and her feet stand tall silver candelabra bearing lighted candles. Finch placed them there, when he stole downstairs to his last meeting with her, after the rest were all in bed. His gaunt young face was that of a mystic as he glided about her, touching each waxen column into flame.

Augusta, in the morning, ordered them to be taken away,

exclaiming against such popish practices, but Nicholas said, "Let them be. Pomp suits her."

By ones, twos, and threes her descendants came to mourn over their progenitress. Nicholas remained by her side all day, refusing food, his leonine head disheveled, one end of his gray moustache caught in his teeth. Ernest wandered in and out, tall and elegant in his black frock coat. He escorted visitors to the casket, drawing their attention to the chiseled features, the beautiful expression of his Mamma. He whispered the word a great many times to himself those days, for soon she would be gone, and he would have no Mamma. All the sarcastic things she had ever said to him were obliterated from his mind, and only the times when she had been kind remained. He remembered how she had been dependent on him for certain things, and tears ran down his cheeks.

It was not so with Augusta. The contemptuous smile on her mother's lips seemed to be especially directed toward her. Every now and again some humorous jibe from those lips would crop up in her mind. She kept remembering the last of them: how, when she had been dressing her for the last tea, she had remarked, "You look nice and bright this afternoon, Mamma," and her mother had returned, "I wish I could say the same for you!"

Augusta recalled happenings of her childhood. They were clearer to her than the events of the past year. She remembered the time of her marriage, when on the eve of her wedding day her mother had said to her, "I don't think I need give you any advice, my dear. Buckley's not much past your shoulder. You needn't be afraid of him!" Mamma could remember his name quite easily then; but once he had come into the title, it had always been Bunkley or Bilgeley or Bunkum!

Augusta reproached herself for recalling such little frictions at a time like this. Her sorrow was real, but her

memory was very uncomfortable. . . . She led Wakefield
to the coffin. It was his first sight of death. She said, in
impressive tones, "Look at her long, Wakefield. Try to
impress her face on your mind. She was a very wonderful
woman."

The little boy was awestruck. He felt dizzy from the
heavy scent of flowers. He gazed long at the calm face —
at the shapely old hands folded in resignation.

"But, Aunt," he exclaimed, his clear treble sounding in-
congruous in that room, "she looks *so* nice! Isn't it a *pity*
to bury her?"

Her old friends — there were not many left — agreed that
they had never seen a corpse look so natural. Down in the
basement Rags declared to his wife and the kitchenmaid,
and a little gathering of workers from the stables, the farm,
and Vaughanlands, "Bless me, if the old lady don't look
more natural than 'erself!"

What of Renny? Like one of the horses among which
he spent so much of his time, his feeling toward death was
one of almost animal alarm. He drew away, shivering,
from the sinister presence that shadowed the house.

After one look at the face of the dead woman, he left the
room and did not return to it until the hour of the funeral.
Death, as he had seen it during the War, had not affected
him greatly. He had been overseas when his father and his
stepmother had died. This experience was to him terrifying.
He left the arrangements for the funeral to Augusta, Ernest,
and Piers. In one matter only he took an interest, the choosing of the pallbearers. These, he decided, must be the four
eldest grandsons. Eden expostulated, he was not strong
enough yet to undertake such a thing. Alayne thought, and
said with some vehemence, that it would be wrong, impossible for him to tax his strength so. But Renny was adamant.
Eden looked to him almost as well as ever; he should and
must take his place among his brothers to bear the body of

their grandmother to her grave. He went to Fiddler's Hut, and the three sat about the table talking excitedly, his red hair in an unkempt crest, his lean narrow face flushed, the sharp lines of his face set against opposition. Eden gave in.

The day of the funeral broke infinitely lovely. There had been a heavy dew, which lay like a sparkling veil across the lawn. It was a still day, except for the chatter of small birds in the evergreens along the drive. There was a tender aloofness about the day, as though summer hesitated, drawing a deep breath before departing. Old Adeline had loved such a day as this. If she had been living, she would have assuredly taken one of her little walks as far as the gate, supported by her sons. But instead she was to take her last ride. During her lifetime she had consistently refused to get into a motor car, but she had asked to have a motor hearse at her funeral. "I like to think," she had said, "that I'll have a ride behind a motor instead of a horse before I'm laid away. No one can say that I was old-fashioned."

Wakefield was awed to see all the family, even to Finch, in deep black. He would have liked a black suit himself, but he had to be content with the black band that Meggie stitched on the sleeve of his gray Norfolk jacket. He felt very conscious of this badge of mourning, very dignified and aloof. He greatly wished that he were big enough to be one of the pallbearers.

The funeral cortège was almost ready to leave the door. The four who were to carry the coffin stood shoulder to shoulder, Eden and Piers near enough to hear each other breathing! Renny had had trouble with Piers before he could persuade him to be, even for so short a time, near Eden. But he had overridden them both. There they were beside him, and he was head of the clan! Short prayers were said by Mr. Fennel. The pallbearers raised the coffin to their shoulders.

The hearse moved slowly from the door, followed by a

car in which rode the four brothers. This in turn was followed by one in which were Augusta, Nicholas, Ernest, and
Mr. Fennel. Next the Vaughans and Wakefield. Pheasant
had made an excuse of some baby ailment of Mooey's to
remain at home. She peeped through a curtain above and
saw Eden's fair head shining among his brothers', and she
made little moaning sounds, remembering her short and
sultry passion for him. It had nearly wrecked her life and
Piers's, but tragedy had been averted — she was safe, safe
with Piers and her baby!

Alayne also had stayed behind. She had gone for one
long look at that aloof old face, which indeed had always
looked kindly on her. Shrewd as old Adeline had been,
Alayne felt sure that she had never guessed that she had
ceased to love Eden, any more than she could be convinced
that she was not an American heiress.

Alayne had left the house in a mood of deep depression.
She had felt, not the aversion of a sensitive animal from the
presence of death, as Renny had, but a profound shrinking
from the mourning of the inanimate Jalna. It had seemed
to her that the solid walls had drawn nearer to enclose that
body, that the ceiling had lowered to shelter it, that the very
doors had narrowed to delay its passage from thence. . . .
Leaving, she had looked back at it from the edge of the lawn,
and it seemed to her that the whole house had shrunken into
itself with grief.

After the chief mourners there followed the friends of
the family, and many people from the surrounding villages
and countryside in motors and old-fashioned buggies, a
long procession. Here was the funeral of one whom the
oldest of them could remember, from their earliest days, as
a married woman. A landmark was gone. Not a tree, not
the steeple of a church, but a living, dominating being!
Many of the mourners had not seen her for years, but her
tall form, her rust-red hair, her piercing brown eyes, were

impressed on their memories forever. Every now and again some story of her temper or her idiosyncrasies would float about. To-day it was remembered how until the last year she had never — or almost never — missed a morning service in the gray stone church built by Captain Whiteoak, driving there in her shabby phaeton behind the two stout bays. And, though she might have been close-fisted enough in some ways, she had each Christmas given a present to every child in her own village of Evandale, built on what was once part of the estate of Jalna. In her last years she had depended on Ernest to buy these presents for her. Next Christmas the children would miss that.

So, though she had been almost as immovable as a tree, her reputation grew, year by year, as girth is added to a tree. Those who had come to pay respect to her remains felt that they were taking part in a momentous and climactic occasion.

To stout Hodge, who had driven her phaeton for the past thirty years, her death had been a tragedy. The meaning of his life was gone. No longer would he groom the bays — each nearing thirty — to satin sleekness, on a Sunday morning, polishing their jangling harness to a bright finish. No longer wash down the creaking wheels of the phaeton or put on his tight coachman's coat with the velvet collar. His dignity was gone. He was nothing but an aging stableman.

He had come to Nicholas with tears on his cheeks, and said, " I suppose, sir, I 'll never need to bring out the old phaeton again. . . . It does seem hard."

And Nicholas had growled, " My brother and I will use the phaeton for a long time yet, I hope." Nicholas would have preferred to go to church in a motor car, now that the widow's veil of his mother would no longer dominate the phaeton, but one could not hurt Hodge. He was the one old servant left. The others came and went, and had no old-fashioned pride in their work.

Renny, in the car with his brothers, was thinking of the phaeton. He was remembering how his grandmother delighted in having her horses possess the middle of the road, thereby preventing him or any other motorist from passing. But him in particular. Yes, she had liked to get the best of him. God, but she was game!

He wished she might have seen the number who had turned out to do her honor. It seemed too bad that she could never know. And the flowers! A car filled with them. He liked that wreath of roses and carnations from the Hunt Club. . . . He looked his brothers over. It was good to see Eden fit again. A summer at Jalna was bound to do it. Good, too, to see him and Piers riding in the same car. It had taken some will power to bring that about. He wondered if it were possible to bridge that chasm. He was afraid not. Wives brought into the family had a way of messing things up. A good thing probably that he had never married. His mind dwelt, for one aching moment, on the thought of Alayne. The funeral procession became a phantom procession. She was in his arms. He closed his eyes, giving himself up to the desire that tore at his heart.

When he opened them again, they rested on Finch, who was sitting between Piers and him, his long legs very much in the way. Finch had been in a detached, almost hallucinated state of mind since his grandmother's death, but now, of all times, with his face exposed to the gaze of Renny and Piers, he had broken down. He was giving way to spasmodic sobs; even the frequent wiping of his eyes on a large folded handkerchief could not keep them dry. Poor young devil, Renny thought, and he put his hand on the boy's bony knee, at which he cried the more. He felt that Piers was regarding him with contempt, but Piers did not see him. His eyes were fixed on Eden's back, before him on the front seat with Wright.

The funeral procession, phantom momentarily to Renny, was nothing but phantom to Piers. The one reality was Eden, sitting before him. Eden well again. Eden ready for more mischief. Eden, whom he longed to beat with his fists into insensibility. Except for that one glimpse of him by the paddock, he had not seen him since that summer day two years ago on the night of which young Finch had come white-faced to tell him that Eden and Pheasant were in the birch wood together. If only Eden had not got away that night! If only he could have had it out with him! Now, he supposed, they would never have it out.

Eden was conscious of Piers's eyes on the back of his head. He would have given a good deal to know what was in Piers's mind. Melodramatic, blood-and-thunder thoughts, no doubt. He smiled a little, as he imagined them, but he shifted uneasily in his seat. He pitied himself, rather. Here he was, on his first outing of the entire summer, and it a funeral! Had been forced, dragged into it, and into a proximity with Piers that, in spite of his cynicism, made his nerves feel shaky. He could not feel as the others did about his grandmother. They had seemed to expect her to go on living forever. She had had a longer innings than he would ever have. He ached all over, had an uncomfortable, trembling sensation, after the effort of carrying his share of her coffin. Alayne had been against it. She had known he wasn't fit for it. And ahead of him lay the journey from the hearse into the church, and from the church to the grave-side. He wished that he had sat behind and looked at Piers's back instead of having Piers glaring, in that early Victorian way, at his.

The car stopped. The first of the cortège was on the driveway of the churchyard. He removed his hat and inhaled the sweet air. He was surprised to see what a crowd had gathered. He looked with apprehension at the steep that led to the church door. They had her out of the hearse.

God, that scented, embalmed breath from its interior! He
shouldered his share of the burden.

Mr. Fennel had met them. All was orderly confusion.
The brothers strove together under that dead weight up the
graveled drive. Piers saw that Eden was overtaxed, half-
fainting, and wished the way were twice as long. As they
reached the church door Maurice came and took Eden's place,
and Eden, his forehead dripping with sweat, dropped behind.

He had heard the rector's words, from a long way off.

"I am the resurrection and the life, saith the Lord: he
that believeth in me, though he were dead, yet shall he
live. . . . We brought nothing into this world, and it is
certain we can carry nothing out. The Lord gave, and the
Lord hath taken away; blessed be the Name of the
Lord. . . ."

He was in a pew between Renny and Finch. He could
not think clearly. His blood was singing in his ears. The
chancel was veiled in a mist. If Alayne could see him, exhausted like this, how anxious she would be! She was always connected now in his mind with anxiety for him.

He became conscious that Finch was breathing in a queer
snuffling way. He turned his eyes toward him, and saw his
drooping boy's figure, and, beyond, Piers's brown hand lying
on his knee. A fist! Surreptitiously his eyes slid to Piers's
face, sunburnt, full-chinned, with strong, short nose. Of
what was he thinking? Of his proximity? Of Pheasant?
Of Gran lying there at the chancel steps?

"My heart was hot within me, and while I was thus musing the fire kindled. . . ."

He became conscious of the voice from the chancel,
resonant, mournful:

"Behold, thou hast made my days as it were a span long:
and mine age is even as nothing in respect of thee. . . ."

Poor old Gran! How she would resent that! He could
fancy her exclaiming. "Not a bit of it! I won't have it!"

The voice swept on: —

"O spare me a little, that I may recover my strength: before I go hence, and be no more seen."

Good poetry David wrote! And he had known life — not bridled himself! Lovely fragments came, clear as crystal: —

". . . seeing that is past as a watch in the night . . . and fade away suddenly like the grass. In the morning it is green, and groweth up: but in the evening it is cut down, dried up, and withered."

Ah, well, he was only twenty-six. He had seen and experienced a good deal, and would experience a deal more. Write poetry that would be remembered — for a day, at any rate. He was almost well. The desire to write surged up in him. He became wrapped in contemplation of his own personality. He forgot to rise when a hymn was sung until Renny touched him on the arm, then he rose hesitatingly to his feet. So long since he had been to church. . . .

> "Day of Wrath! O day of mourning!
> See fulfilled the prophets' warning!
> Heaven and earth in ashes burning!"

He wondered whether anyone in heaven or on earth disliked hymns as much as he did. They made him want to throw back his head and howl like a dog. But he made no sound whatever, meekly taking a corner of the hymnbook Renny offered him. Renny did not sing either, or poor snuffling young Finch, but Piers raised his lusty baritone.

> "What shall I, frail man, be pleading,
> Who for me be interceding,
> When the just are mercy needing?"

From a pew behind a woman's voice rose, clear and beautiful.

> "With Thy favored sheep O place me,
> Nor among the goats abase me,
> But to Thy right hand upraise me."

He recognized the voice as Minny Ware's. He followed it, absorbed by its beauty. He glanced at Renny, wondering if he too was following it, but Renny seemed to be engrossed in the hymn, his lips silently shaping the words.

All through Mr. Fennel's eulogy of the Christian qualities of old Adeline, Eden's mind played with the thought of Minny Ware. He recalled her as he had seen her on various occasions, always in bright colors, full of vitality, ready to give laugh for smile. He thought of her snowy neck rising columnlike from her turned-back collar. He rested his mind on the music of her voice. He decided that he would ask Alayne to have her come more often to sing to them. No, he would go over to Vaughanlands himself, and hear her sing with the piano. He was getting restless. He couldn't loaf about much longer. He must get work of some kind, though what it would be, God only knew!

His brothers were rising. Now it was time to carry the coffin to the graveyard. Surely Maurice would take his place again. Renny left the pew, but Eden did not move, though Finch was pressing behind him. He sent a glance, almost of entreaty, toward Maurice, who seemed undecided what to do. But Eden was not to be let off. Renny had made up his mind that it was seemly for the brothers to bear the coffin, and bear it they must, though one of them faint. He threw a look, half-harsh, half-affectionate, toward Eden, and, with a curt motion of the chin, indicated that he was to follow. The four took up their burden.

They had lowered her into the ground. Earth had been thrown into the grave. The last words were being spoken: "Earth to earth, ashes to ashes, dust to dust." . . . Meggie's soft weeping was mingled with Mr. Fennel's voice. "Who shall change our vile body, that it may be like unto his glorious body." . . .

Ernest's face was white and bleak. His jaw had dropped

a little. He was inwardly sobbing to himself, "Mamma, Mamma!" Now she was to be "no more seen." . . .

Augusta, in deepest black, had drawn back her head, facing the concourse with the dignity of sorrow. If she had been isolated from her surroundings, one might easily have been persuaded that her expression was one of profound offense. Was she, perhaps, offended by death? On her next birthday she would be seventy-seven.

The face of Nicholas was like a rock, scarred by the lashings of long-past storms. He stood, massive, looking stoically into the dark aperture before him. But he did not see it. He saw himself, a little lad of five, sitting in the pew he had just left, leaning against his mother, with three-year-old Ernest on her other side, both getting very drowsy. Mamma was voluminous in a snuff-colored, billowing dress, lovely for tiny boys to curl up against, and the broad satin ribbons of her bonnet delightful to fondle. What a fine rich red her hair was then! Strange how it had slipped a generation and struck fire in Renny! Beyond was Papa's stalwart figure, his fresh-tinted stubborn profile that had descended, first to Philip, then to Piers, but not so aristocratic in the last generation. Well, you couldn't do anything about it. You were hurled into this world, floundered about a while, and were hurled out of it. . . . Ernest had taken his arm. "Come along, Nick," he said. "It's over. We're going."

Ernest led him through the maze of gravestones. His gouty knee gave him some nasty twinges; once or twice he stumbled. Queer how things looked unnatural to him. Even the people who came up to speak to him. The elder Miss Lacey had taken one of his hands in both of hers.

"Dear Nicholas," she said. "It's terrible, isn't it? I know just how you feel! Losing our father as we did, last year. He was ninety!"

He looked at her vaguely. He did not see her as she now was, but as she had looked forty-five years ago when she was making up to him, wanting to marry him. He'd have done a sight better if he'd taken her instead of that flyaway creature he had chosen. He'd have had a family, and his father might have left Jalna to him instead of to his younger brother. He rumbled a few words appreciative of her sympathy, and limped on.

A strong wind, smelling of the hot dry land, had sprung up. The long grasses of the graveyard rippled before it joyously. "It is not yet evening," they seemed to sing. The wind swept low, as though to gather fresh sweetness from the roses, lilies, and carnations mounded in the White-oak plot. A number of white clouds were borne along the sky in orderly procession, like choristers in snowy surplices. The drone of the organ still came from within the church.

Renny moved urgently toward his car, Wakefield dragging at his arm.

"Renny, Renny, may I drive home with you? I see Eden getting in with Meg and Maurice."

"All right, youngster."

He was glad to have the little boy with him, glad to get away from that place. At the grave-side he had stood with raised head, his eyes on the distance, and again something in his attitude suggested the fear of a sensitive horse toward death. Now he snuffed the wind, pressed Wake's hand against his side, and made an effort to restrain his eagerness to leave that place.

Wakefield said, "I don't think my grandmother could have had a nicer day for her funeral, do you? And I think she would be glad, if she could know, what a monstrous crowd there is."

The churchyard was deserted.

The body of Adeline lay at last in the family plot, which was enclosed by a low iron fence around which were festooned rusted chains and little spiked iron balls. Under a burden of earth and sod and drooping flowers, she lay stretched out by the side of all that was left of her Philip, whose bones were now probably bare. At their feet lay young Philip, and at his side his first wife Margaret. In a corner reposed Mary, his second wife, surrounded by a little group of infant Whiteoaks.

All that was lacking was Adeline's name, soon to be graven on the granite plinth that towered above the graves. . . . All was over for her, her tempers, her appetites, her sudden dozes, her love of color, of noise, of family scenes. No more would she sit, velvet-gowned, ringed, capped, with Boney at her shoulder, before the blazing fire. No longer would she entreat, with a sudden tremulousness of that bold heart, "Somebody kiss me — quick!"

She would be "no more seen."

One of meditative mind might, knowing her character, speculate on what sort of tree should possibly be nourished, in far future days, from that grave. A flamboyant, Southern tree would perhaps be favored were this not a Northern land. In consideration of this, a Scottish fir might well draw sustenance from the hardy frame and obdurate spirit.

XX

THE YOUNG PRETENDER

WAKEFIELD scented excitement in the air from the moment
when he first opened his eyes. There was something in the
way the window curtains swelled in the breeze that made
him think of the bellying of sails. There was something
unusual in the smell of the air, as though it had come from
a long way off, a different country, full of strange adventure. A tiny cockerel, just learning to crow, had somehow
escaped from the poultry house and found his way to the
lawn. Every few minutes he raised himself on tiptoe,
flapped his wings, and essayed a plaintive, yet boastful,
crow.

Wakefield, lying across the sill in his pyjamas, watched
him with eyes still soft with sleep, but already lighting into
mischief. The shoulder of his pyjamas was ripped, and a tear
in the seat fluttered as the breeze ran along his back. Since
Meg had married, his clothes were not kept in very good
order, but that gave him no concern; to improve his mind,
to broaden his experience, were of more importance to him
than mere sartorial perfection. The sun warming a bare
shoulder, the fluttering of a torn pyjama suit, were more
stimulating than tame tidiness. He noticed that one feather
of the half-grown tail of the cockerel was awry, and he had
a fellow feeling for him. He watched him strutting about,
between crows picking up nice morsels from the lawn.
Before each peck there was a short, gay period of scratching.
Wakefield felt that he would like to get his breakfast in such
a way. He had a vision of himself energetically pawing the
ground, turning up buttery morsels of toast, or, better still,
chocolate creams wrapped in silver paper.

He thought he would see what time it was. He did not wish to spend too much of his day in meditation. He went to the dressing table where, among Renny's rather meagre toilet articles, lived the alarm clock. It was a temperamental clock, though it bore across its forehead the words "Big Ben." It lost twenty minutes every day, and might have been counted a sluggard but for the fact that its alarm had to be set half an hour later than the time when one wished to be called, so urgent was it in its desire to go off. How many a time the little boy had wakened at night to see Renny half-undressed, his face close to the face of Big Ben, with a look as of determination to keep the upper hand in the constant duel between them! It was twenty minutes to ten. There would be little left of breakfast to tempt one of wayward appetite. He opened Renny's top drawer, and there, among the neat rows of ties and mounds of handkerchiefs, he discovered a small tin box marked "Chest and Lung Tablets." These were richly flavored with licorice and, while not large in bulk, might be counted on to stay one until something more intriguing than half-cold porridge and tepid tea turned up.

He laid one on his tongue and, when he had got into his clothes, dropped a few more into a pocket of his knickers. His ablutions were a miracle of producing the most pleasing effect with the least effort. However, he spent a good deal of time on his hair, for he had found that its sleekness invariably produced a favorable impression on his elders with the exception of Piers, who took delight in rubbing it the wrong way.

He was about to go downstairs when he heard the peculiar bubbly cooing by which young Maurice was wont to express his pleasure in the morn. He glided to the door of Pheasant's room and looked in. No one was there save the infant, sitting on a quilt on the floor, sucking something out of his bottle. When he saw Wakefield he kicked convulsively and took the bottle from his lips, a waggish smile widening his mouth, showing all his pearl-like teeth.

"Nug-nug! Ee-ee! Nug-nug!"

"Hello, Mooey!" returned Wakefield, kindly. "Glad to see your old uncle, aren't you?"

"Nug-nug! Brrrr!" bubbled Mooey, and replaced the nipple in his mouth. He sucked energetically, the muscles in his lip quivering, his eyes turned slightly toward his nose.

Wakefield took him under the arms and raised him to his feet. Mooey stamped his bare soles energetically on the quilt, but the bottle fell from his grasp and a shadow troubled his pink brow. His motto was "one thing at a time and that done thoroughly." This promenading in the middle of a drink confused him.

"Ba!" he declared, trying to see his uncle's face. "Bub-bub-bub!"

Wakefield walked him the length of the room between his knees. "Nice walk," he said, dictatorially. "Bad old bottle."

But Mooey was of a different opinion. There, on the quilt, lay his bottle, still half full of delicious sweetened water, and here was he, leagues away, held by two viselike hands, while tweed-knickered legs and leather brogues imprisoned him on either side.

"Ha-ha-ha-ha!" he cried, but his "ha" was of lamentation, not mirth.

"Hush," said Wakefield, sternly, "or you'll have your mother fussing about! What's the matter with you? Why don't you step out and learn to walk when I'm taking all this trouble with you? Do you know what's likely to get you, if you're naughty? Well, a big wolf is, and gobble you right up."

Happily Mooey was unable to take in the import of this dire possibility, but when he threw back his head, and looked up into Wakefield's face, he saw something in that smooth, alive visage that brought tears welling into his eyes, and made him raise his voice in a despairing wail. Wakefield propelled him to the door and balanced himself on one leg while he shut it with his foot. He then returned him to his quilt, on which he dropped him so precipitately that the infant's faculties were occupied, for the moment, in recovering his balance.

Wakefield picked up the bottle and shook it. He removed the nipple and tasted the insipid fluid. At this sight, an expression so outraged came into Mooey's wet eyes that Wakefield was moved to reassure him.

"Can't you trust your uncle?" he asked. "You're very much mistaken if you think I want any of this beastly stuff. And if you weren't such a little fathead you'd never let them put you off with it! Now I'm going to give you something really nice. And it's good for you, too, 'specially as you sound sort of wheezy."

Mooey made noises indicative of a broken spirit, and watched Wakefield fascinated as he took two of the Chest and Lung Tablets from his pocket and dropped them into the bottle. He placed his palm on the opening and shook the bottle vigorously. It took the tablets some time to dissolve, but at last the water took on a dark, rather poisonous color, and Wakefield assumed that sufficient of the medicinal quality of the tablets had been absorbed. He replaced the nipple and put the bottle into the outstretched hands of his nephew.

"There you are, my boy!" he said, heartily, and a benevolent smile curved his lips as he observed the gusto with which Mooey returned to his drink.

He was not a Boy Scout. He had not the physical strength to take part in their enterprises. However, he liked the idea of beginning each day with a kind act. He was one whom it would be impossible to hamper by sectarianism, but who, nevertheless, was willing to take something of good from any creed.

He descended the stairs lightly.

In the hall below he was interested to see that Rags had just let someone in at the front door. It was Mr. Patton, Grandmother's lawyer. He carried his brief bag, and, as Rags divested him of his coat, he gave Wakefield a pleasant but rather nervous smile.

"Good morning," he said, "and how are you?"

"Thank you, sir," answered Wakefield, "I'm as well as can be expected, after all I've gone through."

He had heard Aunt Augusta make this same remark to Mrs. Fennel the day before, and he saw no reason why a remark so fraught with mournful dignity should not serve for any member of the family.

Mr. Patton looked at him sharply. "H'm," he said, dryly. "I suppose so. Well, well."

Aunt Augusta appeared in the doorway of the sitting room. She held out her hand to Mr. Patton, and Wakefield saw that almost all the family was gathered in the sitting room. Uncle Nicholas sat in an armchair in a corner, filling his pipe; Uncle Ernest was by a window, nervously rubbing the nails of one hand against the palm of the other. Piers and Renny stood together talking, and Mr. Patton was barely inside when Meg and Maurice arrived. Meg was carrying her infant daughter, Patience. Wakefield was consumed by curiosity. He was also humiliated to find that a family conclave had reached such a point as this without his knowledge.

Finch came along the hall, rather more sheepish than usual, and he too made toward the door of the sitting room. Wakefield caught his arm.

"What is it?" he asked, eagerly. "What are they up to?"

"The will. Patton's going to read the will."

"The will? Oh! Then we'll know who's going to be the heir, shan't we?"

"Shut up," whispered Finch, and pushed past him.

But Wake was not to be put off so easily. He followed Finch into the sitting room and drew up a chair beside Mr. Patton where he sat at the square table, with some papers spread before him.

Mr. Patton looked at him over his glasses.

"I don't think the child should be allowed to stay," said Aunt Augusta.

"Oh course he shouldn't," agreed Piers.

"Wake, darling," said Meg, joggling Patience on her knee, "run along and feed your rabbits."

Wakefield did not demur, but he hitched his chair a little nearer the table and pushed Aunt Augusta's bottle of smelling salts within reach of Mr. Patton, in case of need.

"Put that child out," growled Nicholas from his corner, pointing at Wake with his pipe. "I don't see—" began Renny, but Piers took the little boy by the arm and put him into the hall.

He stood there ruffled, like a young robin pushed from the nest, looking at the door so inexorably shut against him. He heard someone hurrying down the stairs and saw that it was Pheasant.

"Oh," she said, as she saw the closed door, "I am late! I had to run upstairs to Mooey. I wonder what I'd better do."

"Go and fetch Mooey," advised Wakefield, glumly. "P'raps they'll let you in if you've a kid in your arms. Meggie's got *her* baby."

Pheasant stared. "How funny! I've heard of women taking babies to police courts to influence the jury. Maybe she thinks . . ."

"There's only the family in there," said Wakefield, "and I think it was filthy to put me out."

"Did they? I wonder if they'll want me! Piers didn't say to come, but then he didn't say not to come. I wonder . . ."

Wakefield could not conscientiously encourage her.

"I think you'd better not go in, my girl," he advised. "You're safer out here with me."

"If they think I'm after the old money!" she cried angrily.

"I bet I get it," he said, boastfully.

"I bet you don't!"

He put his eye to the keyhole. He could see nothing but Mr. Patton's hands fumbling among papers. A good deal of coughing came from within. The family seemed to be collectively clearing its throat. Then Mr. Patton began to speak in a mumbling, unintelligible voice.

Wakefield looked around to where Pheasant had been standing. She was just disappearing up on the landing. He thought he would go out for a breath of fresh air while the will was being read.

"I wonder how long it will take," he said to Rags, who had just missed seeing him with his eye to the keyhole.

"It'll take some time," replied Rags, dusting the mirror of the hatrack; and he added sarcastically, "I expect you'll 'ave time to order yerself a new touring car, in cise you're the old lidy's heir."

"There isn't any 'in case,'" said Wakefield, on a sudden impulse. "I am."

"Of course you are!" jeered Rags. "Sime as I won the Calcutter Sweepstikes! We'll go araound the world on a tour together."

"It's all very well to laugh," returned Wakefield, gravely, "but it's the truth! She told me so herself, not long before she died."

Rags gaped at him, duster in hand. He could not help

being impressed. "Well, if wot you s'y is true, them in there will get the surprise of their lives."

"Yes," agreed Wakefield, "and they'll feel meaner after shutting me out and all."

"I wish I knew if you're telling the truth."

"You'll know soon enough."

Wakefield went out into the morning. He sauntered along the flower border, brilliant with marigolds, zinnias, and asters. Bright cobwebs veiled the cedar hedge where the sun had not yet struck. A birch tree was letting fall little yellow leaves into the moist green of the lawn.

What should he do to pass the time until the reading of the will was over? This was an important hour in his life, he felt, and should be spent in no trivial fashion. He began to feel qualms of hunger, but the thought of reëntering the house was intolerable to him. The blue and gold of the morning, the little breezes that skipped about like young lambs, the spaciousness of open air, were necessary to his mood. He strolled, hands in pockets, to the back of the house, and there came upon a tub set beneath an eave, full of rain water. He squatted beside it, peering at his reflection, darkly bright in the water. So looked the heir to the Whiteoak millions! He lengthened his face, trying to make his nose into a Court nose, and when it began to ache from the strain he eased it with a hideous grimace or two.

The sight of these grimaces reflected made him burst out laughing, and the tiny cockerel, which had followed him, responded with a boastful crow.

"What have you to crow about?" asked Wakefield. "If you were me, you might crow. What are you heir to, I'd like to know? A dirty old nest, and a worm or two. Do you know what I am? I'm heir to the Whiteoak millions, and it'll pay you to crow when I tell you to, and not before!"

The cockerel looked at him so hard that it turned its head

almost upside down. Its bright amber eye glittered with greed.

Then in the rain water Wakefield discovered a black beetle half-drowned, lying on its back, only a feeble kicking of the legs showing it to be still alive. He picked a blade of grass and with it steered the beetle round the tub. A dear little boat making a tour of the world. He made it call at various ports — Gibraltar, Suez, Ceylon, Penang. How he loved these names in his geography lessons with Mr. Fennel! Lucky, lucky beetle!

Alas! Just as they reached Shanghai, it sank. Rather ungrateful of it. Not many Canadian beetles had a chance to go to Shanghai!

He peered down at it, lying on its back in the depths of the tub. It must be rescued. He pushed up his sleeve and put his slender brown arm into the water, found the beetle, and laid it right side up in the sunshine. He lay down beside it, watching with satisfaction the slow but sure return to life. It was his second kind act that morning!

A slender, pale worm was descending on a gossamer thread out of the sky. The lightest breeze swung it, now above the tub of rain water, now above the grass. Unperturbed, it continued its descent, the silver thread lengthening, let out from some invisible reel. A robin ran across the yard, a peewee said "peewee" from a maple tree.

The worm had arrived. An undulation passed through its slender body; it moved delicately beneath a towering blade of grass. But Wakefield was not to discover its destination or why it had descended to this sphere from another. A swaggering black ant fell on it, worried it, choked it, slew it. He was such an important, toplofty fellow that he was quite above conveying the body to the ant hill. Apparently he put his feelers to his mouth and whistled, for a company of little ants appeared from nowhere, snatched it, fought over it, dragged it, trailing palely, through the grass blades, out of sight. Wakefield was not the only spectator of the tragedy, for a strange fellow in a fuzzy yellow waistcoat and a saffron-colored stern appeared on the rim of a burdock leaf, and stared goggle-eyed, now and again wringing his antennæ.

Wakefield did not like the looks of him. He plucked the burdock leaf and turned it upside down on top of him.

"Here endeth," he said, "the second lesson."

The peewee chanted "peewee"; the cockerel crowed.

Wakefield threw him a Chest and Lung Tablet.

"Perhaps this will help your voice," he said. "I've never heard anything so squeaky. Suck it slowly."

The cockerel bolted it, and liked the licorice flavor so well that it came close, on the lookout for another. It was then that it espied the black beetle, making cumbersome attempts to reshoulder the responsibilities of life. The cockerel cocked an eye, pecked, gulped. There was no beetle in sight.

Wakefield rose, dusted his bare knees, and uttered a sigh of bliss. A third kind act, providing the cockerel with a beetle! His cup was full.

But not his stomach! It seemed hard that he, heir to the Whiteoak millions, should go empty.

He crouched before a window of the basement kitchen and peered into the twilight depths below. He could see Mrs. Wragge kneading dough, her red fists pounding it so vigorously that one could not help wondering whether it might not hurt the dough. Bessie, the kitchenmaid, was paring vegetables in a corner, her hair in her eyes. Rags, cigarette in mouth, was cleaning knives, dipping the cork first in a little puddle of water on the knifeboard, then in a small mound of Bath brick, before he angrily furbished the blades. Rags was always angry when he was in the basement. No matter how cool his temper might be above, it rose to boiling point as he clattered down the stairs. No, Wakefield did not want his breakfast from that galley!

He ran across the fields, climbed the sagging rail fence, and was on the road. Soon he was opposite the door of the blacksmith shop, between its tall elms. John Chalk, the smith, was shoeing a gray farm horse. He glanced at Wake from under his shaggy brows, and went on hammering the shoe.

When he dropped the hoof, and straightened his back, Wakefield remarked, "My pony's cast that last shoe you put on her."

"That's queer," said Chalk. "Are you sure it was that one? She'd no right to cast that one so soon."

Wake looked at him dubiously. "Hadn't she? I had my doubts of it when you put it on. I thought it was a very queer-looking job."

Chalk glared. "I like your cheek! There was never a shoe better put on than that shoe, and I'd like you to know it!"

Wakefield folded his arms. "I don't want," he said, "to take my custom from you."

"You and your custom!" bawled the blacksmith. "You and your one little pony that I could pick up under my arm like a sheep! Take it away, and be darned to you. I guess I can make ends meet without it!" He wiped his brow with a blackened hand.

"Well," said Wake, "if it only *was* one pony you might be snifty! But it'll likely be a whole string of race horses before long. You see, I'm the heir to the—my grand-mamma's money."

"A likely story," jeered Chalk. "The old lady 'ud never leave it to a little whippersnapper like you!"

"That's just why she did it. She knew I needed it— what with my weak heart and all. I've known it for a long time, but the family's just finding it out this morning."

Chalk regarded him with mingled admiration and dis-approval. "Well, if that's true, and you've got the old lady's money, I pity them, for of all the high-cockalorum, head-up-and-tail-over-the-dashboard young rascals I ever set eyes on, you're the worst." He began to hammer so loudly on his anvil that further conversation was impossible. Though fast friends, their intercourse was often stormy.

He let the smith feel the weight of his gaze for a few moments, before he moved on with dignity along the straggling street. At the Wigles' cottage he stopped. Muriel, as usual, was swinging on the gate. He brought it to a standstill so abruptly that the little girl fell off. Before she could begin to cry, Wakefield took her by the hand and said, "Come along, Muriel. I'm going to take you with me for a treat."

The door of the cottage opened and Mrs. Wigle stuck out her head.

"Muriel!" she called. "Don't you dare leave the yard! Come back here this instant moment!"

"But he'th taking me out for a treat!" whined Muriel. "I want to go out for a treat!"

"Treat nothing," retorted her mother. "The last time he took you out for a treat you came home in rags and tatters. Treats may be fun for him, but he ain't going to take my daughter to 'em!"

Wakefield listened to this tirade with a reproachful air.

"Mrs. Wigle," he said, "it wasn't my fault that Muriel fell in the stream, and the old sheep tossed her about, and the burrs got in her hair. I did what I could to save her. But I'd forgotten the sheep's name, and she won't come for any other name but her own. You see, all our animals have names, we make such pets of them."

Mrs. Wigle came down the path, her arms rolled in her apron. She looked somewhat mollified.

"Where did you plan to take her this morning?" she asked.

"Only to Mrs. Brawn's shop to buy her something nice to eat."

"Well, fetch her straight back here afterward. And there's one thing I wish you'd tell me. Have you ever heard your brother say aught about mending my roof? It leaks into the best room like all possessed every time it rains."

Wakefield knitted his slender black brows. "I've never heard him say a single word about it, Mrs. Wigle. He doesn't seem to mind what roof leaks so long as the stable roof doesn't. But I'll tell you what I'll do — I'll mend your roof myself!"

"Bless the child! As though you could mend my roof!"

"I mean, I'll have it mended for you. You see, I've inherited all my grandmamma's money, and I'll be wanting to do all sorts of nice things for ladies that have been kind to me. Come along, Muriel."

Mrs. Wigle was dazed before the splendor of it. A little boy with all that fortune! Beautiful to see him holding her Muriel by the hand. She followed them, rolling her arms tightly in her apron, into Mrs. Brawn's shop. She did not give him time to tell his news to fat Mrs. Brawn. She poured it out for him, and the two women stood, wrapped in admiration, while he scrutinized the contents of the window.

"I was so excited," he murmured, half to himself, "that I couldn't eat my breakfast. 'Air,' I said, 'I've got to have air.' . . . I think I'll have two currant buns, a little dish of custard cakes, and three bottles of Orange Crush. Muriel, what would you like?"

He stood before the counter, slender, fragile, the toe of one crossed foot resting on the floor, his dark head bent above the bottle from which the lovely drink ebbed through two straws into his throat. Before him stood the unopened bottles, the custard cakes, a currant bun. He held the other bun, soft, sticky, warm from the oven. At his shoulder was the tow head of Muriel, her eyes raised adoringly to his face, as she munched a bun. She would have followed him to the ends of the earth.

Above his head the voices of the two women babbled on, discussing his wonderful prospects. Mrs. Brawn cared nothing that he owed her twenty cents and was fast running up his account. Mrs. Wigle forgot her leaky roof. She rolled and unrolled her hands in her apron. From the stove in the back room was wafted the insidious smell of burning cakes. Wakefield's head was full of beautiful thoughts — like whirling golden coins.

XXI

BEQUEST

In the hall he almost ran into Mr. Patton, who was putting on his coat. Mr. Patton had the uncomfortable expression on his face of one who has eaten something that has disagreed with him. The expression on the face of Renny, who was accompanying him to the door, was even more uncomfortable. He said, "You're sure there's no doubt of her sanity?"

Mr. Patton puckered his lips. "None whatever."

"Well, she had a right to do what she liked with her own money, but — it's rather hard on my uncles."

"Yes, yes. . . . Yes, indeed."

"And so entirely unexpected. She never seemed to care especially for him. She was much more partial to Piers."

"You never can tell."

"With women — I suppose not."

"Nor men, either. It's extraordinary what some of them will do." Mr. Patton took his hat from the rack, looked into it; then, casting a furtive look into the silent sitting room, he added, in a muffled tone, "I actually tried to dissuade her. I don't mind saying this to you. But — she was —" He shrugged.

"Not very tolerant of interference. I know."

Mr. Patton said, picking up his brief bag, and looking into Renny's eyes with some embarrassment, "It's hard on you, too. Particularly as in most of the former wills —"

Renny scowled. "I'm not worrying about that. How many wills did you say there have been?"

"Eight during the twenty years I have looked after her

affairs. Some changes, of course, were only minor. In most of them you—"

They became conscious of the little boy's presence. He was staring up at them inquisitively. Renny saw a question coming, and took the back of his neck in a restraining hand. Mr. Patton's lips unpuckered into a smile.

"He's looking pretty well," he remarked.

"There's no bone to him. Just gristle. He's got no appetite."

The lawyer felt Wake's arm. "Not very firm! Still, his eyes are bright; but then your family runs to bright eyes."

"Who—" began Wakefield, and Renny's fingers tightened on his neck.

He and Mr. Patton shook hands. The lawyer hurried out to his car.

"But who—" began Wake again.

The master of Jalna took out a cigarette, struck a match on the underside of the hatrack, and, after its flare had lighted the cigarette and been reflected in his eyes, threw it into the umbrella stand. He turned then toward the fantastic silence of the sitting room. Wakefield followed.

This was the strangest room he had ever been in. The drawing-room had seemed strange when Grandmother lay there in her coffin with the lighted candles about her and the presence of death making the air heavy, but this was stranger still. For, though the air was heavy as death, it was pregnant with the life of battling emotions.

Nicholas still sat in the corner with his pipe. He held it in his teeth, and stared at Renny and Wakefield as they came into the room without seeming to see them. He stroked the back of Nip, his terrier, with a large trembling hand, and seemed to be unaware of his presence also.

Ernest was rubbing the nails of one hand against the palm of the other, as though he had never stopped, but now he did stop, and began to tap his teeth with them, as though all the polishing had been leading up to that. Augusta looked more natural than the others, but what disturbed Wake was that her eyes, fixed on Ernest, were full of tears. He had never seen tears in them before.

The eyes of Piers, Maurice, and even the infant, Patience, were on Finch, and Finch looked more miserable than Wakefield had ever seen anyone look in all his life. Certainly he had not fallen heir to a fortune!

"But who?" he entreated, in his penetrating treble. "*Who?*"

All the eyes, dark and light, intense and mournful, turned on him. Words froze on his lips. He began to cry.

"No wonder the child weeps," said Augusta, regarding him gloomily. "Even he is conscious of the outrage of it."

Nicholas took his pipe from his mouth, tapped it over the hearth, then blew it out with a whistling sound. He said nothing, but Piers broke out, "I always knew he had a yellow streak. But how he accomplished this —"

"My mother," declared Augusta, "must have been demented. Let Mr. Patton say what he will —"

"Old ninny," said Piers, "to allow a woman of that age to play ducks and drakes with her money! It's a case for the courts. We must never stand for it. Are you going to let yourself be done out of what is really yours, Renny?"

"Really *his!*" cried Augusta.

"Yes, really *his!* What about those other wills?"

Augusta's glazed eyes flashed away the tears. "What of the will in which all was left to your Uncle Ernest?"

Ernest suddenly seemed to feel weak. He sat down and twisted his fingers between his knees, and his underlip between his teeth.

"That was years ago!" retorted Piers.

"She was sane then. She *must* have been *quite mad* when she made this will."

Ernest held up his hand. "Don't! Don't! I can't bear to hear Mamma spoken of so!"

"But, Ernest, the money should be yours!"

"I can do without the money."

Piers glared at Augusta. "I don't see why the blazes you insist that the money should come to Uncle Ernest! What about Uncle Nick? What about Renny? Renny's had the whole family to keep for years!"

"Shut up!" growled Renny, savagely.

"How dare you insult us?" cried Augusta. "This is my brothers' home! I have been here to look after my mother. What could she have done without me, I should like to know?"

"Kept up an establishment of her own! She'd plenty of money!"

Nicholas pointed with his pipe at Piers. "Say one word more!" he thundered. He struggled to rise, but could not. Ernest sprang up, trembling, and went to him. Grasping his arm, he pulled him to his feet. Augusta also went to him, and the three stood together facing the younger generation.

"I repeat what I said," said Piers.

Renny interrupted, "It doesn't matter what he says! I've never grudged—"

Nicholas exclaimed, sardonically, "Well, now, that's handsome of you! Very handsome of you! You haven't grudged us a roof! Our meals! We ought to feel grateful. Eh, Augusta? Eh, Ernest?"

Renny's face went white. "I don't understand you. You purposely put me in the wrong!"

Augusta drew back her head with an almost snakelike movement. "If I had ever known! If I had ever dreamed! But, never mind, I shall be going back to England soon."

"For God's sake, be fair!" cried Renny. "Have I ever acted as though I didn't want any one of you here? I have always wanted you. I always wanted Gran!"

Piers burst out, "That's the trouble! Renny's been too generous. And now this is the thanks he gets!"

"You to talk!" snarled Nicholas. "You who brought your wife here, when everyone was against it!"

"Yes, and who was she?" thrust Augusta.

Nicholas proceeded, "And what did she do? Made a little hell here!"

"Eden would have been all right," cried Ernest, "if only she had let him alone!"

Piers strode toward them, his hands clenched, but Meg interrupted with "Everyone talks so selfishly! As though his side of the question was the only one. What about me? Put off with an old India shawl and a big gold watch and chain no one ever carries the like of now!"

Augusta cried, passionately, "My mother's watch was a valued possession to her! She thought you, as the only granddaughter, should have it, and those India shawls are priceless nowadays!"

"Yes! I've often seen Boney make his bed on this one!"

Piers was trying to shoulder himself from Renny's restraining hand. "Do you expect me," he muttered, "to let them say such things about Pheasant? I'll murder some- one before I've done!"

Renny said, with composure, though he was still white, "Don't be a fool! The old people are all wrought up. They don't know what they're saying. If you care a straw for me, Piers, hang on to yourself!"

Piers bit his lip and scowled down at his boots.

Meg's voice was heard again. "When I think of the lovely things she had! I could have borne her giving the ruby ring to Pheasant, if she'd treated me fairly afterward. But a watch and chain— and a *shawl* that Boney'd made a nest in!"

"Margaret!" thundered Augusta.

Meg's face was a mask of obstinacy. "What I want to know is who the ruby ring really belongs to!"

"*Belonged* to, you mean, before your grandmother gave it away," corrected Maurice.

"I think," said Ernest, "it was the one she intended for Alayne."

"As though Alayne needed one of my grandmother's rings!" Meg's mask of obstinacy was broken by temper.

Renny said, with a chest vibration in his voice, "Each grandson's wife is to have a piece of jewelry, or the grandson a piece for his prospective wife. As I understand the will, Aunt Augusta and I are to make the choice. Isn't that so, Aunt?"

Augusta nodded, judicially. "Pheasant already has her bequest."

"She has nothing of the sort!" said Piers, vehemently. "The ruby ring was a present entirely outside the will."

"I agree," said Renny.

A sultry lull fell on the room for a moment, in which could be heard the ticking of the clock, the heavy breathing of Nicholas, and the loud tap of a woodpecker on a tree near the open window. The momentary silence was broken by Augusta's contralto tones.

"The whole situation is disgraceful," she said. "I've never known such insensibility. Here I and my brothers are put off with not very valuable personal possessions of my mother's, and expected to be content while all the squabbling goes on among the rest of you over her jewels."

Nicholas added fuel to the flame: "And the memory of our mother is insulted by one nephew who says she sponged on Renny —"

"And we too," put in Ernest.

Nicholas continued, gnawing his gray moustache, "While another nephew benevolently tells us that he's never grudged us shelter and our meals!"

"If you're going to bring that up again," Renny exclaimed, despairingly, "I shall get out, and that's flat!"

Maurice Vaughan said, heavily, "What we should all do is to get down to brass tacks, if possible, and find out why your grandmother did such an extraordinary thing as to leave all her money to Finch."

Augusta reared her head in his direction. "My mother was deranged— there is no doubt of it."

"Have you anything to go on?" asked Vaughan. "Had she been acting strangely, in your opinion?"

"I've noticed a difference."

Meg asked eagerly, "What sort of things, Auntie?"

"For one thing, I overheard her several times talking to herself."

Talking to herself! The phrase produced a strange tremor in the room. Those in the corners appeared to draw toward the centre, as though their intense individualism were about to be merged.

"Ha!" said Vaughan. "Did you notice anything singular in what she said? Did she ever mention Finch's name?"

Augusta pressed her finger to her brow. "M-yes. Yes, she did! She muttered something once about Finch and a Chinese goddess."

Nicholas leaned forward, clasping his gouty knee. "Did you ask her what she meant?"

"Yes. I said, 'Mamma, whatever do you mean?' and she said, 'That lad has guts, though you might n't think it!' . . . I did wish she would not use such coarse expressions!"

Vaughan looked at the faces about him. "I think that is sufficient proof. Do what you like about an appeal, but I think no one who was sane would ramble like that."

Nicholas rolled his gray-crested head from side to side. He growled, "That's nothing. If anyone could hear my mutterings to myself, I might easily be considered insane."

Piers flashed, "You may be, but the rest of us aren't! It's a case for the courts!"

"Yes, indeed!" chimed Meg. "We might easily arrange to have the money divided equally."

Augusta cocked her Queen Alexandra fringe. "If it could be done — it's really the just way out of the difficulty."

Ernest raised his long face from gnawing his forefinger. "It seems to me," he faltered, "that I've never known Mamma brighter than she was that last day."

Meg exclaimed, ironically, "If you call it *bright*, giving away her most valuable ring on a mere whim!"

"For the Lord's sake," shouted Piers, "try to get your mind off that ring! One would think it represented a fortune!"

"It quite probably does," returned his sister suavely. "What can you know of the value of jewels — you, a crude boy who has been nowhere, seen nothing!"

Piers's eyes grew prominent. "I should like to know what you've seen and done?" he inquired, sarcastically. "You spent nearly twenty years trying to make up your mind to marry your next-door neighbor."

Meg burst into tears, and the baby, hearing her mother cry, put her kid slippers in the air and wept with all her might.

Above the noise Maurice called to Piers, "I won't have you insulting my wife!"

"Make her let my wife alone then!" retorted Piers.

Augusta boomed, "Is it our duty, I wonder, to make an appeal? To settle the matter in court?"

"What's that you say?" asked Nicholas. "I can't hear you for the noise those girls are making!"

"I said I wondered if we should go to law about it."

The sound of crying ceased as suddenly as it had begun. All the heads in the room — they seemed to Finch, sitting guiltily on his ottoman, to have swollen to the size of balloons — turned, as though drawn by a magnet, facing Renny. It was one of those volcanic moments when the entire family shouldered all responsibility upon him. The faces, which had been distorted with emotion, gradually smoothed out as though each had inhaled some numbing incense, and an almost ceremonial hush fell on the room. Renny, the chieftain, was to speak. Goaded, harried, he was to give expression to the sentiments of the clan.

He stood, his hands resting on the table, his red hair raised into a crest as though distraught, and said, in his rather metallic voice, "We shall do no such thing! We'll settle our affairs in our own way without any intervention from outsiders. I had rather give up Jalna than take Gran's will into court! As to her sanity — sane or insane, her money was hers to do what she liked with! I believe she was perfectly sane. I think I never knew a better brain than hers. All her life she knew what she wanted to do — and did it. And if this last act of hers is a bitter pill for some of us, all we can do is to swallow it, and not get cockeyed fighting over it. Imagine the newspaper articles! 'Descendants of Centenarian at War over Will'! How should we like that?"

"Horrible!" said Ernest.

"No, no, no. It would never do," muttered Nicholas, indistinctly.

"Newspapers — outsiders gossiping!" Augusta gasped. "I never could bear that!"

"But still —" wavered Meg.

Piers said, "You are the one most concerned, Renny. If you're willing to take it lying down —"

Nicholas heaved himself about in his chair and looked sombrely at Piers. "I can't see why you persist in regarding Renny as the one chiefly concerned. It's very irritating. It's impertinent."

Renny broke in, "That's beside the point, Uncle Nick!

The point is that we can't go to law over Gran's will, isn't it?"

Nicholas gave a proud and melancholy assent. No, they could not go to law. The wall about them must be kept intact. Their isolation must not be thrown down like a glove, to challenge notoriety. Bitter as the disappointment was, it must be borne. The Whiteoaks would not supply a heading for a column in any of the tawdry newspapers of the day. Gossip for the neighborhood! Their affairs settled by a court! They were a law unto themselves.

The temporary breach in their protective wall closed up, knitting them together, uniting them against interference. Renny had spoken, and a sigh of acquiescence, even of relief, rose from the tribe. Not one of them — not, in his heart of hearts, even Piers — wanted to go to law over the will. That would have been to acknowledge weakness, to have offered submission to a decree from outside Jalna.

Even Maurice Vaughan felt the hypnotic spell of the family. Impossible to fight against it. Knuckle under and bear with them, that was all one could do. They raised Cain, and then they took hands and danced in a circle around the Cain they had raised. They sowed the wind and reaped the whirlwind, but they wanted no outside labor to help garner that harvest. . . . Maurice took his baby daughter and dandled her. She was the image of her mother. He wondered if she would have her mother's nature. Well, she might do worse. Meggie was almost perfect. He was lucky to have got her. And the baby, too!

Piers was standing with his back to the mantel, looking at Finch with narrowed eyes. "There's one thing I think we should find out," he said.

He got no further, for at that moment a tap sounded on the folding doors, they were drawn apart, and the dining room was discovered, with the table set for dinner.

Rags said, addressing Augusta, "The dinner has been

ready for some time, Your Ladyship. You seemed so occupied that I thought I 'ad better not disturb you before." His eyes flew about the room, his impudent nose quivered, scenting trouble.

Augusta rose and passed her hands down her sides, smoothing her dress. She said to Renny, "Shall you ask your sister and her husband to dinner?"

He thought, "She's punishing me for what Piers said about her and the uncles stopping here so long. She won't take it on herself to invite Meg and Maurice to dinner. Lord, as though there weren't enough trouble!" Well, he would not give her the satisfaction of appearing to notice anything. He said, "Of course you two will stay to dinner."

"There's Baby," said Meg.

"Tuck her up on the sofa. She's all but asleep."

"Oh, I don't think I had better!" Her tears overflowed again.

Nicholas hobbled up, stiff after sitting so long in one position, and tucked his hand under her arm. "Come, come, Meggie, stop your grizzling and have a good dinner," he rumbled. "'More was lost at Mohac's Field.'"

Even with old Adeline gone, they retained the air of a procession as they moved into the dining room. Nicholas first, holding by the arm plump-cheeked Meg; next Ernest, struggling against self-pity, comforted by Augusta at his side, full of pity for him. Then Piers, Finch, and Wakefield. Finch looked as though he did not see where he was going, and when Piers jostled against him in the doorway he all but toppled over. Maurice and Renny came last.

Maurice said, grinning, "So you 're to have the old painted bedstead! What are you going to do with it?"

"Get into it and stay there, if this sort of thing keeps up," returned the master of Jalna.

He sat down at the head of his table and cast his sharp glance over the clan. Still a goodly number, even though

Gran and Eden were missing. After a while young Mooey would be big enough to come to table. . . . But Pheasant was not there. He frowned. Just then she entered timidly, and slid into her place between Piers and Finch.

"Where have you been hiding all morning?" asked Renny.

"Oh, I thought I was superfluous," she answered, trying to appear sophisticated, entirely grown up, and not at all nervous.

Piers pressed his ankle against hers. She trembled. Was it possible that he was signaling her — telling her that Mooey was the heir? Her eyes slid toward his face. No jubilation there. A grim, half-jocular look about the firm, healthy lips. Poor little Mooey had not got the money. Then who had? Her gaze, sheltered by long lashes, sought one face after another, and found no answer. Had there been a mistake? Was there perhaps no fortune after all? Under cover of the voices of Maurice and Renny, discussing the points of a two-year-old with determined cheerfulness, she whispered to Finch on her left, "For goodness' sake, tell me, who is the lucky one?"

His voice came in a sepulchral whisper: —

"Me!"

She whispered back, "There may be thousands who would believe you, but I can't."

"It's true."

"It is not!"

Yet, looking into his eyes, she saw that it was. She began to laugh, silently, yet hysterically, shaking from head to foot. It was too much for Finch; he too shook with soundless mirth, very near to tears. The eyes of all at the table were turned on them in shocked disapproval or disgust. Finch — an indecent young ruffian. Pheasant — a hussy.

Augusta saved the moment from tragedy by declaring, sonorously, "They're mad! They must be mad."

The meal proceeded. With decisive movements of his thin muscular hands Renny cut from the joint portions to the taste of each member of the circle — for Nicholas, it must be very rare, with a rim of fat; for Ernest, well done, not a vestige of fat; for Augusta, well done *and* fat. For all, generous pieces of Yorkshire pudding. For Wake always fat, when he hated fat! " See that he eats it, Aunt!" And — " Wakefield, you must or you won't grow strong!" Then the usual slumping on his spine until Meg transferred the despised morsel from his plate to hers.

To a family of weaker fibre such a scene as the one just passed in the sitting room might have ended all appetite for dinner. It was not so with the family at Jalna. The extravagant and wasteful energy of their emotions now required fresh fuel. They ate swiftly and with relish, only in an unusual silence, for they were still oppressed by that empty chair between Nicholas and Ernest, and into their silence was flung, every now and again, the sharp memory of the harsh old voice, crying, " Gravy! I want more gravy! Dish gravy, please, on this bit of bread!"

Ah, how her shadow hung on them! How the yellow light, sifting through the blinds, threw a sort of halo about her chair! Once Ernest's cat crept from his knee to the empty chair, but no sooner was she seated there than Nicholas's terrier leaped to drag her down, as though he knew that empty seat was sacred.

Renny fed his spaniels with scraps from his plate. He shot swift glances at the plates of his aunt and uncles. He urged their replenishment, but they steadfastly refused. He set his teeth. They were remembering, he was sure, what Piers had said; out of hurt pride they were refusing second helpings.

When a steamed blackberry pudding came, with its syrupy purple sauce, deep melancholy settled on them. It was the first pudding of this kind they had had since her death. How she would have loved it! How her nose and chin and cap would have pressed forward to meet it as it advanced toward her! How she would have mashed the pudding into its sauce, and dribbled the sauce on her chin! Ernest almost found himself saying aloud, "Mamma, must you do that?"

They ate the pudding in heavy silence. Finch and Pheasant were barely able to restrain their insane laughter. Wakefield's eyes were bright with admiration as they rested on the tall silver fruit dish in the middle of the table. From its base sprung a massive silver grapevine, beneath the shelter of which stood a silver doe and her fawn. It was heaped with glowing peaches and ripe pears. Aunt Augusta had had it brought out on the day of the funeral, and it had remained. Wakefield wished it might remain forever. He wished he might have been placed opposite it instead of at the far end, so that the nearness of the darling little fawn might take his mind off the terrible silence. He knew now quite definitely that he had not inherited Grandmother's money, and he did not so very much mind. He had had a nice morning pretending that he was the heir, and he did not see why the others could not accept their disappointment as he did. . . . Funny to think of Finch. . . . Would Finch take Gran's room now and sleep in the painted bed? He pictured Finch propped on the pillows with Boney perching at the head. Finch, in a nightcap and teeth like Grandmother's! Wake was rather frightened by this picture. He put his head to one side and reassured himself by the sight of Finch looking wretched, beyond the fruit dish. A queer grayish color over Finch's face made him remember something. He puckered his forehead, winked fast, and then broke the silence.

"Renny," he questioned, with great distinctness, "was Finch born with a caul?"

The steaming cup of tea halfway to the lips of the master

of Jalna was suspended; his eyebrows shot upward in astonishment.

"A *caul!*" he snapped. "A *caul!* What the devil — what put that into your head?"

Meg broke in. "I think it is too bad of you, Renny, to swear at Wake! He was only asking a natural question!"

"A *natural* question! Well, if you call *cauls* natural, I'll be —"

"There you go again!"

"No, I don't."

"Only because I stopped you! Really, you can't *speak* without swearing!"

Piers asked, "But was he?"

"Was who?"

"Finch. Born with a caul."

"Yes, he was," answered Meg, stroking Wakefield's hair.

"Extraordinary!" said Nicholas, wiping his moustache and staring at Finch. "I had never heard of one in the family."

Meg said, "His mother kept it in a little box, but after she died it disappeared."

Ernest observed, "It is supposed to be a good omen. To bring luck."

Piers laughed. "Aha! Now we've hit it! Good luck! It's the caul that did it!" He laughed into Finch's face. "Why didn't you let us know about it before? We might have been on our guard. Gosh, you're a dirty dog, Finch, to go sneaking around with a caul on your head, rounding up all the ducats in the family!"

Finch pushed back his chair and rose, shaking with rage. "Come outside with me!" he said, chokingly. "Only come outside with me! I'll show you who's a dirty dog — I'll —"

"Sit down!" ordered Renny.

Nicholas thundered, "Have you no sense of decency, you young ruffian?"

Everyone began to talk at once. Wakefield listened, astonished yet not ill pleased, as one who had sown the seed of a daisy and raised a fierce, thorny cactus. A caul. To think that one little word like that should raise this storm.

Finch sat down and rested his head on his hand.

Ernest looked across at him not unkindly. "You need never be afraid of the water," he said. "One who is born with a caul is never drowned."

Augusta asked of Wakefield, "But, my dear, however did you hear of such a thing?"

"Finch told me himself. I wish I'd got one!"

"So do I!" said Piers. "It seems a shame that Finch should have all the luck."

Pheasant could remain in doubt no longer. "But what *are* they?"

"One doesn't explain them," replied Augusta, looking down her nose.

Renny regarded Finch with no good eye. "I don't like your telling the youngster about such things. I don't like it at all. I'll have a word with you about this. Another cup of tea, Aunt, please."

Good appetite had attended all the Whiteoaks at dinner, but Finch had eaten as though famished. In spite of the fact that he was in acute disfavor, looked upon with suspicion and reproach, something inside him was ravening for food. He felt that if he could appease that something he might not feel so light-headed. But he rose from the table unsatisfied. . . . If only he could escape and hide himself in the woods! Press his hot forehead against the cool earth and his breast upon the pine needles! He made a stumbling effort to go into the hall instead of returning to the sitting room with the others, but Nicholas laid a heavy hand on his shoulder.

"Don't go away, boy. I should like to ask you a few questions."

"Yes," agreed Ernest, on his other side, "I should like to find out something of the inside of this affair, if possible."

Finch returned, as between jailers, to the torture room. He heard the clock on the landing strike two, and this was echoed in a silvery tone by the French clock in the drawing-room, and in an abrupt metallic voice by the clock on the mantelpiece of the sitting room. Nicholas took out his large hunting-case watch and looked at it. . . . Ernest looked at his nails. . . . Meg hung over her baby. . . . Maurice dropped into a comfortable chair and began to fill his pipe with his active hand, the disabled one lying, unmoved and smooth, on the leather arm of the chair. Finch, seeing it, felt a sudden morbid envy of it. It was hopelessly injured, neglected, let alone. . . . Renny took the muzzle of one of his spaniels in his lean brown hands, opened it, and examined the healthy white teeth. . . . Piers, in a corner, laughed at Pheasant. . . . Augusta produced a piece of crochet work from a bag, and a long, stabbing crochet hook. . . . Finch saw them all as torturers.

There was Rags, closing the folding doors upon them, seeming to say, "There naow, I leave you to your own devices! Whatever you may gaow through, it's all the sime to me!"

But not yet were they to settle down. A voice came from Grandmother's room, crying, "Nick! Nick! Nick!"

Ernest clapped his hands on his ears.

"Boney!" ejaculated Nicholas hoarsely. "God, what has come over the bird?"

"He has made up his mind," said Augusta, "to torture us."

Ernest cautiously removed his hands from his ears. "It is unbearable! I don't know what we are going to do about it."

Maurice suggested, "Perhaps it would be better to put him away, as he seems to be out of sorts and all that."

Every blazing glance in the room branded him as an outsider.

"He will be all right," said Renny, "as soon as he's done moulting. He ought to have a few drops of brandy in his drinking water. I remember Gran used to give him that for a tonic. Fetch him in here, Wake. He needs company."

The parrot was brought, squatting glumly on his perch, and placed in the middle of the room beside the ottoman on which Finch had uncomfortably disposed his lanky form. Boney ruffled himself, shook his wings, and three feathers drifted to the floor.

"It's uncanny," muttered Nicholas, "that he should have forgotten his Hindu, and should say only my name."

"It's dreadful," said Ernest.

"I think," declared Augusta, "there's something portentous about it. It's as though he were trying to tell us something."

"He looks strangely agitated," said Ernest.

Everyone looked at Boney, who returned melancholy stare for stare out of cold yellow eyes.

After a silence, Nicholas heaved himself in his chair and turned to Finch. "Did my mother ever give you reason to believe that she was going to leave her money to you?"

"No, Uncle Nick." Finch's voice was scarcely audible.

"Did she ever speak to you of the disposal of her property?"

"No, Uncle Nick."

"Did she ever speak to you of having made a new will?"

"No — she never spoke of any will to me."

"You had no faintest idea that her will was in your favor?"

"No."

"Then you would have us believe that you were as much

surprised as we were this morning when Patton read the will?"

Finch flushed deeply. "I—I was terribly surprised."

"Come, come," put in Piers, "don't expect us to believe that! You never turned a hair when Patton read the will. I was looking at you. You knew damn well what was coming."

"I didn't!" shouted Finch. "I didn't know a thing about it!"

"Stay!" said Nicholas. "Don't get blustery, Piers. I want to untwist this tangle, if possible." His eyes, under his shaggy brows, pierced Finch. "You say you were as astonished as the rest of us by the will. Just tell us, please, what in your opinion was my mother's reason for making you her heir."

Finch twisted his hands between his knees. He wished some tidal wave might rise and sweep him from their sight.

"Yes," urged Ernest, "tell us why you think she did such a thing. We are not angry at you. We only want to find out whether there was any reason for such an extraordinary act."

"I don't know of any reason," stammered Finch. "I—I wish she hadn't!"

He did himself no good by this admission. The words coming from his mouth, drawn in misery, made him the more contemptible.

Nicholas turned to Augusta. "What was that about Mamma's talking to herself? Something about a Chinese goddess."

Augusta laid down her crochet work. "I couldn't make it out. Just some mumbled words about Finch and the goddess Kuan Yin. It was then she said that he had more —you know what. I prefer not to repeat it."

"Now, what about this Chinese goddess, Finch? Do you

know what my mother meant by coupling your name with such a strange one?"

"I don't see why she should have," he hedged, weakly.

"Did she at any time mention a Chinese goddess to you?"

"Yes." He was floundering desperately. "She said I might learn — she — that is, she said I might get to understand something of life from her."

"From her?"

"Yes. Kuan Yin."

"This is worth following up," said Vaughan.

"It sounds as though Gran and Finch were both a little mad at the time," said his wife.

"At the time," repeated Nicholas. "Just how long ago did this conversation take place?"

"Oh, quite a bit ago. At the beginning of summer."

Nicholas said, pointing at Finch with his pipe, "Now, tell us exactly what led up to this conversation."

Ernest interrupted him, nervously, "The little Chinese goddess Mamma brought from India! Of course. I have not seen the little figure for some time. Strange I didn't miss it! Have you noticed it lately, Augusta?"

Augusta tapped the bridge of her nose sharply with her crochet hook, as though to stimulate her faculty of nosing out secrets. "No — I have not. It is gone! It is *gone from Mamma's room!* It has been stolen!"

Finch burned his bridges. "No, it hasn't. She gave it to me."

"Where is it?" demanded Nicholas.

"In my room."

"I was in your room this morning," said Augusta. "I thought I smelled something strange. The goddess was not there! I should have noticed instantly!"

Finch cared for nothing now but to have this cross-questioning done with. He said, with weary contempt for the consequences, "You did not see her because she is hidden. I keep her hidden. The stuff you smelled was incense. I was burning it before her at sunrise. I forgot to shut my door when I came down."

If Finch had suddenly produced horns on his young brow, or hoofs instead of worn brown shoes, he could scarcely have appeared as a greater monstrosity to his family. The monotonous pressure of their various personalities upon his bruised spirit was violently withdrawn. The recoil was so palpable that he raised his head and drew a deep breath, as though inhaling a draft of fresh air.

They drew back shocked from a Whiteoak who had risen at sunrise to burn incense before a heathen goddess. What sort of abortion had the English governess—young Philip's second wife—produced? That they, Courts and Whiteoaks,—gentlemen, soldiers, "goddamming" country squires,—should come to this! A white-faced, wincing boy who did fantastic things in his attic room while his family slept! And to this one had old Adeline, toughest-fibred of them all, left her money!

Their invincible repugnance toward such a deviation from their traditions caused a tremor of bewilderment to shake their tenacity. Finch, slumping on his ottoman, seemed a creature apart.

But this spurious advantage was soon past. The circle tightened again.

Nicholas, his chin gripped in his hand, said, "When I was at Oxford there were fellows who did that sort of thing. I never thought to see a nephew of mine . . . "

"He'll be turning Papist next," said Piers. "Look at those candles he set up around poor old Gran!"

"Yes, and you allowed him to do it!" exclaimed Augusta, accusingly to Nicholas.

Nicholas ignored this. He continued, "You expect us to believe that you hoped to gain nothing by my mother's will, when in secret she was giving you valuable presents?"

"I didn't know it was valuable."

Meg cried, "You must have thought it was very strange that she should be giving away things she had treasured all these years! The goddess — the ruby ring!"

"What motive had you in hiding the present?" probed Nicholas.

"I dunno."

"Yes. You do know. Don't lie. We're going to get to the bottom of this!"

"Well, it was hers, I thought. I didn't think — I knew she wouldn't want it mentioned."

"And what else?"

"I thought I'd get into a row."

"Just for having a present given you? Come, now!"

Ernest interjected, "But why should she have given him anything? I can't make it out!"

Piers grinned sarcastically. "Look at him, and you'll understand. He's such an intriguing young devil. I am always longing to give him something."

Renny spoke, from where he sat on the window seat. "Cut that out, Piers."

Nicholas continued, "Were you often alone with my mother? I don't remember ever finding you together!"

Finch writhed; his chin sank to his breast. He set his teeth.

Renny said, "Make a clean breast of it, Finch! Hold your head up."

He was intolerably miserable. He could not bear it. Yet he must bear it. They would give him no peace till they had everything out of him.

"Buck up!" said Renny. "You didn't steal the goddess, or the money either. Don't act as though you had!"

Finch raised his head. He fixed his eyes on Augusta's crochet work, which lay on her lap, and said in a husky voice : —

"I've been going to the church to practise on the organ at night. Once, when I came in very late, Gran called me. I went into her room and we talked together. That was the night she gave me the goddess. After that I went often — almost every night." He stopped with a jerk.

There was a sultry silence while they waited for him to go on.

Nicholas nudged him, almost gently. "Yes? You went every night to my mother's room. You talked. Would you mind telling me what about?"

"I talked about music, but not much. She did most of the talking. The old days here — her life in India, and about when she was a young girl in the Old Country."

Ernest cried, "No wonder she was drowsy in the daytime! Awake half the night talking!"

Finch was reckless now. They might as well have something to rage about. "I used," he said, "to go to the dining room and get biscuits and glasses of sherry, and that made her enjoy it more. It helped keep her awake."

"No wonder she was drowsy! No wonder she was absent-minded!" cried Ernest, almost in tears.

Augusta said, with dreadful solemnity, "No wonder that for the last month her breakfast trays have come away almost untouched!"

"I saw her failing day by day!" wailed Meg.

Nicholas cast a grim look at those about him. "This has probably shortened her life by years."

"It has killed her!" said Ernest, distractedly.

"He's little better than a murderer!" said Augusta.

He could look them in the eyes now. They knew the worst. He was a monster, and a murderer. Let them take him out and hang him to the nearest tree! He was almost calm.

Their tempers were surging this way and that like waves driven by variable winds. They were all talking at once blaming him, blaming each other, desperately near to blaming old Adeline! And the voice of Uncle Nicholas, like the voice of the seventh wave, was the most resonant, the most terrible. It was the voice of the wronged eldest son.

Presently the voice of Piers, full of malicious laughter, disentangled itself from the others. He was saying, "The whole thing is a tremendous joke on the family. We thought Finch was queer. A weakling. But, don't you see, he's the strongest, the sanest, of the lot? He's been pulling the wool over everybody's eyes for years. Poor, harmless, hobbledehoy Finch! Well-meaning, but so simple! I tell you, he's as cool and calculating as they make them! He's had this under his hat ever since he came back from New York!"

"Rot!" said Renny.

"You'd stand up for him, Renny! Why, he's fooled you all along! Didn't he trick you into thinking he went into Leighs' to study, when he was up to his eyes in play-acting? Didn't he trick you nicely over the orchestra? He was supposed to be studying then, and he was playing the piano in cheap restaurants, and coming home drunk in the morning! And now he's tricked you out of Gran's money!" The laughter had died out of his voice—it was savage.

Enraged, Finch cried out, "Shut up! It's a pack of lies!"

"Deny that you ever set out to deceive Renny!"

"What about you? You deceived him when you got married!"

"I wasn't *cheating* him out of anything!"

Finch rose to his feet, his arms rigid at his side, his hands clenched. "I'm not cheating Renny! I don't want to cheat anyone. I don't want the money! I want to give it back! I won't take it! I won't take it—I won't take it—"

He burst into despairing tears. He walked up and down the room, wringing his hands, entreating Nicholas—entreating Ernest to take the money. He stopped before Renny, his face broken into a grotesque semblance to that of a gargoyle by devastating emotion, and begged him to take the money. He was so distraught that he did not know what he was doing, and when Renny pulled him on to the window seat beside him he sank down bewildered, dazed by his own clamorous beseechings. His throat ached as though he had been screaming. Had he been screaming? He did not know. He saw them looking at him out of white, startled faces. He saw Pheasant run from the room. He saw Meggie clutching her crying baby. He heard Renny's voice in his ear, saying, "For Christ's sake, get hold of yourself! You make me ashamed for you!"

He put his elbows on his knees and hid his face in his hands. Against his cheek he felt the roughness of Renny's tweed sleeve, and he wanted to rub against it, to cling to it, to cry his heart out against it like a frightened little boy.

In a heavy undertone the talk went on and on, but no one addressed him. They were done with him now. They could not or would not take the money from him, but they would let him alone, and they would talk and talk, till from afar off the tidal wave he had been praying for would come roaring and sweep them all into oblivion. . . .

The tidal wave came, and it was Rags; the oblivion, tea.

XXII

SUNRISE

As he walked swiftly along the country road that led to the lake, the feel of the thick fine dust through the thin soles of his canvas shoes gave him an aching sense of pleasure. The balls of his stockingless feet, his toes, seemed to have acquired a new sensitiveness that morning. They pressed the earth hungrily as though to imprint on it a palpable and lasting caress.

His eyes, dark-ringed after a sleepless night, moved constantly, as though to drink in all possible beauty from the dew-drenched burnished land. They swept over a field of ripe corn, from which came a dry, sweet whisper as though all the tiny imprisoned kernels sang together. They swept hungrily over a swarthy stubble field, from which a great flock of crows rose into the blueness of the sky. They espied, bluer than the sky, the clump of chicory by the roadside. Nothing could escape them. Not the spider's web, red as copper in the red sunrise. Not the sudden sparkle of dew on a tilting leaf. Not the slender imprint of a bird's foot on the dust before him.

He loved it so, and he was going to leave it. So often had he traversed this road, afoot and on his bicycle, and now this was to be the last time!

He could endure his life no longer. He had thought it all out through the long night, reviewed its nineteen years of blundering, cowardice, and terrors, and he had reached the certainty that he could endure it no longer. If he had had one friend — one person who could have understood, and pitied his forlornness! There was Alayne, but she was inaccessible because of the presence of Eden. And, even

if he could have gone to her and poured out his miserable
heart, it would not have sufficed, for there was the
family, a solid hostile wall, impervious to his tears as to his
batterings.   It was not to be borne!   In that wall of his
own flesh and blood there was no relenting crevice through
which he might creep and timidly touch hands with those
he loved again. . . . He had wronged them, and there was
only one way to make it right. . . . The old uncles —
wondering all these years about their mother's money — and
it had come to him! And Renny! But he could not think
of Renny, and that look of shame for him on Renny's face!

All night it had been necessary to compel his mind from
the remembrance of that look.   There had been moments
when he had felt that he must run down the attic stairs,
throw himself on his knees at Renny's bedside, and beg him
to forgive him, to comfort him, as he had comforted him
after childish nightmares.   Renny, whom he had wronged
most of all!   Well, now he was going to do what lay in
his power to set things right.   They would have to take the
money now and divide it among them!

This morning it required no effort to keep his mind clear.
It was as clear as crystal, exquisitely empty, as though
washed clean by a hurricane.   It was like an empty crystal
bowl held up by the hands of his soul to receive the wine
of beauty.   From every side that wine ran into it, from the
pine-sweet darkness of the ravine, from the reddening fields,
along the slanting rays from the sun through which God
spoke to him.

He passed the crossroad.   Here once they would have
buried him, when his drenched body had been taken from
the lake, with a stake driven through his heart.   A warning
to those who contemplated suicide.   He did not think he
would have minded that.   He would have been no lonelier
buried at the crossroad than in the churchyard with his kin
around him.   What he was about to do seemed so natural

that it seemed to him that all his acts for years had been leading up to this. To obliterate himself — to dash from his lips the bitter cup of living. He had brought with him into the world not much but the power of loving beauty. He would take out with him all that he could absorb of beauty, and perhaps God would leave that with him, while he slept, as compensation for the pain.

Oh, the caressing softness of the dust! For this last little way he would have nothing between his soles and it. He threw off his shoes and ran barefoot. He threw back his head, drinking in the cleanness of the breeze from the lake. Now he ran over dry, coarse grass, now over shingle that cut his feet, now over fine sand, hard as a marble floor.

The sun was hanging, a great lantern, just above the horizon. A red pathway crossed the lake from it to his very feet. The morning was as pure, as crystalline, as though it was the first morning that had broken over the earth. As he ran splashing into the water, fiery drops were flung up all about him. Translucent ripples disturbed the glassy surface of the lake. He ran out, his bare head empty and untroubled. He was not afraid. He sank into the water and swam outward on his side, following the red pathway. He would swim till he was tired, and then . . . He embraced the gently heaving water. He flung his arm again and again across the early morning ruddiness. He closed his eyes and saw bright panels set in amethyst walls against the lids. . . . There was no thought in him; he was empty as a crystal bowl moving through the water; feeling neither pride nor shame, exquisitely unconcerned; fragile, yet capable of receiving and holding fast the beauty that was flowing with him. . . . He heard music. . . .

Slowly he relaxed, and surrendered himself. . . .

The music became by degrees blurred, resolving itself into an overpowering humming, as though the arch of the

sky were the dome of a vast beehive. His ears ached with
the burden of it. He longed, with a sad longing, to be free
of the fantastic, terrible droning, to hear the music, pure
and clear once more. . . . It was no longer morning, red
sunrise, but night, black night, and all the stars were bees,
filling the universe with their humming. They swarmed in
the cold black heavens, hungry for honey, ceaselessly humming. . . .

He must conceal the fact that he is a flower, full to the
brim, overflowing with honey, for, if they discover this,
they will swarm down upon him and suck the sweet essence
out of him, leaving him empty, bruised and forlorn. . . .
He shudders and draws his petals close about him to conceal
the treasure. He is rocked on his stem, and is terrified that
he will be broken from it and fall into the dreadful abyss
below. . . . His petals are now white, now red, changing
their color constantly, veined with violet and gold, drawing
and withdrawing above the honey that is the centre of
him. . . .

He is convulsed with agony, for the bees have found
him out. Their humming is becoming deafening, their wings
clash like armor; they fly down, carrying lances to pierce
him. . . . There is one golden bee that has seized him.
They struggle. He curls up his petals desperately. He tries
to scream, but knows that flowers have no voice. The
abyss yawns below.

The great golden bee clutches him and will not be thrown
off. Another comes to its aid. They are dragging him
away now, helpless, fainting. No use to struggle. His
petals, red and white, are falling into the abyss. He is torn
to pieces.

Eden's face was close to his. Eden's face, white and
dripping, with a wet lock plastered over the forehead.
Someone else was there too, someone who had been doing

strange things to him, knocking him about. He felt weak and sick, but he managed to gasp out, "All right . . . all right . . . pretty well, thanks."

He didn't know why he said that, unless they had been asking him how he felt, and he knew he must conceal the terrible truth. He had completely forgotten what the truth was, but he was poignantly conscious of its terror.

Eden was saying, in a staccato way, as though his teeth were rattling, "God, what a mercy that you were here! I should never have saved him alone!"

It was Minny Ware's rich voice that answered.

"I'm afraid you'd both have been drowned."

"And this first-aid business — you're simply wonderful! I've never felt such a duffer in my life!"

"You were splendid the way you plunged in! He'll be all right now, I think. It's you I feel worried about. You've been so ill. I must get help at once!"

Eden's hand was on Finch's heart. "It's beating more regularly. You're better, old chap? You know who I am?"

"Yes, Eden."

With a great effort he raised his eyelids again and saw Minny Ware standing straight and flushed, a dripping undergarment clinging to her rounded body, her breast still heaving from her exertions, her hair, like Eden's, plastered against her head. When she saw him looking at her, she smiled and said, "You naughty boy! I hope you're sorry for what you've done. Giving us such a fright!"

A shiver shook Eden from head to foot. She snatched up her dress and struggled, dripping as she was, into it. "I shall run to the house and get Mr. Vaughan as quickly as possible."

"No — no. Get Renny. He'd not like it if we didn't send for him first. Besides, he'll get here in half the time Maurice would."

She hesitated, disappointed. She had thought to come back with Maurice. The idea of missing any of the excitement, of losing any of the savor of being with these two males, half-drowned as they were, was intolerable to her exuberant femininity. She said, " I think it would be better to fetch Mr. Vaughan."

" Why ? " Eden asked sharply.

" Because — he would take you straight to his house. You 'd like that better, would n't you ? "

" Telephone Renny — I 'll have him take us to the Vaughans'. Please be quick, Miss Ware. This poor youngster is half-frozen — and I — " He shivered and smiled.

" What a beast I am ! " she cried. " I 'll run every bit of the way ! "

She did, and felt as though she could never tire, elated by the strange happenings of the morning. Her life at the Vaughans' was so quiet ! Her mind was fervently preoccupied with the young men at Jalna. Married or single, their doings filled her thoughts. She discussed their dispositions, their talents, and their prospects endlessly with Meg. Meg pushed her always in the direction of Renny. Rich-voiced, yearning-bosomed, she was willing to be pushed in any direction.

She had risen that morning shortly after dawn, and sat at her open window, from which she could see the road. Along it she had seen the figure of Eden sauntering. She was almost sure it was Eden, but not quite sure. At any rate, it was one of the Whiteoaks. The red sky in the east, the figure of the young man sauntering, the sudden cry of a blackbird in the elm tree near her window, had filled her heart with loneliness, with longing. She had changed into a prettier dress, stolen from the house, and followed him to the shore. She had found him nursing his knees and a pipe. She had made her presence known by singing softly as she approached along the sand. He had confessed to her that he had been too restless to sleep — a lyric that struggled toward birth, and yet was perversely reluctant of delivery. She had sat down beside him, at his invitation, hugging her knees and the smell of his tobacco smoke. Together they had rescued Finch.

They had watched him run into the water and swim outward without suspicion dawning, until Minny had exclaimed over the fact that he wore trousers and shirt instead of a bathing suit. And there had been something strange, wild, and exalted about the running young figure. . . .

He lay stretched on the sand now under Eden's coat, his face, of a deathly pallor, half-hidden in the crook of his arm. Eden crouched beside him, gripping between shaking jaws a pipe that had long been out. He patted Finch's shoulder. "Someone will be here, old chap! Do you feel sick?"

An inarticulate sound came from the prostrate figure. Eden patted him again. "You'll soon be all right. Those feelings come to us, but they pass. I've felt like doing it many a time."

"Ugh!" He shuddered from head to foot.

Disgusted at being brought back, poor young devil, thought Eden. Preferred oblivion out there to that tidy little fortune of Gran's. Ah, he'd been having a rough time of it — no doubt about that! But he'd get over it — live to play the fool with the money. . . . Money. What must it be like to have money! Why the hell didn't Renny come? If only Gran had left the money to him! He'd have snapped his fingers in the family's face. There he went — shuddering again! Poor little devil!

The Whiteoak car! Rattling down the stony road as though it would fly to pieces. Bang! Some rut that! Rattle, jiggle, bump. Ungodly racket, but how the old car could go! There was Renny at the wheel, his face set, too weather-bitten to show pallor even though he'd had a fright.

Serve him right! Serve them all right if the kid had been drowned. Eden guessed at the scene which had brought about this reckless act.

"Hullo!" he shouted. "Here we are!"

The car bumped on to the beach, stopped with a jerk, and the master of Jalna leaped out.

He came with a long, crunching stride. "What's this?" he asked sharply.

Eden got to his feet. "This boy's been trying to do away with himself."

"Do away with himself! Minny Ware told me that he'd got cramps swimming!"

"She was trying to spare your feelings! I'm not." Eden's face was set also. His characteristic half-smile was frozen into a queer grin. "He hasn't been able to tell anything, but I'll venture to say he was hounded into it!"

Renny bent over Finch. He looked into his eyes, felt his heart. "I must get him into bed. I've brought brandy with me." He held the cup from a flask to Finch's mouth, and, when he had gulped the brandy gaspingly, Renny re-filled the cup and handed it to Eden. "This has been enough to kill you," he said grimly, "after all you've been through!"

Eden shrugged, then looked steadily into Renny's eyes. "I have an idea," he said, "that I've done the best thing in saving this youngster that I've done in all my life."

"Minny Ware told me that you'd never have got him if it hadn't been for her."

Damn Renny! How he took the wind out of one's sails!

"She was there," he admitted, "and I guess *she* never did a better thing! He must have had a hell of a time to make him do this!"

"Time to talk of that later." Renny picked up the boy, too light for his length, and carried him to the car. He supported him against his shoulder while Eden drove. Meg met them on the steps. The old people at Jalna must not get a fright. Meg's full, soft lips were ineffably tender, and behind her stood Minny Ware. Maurice helped to carry Finch up the stairs.

He was rolled in blankets before a fire, drowsy, perspiring, sensing already the sweet, sticky smell of petunias that came in on the hot sunshine through the open window. But he had something to say to Renny, who stood drawing down his shirt sleeves. He had been rubbing Finch with alcohol.

"Renny," he said hesitatingly, "you won't tell them what I did . . . you won't let the others know?"

"All right," returned Renny, looking down on him with brusque compassion. His mind flew back to other times when Finch had entreated, in the very same tone, "You won't tell them that you licked me, will you, Renny? You won't let the others know?" And he had answered then as now, "All right, I won't."

Meg came in with a step which she tried to make noiseless, but she was getting heavy, and the things on the bedside table jiggled. She bent over the sausagelike form on the bed and stroked the damp hair.

"Comfy, now?"

"Uh-huh."

She asked Renny, "How is he, really?"

"Half-lit and as hot as blazes."

"Poor fellow!" She sat down on the side of the bed and tried to see his face. "Finch, dear, how could you do such a dreadful thing? Frightening me almost to death! As though *I* minded you having the money! What upset *me* was Gran's giving her ruby ring, that I always understood *I* was to get, to Pheasant. You must understand that. Do you?"

He pushed his head against her palm as a dog urgent for caresses. He felt broken. He tried to drag his mind from the well of muddle-headedness, exhaustion, and submission, into which it had sunk, and reply to her, but he could not. He could only feel for her fingers with his hot lips and kiss them.

"He feels so hot!"

"That's the way he ought to feel. Come along and let him sleep."

She led Renny into the sitting room, bright with glazed chintz. Eden was seated before a tray on which were a dish of poached eggs on toast, a pot of tea, and a jar of quince jelly. The shadow was lifted from her face. The agitation caused by Finch was eased. He was safe in bed, and here was a delicious breakfast tray.

She exclaimed, "This is Minny's doing! She has had breakfast brought up for the three of us. She knew we must be faint for food. What a girl!"

"She carried it in herself," said Eden, "but she wouldn't stay. By George, she can swim! And to look at her just now you'd never think she'd been through anything. I admire her awfully." He helped himself to an egg.

"She's a darling," said his sister. "I shall feel very blue when she goes."

"Is she going?" Eden looked almost dismayed.

"Of course. A girl like that couldn't stay here forever. She's getting unsettled. But I don't know what she'll find to do—"

Renny put an egg on Meg's plate and two on his own. He said, easily, "She'll find something to do! That sort always fall on their feet."

"What sort!" cried Meg, offended.

"Adventurous. Grabbing at life with both hands."

"I'm awfully keen about her," said Eden.

"You'd make up to anything in petticoats," said Renny.

"Petticoats! Listen to the man!"

"She could do with one. She's too—"

"Too *what*, dear?" asked Meg.

"H'm   Provocative. A little hampering might be good for her."

Meg pondered on this remark, not knowing whether or not to be displeased. She changed the subject. "How lovely to be breakfasting together!"

"I thought you liked eating alone," observed Renny, taking a third egg.   Have another, Eden?"

Eden shook his head. "I wonder," he said, "what the upshot of this is going to be! Brother Finch and the money. I wish the old lady might have left me a thousand."

"Poor darling!" sighed Meg. "I wonder what you're going to do now that you're better."

"Fall on my feet, I suppose, like Minny. I suspect I'm that sort, too — grabbing life with both hands."

Meg said, spreading quince jelly on toast, "Finch has been getting out of control for a long time. I've seen it, though I haven't said anything."

"I commend your reticence," said Renny, looking down his nose.

Meg looked pensive. "Finch is really a nice boy — underneath. He's ever so generous. Don't you think he might do something for Eden?"

"He doesn't come into the money until he's of age. Almost two years. By that time Eden will probably be famous."

"Oh — his poems! But they pay so badly for them, don't they? Can't Alayne do something for you, Eden?"

"Good God," exclaimed Renny, irritably, "she's done almost enough for him, I think! Giving up her work and coming here to nurse him!"

"But why not? He's her husband. I think she'd a perfect right to nurse him."

"And yet," retorted Renny, "you were angry with her for coming!" And he added bitterly, "But she could never do anything right in your eyes!"

Eden's eyes, full of mocking laughter, looked from one face to the other.

"Quarrel over me, do!" he said. "It makes me feel so important. And I haven't felt very important of late. I'm quite well again, I've no job, and my wife doesn't care a damn for me. In fact," his eyes narrowed with malice, "it's my opinion that she only came back to Jalna to nurse me so that she could be near Renny!"

Renny sprang up, with lean red face redder with anger. The table was jarred, a miniature squall slopped the tea from the cups.

"I don't expect anything better of you, Meggie," he said. "But I thought that you, Eden, might have a little gratitude—a little decency!" He strode to the door. "I must go. If you want me to drive you home, come along."

This day seemed set apart for one emotion on top of another. He could not endure the indoors. Meg followed him to the porch. Before the bed of purple petunias, whose sweetness had risen to Finch's window, knelt Minny Ware, her face close to the flowers, absorbing their perfume drawn out by the sun. She liked the untidy, luxuriant, sticky things. They hadn't troubled themselves about delicacy, precision of form, like some flowers, but had given themselves up to sucking in all the sweetness possible and wastefully exuding it. Though she was conscious of the two in the porch, she made no sign, keeping her head bent over the flowers.

Meg clasped Renny's arm in both her hands. "There's someone," she said, indicating Minny with a glance, "who is deeply disappointed for your sake."

"I like her nerve! I don't want her sympathy. . . . Meggie!" He turned his dark eyes reproachfully on her. "Why will you try to shove that girl down my throat when you know that I love Alayne—and Alayne only—and always shall?"

Meg said, with a melancholy vibration in her voice, "No good will come out of this! Why should she have come back? She is full of deceit. It's just as Eden says — she made his illness an excuse to be near you! I'm glad he's not grateful to her! I'm not grateful to her. I despise her, and hate her."

His carved profile showed no sign of emotion. He let his arm remain in his sister's clasp and his eyes rested composedly on the bright head of Minny Ware, but Meg was aware of an inexplicable magnetic current from him which, if she had been more sensitive, she might have interpreted as a volcanic disturbance in the restrained tenacity of his passion.

Eden appeared in the hall, slid past them, and went to where Minny crouched above the purple mass of petunias. She was not aware which of the brothers had approached, and scarcely knew whether to be pleased or disappointed when it was Eden's voice that said, "I'm afraid you feel very tired. Heroic exertion, that — saving the lives of two able-bodied men."

She tilted her head so that he looked down into her eyes, and saw the sunlight on the satin prominence of her cheek bones. She denied heroism emphatically. "I only helped you a bit with Finch. He would struggle. But — I am tired — I don't sleep well — I'm restless."

He said, "If you should be taking another early stroll to-morrow, we might meet again by the lake. We could talk."

"I'd like that. . . . Mrs. Vaughan's a darling, but — I'm getting bored. Oh, I'm a beast! I'm always like that."

He laughed. "So am I. We'll meet and compare our beastliness. It's going to be fine to-morrow."

In the car the brothers rode in silence, broken at last by Eden's saying rather fretfully, "Sorry, old chap."

The Whiteoak car was an inauspicious place for an apology to a driver whose ears were not only assailed by its rattle, but who was trying to fathom the meaning of a new jerking movement in its anatomy.

"What'd you say?" he demanded, turning his head with a gesture so like old Adeline's that Eden's apology was marred by mirth. He repeated, "I say I'm sorry for what I said — about Alayne, and all that."

Renny had caught nothing but the name of Alayne. He stopped the car with a jerk and gave Eden a look of mingled encouragement and suspicion.

"Yes?"

"If I have to repeat it again," said Eden, sulkily, "I'll take it back. I was trying to apologize for what I said about Alayne." He continued with a frown, "The fact is, I'm absolutely fed up with being grateful. I've spent the summer oozing gratitude to Alayne. It's got on my nerves. I suppose that's why I said what I did. I'd no right to say it, but — it's true, and you shouldn't mind that. She'd go through hell — and being under the same roof with me is a fair imitation of hell for her — for the sake of setting eyes on your red head once in a while. She can't help it . . . I can't help it . . . we're caught in a net. . . . She's not suited to any Whiteoak that ever lived. But neither of you can ever be happy as things are. I want you to believe I'm sorry — horribly sorry."

Renny said, "I hope this affair hasn't given you any cold. If you feel a chill we must have the doctor to you. You mustn't be running risks."

He started the car and concentrated once more on that dubious, jerky movement in its interior. What could it be? He was afraid the time was at hand when he would have to buy a new car.

Eden slouched in his corner. What a baffling devil! If only one could take him apart as one could the car, and find out what was inside! A queer, fiery, cantankerous interior, he'd be bound!

XXIII
RENNY AND ALAYNE

RENNY WHITEOAK wandered about that afternoon with a grievous sense of being cut off from the activities of the life he loved by the flaring up of a passion he had thought to have under control, the futility of which was so definite that to brood on it was to hunger for painted fruit in a picture.

He had thought to keep his desire for Alayne under control, as he controlled a vicious horse by a curb bit, and he was humiliated to find that Eden's reckless words at the breakfast table had broken the bit and set his passion galloping. That, and the sting of Meg's determination to marry him to Minny Ware, her fond hope of transforming him into a placid husband and father. Now he was conscious of only one thing — that, close at hand, beyond the orchards heavy with fruit and thick autumnal sunshine, was Eden's wife whom he loved, who, as Eden had said, would live in hell for the sake of sometimes setting eyes on his red head. Had the summer been hell to her, he wondered? But he was only faintly curious. Her mind was to him, as woman's mind, a book in a foreign tongue, the pages of which might flutter with subtle charm before him, but which he knew himself to be incapable of reading. Hesitatingly he might recognize a word, a phrase, which resembled the language spoken by himself; indolently he might form its syllables with his lips, trying to become familiar with its tones, but the language must ever remain for him a tenuous whisper between girl and girl.

Vehemently he was occupied by the clamor in his own being. At times he surrendered himself to it, plunging all

his senses into its depths, so that he was unconscious of
where he was, what he saw or heard, moving like a storm
cloud through his stables, fields, and woods. Piers avoided
him, while sympathizing with the evil mood, brought on,
as he thought, by disappointment over the will. The stablemen pronounced him vicious. As he was passing a field of
potatoes he came upon the bent figure of Binns brooding.
The old man straightened himself with difficulty, and cast
a disgruntled look across the brown loam at the master of
Jalna.

"Hi!" he called.

Renny wheeled and stared at him blankly.

"No gettin' away from blight," called Binns. "Taters
got it. Tomaters got it. Corn's got it. It's a terr'ble year
for blight." He began to dig lustily, fearing he would again
be told to cease work, for he was a day laborer. But when
the tall figure had moved on without answer he leaned on his
spade and followed him with vindictive little eyes. "Blight's
got him, darn him," he muttered. "It's got the whole
fam'ly. They be crazy, I tell you," he said to the potatoes,
"rampagin' over the country, playin' the organ in pitch
dark. They've women on the brain — that's what. . . .
I tell Jim Chalk to keep his girl in at night. He just laughs.
Serve him right if she's ketched. High or low, it's all
one to that kind. Rips!" His eyes looked sagaciously into
the eyes of the potatoes.

Renny loitered by the paddock, where a two-year-old was
being put at a gate by Wright. He felt more peaceful as he
followed the lift of the splendid, lustrous body, the straight
hocks, the strong neck. When the practice was over, bridle
and bit were removed; the two-year-old came to the paling
and nozzled him. He plucked a handful of short clover
and fed it to her, watching the beam in her liquid eyes become ecstatic, watching the firm muscles above the eyes swell
and contract into hollows as she munched. He took her

head between his hands and kissed her nose. "Sweet girl,"
he murmured. "Pet Jenny!"

But he could not rest. He left her, though she whinnied
to him. Restlessly he turned his steps in the direction of
the bridle path, following it into the green well of the pine
wood. The damp summer had produced a rich crop of
mushrooms here. They followed the path, ivory-white,
brown, and rust-red, fantastically shaped, pushing through
the grass or half-hidden beneath prickly brambles laden with
berries. By a curve where the sun had access a tall clump
of pennyroyal scented the air with its acrid sweetness. A
tiny green snake hesitated for a moment, with quivering
tongue, before it slid under the grass. On the path were
hoofprints of Wake's pony. He had passed that way, and
was returning, Renny judged by the small thunder of an
approaching canter. He pressed his way through the
brambles under the pines and watched boy and pony go by,
Wakefield sitting erect, with folded arms, a look of exaltation on his face. Renny made a grimace of disgust with
himself for hiding from the little boy, yet speech with even
Wake was abhorrent to him. He stood motionless as one
of the mastlike trunks, his eyes fixed on the sombre wasted
red of pine needles thick on the ground. He recalled certain
amorous adventures of his past. How lightly forgotten!
But now there was neither fulfillment nor forgetting.

Eden was well now, but unfit for responsibility. He must
be sent to some warm climate for the winter. And Alayne
would return to New York. Unless — but what was the
alternative? His mind moved in the old relentless circle.
There was no way out. If only she was gone to-day! If
only he could force himself to go away until this fever
subsided and he could endure her nearness with the same
stoicism as before. He made up his mind to go away — to
breathe a different air.

He reëntered the bridle path, and in a sunny space, where

the berries were large and ripe, he found Minny Ware filling a small basket. He felt a quick annoyance with her for being in his path and, after a nod, passed on. Then he remembered that he had not thanked her for what she had done that morning. He reversed his steps hastily and came to her side.

"I want to thank you — I can't thank you enough for your courage this morning. God knows what might have happened if you had not been on the shore!"

The sound of his own words raised suspicion in his mind. "How did you come to be there," he asked abruptly, "at that hour?"

"Oh, it was just a coincidence. I like the early morning."

But he saw warm color creep up her cheeks. Why had she been there? Odd that neither he nor Meg had seen anything strange in the presence of Eden and her on the shore at sunrise.

She knew that he was suspecting her, but she went on picking berries. She selected the largest ones and dropped them almost caressingly into her basket. He noticed that her finger-tips were stained and also her lip, giving her a look of childlike innocence. The trivial act of her laying the plucked berries so gently in the basket, the stain on her fingers and her lip, seemed suddenly of enormous importance to him, as though she were performing some rite. The harassment of his thoughts ceased, his mind became concentrated on the ritualistic act.

She said, dreamily, "Do you care for these? Shall I pick you some?" Her eyes slid toward him speculatively.

"No," he answered, "but I'd like to stay and watch you pick them, if you don't mind."

"Why should you want to watch me do such a simple thing?" Her eyes searched his face. She had a great longing for love.

"I don't know," he answered, perplexed. And, seeing

that she looked rebuffed, he took her hand in his and kissed her bare arm on the white crook of her elbow.

He was not conscious of the approach of a third person, but he felt her arm quiver and he heard the quick intake of her breath. She was startled, but not by the caress. She said, "Oh!" in a defensive tone, and, turning his head, he saw across the bushes the pale, set face of Alayne.

She had come upon what looked to her like a radiant understanding between the two. She saw Minny's exuberance responding to a calculated caress for which Renny had led her to this secluded spot.

She drew back and stammered something incoherent. Minny, not much put out, regained her composure and smiled, not ill-pleased to be discovered by Alayne in such a situation. Renny retained his grasp on her wrist.

In the silence that followed Minny's exclamation, a delicate trilling sound became audible, as though some bizarre but diminutive instrument were being played beneath a leaf of bracken. The performer seemed to be so unconscious of the existence of the giant beings towering above him that his very egotism reduced them to something less than his own size; his shrill piping rose higher and higher, triumphant over mere bulk, was taken up by other players just as insistent, just as impressive in their purpose, till the sound of their trilling became universal. The locusts were singing of the death of Summer.

An inertia had crept over the three, who had, without their own volition, become listeners rather than performers in the woodland drama. Minny held a warm, too soft berry in her hand; Renny looked entreatingly yet dreamily at Alayne, who stood, as though she had lost the power of motion, regarding the linked hands of the other two.

The spell was broken by the reappearance of the little green snake, who, unlike the orchestra of locusts, was conscious of the intruders from tip to tip, quivering with fear and hatred of them, rearing his head against their presence, determined to separate them into the three lonely wanderers they had been when they entered the wood.

Without speaking, Alayne turned and walked swiftly along the path, a curve of which soon hid her from their sight. Their hands fell apart. Renny stood irresolute for a short space, feeling a kind of anger against both girls, as beings of a different texture from himself who had a secret in common that was in its essence antagonistic to him. Then, without looking at Minny, he crashed through the underbrush and strode after Alayne.

Minny's eyes, as she resumed her berry picking, had in them more of amusement than chagrin. After all, it was an amusing world. Mrs. Vaughan's schemes come to nothing. . . . Renny Whiteoak in love with that cold-blooded Mrs. Eden. . . . Eden, himself — a wayward dimple indented her round cheek. She began to sing, softly at first, but gaining in volume, till the locust orchestra was silenced, believing Summer to have returned in all her strength and beauty.

Alayne was conscious that he was following her and, dread-ing a meeting with him, she turned from the path at the first opportunity and took a short cut through the woods toward a gate that opened on to the road. He followed the wind-ings of the bridle path, believing her still to be ahead of him, but when he did not overtake her he suspected that she was willfully eluding him, and retraced his way to the short cut. He overtook her just as she reached the road. She heard the opening of the gate and turned to him. Here in the public road she felt more courageous than in the quiet of the wood, less likely to show the feeling which she fought so desperately to control. He had been the permanent object of her thoughts all the summer, yet this was the first time they had been quite close together. She had desired to return to New York without such a meeting. Now that it had been forced upon her, she felt her strength drained by the effort of resisting her own love for him no less than by the bitterness of having discovered him in the act of kissing Minny Ware.

"Alayne," he said, in a muffled voice, "you are trying to avoid me! I don't think I deserve it. Upon my word I don't!"

"I would rather be alone. It's nothing more than that." She began to walk slowly along the road.

"I know—" he exclaimed. "You're angry. But I give you my word—"

She interrupted furiously, "Why should you explain things to me? As though it mattered to me! Why did you leave her? Why did you follow me?" Though her lips questioned him her eyes looked fixedly ahead.

He walked beside her in the dust of the road. A jolting wagon loaded with turnips overtook and passed them.

He said, "You can't refuse to have this much explained, surely. I had not been two minutes beside Minny when you came up. My kiss on her arm was no more than her eating a blackberry. A few minutes before that, I had stopped by the paddock and kissed a two-year-old mare. One kiss was as important as the other. To me—to the mare—to Minny!"

He looked down into her pale, firmly modeled face, with its look of courage, of endurance, its what she called "Dutch" look of stability. Yet about her mouth was a look of fatigue, as though she were played out by the isolation and the ingrown emotions of the last months.

He continued, "I wish I could make you believe in my love as I believe in it myself. There's nothing on earth I could want so much as to have you for my own. Do you believe that?"

She did not answer.

A motor car whizzed by them, raising the dust in a

cloud. "Come," he said, "let us get off this road. It's so hot and dusty, it will give you a headache."

But she trudged doggedly on.

"Alayne," he persisted, "why don't you say something — if it's only to say that you don't believe me — that you're sick of the sight of me?"

She tried to answer, but her mouth was parched and her lips refused to move. She felt that she must go on forever, walking along this road, with him following her, longing to cry out, yet unable to speak, as in a nightmare. She would go on till she stumbled and fell.

He did not speak again, but walked beside her, trying once rather pathetically to suit his stride to hers. At the foot of the steps that led to the church he stopped.

"Where are you going?" he asked.

"To your grandmother's grave. I haven't seen it yet. Do I hear Finch playing in the church?"

"No, no. Finch is in bed. He tried to drown himself this morning." Let her have that. Perhaps it would shock her out of this terrible quiet.

"Yes," she said calmly. "Eden told me. No wonder!"

"God, how you hate us!"

"No — I fear you."

He said, almost irritably, "All this is so unreal! Can't you, or won't you, talk about our love? You know it exists. Why blink it? We can't come together, but surely — just before we part we can speak of it. I am going away to-night. You needn't be afraid that you'll see me again."

She began to go up the steps toward the churchyard. He caught her dress and held it. "No. You shall not go up there! I can't follow you there."

She raised her face to his with a sudden piteousness in her eyes. "Where shall I go, then?'

"Back into the woods."

They turned back, and had to step into the ditch, rank

with dusty goldenrod and Michaelmas daisies, out of the way of a truck loaded with calves. She stumbled; he put his hands on her and supported her. She felt that she must fall.

Again they were in the golden-green well of the woods. The red sun was low. Overhead the half-moon drifted, a pale feather, along the sky.

They stood for a moment listening to the beating of their own hearts. Then she raised her heavy eyes to his and whispered, "Kiss me — "

He bent. She drew his head down, closed her eyes, and felt for his mouth with her lips.

With their kisses they mingled the endearments pent up so long in their hearts.

"Alayne, my precious one."

"Renny — oh, my darling love."

He drew away a little and cast an oblique glance at her. "Is it true — "

"Is what true?"

But he could not go on. He could not ask her if what Eden said to him were true — that she would be willing to live in hell for the sake of seeing him now and again — that she had come back to Jalna to be near him, and not for Eden's sake.

"Is what true?" she whispered again.

"That we must part."

She broke into restrained but bitter crying.

A great flock of crows passed above the treetops, calling to each other, crying wildly.

"They are mocking us!" she said.

"No, we don't exist for them. We only exist for each other. . . . Alayne, I can't go away to-night as I said."

"No, no! We must meet sometimes and talk — while I am still here. Oh, Renny, hold me close — I want to get strength from you."

"And I want to make you as weak as I am," he murmured, against her hair. He drew her closer. Some magnetic current from his hands frightened her. He began to kiss her again. What mad thoughts were born of his kisses against her eyes, her throat, her breast!

She disengaged herself and began to return along the bridle path. He followed her, his eyes dark and brilliant, the lines about his mouth patient and stubborn.

It seemed that he could follow her thus across the world, lean, primitive, untiring.

Where their paths separated, they said a muttered good-bye, not looking at each other.

XXIV

WEAVING

FINCH did not return home for a week. He remained under Meg's protective care, feeling the not unpleasant languor that follows the overstrain of hysterical emotion. He spent the first days in bed, listening indolently to the various noises of the house, the cooing of Patience, the singing of Minny Ware, the activities of the old Scotch housekeeper. Over and over again, as he lay there, he reviewed the events of his life since the New Year. His playing with the orchestra, his shadowy acquaintance with the other members of it: Burns, from the abattoir, Meech, the tailor's assistant. Their faces came and went. He thought oftenest of his friend, George Fennel, with his square hands, so deft on the banjo strings, his thick-set figure, and his eyes beaming beneath his rumpled hair. He had not seen George since his return from New York. George had spent his summer as swimming instructor at a boys' camp, and they had not written to each other. Friendship with George was such an easeful thing. When you were separated from him you did not write to him or perhaps often think of him, but once you were together again the gap of separation was bridged as though it had never been. Looking back on the cold nights when he and his friend had slipped from the house of George's aunt, and hastened to some dance hall to play with the orchestra, Finch thought that this had been the happiest time of his life. The adventurous freedom of it, the exciting risk, the playing of dance music for the rhythmically swaying bodies of bright-eyed boys and girls, the creeping home toward morning with money in their pockets! As he lay in bed he hummed their favorite dance tunes.

He reviewed his friendship with Arthur Leigh. How different from his friendship with George, which had begun in babyhood and continued at the same temperate level to their school days. He had not seen Arthur either since his return. Leigh had been in Europe with his mother and sister. Difficult to bridge a gap of absence with them, Finch feared. He had an inexplicable dread of meeting Leigh and, more especially, his sister Ada again. Now that he had passed his exams, he would be going to the University in October. Arthur would be there. What would he think of Finch's having all that money left him? Perhaps it would not seem so very much to Arthur, for the Leighs were rich. Their faces rose before him too, Arthur's sensitive, questioning, rather supercilious; Ada's ivory-pale, heavy-lidded, provocative; and Mrs. Leigh like a sister rather than a mother, more golden, less bronze than Ada, her eyes more blue than gray, desiring to please rather than dubiously offering to be pleased. How little he knew of girls! And yet they were often in his mind, when, lying awake, he would make fantastic pictures of the girl who might possibly love him. Sometimes their faces were mocking variations of the face of Ada Leigh, sometimes they were impossible faces with disproportionately large, mournful eyes or wide red mouths like flowers. Sometimes they showed no face at all, only a flat, white disc borne above heavy breasts that pressed against flowing garments.

He reviewed his life in New York as costing clerk. His determined efforts to learn the routine of business, his rides on the Fifth Avenue buses, his visits to Alayne's apartment, the jolly kindness of Rosamund Trent. Looking back at this period, he seemed not to have been himself at all, but a strange translation into a being of another world, already becoming so shadowy that it was hardly to be grasped at.

He went over the happenings of the summer — his practising, his playing in the church at night, the walks home by moonlight, the secret meetings with his grandmother. When his imagination reached the point of her death, her funeral, the reading of the will, and the scene afterward, a protective instinct drew a film, like a fine veil, between the eyes of his spirit and these pictures, so that it might not be bruised by the cruelty of them.

These various experiences presented themselves as sections of a screen, which shut him off from what might have been a shrinking contemplation of his future at Jalna. He lay supine, indolently dreaming of life, not daring to think how close he had been to death.

Meg's notion of rehabilitating him in his old niche, or something better, was to feed his body with the best that her kitchen could provide. Her intuition, and some self-reproach, told her that he needed tempting food and plenty of it. He was tempted like an invalid and ate like a field laborer. Renny, coming to visit him and finding him propped up over half a broiled chicken, thought, and declared vehemently at Jalna, that Meggie was perfect. Her remarks about Alayne had faded as breath from a glass. These were women's ways and beyond his ken. But he could take in the significance of Meggie's plump white hand stroking Finch's lank hair, or a crisp section of broiled fowl surrounded by green peas. The family at Jalna were told that Finch had had a "nervous breakdown" (most convenient of illnesses) just as he arrived at the Vaughans' house, had been taken in, and was being nursed back to health by the blameless Meggie, and that it would be a good thing if they could bring themselves to treat him with indulgence on his return. It was a relief to all to have him out of the house for that week. The sight of his angular, drooping form and the knowledge that here was the heir to old Adeline's fortune might have produced other nervous breakdowns. As it was, the talk rolled on and on without even the insignificant let or hindrance of his presence. Augusta was shortly returning to England. Never again would she endure another Canadian winter. She had had the good fortune not to have been born in Canada. She had no intention of dying there of the cold. This she affirmed with the thermometer at eighty-five degrees in the last fever of summer. She urged her brothers to return with her for a visit.

Meg thought that a talk from Mr. Fennel would be good for Finch. She did not tell the rector that he had done anything so desperate as attempt to take his own life, but she intimated that he had lost control of himself in a very strange and inexplicable fashion. Mr. Fennel shrewdly guessed that there had been a disturbance at Jalna over the will, and that Finch, made ill by the excitement, was being kept at the Vaughans' till the smell of the fat died away. He came to see him and talked, not religion or behavior, but about his own young days in Shropshire, and how he had wanted to be a stage comedian, and did Finch so much good by his wit and sagacity that he was able to be out of bed that evening, and the next morning steadied himself still more by an hour at the piano.

The next day George Fennel, back from camp, came to see him, and still further forwarded his recovery. George was beaming over his friend's good fortune, and blithely indifferent to the disappointment of the rest of the clan. He sat, solid, rumpled, sunburned, on the side of the bed, and discussed the endless possibilities of a hundred thousand dollars.

"Why, look here," he said, "you can get up a *regular* orchestra of your own, if you want. We could take it on a tour across the continent. Some sort of striking uniform— blue with lots of gilt. I suppose your family would object. My father would, too. He hasn't much imagination. Hates anything stagy. But it's the sort of life I'd like." His eyes shone. He took from his pocket the usual crumpled cigarette package that invariably contained from one to three enervated cigarettes, and offered Finch one. They puffed together in the sweet renewal of good-fellowship after absence.

"And look here," he went on, "you should get yourself a concert grand piano. I'd like to hear you on a concert grand. Playing some of those things from the *Chauve-Souris*. It would make a tremendous difference to you, having a piano like that. You might become famous. . . . Of course, for my part, I like the idea of a swell orchestra. Great Scott, we had some fun with the old one, didn't we? And we worked for what we got! My finger-ends used to get so sore that the banjo strings seemed red-hot. Do you remember the last night, and that girl who tried to make up to you? They were a pretty tough crowd. Do you remember what a time we had getting home, and how we bought milk from a milkman and it was frozen? I should never have got home if it hadn't been for you."

George broke into his peculiar, sputtering laughter, then became serious. "Last night I had dinner in town with a Mr. Phillips. He's got absolutely the best radio I've ever heard. It's an expensive one, but he says it gives perfect satisfaction. We heard wonderful grand-opera music and some fellow on the piano — just the sort of thing you'd like. You really ought to have one of those. It would be good for you, too, because you could hear all the best things and not bother about the jazzy stuff. . . . Good Lord, do you remember the way we used to pound out 'My Heart Stood Still'?"

He sputtered again and then made an even more significant suggestion. "Do you know, Finch, up in the North where I was there was a wonderful bargain in a summer cottage. It was a log-cabin sort of thing built by some American who finds it too far to come. He's going to sell it awfully cheap. It would be splendid for you to own such a place to rest in, in the summer, and take your friends to, and recuperate and all that. It's got an enormous stone fire-place and raftered ceilings, and the deer come almost up to the door. Why, one night this American said a porcupine kept him awake gnawing at the foundation."

"It would be splendid," agreed Finch, his head suddenly very hot with excitement.

"And there's another thing I've just remembered," pursued George. "There's a chap up there who has a motor launch for sale. It's the fastest one I've ever been on. Goes through the water like a knife. If you had that, with the cottage, you could have no end of fun. I wish I'd found out more about the launch. However, I think you'll be safe in risking it. It's quite different with a motor car. When you buy a car you should get one of the best English makes. There's nothing like them for standing the wear and tear."

"The trouble is," said Finch, "that I don't get this money till I'm twenty-one."

"The time will soon pass," said George, easily. "I dare say these people would hold the cottage and launch for you. I'll bet that you could raise money any day on your prospects. That's often done."

Finch lay bewildered, speechless before the vista opening before him.

His meeting with Arthur Leigh was very different and, though less riotously stirring, had an equally healing effect on his bruised spirit. He had a note from Arthur that ran : —

My dear old Finch, —

What is this dazzling news I hear of you? I met Joan on the street and she told me something about a huge bequest. I am delighted, and mother and Ada almost as much so. Please come and spend a week with us (my womenfolk insist that it shall be no less) and we can talk day and night. It will take seven of them for all I want to say to you.

To think that I have never seen you since your mysterious disappearance to New York! And in all this time I have never had so much as a line from you!

Yours ever,
ARTHUR.

Finch's heart was quick with love for his friend when he had read this note. The plain but heavy note paper, bearing the Leighs' crest and Arthur's small black handwriting, symbolized for him the dignity and elegance of Arthur's life. The fact that he was a Court and a Whiteoak meant nothing to Finch; this note written by Arthur's small, exquisite hand was truly impressive. He carried it in his pocket as a kind of charm when he returned to Jalna.

It required great fortitude to return. So tremulous were his nerves when he entered the house, he feared a wry look or word lest they should betray him into an hysterical outburst. The very smell of the house sent a quiver through him. The smell of the thick, heavily-gilded wall paper, the shabby tasseled curtains, the faint Eastern odor that hung near his grandmother's room, where now reigned inviolable stillness. Did he imagine it, or was there still the odor of coffin and funeral flowers in the empty drawing-room? He stood in the hall, not knowing where to go, listening to his own heartbeats. He felt desolate and afraid in spite of George's visit, of Arthur's letter. For the first time he realized his grandmother's death, and the loss those visits to her room would be to him. He realized with a constriction of the throat how much confidence he had got from those weeks of intimacy with her fierce and extravagant nature.

Standing in the hall, he saw himself, a tiny boy not more than three, descending the stairs, a step at a time, on his little seat, lonely even then, a pathetic infant with a limp fair lock dangling over his eyes. It had seemed a tremendous journey down those stairs, and the smells then had been strange and disturbing as now. He remembered the long-legged, red-haired big brother who, striding in leather leggings along the hall, would snatch him up and throw him, screaming with frightened laughter, across his shoulder. He remembered the smiling, teasing boy of ten that was Eden, and the ruddy-cheeked one of seven, whom he worshiped and feared, that was Piers. And the uncles. . . . Standing there, he meditated a separate penitential apology to each for the trick he had played them. For, however unwittingly, he felt that there must have been something tricky in the way he had supplanted the others. Else they could not have felt toward him as they did. He feared that among them all there was not one who had not inwardly withdrawn from him, unless it were perhaps Eden. Eden! What a muddle! Could he go to them separately, make them understand, and still keep his self-control?

The very thought of it took the sap out of him. His knees felt weak. He pictured the interviews as a series of fine-drawn agonies. No — he could not do it. They must think of him what they would, endure his moneyed presence as best they could.

He heard a step behind him and turned. Augusta was coming down the hall. In the dim light cast by the stained-glass window he saw that she was very pale and looked troubled. He raised his eyes humbly, wondering how she would greet him. She was beside him before she noticed his presence. Then she concentrated on him a look of melancholy relief.

"It is you, Finch! I'm very glad you have come. I wish you would come to my room so that I may discuss something with you. I believe you are just the one I need to help me."

To be needed! Oh, sweet words! He followed her up the stairs, wishing that he might lift the hem of her black cashmere dress and bear it as a train. To be regarded without bitterness! To be taken under Aunt Augusta's crêpe-trimmed wing!

In her room, she said, "It is about my dear canary that I am worried. I actually made my plans for returning to England without considering him. Now I cannot turn back. He will die unless he is tenderly cared for. Finch, dear, can I trust him to you? Will you do this for me?" Her Queen Alexandra fringe drooped above the gilded cage where the canary, trig as a daffodil, searched for hempseed in his cup.

"Tweet, tweet!" said Augusta. "Thank Heaven, he can know nothing of what is passing in my mind. Tweet, tweet! I tell you, Finch, he knows more than all the cats and dogs of the family put together. I do not boast about it, but I take the greatest pleasure in his sagacity. Can I, *can* I trust you to care for him?"

"Yes, Aunt, I'll do my very best for him. I suppose he's pretty delicate."

"His health is perfect. But he needs perfect care. I shall give you minute directions about his bath, his seeds, his lump sugar, and his lettuce leaf."

The canary wiped his bill vehemently on his perch and cocked an eye at them.

"Tweet, tweet," said Augusta, in a mournful contralto.

"Tweet, tweet," echoed Finch hoarsely.

Poor bird, he was to know some vicissitudes under Finch's care!

Finch kissed his aunt fervently and, with a lightening of the shadow that hung over him, ran upstairs to his attic room to look over his clothes. He took them from the closet, examined them near the window, then laid them on the bed. The more he looked at them, the more certain he became that he must refuse Arthur Leigh's invitation to spend a week with him. The new black ready-to-wear suit which had been hastily bought him for the funeral did not seem to help things out at all. Most of his underthings and socks had holes in them. His best hat was no better than his worst. Some ties he had bought in New York were satisfying, but scarcely enough to make him presentable. His visit to Leigh's must be short, for, even if he could persuade Renny to buy him new clothes, they would not be ready at once, and Leigh wanted him at once.

In the upstairs hall he met Nicholas, the one he dreaded most of all.

"Home again?" Nicholas said, in his brusque way. "Do run down to the dining room and fetch me my glasses. I've left them on the table by the window."

Finch flew for the glasses. Nicholas took them, with a rumble of thanks, not looking at him, and retired into his room. Finch drew a deep breath of relief. Nicholas had been aloof, but not austere — not terrible as on that last day. His home-coming might not be so harrowing after all.

Ernest came to the door of his room and beckoned to Finch. He looked delicate and distinguished. His person and his room were exquisitely neat, as though the disappointment, the hopelessness of ever possessing greater scope for self-expression, had moved him to perfect, as much as lay in his power, his restricted field of action.

The water colors on the walls had been rearranged, the china ornaments on the mantelpiece. A black glass vase holding a few sprays of the delicate white blooms of Queen Anne's lace stood on his desk, where the books and papers relating to his Commentary on Shakespeare had been recently put in order. Ernest's clothes, his tie, even his studs, were black. There were dark shadows below his eyes. Their expression, however, was gentle as they rested on Finch.

He said, rather nervously, "Come in, come in. I'm not going to keep you." He really meant, "But please don't stay long." He fidgeted to the window and settled the blind.

Finch tried to smile without grinning, to look sympathetic

without looking lugubrious. His features had never felt so large and so difficult to control.

"I'm afraid," said his uncle, hesitatingly, "that we — that I — all of us, indeed, have been too hard on you. I feel sure that there is nothing underhand in you, Finch. You simply didn't realize the danger to my mother's health in such late hours. I think I remember saying that it had killed her. In my excitement I may have said even worse things. I don't remember. I do remember hearing someone say that you were no better than a murderer. But I think that was your aunt. I don't think I said that."

"No. You just said I'd shortened her life."

Ernest flushed. "Yes. That was it. . . . I'm sorry, my dear, that I said that. It is quite probably not true. She was quite old — very old, in fact — she might have died in any case."

"Uncle Ernie," burst out Finch, "I had rather any one of you had got Gran's money than me! I tell you, it's a torture to me!"

Ernest smiled bleakly. "You will get over that feeling. It will be wonderful for you. Open the world before you very beautifully. It's an exhilarating thing for a young man to have money, it is indeed. My father was very generous with me when I was a young man. I had a very good time, but I was foolish, credulous. It slipped through my fingers. I want you to take better care of — your money." He pronounced the last two words with an uncontrollable wryness, as of one who had set his teeth into bitter fruit.

Finch gulped, then said in a shaky voice, "There's one thing certain. When I get the money I'm going to — do things for those who have a better right to it than me. If I can, I want to do something for each one that he would have liked to do if he had got the money." He looked beseechingly at Ernest. "I want you to go to England for a trip, and to consult those books in the British Museum for your Commentary — " He jerked his head toward the desk.

Ernest was touched. "Oh, no. I could not think of doing that."

"Yes, you will! To please me. And Uncle Nick — and the others — something nice for each one!" His eyes were almost radiant.

"Well, well, we'll see. It's very handsome of you, anyhow." A light was roused in his eyes, too. Then he looked meditative. He said, "There's one person for whom I should like you to do something. Someone who, at present, can't do much for himself. He does need help, and he's so very brilliant. I don't want to see him forced into some work that will take away his impulse toward poetry."

"You mean Eden?" Great Scott, he had never thought of Eden! Yet it was true enough what Uncle Ernest said.

"I wonder what I could do for him?"

Ernest said, almost cheerfully, "You will know when the time comes. I only wish something could be done now. He's so much stronger, but he must be taken care of. He could come home if it weren't for Piers."

"Well, I'll see what I can do," and Finch left, feeling an almost tumultuous sense of responsibility for his family.

He did not see Piers until dinner, when he came in barethroated, healthy, bright-eyed, after driving a good bargain for a carload of apples. He grinned at Finch, with derision rather than malice, and, after they were seated at table, said, "No wonder you took to your bed! I'd have done the same if I had got it."

"For God's sake," returned Finch, in a whisper, "shut up!" But even this meeting was much easier than he had expected. Life was going on at Jalna, the loom was moving slowly, creakingly, but it was moving, and Finch, in his new aspect, was drawn into the changed pattern.

He was undressing that first night when he heard soft steps ascending the stairs. He was startled, for he seldom had a visitor. Wakefield appeared in the doorway.

He advanced with an ingratiating smile. "I simply couldn't sleep, Finch. Renny's out for the evening and he didn't tell me where, so I can't be sure what time he'll come in." He added rather patronizingly, "I thought you might feel nervous up here all alone after your breakdown. I thought I'd better come and bear you company."

Finch returned, in the same tone, "Well, I'm afraid you will repent you of your folly. I'm a beastly bedfellow, and I'm going to have the light on and read for a bit."

"That will just suit me!" cried Wake gayly, scrambling into the bed and clutching the sheet defensively. "I really want to talk with you about your plans, and give you a little advice about looking after all your money. You see," he proceeded, hugging his knees, "I know more than you'd guess about money. What I mean is, that I know a lot about making *a little bit of money* go a long way. I could make a hundred thousand dollars seem almost like a million. If you were to make me a little allowance — I wouldn't ask for more than twenty-five cents a week, just enough to keep Mrs. Brawn from nagging at me all the time — I'd give you advice that would be worth a lot to you. I can tell by the looks of you that you haven't got a good head for business. Piers says you won't have your money any time until you'll lose it. I say, Finch, how would you like to divide it equally with me? Then we'd have loads of fun seeing who could make the most out of his share. Like the Parable of the Talents."

"Your particular talent," said Finch, sitting on the edge of the bed, "is nerve. You've got more than anyone I know. I don't know how you've reached the age you have without someone giving you a bang that would finish you, you're so darned cheeky. As though I'd trust you with any of my money!" No doubt about it, there was a thrill in "my money"!

Wake successfully assumed the expression of his aunt when displeased. "I hope," he reproved, with his upper lip lengthened, "that you're not going to be close-fisted the moment you get rich."

"For goodness' sake!" shouted Finch, "have a heart! I'm not rich! How much money do you suppose I've got? Ninety-eight cents — that's what. And I'm invited to spend a week with Arthur Leigh!"

Wake looked pleased. "That's nice, isn't it? Because when you're visiting a rich fellow like that you'll not need any money. You might just as well leave the ninety-eight cents with me. It'd pay my salary for nearly a month."

"If I was some brothers," declared Finch, "I'd give you a good hiding and send you downstairs. I suppose you'd tell, though."

Wake shook his head firmly. "No, I shouldn't. I'd bear the pain with all the fortitude I could muster."

Finch groaned. "Gosh — the language you use! It's awful to hear a small boy talking like an old gentleman of seventy. That's what comes of having no other kids to play with."

Wake's luminous eyes darkened; he played his never-failing trump card. "No — no, Finch, I don't think it's that. . . . I think it's because I'm pretty sure I'll never live to be seventy — or p'r'aps even grow up. I want to use all the language I can in the short while I'm here."

"Rot!" But it was too bad to be rough with the poor little fellow. . . . When he got his money he'd do something nice for Wake!

He got up, undressed, changed his mind about reading, and was just going to put out the light when Wakefield said, in a cajoling tone, "I say, Finch, aren't you going to do — you know what?"

"No, I don't."

"Oh, yes, you do!" His smile was sly. "Shut the door first."

Finch, about to blow out the candle, growled, "Haven't an earthly idea what you're babbling about."

"You said — that day — that you — oh, Finch, please do it!" He made a gesture to express mystery. "That lovely thing you said you did — in front of the little goddess."

"Oh, that!" He stood motionless above the candle flame, an odd pointed shadow on his forehead, the hollows of his eyes dark.

"You wouldn't like that. It would frighten you."

"Frighten me! Never! I shan't tell a soul of it."

"Swear!"

"I swear."

"If you breathe a word of this I'm done with you forever and ever, remember!"

He went to the cupboard. There was a mysterious rustling, while Wake sat upright on the bed shivering in ecstasy.

Finch brought forth the figure of Kuan Yin and set it on the desk. He took from a drawer a packet of small pyramids of incense, and stood one at her feet. The moon had risen above the treetops and was sending a shaft of light, clearly defined as the blade of a sword, in at the window. Finch blew out the candle. The various objects in the room were reclaimed by darkness; only the delicate porcelain figure of Kuan Yin held the light like a jewel. He lighted the incense. A blue spiral of smoke arose from it, and spread like a tremulous veil to the verge of the moon-shaft. A pungent, exotic scent sought the expectant nostrils of the boys. They became still as the statue herself; their faces, drained of color by the moon, seemed also shaped in porcelain. A sudden gust had arisen; the oaks began to sigh and then to shake. The moon, which had seemed clear of the treetops, now was caught in their upward straining, her light shattered into bright prisms dissolving, rejoining, dancing across the darkness. The spirits of the boys were not in their bodies, but were liberated by the incense.

Under the guidance of Kuan Yin, patroness of sailors, they floated through the casement into moonlit seas of an unearthly beauty.

XXV

A LOAN

"WHAT do you suppose I dreamed?" asked Wake. "You'll never guess."

Inarticulate sounds came from Finch's pillow.

"I dreamed that you were a flower!"

A grunt that weakened into a chuckle. Finch opened an eye. "What sort of flower?"

"Not a very pretty one, I'm afraid." His voice was gently regretful. "I don't know the variety. A long, yellowish sad-looking flower . . ."

"Hmph."

"But" — gayly — "just *crammed* with honey!"

"The deuce I was!"

"Yes — and I was a *bee!* One of those jazzy little brown bees that go gathering — "

It was enough. Finch smothered him under a pillow and did not release him until he admitted that he was a liar, a toady, and an altogether filthy little reptile.

No mention was made, while Finch dressed and Wake splashed in the basin, of the ceremony of the night before. In the darkness the figure of Kuan Yin had disappeared, but Wake's sensitive nose was aware of a subtle fragrance in the room, a delicate elation of the spirit as from a lovely half-remembered dream.

It was a morning of swinging white clouds against an ardent blue sky. The thick yellow sunshine was flung on the gray walls of the attic room as though with a brush. More gold than gold it seemed; the sky bluer than blue; the grass and trees more green than ever green had been. That querulous artist Summer, who had given them during her season so many blurred and wanly tinted pictures, now seemed intent on splashing her last color on the final canvas with furious brilliance.

"What a day," cried Wake, "for going on a visit! How I wish I were!" He paused in the scrubbing of his face with a washcloth to look pensive. "Do you know, Finch, I've never been on a visit in my life. Not one little visit! I wonder if ever I shall!"

"Of course you will. I'll take you somewhere — some-time," promised Finch.

He was excited about his own visit this morning. He recklessly made up his mind to stay the week with the Leighs, and, before he went down to breakfast, he put the pick of his wardrobe into a suitcase. Renny must be approached for money.

He found him on the rustic bridge. At this time of the year the stream was usually little more than a rivulet pushing its way through a rank growth of rushes and water weeds. But this year it had the fullness of spring and, beneath the bridge, had widened into a pool encircled by a thick new growth of watercress. The rippled, sandy bottom reflected swarthy sunlight. Renny was not alone. Perched on the rail beside him was Eden, lazily dropping bits of twig into the pool. They were not talking, but seemed to have finished a conversation which had left each absorbed in contemplation of his own position. Finch noticed the great improvement in Eden's appearance. His face and neck had filled out and showed a healthy pinkish-brown. Nevertheless he retained a look of delicacy in contrast to the sharp vigor of Renny. Finch thought, "Eden looks indolent and good-humored and yet I'm glad it's old Renny I must ask for money and not Eden."

He approached, feeling self-conscious, and stood beside the elder, from whose clothes came the smell of pipe tobacco. Finch muttered, out of the side of his mouth, "I've had a letter from Leigh inviting me to stay with him for a week. I thought I'd go to-day."

"Oh, all right. It will do you good."

"I suppose — I think — I'll need to have some money." It was difficult to say the word "money." It had an ominous sound, since its disposal had lately been the subject of so much wrath.

Renny put his hand in his trousers pocket. His expression was forbidding, but, after he had scrutinized the silver and the one crumpled banknote on his palm, he replaced them and produced from the breast pocket of his coat the worn leather pocketbook upon which the eyes of his family had so often rested in expectancy. He drew from it, with his accustomed air of trying to conceal exactly how much he had, five one-dollar bills, and handed them to Finch. Eden craned his neck to observe the transfer.

"A couple of years more," he said, "and your positions will be reversed."

Finch's face grew scarlet. Was he never to have any more peace? Was the legacy always to be a subject for sportive comment? He pocketed the money glumly with a muffled "Thanks awfully."

"In the meantime," said Renny, "he has a lot of hard work before him and I don't want him ragged about his money. I've told Piers so, too. You're a poet. You ought to know what it is to be sensitive and melancholy and neurotic, and all that. If he gets too much teasing he may give you another chance to save his life, eh, Finch?" Reticence was not a characteristic of the Whiteoaks.

Eden laughed, but his face reddened. He said, "Next time you try it on, brother Finch, choose the stream here, and I'll fish you out from the bridge without wetting my feet."

Finch grinned sheepishly and was about to turn away when Eden said, "Don't go! Stay and talk to me. Renny is off. Aren't you, Renny?"

"I'm late, now," said Renny, looking at the battered gun-metal wrist watch that had gone with him through the War. Always hurrying to mysterious appointments concerning horses was Renny, appointments which tended to make thinner rather than thicker the worn leather pocket-book.

Finch and Eden were alone. They stared into the darkly flashing pool in embarrassed silence for a few minutes, then Eden said seriously, "I told Renny the other morning that I believed I had done the best thing in my life when I saved yours. Quite apart from brotherly love, I make a guess that you're the flower of the flock. I'm damned if I know why I think so. I suppose it's intuition — I being a poet, and sensitive along with those other attributes ascribed to me by Renny. God, isn't he an amusing fellow?"

"He's splendid!" said Finch, hotly. "I don't want to hear anything against him."

"You won't. Not from me. I admire him as much as you do — though in a different way. I admire and envy the side of him that you don't know at all. . . . Tell me, Finch, what are you going to do with your life? Do you mind talking to me? Are we friends?"

"Rather! I hope I have gratitude —"

"Stop! Don't say that word. It's a vile word. Not one pleasant word will rhyme with it. Try! See what you'll get. Prude — dude — spewed — lewd —"

Finch added heavily, "There's nude, too."

"Preposterous! It's an unholy company." He looked into the brightness of the stream in silence for a little, then said, with sudden gravity, "Why on earth should you be grateful to me? I want your friendship. Have I got it?"

"Yes. . . . I mean I like you, Eden, but it will be strange being friends with you. Something quite new."

"But you'll try? Good. Have a cigarette." He offered

a silver case filled with an expensive brand. Finch recalled the figure on the bench in Madison Square Gardens — shabby, despairing, ill. How thoroughly Eden had recovered, acquired a look of well-being! If he himself had been is such a plight, he doubted whether he could have recovered, and here was Eden, amused, contemptuous of sentiment, ready for another fling at life.

He accepted the cigarette and a light.

Eden said, " I believe we are more alike than you 'd ever guess. I think we both got a good deal from our — what was it Gran called her? — our 'poor flibbertigibbet mother.' "

" Don't! " interrupted Finch harshly.

" I don't mean anything disrespectful. I mean that we inherited from her the qualities that are 'flibbertigibbet' to the Whiteoaks — love of poetry, love of music, love of beauty. Don't you agree? "

" I think she must have been awfully different."

" Of course she was. So are we. . . . Acknowledge, now, you could say things to me that you couldn't say to any of the others without getting laughed at."

" Yes, I guess I could. Still — "

" Well? "

" Renny's been awfully good to me about my music."

" Certainly. But why? Because he understands your feeling for it? No! Because he looks on you as a weakling, and is afraid you 'd go dotty without it! He has an equal contempt for me as a poet. He only tolerates me because of the blood tie. He 'd be loyal to Satan himself if he was his half brother! "

" I wish I were like him," muttered Finch.

" No, you don't! You can't make me believe that you would exchange your love of music for love of horses and dogs."

" And women," added Finch.

"Ah, we all love women! But you must be like me —
love and forget. Uncle Nick was like that as a young man,
too. He told me once that he's forgotten the names of the
women he once cared for — excepting, of course, the one he
unhappily married."

Finch said, "Eden, do you mind telling me something?
Don't you care for Alayne any longer?"

"I don't love her as a woman, if that's what you mean.
Perhaps I should have forgotten her name, too, if we had n't
married."

"Strange — when she is so — lovely, and so good."

"She loved my poetry first. Then me, as the author of
it. And I suspect that I loved her for loving my poetry.
It's all over."

"But she loves your poetry still, does n't she?"

"I believe she does. But she loves it as disembodied art.
It's Renny she loves now."

Finch turned away and crossed to the other side of the
bridge. Here the stream lay in shadow. He rested his
eyes on the cool shallow of it for a moment of silence, and
then asked, "Are you writing anything now, Eden?"

"A good many things in the last month."

"I should like to see them."

"I'll bring them here some afternoon, and read them to
you. I'll bring the first things I wrote after I came home.
I don't believe they're of much value, but I'd like you to
hear them because the theme of nearly all is the sweetness of
life. I've never questioned that. No matter how despondent
I may have seemed when you found me in New York, I had
never once thought of taking my life. Good God, I'd
sooner have spent the rest of my days and nights on that
park bench where I could look up at the clouds and the
stars than to have done away with myself." He crossed
to Finch's side and put his arm about his shoulders. "You've
read *Lavengro*, of course?"

"Part of it. I did n't care much for it."

"Well, Borrow said one thing — it does n't matter how often it 's quoted, it 's always just as splendid. 'There 's night and day, brother, both sweet things: sun, moon, and stars, brother, all sweet things: there 's likewise a wind on the heath. Life is very sweet, brother.'" He squeezed Finch's shoulder. "Keep that in mind, brother Finch, the next time the family concentrates on making you miserable."

"I 'll try," said Finch, in a muffled voice. Eden glanced at him shrewdly, then, as though fearing he had been too solemn, said, "I was rather glad to hear that the family could stage such a thoroughgoing row without Gran. I was afraid they might degenerate into futile wrangling. She had such gusto for life. You should try to be like her. Get the most out of it."

Finch, sprawling against the railing, said, "I was watching that frog diving about under that big mound of honeysuckle — thinking what a good time he has."

"Yes. Amusing little devil. I wonder how often he 's gone a-wooing this summer."

Finch grinned. It was Eden, he thought, who was amusing. Inquisitive. He could n't watch even a frog without speculating about its private life.

They watched the frog sit goggle-eyed on the mossy rim of the pool, his fingers spread, his full wet throat pulsing. They watched him galvanize, without apparent reason, into the green arc of a leap. When the surface of the pool had cleared, they saw him sitting under water, his fingers spread on the yellow sand, goggle-eyed, hallucinated as ever.

"If you don't mind," said Eden slowly, "I 'm going to tell you something. Something I have not told anyone else."

Finch was immensely flattered. He turned his long face receptively toward his brother.

"I have it in my mind to write a narrative poem of the

early history of French Canada. There's tremendous scope in it: Jacques Cartier. The perilous voyages in sailing vessels. The French Governors, and their mistresses. Crafty Intendants. Heroic Jesuits. The first Seigneurs. Voyageurs. The Canadian chansons. Those poor devils of Indians who were captured and taken to France, and put to work in the galleys. Think of the song of homesickness I could put into their mouths! Think of the gently bred French women who came over as nuns! Think of their chant of homesickness for France — and ecstasy of love for Christ! If only I can do it as it should be done, Finch!" His face shone. He made a wide gesture expressing fervor and half-tremulous hope. Finch saw that the cuff of the gray tweed sleeve was frayed, that the wrist, in spite of its roundness, still looked delicate. His heart went out to meet Eden.

It was the first time that he had been treated as an equal by one of his brothers. And now, not only treated as an equal, but made the recipient of confidence! His face reflected the glow from Eden's. He felt a passionate desire to be his friend.

"It will be splendid," he said. "I'm sure you can do it. It is awfully good of you to tell me."

"Whom else could I tell? You are the only one who can understand."

"Alayne could."

Eden said irritably, "I tell you, there's nothing — less than nothing — between Alayne and me now! When you're older you'll find out that there is no one so difficult to confide in as someone you have ceased to love — no matter how much you may have in common. We're always on our guard now that I am better."

"I don't see how you can live in the Hut together — if things are like that."

"We can't! She's going back to her work. I'm going

away. Drummond says I must be in the open air all winter.
That's the trouble." His fair face was shadowed by some
disturbing thought. "Renny wants to send me to California. But I've made up my mind that I shan't go there.
I must go to France. It will not only be a thousand times
more congenial to me, but I'll be able to search out the
beginnings of French Canadian history. I want to get at
the roots. In fact, I must, or I'll never do this thing as
I want to do it. I want to spend a year in France,—stay
till I've finished the poem,—but how am I to do it? Renny
can never afford money enough for that." The shadow
on his face deepened to an expression of melancholy. "I'm
helpless. I suppose I'll have to go just where I'm sent.
There is no one to lend me an extra two thousand. I'd
need that much."

"If only," cried Finch, "I had my money! I'd help you
like a shot."

Eden gave him a warm look. "You would! I believe
you. You're a trump, Finch! I'd take it, too, but—not
as a gift. I'd pay it back with interest, once I'd got on my
feet. But what's the use? Your money's tied up for
ages."

Finch was tremendously stirred. If only he could help
Eden! This new Eden who had talked to him about his
poetry—while it was still seething in his poet's mind. A
passionate desire to help him surged through all his being.
Why, it was only right that he should help him, give him all
the money he needed! Hadn't he risked his life to save
Finch's? He took excited turns on the narrow space of the
bridge.

"If only I could get at it!"

"I hope," said Eden, "that you're not being stirred by
any ridiculous sentiment—gratitude. You know how I
hate the idea of that."

"But how can I help it?"

"Just don't let yourself. As Gran used to say, 'I won't have it!'"

Finch burst into loud laughter. He was almost beside himself with excitement. He had got an idea. A marvelous, a gorgeous idea! He stopped in front of Eden and grinned hilariously into his face.

"I have it! I can get the money for you! I 'm sure I can."

Eden was regarding him with his odd, veiled gaze. "How could you possibly?" His tone was weary, but his heart was beating quickly. Was it possible that he was going to be able to save his face? Not going to be forced to suggest ways and means to the youngster?

"Why, it 's like this," jerked out Finch breathlessly. "There 's my friend, Arthur Leigh! He 's got any amount of money. He 's of age and he 's in control of a fair-sized fortune already. He 'd lend it to me. I 'd give him my note, — with good interest, you know, — then I 'd be able to fix you up with just what you want!" Finch's face was scarlet; he had run his hands through his hair, standing it on end; his tie was gone askew; he had never looked wilder, less like a philanthropist.

Eden's eyes lighted, but he shook his head almost gloomily. "It sounds feasible enough, but I can't do it."

"Why?" Finch was thunderstruck.

"What would they say — the others? Renny 'd never stand for it. He 's putting up the money for California, and he thinks there 's nothing more to be said."

"He need never know. No one need know, but ourselves — and Leigh. And I 'll not let Leigh know what I want the money for. Oh, he 's the most casual fellow you ever saw! He 'd never ask a question. Just say, 'All right, Finch, here 's your money!' and stuff my note in his pocket. He does n't know what it is to higgle over money as we do. Eden, you must let me do this! I 've hated like the devil having this money. It's hung over me like a curse. If I could do something splendid with it — like helping you — making it possible for you to write your books — it would seem quite different." His eyes filled with tears.

"What put the idea of borrowing from Leigh into your head?"

"It just came. A sort of inspiration, I guess." He must not admit that George Fennel had made the suggestion.

"If I took the money," said Eden, frowning, "I should insist on paying it back with a higher interest than you would pay your friend."

"The hell you would!" said Finch grandly. "You'll pay the money back just when you can — without any interest. I tell you, I've made up my mind to do something for each one of the family out of this money. Then I shan't feel such a — such a — sort of pariah! It just happens that you're the first one I'm tackling, and it's got to be kept an absolute secret."

Eden's face broke into a smile that was almost tender. He caught Finch's hand and squeezed it. "My poor wretch," he said, "how quickly you're going to be rid of your money!"

XXVI

LIES AND LYRICS

"You are a most amazing person," said Ada Leigh.

"I don't see why," answered Finch. "Arthur doesn't think so, do you, Arthur?"

"I'm not sure that I don't."

"But why?" Finch, who so hated being under discussion at home, yearned for the analytical interest of the Leighs. "I think I'm a chap who will never be noticed."

"Don't deceive yourself," said Leigh. "People are always going to stare at you."

"I know I'm ill-favored, but please don't rub it in." For the first time in his life he was feeling conceited. It was delicious.

Ada said, "When we heard that your grandmother had left you her money, we said at once, 'How natural! He's bound to have spectacular things happen to him!'"

"You're ragging me!"

"I never could do that. I should be afraid. You're so sensitive."

"It's a pity my people don't feel that way about me."

"I suppose it came rather as a surprise to them—your getting all the money," said Leigh.

"A tremendous surprise."

"I hope they took it well." Leigh tried to keep curiosity out of his voice. That family! He could imagine their being pretty formidable, especially the peppery fox-faced fellow from whom he had bought a horse he didn't want.

"Oh, they were very decent about it!" How easy to lie — to picture Jalna as running on oiled wheels — in this rose-and-ivory drawing-room! He expanded more and more in

the warmth of their interest. They drew him on to talk of
his music, what he had been practising that summer, his
experiences in New York, plans for his future. Arthur's
interest in Finch was generous and affectionate, but Ada's
was mingled with chagrin at the feeling which his presence
aroused in her. His awkwardness repelled her to the point
of dislike, yet the sadness of his face in repose, the lank
fair lock on his forehead, his shapely hands, in contrast to
his bony wrists, had a disturbing fascination for her. She
knew that he was mystified and attracted by her. It amused
her to think that she could play on his sensibilities, yet she
had a subtle suspicion that to do so was to risk her own
detachment.

Mrs. Leigh joined them, still more like a sister to Ada
than a mother, after the exhilaration of their European
trip. With her desire to please, she had almost the effect
of being younger, or, at any rate, more ingenuous. They
talked of Europe. Arthur said, "As soon as you come into
your money, Finch, we'll go to Europe together!"

"I shall go, too," said Ada.

"Never! This is to be a vagabond journey. Little girls,"
he included his mother in his glance, "will be safer at home.
Finch, do you remember, when I talked of our going to
Europe last spring, you scoffed at the idea? You said you'd
never have the money to go abroad. Now look at you!"

"Yes," agreed Finch serenely. "There's quite a difference."

Mrs. Leigh said, "We didn't know of your grandmother's
death until we heard of the legacy. I'm afraid that when
Arthur wrote to you he was excited and perhaps forgot to
say how sorry we are to hear of your loss."

"I'm afraid I did forget," said Leigh.

"You must miss her. She was extraordinarily vigorous
for her age, wasn't she?"

"Yes." . . . The strong old face came before him —

blotted out the pretty room, the pretty women. He saw the rust-red eyebrows raised in humorous disdain of such. He saw the toothy grin with which she would have dismissed them. His face lost the animation that had made it attractive and became blank.

"I wish I might have seen her. We must get to know your family, Finch."

"Y-yes. Thanks. I'm sure they'd like it."

"Are you really? Then I shall motor out to Jalna one day and call on your aunt, Lady Buckley!"

Finch hastened to say, "She's going home to England. She is just here on a visit."

"Does she like England better?"

"Oh, yes, she hates the Colonies."

Leigh exclaimed, "Colony! I like that! We're an independent part of the Empire."

"Of course. But I'm used to hearing us called a colony at home."

"I should think you younger ones would object," demurred Leigh.

"I don't see why. If you're a part of anything, how can it matter what you're called?"

Mrs. Leigh said, "It doesn't matter. We all love England, that is what matters."

"I don't," said Ada. "I love Russia. I have a Russian soul."

"But how can you tell?" asked Finch, wondering if possibly he had one.

"Because it's never satisfied."

He sighed. "In that case, I'm afraid it's my stomach that's Russian!"

Mrs. Leigh noticed that he looked as though he had been ill and asked him about his health.

"I'm awfully fit," he insisted. "I've never been better. I'm just naturally cadaverous."

"Perhaps. But more probably you have been growing very fast." Her mind flew back to his family. "You have sisters-in-law at home, haven't you? And one of them — the wife of a poet brother — is an American?"

"Yes . . . that is — they live in another house — just a little place. He's been ill."

"We were *so* intrigued when we were crossing! A young man from Philadelphia was enthusiastic over both books of your brother's poems. The lyrics, and—" She could not recall the other.

"*The Golden Sturgeon.* It's a narrative poem. I'll tell Eden. He'd like that."

Mrs. Leigh said eagerly, "Let me tell him myself! I shall go out and call on him and his wife."

"They are leaving, too," said Finch desperately. "I'm sorry. . . . You see, he has recovered, but he has to go to a warm climate."

Her pretty face fell. "I'm doomed not to meet your family! Still — there's another sister-in-law."

"Young Pheasant. She is scarcely grown up. My uncles would be frightfully pleased if you were to call on them. There's nothing they like better than calls. It would be better to let them know which day you're coming. They'd make you very welcome." But his tone was a little anxious.

She leaned forward, smiling, her lips drawn back from her teeth. "Do you think I might just *rush* out for a very few minutes and entreat your brother to autograph his books for me? I bought them both yesterday. Do you think that would be too much to ask him?"

Leigh intervened. "I'll take them out for you, if Finch thinks he would do it."

Finch wished that Mrs. Leigh were not so interested. He began to feel that a somewhat ruthless interest was the key-note of her character. He assured her rather glumly that Eden would sign as many of his books as she desired. It was probably the first time he had been asked to autograph his poems, he added, and instantly wished he had not given his brother away.

When he had been two days at the Leighs' he reached the point of moral courage when he could ask Leigh for a loan. It was not so easy to frame the words as he had thought. He was hot all over, and Leigh was not so casual as he had expected.

His bright glance dived into the turgid pool of Finch's soul.

He asked, "Are you sure that you want this for yourself, old fellow? It's quite a lot of money, you know."

Finch nodded.

Leigh smiled. "I'm afraid you're lying, and I love you for it. But it makes me sick to think that someone has perhaps been working on your sympathies. Perhaps trying to get money out of you that he'll never pay back. Upon my soul, I'm afraid to lend it to you for fear you've got some quixotic idea in your head about helping someone who isn't worth it."

"But he is!" burst out Finch.

"There, you admit it! It is for someone else."

"I'm borrowing it to please myself, but I admit I'm going to help someone — with some of it."

"Not all of it?"

Finch said hotly, "Very well, don't lend it to me!"

"Finch, you're angry with me. But I'm not going to get angry with you. It would be too unreal." Leigh's voice shook. "I'll lend you the money. For heaven's sake get some security, if you can, from this friend of yours!"

"I can't take it when you feel like this about it, Arthur."

"But you must. You know that all that's troubling me is the fear that you'll lose it."

"You don't give me credit for any common sense, then!"

"I know that your generosity is greater than your common sense. I'm terribly afraid that if you start off like this — lending your money before you're in possession of it — you're going to be an easy mark for unscrupulous people."

It was easy to lie in the rose-and-ivory drawing-room, but how difficult up in Leigh's study, among his intimate things, and with his clear eyes full of trouble for one's sake.

"Arthur," he said, "I can't take it without telling you who it's for, now that you've put things as you have. It's for Eden."

"Aha, one of the family!"

"Yes, but he didn't ask me for it! I offered it. He's been ill, you know, and he wants to go to the South of France for the winter for his health. And it isn't only that. He has it in his mind to write something perfectly splendid. He's got to have a year for it. It's not like the other things he's written — it will be a tremendous piece of work. I wish I could tell you all about it. Renny's willing to send him to California for the winter, but that won't do at all. There's a special reason why he must go to France and not be bothered by a job or anything for at least a year. Look here, Arthur, you know that Eden's poetry is good. He's had splendid reviews. Alayne gave up her job to come and nurse him because she's so keen about his poetry. She's not very keen about him now, you know. They'd been separated. I think it would be beastly selfish of me if I wouldn't put out my hand to help my own brother when he's so clever, and his wife did, and there's no one else!"

Leigh sprang up and came and took him by the shoulder.

"Of course I see it! But why didn't you tell me all this at first? It's splendid of you. And look here, I won't take a cent of interest. I want to help, too. Darling Finch, I want everything to be as clear as crystal between us!"

Even while Finch's soul drew strength and happiness from Arthur's love, it shrank within him at the thought of what Renny and Piers would have said if they could have heard that "darling Finch." But it was all right. Arthur was exquisite, and could use exquisite words; Renny and Piers were vigorous, and used vigorous words. And somewhere in between he floundered.

A note went to Eden that day: —

DEAR EDEN, —

Everything is arranged, so don't worry. Shall be home Wednesday and will bring a cheque for the amount mentioned. My friend Leigh is coming out with me. He's anxious to meet you. He knows a great deal more about poetry than I do, so I thought perhaps you wouldn't mind reading some of your new poems to us both. We'd be pretty safe from interruption on the bridge. Leigh is bringing out your books for you to autograph. They belong to his mother, so perhaps you might think up something clever to write in them as well as your name. I guess you'll be pleased about the money. Some financier, eh?

Yours,
FINCH.

Now that the strain of borrowing the money was over, his promissory note carefully made out and handed to Leigh, Finch began to be almost happy. He began to realize the new amplitude which the possession of money would give to his life. He not only realized, but greatly magnified its possibilities. He had seen so little money; he had seen Renny and Piers jubilant over a small unexpected gain. Piers would be in a gale of good spirits if he got more than he had hoped for from a consignment of apples, or if one of his Jerseys had healthy twin calves. Renny would raise his voice and shout his winnings at the races. From the time Finch had been in sailor suits he had known that his grandmother's money was the subject of jealous conjecture. He had seen the rivalry for first place in her affections from the point of view of an outsider, never in any flight of fancy picturing himself as her heir. Her decision to leave all her money to one person had always seemed to him cruel and unjust. He secretly believed that she had expressed such an intention with the direct purpose of keeping the family interest in her always at high tide, their nerves at concert pitch. She had succeeded. But now tide had ebbed into darkness, suspense no longer tightened the nerves, and Finch, looking about him, inexperienced and hungry-eyed, believed there was no limit to his power.

It was sweet to help Eden. They were travelers in a region which the rest of the family did not enter, and even though neither could fully understand the experiences of the other in that mysterious region, they knew each other as palmers to the shrine of beauty.

Finch found himself able to play the piano in front of the Leighs. His paralyzing shyness under Ada's eyes was gone. Sitting before the keyboard, more erect than at any other time, with motionless head and flying hands, he looked and felt sure of himself. He seemed, to Leigh's ardent eyes, capable of glorious things.

As Ada sat curled in the corner of a sofa while he played, Finch exulted in the fact that in these moments he was fascinating to her. He could tell that by the look in her eyes as they gazed at him through a veil of cigarette smoke. Yet no matter how balanced, how firm he felt, he could not recapture the amorous energy that had made it possible for him to embrace and kiss her on the evening of the play.

It was not until the night before he left that he had the courage again to approach such intimacy. They had been at a dance. She had been kind to him, dancing with him repeatedly because he was shy of other girls, and now and then throwing him an encouraging look from the arms of another partner while he stood glumly in a doorway. It was a night of sudden, intense chill; the white fur collar of Ada's cloak was turned up against her cheeks during the ride home. Seeing her thus muffled, with only her hair, her white forehead and eyes, exposed, made Finch feel suddenly inexpressibly tender toward her. She seemed like some flower bud wrapped in a protective sheath from which he longed tenderly to disengage her.

Arthur took the car to the garage, and as the two ran up the steps Finch put his arm about her and pressed her to his side. He put his face against her hair and murmured, "Darling Ada! You were so good to me to-night."

"It isn't hard for me to be good to you, Finch."

"And I used to think you didn't like me!"

"I like you far too well."

"Ada, will you kiss me?"

She shook her head.

"Then will you let me kiss you?"

"No."

"But you let me kiss you once."

"I'm afraid."

"Of me?"

"No, of myself."

"You said something like that once before — about being afraid. Are you afraid of life?"

"Not a bit. I'm just afraid of my own feelings."

To hear that she was afraid made Finch afraid, too. A shiver of sympathy, ecstatic yet terrified, ran through him. There seemed a menace in the bitter nip of the night air, in the large glittering stars. His arm relaxed and dropped to his side. He took off his hat and passed his hand over his hair, looking down at her pathetically.

"It's frightful to be afraid," he said. "I'm afraid of myself, too, often. And of my feelings. It takes the strength right out of me."

She gave him a scornful little smile.

"I don't think I understand your kind of fear."

"I think I understand the difference," he said. "I think yours is a hot fear, and mine is a cold. Yours makes

you want to fly away and mine paralyzes me." His eyes
sought hers, eager for understanding.

She was searching for her key in a brilliant-studded
handbag. He saw the shadow of her lashes on her cheek.

"If only you would let me kiss you," he breathed, "I
think we could understand each other."

"Too well," she answered, with a catch in her voice. She
fumbled with the key against the lock.

He took it gently from her and opened the door.

The next morning he and Leigh left early for Jalna.
Finch would have liked to linger in the hope that he might
have a few minutes alone with Ada, but Leigh was impatient
to be off. Having it in his mind to meet Eden and hear him
read his poetry, he could tolerate no delay in reaching the
appointed spot, even though Finch declared that Eden
would scarcely be there so early. Leigh left his car near the
gate, and, descending into the ravine, they made straight
for the rustic bridge across the stream. Eden was not there.
Still, Leigh's desire for haste was gratified. He perched on
the railing of the bridge and extolled now the beauty of the
sky, now that of his own reflection in the pool below.

"If I were as charming a fellow," he said, "in my actual
person as I am in that shadowy reflection, I'd have the world
at my feet! Lean over and look at yourself, Finch."

Finch peered into the pool, as he had done a thousand
times. "Mostly nose," he grumbled.

Leigh chattered on for a while, but soon the coolness of
the ravine penetrated him. There had been a dew almost as
heavy as a rain. Even now moisture fell from the tips of
leaves in clear drops like the first scatter of a shower. While
Finch was absent the Michaelmas daisies had come into
bloom. Their starry flowers, varying from deepest purple
to the blue of the September sky, hung like an amethyst
mist above the banks of the stream. The leaves of fern and
bracken showed a chill sheen, as though they had been cut

from fine metal. The clear delicate sunlight had not yet dispelled the heavy night odors of the ravine.

"I wonder," said Leigh, "whether your brother should come here this morning. It doesn't seem quite the right spot for anyone with lung trouble."

"He's over that. At any rate, he looks pretty fit. Our doctor says that he needed rest and good food more than anything. Still," he looked dubiously at the wet boards of the bridge, "it does seem rather damp for him."

"Perhaps we had better go to him." Leigh would have liked to tell his mother that he had sought the poet in his retreat, perhaps glimpsed the wife about whom an atmosphere of mystery seemed to have gathered.

"I think I hear him coming."

"Hullo, what's that?"

"An English pheasant. Renny is stocking the woods with them."

She whirred heavily out of sight, young ones fluttering after her. A rabbit hopped down the path, but, seeing the two on the bridge, turned, showed a snowy stern in three successive leaps, and disappeared into a thicket.

Eden's legs appeared, descending the path; then his body became visible, and last his head, touched by the flicker of sunlight between leaves. He was carrying some rolled-up papers. "A poet, and beautiful!" thought Leigh. "How I wish the girls were here!"

"Hullo," grinned Finch, "we thought you had got stage fright."

Eden stood at the end of the bridge, his eyes on Leigh. Leigh thought, "He's smiling at me, looking at me, and yet he doesn't really seem to see me. I don't think I like him."

Finch said, "This is Arthur Leigh, Eden. . . . He has been wondering if it's too damp for you here."

"I'm as seasoned to damp as an oyster," answered Eden,

shaking hands with Leigh so warmly that he obliterated the first impression of inviolable detachment.

Leigh said, "I hope you are not going to be as reticent as one. I'm very keen to hear some of your poems, if I may. Did Finch tell you?"

"Yes." The eyes of the brothers met. Understanding flashed between them. Finch thought, "I've made him happy. It's glorious, this doing things for others. I can't imagine why other rich people don't try it!"

Eden talked freely to Leigh of his coming trip to France, unconscious that Leigh knew Finch's motive for borrowing the money. Leigh thought, "Doesn't he think me capable of putting two and two together? Perhaps he doesn't care. He knows he can make three or five of them whenever he wants."

The sun rose high, pouring warmth into the ravine, which appeared to stretch itself, languorous and supine, under that delayed caress.

They sat down on the bridge, which was now dry, while Eden, in his deep mellow voice, read poem after poem. Some had been read before, to Alayne, but not all. They were the essence he had drawn from the past summer, what he had formed into strength and brightness from those shadowed months. As he listened to his own words, and saw the rapt faces of the two boys, he wondered whether the solution of his life might not lie in such moments. Might not the suffering he knew he had caused in the lives nearest him be justified, even be necessary to the creation of his poetry? The evil in him was inseparable from the good, like the gods, whose energies were directed first into one channel, then another. So he seemed to himself, and so less coherently he seemed to Finch, who never dared to hope that anything he might create would justify his own clumsiness in life.

There was a third listener to the reading, of whom the others were unaware. This was Minny, who, wandering into the ravine from the direction of Vaughanlands and hearing voices, had stolen from trunk to trunk of the trees till she was within sight as well as hearing. It chanced that this morning she wore a dark dress instead of the usual gay colors, so she was able to conceal herself behind a great clump of honeysuckle within a few yards of the bridge. She crouched there, her feet pressing into the moist earth, the succulent growth all about her exhaling a sweet, sticky odor, and, almost touching her face, a large and meticulously woven spider's web in which two jewel-like flies were caught. She felt no discomfort in her situation, but rather an increased sense of adventure. As a doe might have crept close to watch the browsing of three stags, she observed with ardent interest every detail of their faces, their attitudes and gestures. She absorbed the beauty of Eden's voice, but the words he uttered made no more impression on her than the words of the songs she sang. Though her body ached from its crouching position, she did not grow tired or impatient, remaining after the reading was over to listen to the discussion of the poems which followed. She heard their titles without hearing them, — "The Dove; Thoughts of You and Me; Resurgam; Thoughts on Death; The New Day," — yet so sympathetic was she that when Leigh's bright face broke into merriment she smiled, too, and when the voice of Eden took on a tragic note her lips reflected this in a mournful curve. When the smoke of their cigarettes drifted about her she pitied herself that she could not share this pleasure. When Eden, dropping his voice, related something that produced a gust of hilarity, she would have given all she possessed to have known what he said.

She hoped, and tried to will it so, that the two boys would depart first, leaving Eden on the bridge. Contrary to the usual vanity of such hopes, this was what happened. All three got to their feet, but Eden did not accompany the boys when they ascended the path. Instead, he stood motionless, looking in her direction, and, after a few moments in which she was wondering whether or not to reveal herself, he called, "Come along, come along, Minny! Don't you think you've been hiding long enough?"

She stood up, straightening her dress. She was not at all ashamed, but advanced toward him, laughing.

"How long have you known I was here?"

"All the time. I saw you playing at Indian, creeping from one tree to another. You're a little hussy!"

She liked that. Her laughter became teasing.

"I heard every word you said!"

"No, you didn't!"

"Yes, I did!"

"What was it I told them that made them laugh?"

"Shan't repeat it!"

"Because you did not hear."

"I don't care! I heard all your poetry."

"It isn't becoming in a young girl to spy on men."

"*Men!* Listen to the child!"

"Well, the others are boys, but I suppose you'll admit that I'm a man."

"*You!* You're the greatest baby of all!"

"Me! I'm a disillusioned profligate."

"Then you're a profligate baby! Your wife has made a baby of you. Coming all this way to nurse you when she doesn't really care a damn for you."

"I suppose you wouldn't have done that?"

"Of course I should."

His laughter joined hers. They sat down on the bridge together.

As he held a match to a cigarette for her, he looked deep into her narrowed, mirthful eyes. "I wish I understood you!"

"It's a good thing for your peace of mind that you don't."

An obscure pity moved him to change the subject.

"How did you like my poems?"

"Ever so. Two of them sounded awfully like two songs I sing."

"It's a wise poem," he replied gravely, "that knows its own creator."

"I suppose they'll make you famous one day."

"I hope so."

"What a pity you didn't get any of the money!"

"Ah, my naïve young brother saw to that!"

"I should think you'd hate him for it."

"I don't hate anyone. I only wish people were as tolerant of me as I of them."

"I hate someone."

"Not me, I hope."

"You'd never guess."

"Tell me, then."

"Your wife."

"Do you really? My sister has done that."

"Not at all. I hate her on my own."

His gaze slid toward her swiftly, but he made no comment on this. They puffed in silence, each acutely aware of the other. He heard her suck in her breath once as though putting some sudden restraint on herself. Now the sun beat down on them hotly, inducing a mood of dreamy acquiescence.

After an interval, she said, "I've been to the shore on the last three mornings. It seemed lonely there without you."

He was astonished.

"Have you really? What a shame! And you didn't let me know!"

"I thought you'd expect me. I wouldn't disappoint you."

"My dear child!" He took her hand in his.

At his touch her eyes filled with tears, but she laughed through them. She said, "What a silly I am to care so much!"

XXVII

THE FLITTING

THERE followed a succession of perfect September days, so alike in their unclouded sunshine — a sunshine which was without the energy, for all its warmth, to produce additional growth — that it seemed possible they might continue forever without visibly changing the landscape. Michaelmas daisies, loosestrife, with here and there a clump of fringed gentian, continued to cast a bluish veil beside the paths and stream. In the garden nasturtiums, dahlias, campanula, phlox, and snapdragons continued to put forth flowers. The heavy bumblebee agitating these blossoms might well think, "I shall suck honey here forever." The cow in the pasture, which this year had never turned brown, might well think, "There will be no end to this moist grass." The old people at Jalna might well think, "We shall not grow older and die, but shall live on forever." Even Alayne, collecting her belongings in Fiddler's Hut, did so as in a dream. It seemed impossible that she should be going away, that life held the potentialities of change for her.

The action of the life to which she was returning seemed desirable to her. She could picture the things which she would do on her return with perfect precision, yet when she pictured herself as doing them it was not herself she saw, but a mere shadow. She thought, "There is no real place for me on earth. I was not made for happiness. I am as unreal to myself as a person in a play — less real, for I could laugh at them or weep for them, but I can only stare stupidly at myself and think how unreal I am."

She wondered whether the things with which the Hut

had been so overfurnished would be left there. She had
grown used to them, and they no longer seemed grotesque
in the low-ceilinged rooms. She went about collecting the
few things she wished to take away with her, and wondered
what were Eden's thoughts as he lay on the sofa reading,
now and then giving her a swift look across the page.

An odd embarrassment had arisen between them. He
no longer had need of her care; their relationship was
meaningless. They were like two travelers, forced by the
exigencies of the journey into a juxtaposition from which
each would be glad to escape. If he came in tired, he no
longer demanded her sympathy, but sought to conceal his
weariness. She no longer tried to prevent his doing things
which she thought would be bad for his health. His rest-
lessness was a source of irritation to her, while her reserve,
and what he thought her stolidity, made her presence weigh
upon him.

Yet on this, the second day before her departure, a mood
of pensiveness had come upon Eden. He felt a somewhat
sentimental desire to leave a memory, not too troubled, of
himself with her. He would have liked to justify by some
simple, yet how impossible, act their presence together in
these last weeks. They avoided each other's eyes.

Eden, to override his embarrassment, began to read aloud
scraps from his book: —

"'My idiot guide was on his way back to Aldea
Gallega. . . . And I mounted a sorry mule, without bridle
or stirrups, which I guided by a species of halter. I spurred
down the hill of Elvas to the plain . . . but I soon found
that I had no need to quicken the beast which bore me, for,
though covered with sores, wall-eyed, and with a kind of
halt in its gait, it cantered along like the wind.'"

Alayne was about to empty a vase holding some faded
late roses. She stopped before him, drew out one of them,
and slid it down the page on to his hand.

He took it up and held it to his face.

"Still sweet," he murmured. "A queer kind of stifling sweetness. But it's beautiful. Why are dying roses the most beautiful? For they are — I'm sure they are."

She did not answer, but carried the flowers to the doorstep and threw them out on the grass. When she returned he was reading sonorously: —

"'We soon took a turn to the left, toward a bridge of many arches across the Guadiana. . . . Its banks were white with linen which the washerwomen had spread out to dry in the sun, which was shining brightly; I heard their singing at a great distance, and the theme seemed to be the praises of the river where they were toiling, for as I approached I could distinguish "Guadiana, Guadiana," which reverberated far and wide, pronounced by the clear and strong voices in chorus of many a dark-cheeked maid and matron.'"

She went into his room and reappeared carrying his laundry bag. She took it to the kitchen, and he heard her talking to the Scotch maid. She returned and put a slip of paper into his hand.

"Your laundry list," she said. "You had better look it over when it comes back. They're very careless."

He crushed the neatly written list in his hand.

"Why, oh why," he said, "can't *my* washing be done on the bank of a river by a singing dark-cheeked maid or matron? Why was I pitchforked into this prosaic life?"

"I dare say it can," she returned absently, "if you go far enough. . . . I don't know why, I am sure."

She began to take things from the desk. From her writing folio she turned out some Canadian stamps.

"Here are stamps I shan't need. On the blotter."

"Oh, all right. Thanks."

He looked at her half-quizzically, half-reproachfully, then impulsively got up and went to the desk. He smoothed out

the laundry list, then, licking the stamps one by one, he
stuck them in a fantastic border round the edge. He discovered a picture tack and pinned the paper to the wall.

"A memorial," he said, tragically.

She did not hear him. She was gone into her room.

He followed her to the door and stood looking in. She
had changed into a thinner dress; her cheeks were flushed.

"Do you know," he said, "you are the most matter-of-
fact being I have ever known."

She turned toward him with raised brows. "Am I? I
suppose so, compared to you."

"No other woman living," he returned, "could keep
such orderly habits with such a disturbed mind." And his
eyes added, "For your mind is horribly disturbed, you can't
deny it!"

"I guess it was my training. If you could have known
my parents and our way of living! Everything in such
perfect order. Even our ideas pigeonholed."

"It's deeper than that. It's in your New England blood.
It's a protective spirit guarding you, eh?"

"Possibly. Otherwise I might have gone mad among
you."

"Never! Nothing would send you off your head. In
spite of your scholastic forbears, I seem to see in you the
spirit of some grim-lipped sea captain. His hands on the
wheel, consulting the barometer, making entries in the log,
while the blooming tempest raged and the bally mast broke
and the ruddy blooder — I mean the bloody rudder — got
out of commission. I can hear him saying to the mate,
'Have you made out the laundry list?' — while the heavens
split! And taking time to stick a stamp on the brow of
the cabin boy so that his body might be identified when it
was washed ashore."

Alayne began to laugh.

"How ridiculous you are!" she said.

"Tell me the truth, don't you feel that old fellow's chill blood in your veins?"

"I feel it boiling sometimes. My great-great-grandfather was a Dutch sea captain."

"Splendid! I knew you had something like that somewhere. Now if only he had been a Spanish sea captain, how we might have got on together!"

She made no response, but began to take things from a bureau drawer and lay them carefully in the tray of her trunk.

"I wish I could help you," he said, almost plaintively. "Do something for you."

"There's nothing you can do." She checked an impulse to say, "Except to leave me alone."

"I wonder if you will be angry with me if I ask you something."

She gave an unhappy little laugh. "I don't think so. I feel too tired for temper."

"Oh, I say!" His tone was contrite. "I've bothered you all the time you've been packing."

"It's not that. It always upsets me to go journeys. What did you want to ask?"

"Turn round and face me."

Alayne turned round. "Well?"

"Would you have come here to nurse me if Renny had not been here?"

The flush on her cheeks spread to her forehead. But she was not angry. The shock of what he had asked was too deep for that.

"Certainly, I should."

A look, antagonistic but shrewdly understanding, passed between them.

He said, "I believe you, though I'd rather not. I'd like to think that it was your love for him that dragged you here, against your reason. I hate to think that you did such a tremendous thing for me alone. Yet, in spite of what you say, you can't quite make me believe that you would have come back here if you had never loved Renny. The place itself must have had a fascination for you. I believe places keep some essence of the emotions that have been experienced in them, don't you? Do you think the Hut will ever be the same again after this summer? Alayne, I honestly believe that Jalna drew you back, whether you realize it or not."

She muttered, "How can you be sure that Renny and I care for each other? You talk as though we had had an affair!"

"When we came to Jalna after we were married, I saw that Renny had made a disturbing impression on you. Before many months had passed, I saw that you were trying desperately to beat down your love for him, and that he was trying just as hard to control his feeling for you."

Under his scrutiny she lost her air of reticence. She pressed her hand to her throat. She had woefully failed, then, in her first effort to conceal her love for Renny. Eden had watched this smouldering passion with an appraising eye from the beginning!

She asked brokenly, "Did that make a difference to you? Knowing so long ago that I loved Renny? I thought you had only guessed it, later — believed that I had turned to him when I found you didn't care any more —"

He answered mercilessly, "Yes, it did make a difference. I felt an outsider."

"Then," she gasped, "I am to blame for everything! For Pheasant —"

"No, no. It would have come, sooner or later. It's not in me to be faithful to any woman."

She persisted doggedly, "I am to blame for everything."

He came into the room and touched her with an almost childlike gesture.

"Alayne, don't look like that. You're so — it's stupid of you. You can't help what you are. Any more than I can help what I am. My dear, I suspect that we are much more alike than you would let yourself believe. The great difference between us is that you analyze yourself while I analyze others. It's better fun. . . . Alayne, look up —"

She looked at him sombrely.

"The whole trouble has been," he said, "that you were a thousand times too good for me!"

She turned away from him and returned blindly to the arranging of her trunk.

He said, "I told old Renny one day that you'd go through hell for a sight of his red head."

"Oh! and what did he say?" Her voice was without expression. Eden should not bait her again.

"I forget. But of course he liked it."

She turned and faced him. "Eden, will you please leave me to pack in peace? You know that I have promised to spend the evening with your aunt and uncles. I have no time to waste. Are you coming?"

"No, you will be happier without me. Give them my love. Will Renny be there?"

"I don't know." How cruel he was! Why could he not let her be! How she would rejoice to be far away from all this in another twenty-four hours!

When he had returned to the living room, he hung about miserably. He hated himself for having upset her. If he had! Perhaps it was the thought of going away that made her look like that. And he had meant to say something beautiful to her at the last! The whole situation was ludicrous. The sooner this impossible atmosphere was dispelled the better. . . . Did he hear a sob from the other room? Lord, he hoped not! That would be horrible. He stood and listened. No, it was all right. She was only clearing her throat. He fidgeted about till she came out, ready to go. She looked pale, calm, her hair beautifully cared for, as always. She had a pathetic air of serenity, as though the final word had been said, as though she were now beyond the reach of emotion. He saw that she had indeed been crying.

The sun had sunk below the treetops and had left them almost instantly in a well of greenish shadow. There was no afterglow, scarcely any twilight. After the rich radiance of the sun came shadow and chill. It was like the passing of their love, he thought, and mocked at himself for being sentimental.

" Alayne —" he said.

" Yes ? "

" Oh, nothing — I forgot what I was going to say." He followed her to the door. "You must have someone bring you home. It will be very dark."

She hesitated on the flat stone before the door. She turned suddenly to him, smiling.

"Home!" she repeated. "It was rather nice of you to say that."

He came out, took her hand and raised it to his lips. "Good-bye, Alayne!"

The crows were returning to their nests from some distant field. She heard their approach beyond the orchards, first as the humming of a vast hive of bees which, as it drew nearer, swelled into a metallic volume that drowned all other sound. The air rocked with their shouts. Separate cries of those in advance became audible, raucous commands, wild shouts, vehement assertions, shrill denials — every brazen, black-feathered throat gave forth an urgent cry. They passed above the orchard, against the yellowish sky, hundreds of them, seeking the pine wood. Some battled with the air to overtake those ahead; some swam steadily with forceful movements of the wings, while others drifted with a kind of rowdy grace.

As Alayne followed the orchard path beneath them she wondered if it were possible that in a few hours she would have left all this behind and returned to a life so alien.

There was no mistake about the welcome from those at Jalna. Piers and Pheasant were in Montreal. Renny, although the old people said they expected him, did not appear at supper. The summer had gone like a dream, Nicholas said. A strange, sad dream, Ernest added. Augusta tried to persuade Alayne to go to England with her instead of returning to New York. Augusta dreaded traveling alone, she dreaded returning to her lonely house, and Alayne had never seen England! Why could she not come? Alayne felt a momentary impulse to accept the invitation. Why not go across the ocean and see if she could find forgetfulness there? But how could she forget with one of that family beside her, with constant references being made to the others? No, she could not do it. Better cut loose from them entirely, and forever. Finch played for her during the evening and she was filled with delight by the improvement in him, pride that it had been she who had persuaded Renny to have him taught. The air in the drawing-room, though subdued, was genial. It was full of a melancholy gentleness. Wakefield was allowed to take the jade and ivory curios from their cabinet to show them to Alayne, and afterward arrange them on the floor to his own satisfaction.

Alayne had never spent such an evening at Jalna. Something in it hurt her, made her feel more acutely the impending parting. And yet the old people were cheerful. They had been pleased by a call from Mrs. Leigh. "A pretty woman, egad!" from Nicholas. "Very modern and yet so sweet, so eager to please!" from Ernest. "She was for going to hunt you out at the Hut,—you and Eden,—but I told her you were out. I thought it best," from Augusta.

Wakefield curled up beside Alayne on the sofa. He took

off her rings and adorned his own small fingers with them. But when he went to replace them she shut her hand against the wedding ring.

"I am not going to wear it any more," she said, in a low tone.

"But what shall I do with it?"

"I don't know. Ask Aunt Augusta."

"What shall I do with this, Aunt?" He twirled the ring on his finger.

Augusta replied, with dignity, "Put it in the cabinet with the curios."

"The very thing!" He flew to the cabinet. "Look, everybody! I've put it on the neck of the tiny white elephant. It's a jolly little collar for him."

Alayne watched him, with a smile half-humorous, half-bitter. So that was the end of that! A jolly little collar for a white elephant. And the glad thrill that she had felt when it had been placed on her finger. She fidgeted on the sofa. She had waited past her time in the hope that Renny would return. Why was he avoiding her? Was he afraid? But why should he be, when it was her last night at Jalna? All day she had hugged the anticipation of the walk back to the Hut at night. For surely he would take her back through the darkness! What he might say to her on the way had been the subject of fevered speculation all day. She had dressed herself, done her hair, with the thought that as he saw her that night, so would she remain in his memory. And he had taken himself away somewhere, rather than spend the evening in the room with her!

Augusta was murmuring something about a horse — Renny — he had been so sorry — his apologies.

"Yes? Oh, it is too bad, of course. Say good-bye to him for me."

"Oh, he will see you again," said Ernest. "He's driving you into town himself to-morrow."

No peace for her. The feverish speculations, the aching thoughts, would begin all over again.

She said, "Tell him not to trouble. Finch will drive me in, won't you, Finch?"

"I'd like it awfully."

"What do you suppose, Alayne?" cried Wake. "I've never been on a visit."

"What a shame! Will you visit me sometime? I'd love to have you." She pressed him to her, on the sofa, and whispered, "Tell me, where is Renny?"

He whispered back, "In the stables. I know, because he sent Wright to the kitchen for something, and I was there."

Finch was to see her back to the Hut. He ran upstairs for his electric torch.

Alayne was enfolded in the arms of Augusta, Nicholas, and Ernest.

Ernest said, "How shall we ever repay you for what you have done for Eden?"

Nicholas growled, "How shall we ever make up to her for what he has done? Turned her life topsy-turvy."

Augusta said, holding her close, "If you change your mind about coming to England with me, just let me know. I'll make you very welcome."

"I advise you not to," said Nicholas. "She'll freeze you in that house of hers."

"Indeed I shan't! I know how to make people comfortable if anyone does. It was I who arranged the cottage for her, though Mamma took all the credit." From her was exhaled a subdued odor of the black clothes she wore, and of a hair pomade with the perfume of a bygone day.

Finch and Alayne were out in the darkness, the beam from the electric torch thrown before her. Cold, sweet scents rose from the flower beds. The grass was dripping with dew.

"Let us go though the pine wood," she said. She had thought to return that way with Renny.

They spoke little as they went along the bridle path beneath the pines. Her mind was engaged with its own unhappy thoughts, Finch's was filled with the sadness of life, its reaching out, its gropings in the dark, its partings. It was cold under the trees. From a cluster of hazels came the troubled talking of small birds passing the night there on their migration to the South.

Finch flashed the light among the branches, hoping to discover the small things perching. His attention was diverted to a more distant sound, as of footsteps moving among the pines.

"What are you listening to?" whispered Alayne.

"I thought I heard a twig break. Someone in there. Wait a second." He left her and ran softly padding toward the sound.

She strained her ears to listen, her eyes following the moving beam of the electric torch. The sound of Finch's padding steps ceased. The light was blotted out. She was in black silence except for the infinitesimally delicate song of a single locust on a leaf near her. She was frightened.

She called sharply, "Finch! What are you doing?"

"Here! It was nothing."

The torch flashed again; he trotted back to her. "One of the men hanging about." He thought, "Why was Renny hiding in the wood? Why didn't he turn up at the house? If looks could kill, I'd be a dead man! Gosh, he looked like Gran!"

The Hut lay in darkness, save for starlight sifting among the trees. A tenuous mist hung among their trunks, weighted with chill autumnal odors, dying leaves, fungus growths such as wood mushroom and Indian pipe, and the exhalations of deep virgin soil.

Alayne opened the door. Dark and cold inside. Eden

had gone to bed early. He might have left the lamp burning and put wood on the fire! Finch flashed the light into the interior. She found a match and lighted two candles on the table. Her face in the candlelight looked white and drawn. A great pity for her welled up in the boy's heart. She seemed to him the loneliest being he knew. He glanced at the closed door of Eden's room. Was Eden awake, he wondered?

Alayne said, "Wait a minute, Finch. I must get that book I want you to read." She went into her room. "Goodness, what a muddle I have here!"

"Oh, thanks! But don't trouble now." The laundry list decorated with postage stamps caught his eye. What the dickens? He peered at it, puzzled. Some of Eden's foolery, he'd bet. The stamps not used ones either. If they went away and left that pinned to the wall, he'd come and get the stamps.

When she returned, after what seemed a long while to Finch, what little color she had had in her face had been drained from it. She laid the book on the table.

"There," she said in a strained voice, "I hope you will like it." She went on, with an odd contraction of her mouth, "I have just had a note from Eden." He saw then that she had crumpled a piece of paper in her hand.

"Oh," he said stupidly, his jaw dropping, "what's he writing a note about?"

She pushed it into his hand. "Read it."

He read:—

Dear Alayne,—

After all your preparations it is I who am to flit first! And not to flit alone! Minny Ware is coming with me. Are you surprised, or have you suspected something between us? At any rate, it will be a surprise for poor old Meggie. I'm afraid I am never to have done taking favors from your sex. There is only one thing for you to do now, and that is divorce me.

I am giving you good grounds — and not so impossibly scandalous as the first time. My dear child, this is the first really good turn I've ever done you. My withers are wrung when I think what you must have gone through this summer!

If you and Renny don't come together, I'll feel that I have sinned in vain.

We are not going to California, but to France. I shall be writing to Finch from there, so he will be able to inform your lawyer of my exact whereabouts.

Thank you, Alayne, for your magnanimity toward me. I can say thanks on paper.

Yours,
EDEN.

Finch read the letter through with so distraught an expression that Alayne burst into hysterical laughter.

"Oh, Finch, don't!" she gasped. "You look so funny, I can't bear it!"

"I don't see anything funny about it," he said. "I think it's terrible."

"Of course it's terrible. That's what makes it so funny. That, and your expression!" She leaned against the wall, her hand pressed to her side, half laughing, half crying.

He strode toward Eden's room and flung open the door. It was in a state of disorder such as Eden alone could achieve. Alayne came and stood beside Finch, looking into the room. He could feel that she was shaking from head to foot. He put his arm about her.

"Dear Alayne, don't tremble so! I'm afraid you'll be ill."

"I'm all right. Only I'm very tired, and Eden's way of doing things is so unexpected!"

"I'll say it is! I'm the one that ought to know. He didn't tell me he was going to take a girl with him when he borrowed the money."

She was bewildered. "Borrowed the money? What money?"

"The money for the year in France. I raised it for him.

But for heaven's sake don't tell Renny of it or I'll get into a frightful row!"

She ceased trembling, her face set. "He borrowed money from *you* — to go to *France?*"

He assented, not without self-importance.

"But, Finch, Renny was paying for a winter in California!"

"I know. But Eden didn't want to go to California. He wanted a year in France. He must have it because of something he's going to write. I can't explain. You understand how it is. You left your work and came here to nurse him because of his poetry. It makes you feel that what he is doesn't really matter. You and I feel the same about art, I think. I hope you don't think I'm a fool." He was very red in the face.

She must not hurt his feelings by deprecating his act. Ah, but Eden would never pay him the money back! She put a hand on each of his cheeks, and kissed him.

"It was a beautiful thing to do, Finch! I'll not tell a soul. . . . Strange how he uses us, and then leaves us standing staring at the spot where he has been."

She took the letter from Finch and read it again. The color returned to her face in a flood.

"I wish I hadn't let you read it. Because of — things he said. You must forget them. He's so — ruthless."

Finch grunted acquiescence. Of course. That about Renny and her. Still . . . he stared into the deserted nest from whence the singer had flown. How desolate! How lonely it was here! No place for a woman.

He broke out, "You can't stop here to-night! You must come back with me."

"I am not afraid."

"It's not that. It's the gruesomeness. I couldn't stick it myself. I'll not leave you."

"I would rather be here."

"No. It won't do! Please come. Aunt will like to have you. There's your old room waiting."

She consented. They returned.

There were lights upstairs now, but a light still burned in the drawing-room, and from it came the sound of the piano. Nicholas was playing.

From the hall they could see his gray leonine head and heavy shoulders bent above the keyboard. Alayne remembered with a pang that she had not asked him to play that evening, though she had urged Finch.

He was playing Mendelssohn's "Consolation." When had one heard Mendelssohn! His terrier sat drooping before the fire waiting for him to come to bed.

Finch whispered, "Shall you tell him?"

"Yes. Wait till he has finished."

They stood motionless together. When the last notes had died, Alayne went to his side. He remained looking at his hands for a little, then slowly raised his eyes to her face.

Startled by her reappearance, he exclaimed, "Alayne, my dear! What is wrong?"

"Don't be alarmed," she said. "It's nothing serious. It's only that Eden has gone away a little sooner than I expected. He left a note at the Hut for me. Finch wouldn't let me stay there alone — so I'm back, you see." Her head drooped; she twisted her fingers together. Her voice was scarcely audible as she added, "He took Minny Ware with him."

Nicholas's large eyes glared up at her. "The deuce he did! The scoundrel! He ought to be flogged. My poor little girl —" he heaved himself around on the piano seat and put his arm about her waist. "This is the return he makes you for all your kindness! He's nothing but a young wastrel! Does Renny know of this?"

"I haven't seen Renny." She was filled with shame at

the thought of Renny. Now she did not want to see him. She would leave this house and never return to it again.

Augusta was calling from upstairs, "Did I hear Alayne's voice? What is wrong, Nicholas?"

Full of excitement, he limped vigorously to the foot of the stairs.

"Gussie!" He had not given her this diminutive for years. "Come along down, Gussie! Here's a pretty kettle of fish. Young Eden has run off with that hussy Minny!"

He turned to Alayne and Finch, who had followed him into the hall. "Do you know where they've gone?"

Finch was getting excited, too. "To France!" he shouted, as though his uncle were deaf.

Augusta began to descend the stairs, dressed in petticoat and camisole, a tail of hair down her back. If ever she had looked offended, she looked offended now.

"Nick, you don't mean to tell me!"

Ernest appeared at the top of the stairs in nightshirt and dressing gown, the cat Sasha rubbing herself against his legs.

"What's this new trouble?" he demanded.

Augusta on the stairs, midway between the brothers, answered, "Some scrape of Eden's. I'm afraid that Ware girl has been leading him into mischief. Nicholas does get so excited."

Just as they drew together at the bottom of the stairs, and Nicholas was demanding to see Eden's letter, and Augusta was declaring that she had always expected something like this, and Ernest was saying what a blessing it was that Mamma had not lived to see this night, and Nicholas was retorting that no one enjoyed a to-do better than Mamma, quick steps were heard in the porch and the door was opened by Renny.

Before he had seen her, Alayne fled down the hall. She

could not face him there before the others. She would
escape to her room and not see him before morning.

She heard his question: "What's up?" She heard
Nicholas put the situation pithily before him. He made no
audible comment, but she could picture his expression, how
the rust-red eyebrows would fly up, the brown eyes blaze.
Then she heard Augusta's voice.

"Alayne is here, poor girl. She is staying the night.
Why, where has she gone? Alayne, dear, Renny is here!"

She did not answer. The door of Grandmother's room
stood open; she stepped inside and drew it to after her. She
was startled to find the night light burning. By its faint
radiance the room was revealed to her in an atmosphere of
sombre melancholy: the tarnished gilt flourishes on the wallpaper, the deep wing chair before the empty grate, the heavy
curtains with their fringe and tassels, the old painted bedstead, on the headboard of which perched, above the fantastically pictured flowers and fruit, Boney, his head under
his wing.

The room seemed conscious of this intrusion. It had
absorbed, during the years of old Adeline's occupancy,
enough of human emotions to give it food for brooding
while its walls stood. Every article there bore the imprint
of that trenchant personality. Now, dimly revealed by the
night light, these inanimate objects had the power to re-
create her presence. The bed was no longer smooth and
cold, but rumpled and warm from the weight of that heavy,
vigorous old body. Alayne thought, "If I had come into
her room like this, how she would have held out her arms,
and grasped me, and begged, 'Kiss me. . . . Kiss me,
quick!'"

Alayne stood by the bed, listening. Had they gone upstairs again, or into the drawing-room to talk? She could
hear voices, but Renny's voice, which carried so distinctly,
was not audible. The impetus given to her passion for him

by her surroundings, by his sudden appearance, made her heart beat painfully. She steadied herself by her hand on the footboard.

He was coming.

Involuntarily she moved toward the door, as though to bar it against him. But he was there before her. He pushed it open and came inside. In the clouded radiance of the night light, against the background of a heavy maroon curtain, she saw the face she loved. The face she called up in the night, the face that haunted her by day. There he stood—she could put out her hand and touch him. He lived in her, and the urge toward him would not be denied. But what did she really know of him? What was really his conception of love and happiness? She did not know. He was an enigma to her to which the only answer was the cry of her heart.

He said, scanning her face, "Shall you divorce him, now?"

She breathed, "Yes."

"And marry me?"

"Yes."

Her eyes fell; she was afraid of their nearness. Against it she raised the barrier of a question.

"Why did you not come to-night?"

"I couldn't," he answered, "because I knew they had gone."

"You knew Eden and Minny had gone?"

"Yes." He gave a short, strained laugh. "I was riding. The gates at the crossing dropped as I got there. It was just light enough for me to make out their two figures on the platform. They were carrying bags. And when the train passed I saw him again at a window." His grimness was dispersed by the sudden arch grin so amazingly like old Adeline's. "He saw me and waved his hand!"

"And that is why you didn't come in to supper?"

He nodded.

"But why?"

"I can't tell. I simply could n't — knowing that."

In sudden pain, she asked, "And you were n't going to tell me? You were going to let me go back to the Hut and find out for myself?"

"I suppose."

"But how cruel of you!"

He did not answer; his eyes were on the little pearl-white hollow of her throat.

Now her eyes searched the dark depths of his. Was he really cruel, or only shy as a wild animal is shy, afraid of things he does not understand? She remembered the sound of someone moving in the pine wood, of Finch's odd look when he returned from searching.

"Were you in the woods? Was it you Finch and I heard, then?"

Again he did not answer, but this time he came and put his head against hers, and whispered, "Don't ask me questions. Love me."

She felt the fire of his kiss on her neck. She clung to him, her forehead pressed against his shoulder. They could find no words, but their hearts, pressed close, talked together in the language of the surging tides, the winds that bend the branches to their will, the rain that penetrates the deep warmth of the earth.

XXVIII

WILD DUCKS

A MONTH later a party was setting out one morning from Jalna for the wild-duck shooting. They were going by motor to the lakes and marshlands haunted by canvasback, mallard, and snipe. With Maurice Vaughan were to ride two friends of his, Mr. Vale from Mistwell, and Mr. Antoine Lebraux from Quebec. Piers and Renny were to take the dogs, which, filled with gladness by the sight of the guns, trotted without rest from point to point of interest — the dunnage bag, the provisions, the weapons, and their masters' legs clad in thick woolen stockings or leather leggings. The sky was gray, broken by small patches of cold blue, while the scattered sunshine seemed deliberately to seek out the burning red of the maple trees. A strong wind was blowing from the southeast, bringing with it the smell of the lake and the sound of its thunder on the beach.

Wright came from the house, carrying a heavy canvas-covered hamper, and stowed it in the back of Renny's car.

"The bacon's in this one, sir," he observed, "and the small tinned stuff. The bag of dog biscuits is in this corner. And this here's the sperrits."

"Good." Renny stuck his head into the car. "We can start directly. . . . All set, Maurice?"

"Yes, it's time we were off."

Nicholas, Ernest, Finch, Wakefield, Pheasant, and Mooey were out bare-headed to see the party off. Nicholas wore a heavy red-and-green-plaid dressing gown; his iron-gray mane had not yet been combed, and rose in a crest above his strong features. Ernest stood chatting to the strangers, hands in pockets, looking slender, feeling young again, exhilarated by the bustle. Pheasant, her short brown hair fluttering, was everywhere in pursuit of her son, who, on his feet now, wrapped in a muffler of Piers's, his small nose blue, was in imminent danger from cars, dogs, men, and the excited racings of Wake.

How Finch wished he were going!

He stood curved like the new moon, hands in his pockets, shoulders hunched against the wind, watching with a wistful grin the fascinating activities of the hunters.

Piers was passing him with a pointer on a lead, when he stopped abruptly and stared at him. The grin faded from Finch's face. He stiffened, expecting a sneer. Piers said, "Why don't you come along?"

Finch returned pleasantly, "Yes, I see myself!"

"I'm in earnest. It'd do those fool nerves of yours good. Set you up for the winter." He called to Renny, who was peering suspiciously into the engine of his motor. "Why don't you let young Finch come? He might be of some use."

"He'd be more likely to put a shot into one of us! He's never been. Why take him?"

"Why not?" persisted Piers. "Look at him! He'll never live to enjoy his money if he goes on like this. He's all legs and nose."

The two surveyed him. Finch giggled distraughtly, feeling himself to be dangling in mid-air.

"Very well," agreed Renny laconically. "But don't waste any time getting ready."

Finch flew toward the house.

"Why, he's as keen as mustard," said Piers, approvingly.

"Me, too!" clamored Wake. "I want to go!"

Piers tried to quiet him by standing him on his head, but the moment he was released he got into the car and established himself on the dunnage bag, whence he had to be forcibly ejected.

"Do you know," he said, tears in his eyes, looking up into

Renny's face, "that I have never been anywhere in my life?"

"You can't come." Renny took out some silver and put two fifty-cent pieces into the little boy's hand. "Try to have a good time on this."

Wake had never had such a magnificent sum given to him before. He was effectually quieted, even made solemn by the responsibility.

In his room Finch was throwing clothes and boots into a suitcase. In a fury of haste he dragged a bottle-green sweater over the dark red one he wore. He surveyed himself in the glass. He remembered Wake's dream of his being a "long, yellowish, rather sad-looking flower." He burst out laughing. "Gosh," he exclaimed, "this is fierce!" What he designated as "fierce" can only be guessed, but probably referred to the furious speed with which life was moving. There were Eden and Minny Ware mysteriously disappeared, there were Aunt Augusta and Alayne in England, and here was he off hunting with the other men.

He tore down the stairs, the suitcase bumping against his legs, and appeared wild-eyed before the others. He sprang, bag in hand, into his brother-in-law's car.

"Here," objected Vaughan, "you can't ride in this car! You'll have to go in the other."

"Get in here with the dogs," said Renny.

He put his suitcase on top of the mound of luggage, and wedged himself in with the two spaniels and the pointer. They were trembling with excitement. They licked his hands and face and cried with glad eagerness to be off.

They were off! Maurice's car was turning into the drive, its three occupants waving and calling out to the group who were left. It was impossible to believe that he was in the car behind Renny and Piers. He put his head out of the window and shouted, "Good-bye, Uncle Nick! Good-bye, Uncle Ernest! Good-bye, kids!"

They shouted back. Wake was dancing up and down with excitement. Uncle Ernest had Mooey in his arms. Pheasant and Mooey were throwing kisses. The joy, the abandon of it pained him. He could bear unhappiness, but he had no defenses against joy.

On either side of the road the oaks and the maples stood up showing their scarlet and mahogany-colored leaves, a few of which, with every gust, were swept from them and flew a short way like bright birds before they sank to the roadside. As they neared the church the cedars of the graveyard rose in a dark green cluster against the sky. Renny touched Piers's hand on the wheel. "Go slow here," he said.

The car crept past the graveyard. The brothers looked up the steep path, remembering how only a short while ago they had carried a coffin up there. Renny took off his cap. He shot a quick glance at the others, and they too pulled off theirs. Piers held his in his brown hand, glancing out of the corner of his eye at Renny for the signal to replace it. But Renny looked over his shoulder and said to Finch: —

"Finch, do you remember what her last word was?"

"Gammon," answered Finch.

THE END